Honor sighed. "I don't want to kill anyone we don't have to kill. But if Filareta's determined to fight anyway, then I want him hammered so hard even *Sollies* have to get the message that going after us is a really, really bad idea. That it's a *war*—and that wars have consequences. We didn't start it; they did, when Byng massacred Chatterjee's destroyers. And we didn't send a fleet to attack the Sol System; they've sent one to attack *us*.

Honor's eyes were hard, and even as she spoke, she wondered how much of the grim, cold determination she felt inside was aimed at the Solarian League and how much of it was aimed at any convenient target. Was her anger the product of New Tuscany and Spindle? Or was it the product of the Yawata strike, directed at the Solarian League because she couldn't get at the ones who'd actually murdered so many people she'd loved?

And did it matter which it was?

"They're bringing this war to us, when they don't have to," she went on coldly. "There's a limit to what *we* owe *them*, how far over backward we're required to bend to keep from killing people who're here for the express purpose of invading and conquering our star system and our homes. Don't let them off. Smack them down in a way that *forces* them to admit the stupidity of sending Filareta out here, and then see how well Kolokoltsov and his Mandarins deal with the fallout!"

IN THIS SERIES BY DAVID WEBER:

HONOR HARRINGTON

On Basilisk Station • *On Basilisk Station 20th Anniversary Edition* • *The Honor of the Queen* • *The Short Victorious War* • *Field of Dishonor* • *Flag in Exile* • *Honor Among Enemies* • *In Enemy Hands* • *Echoes of Honor* • *Ashes of Victory* • *War of Honor* • *At All Costs* • *Mission of Honor* • *A Rising Thunder* • *Shadow of Freedom*

HONORVERSE

Crown of Slaves (with Eric Flint) • *Torch of Freedom* (with Eric Flint) • *Cauldron of Ghosts* (with Eric Flint, forthcoming) • *The Shadow of Saganami* • *Storm from the Shadows*

THE STAR KINGDOM

A Beautiful Friendship • *Fire Season* (with Jane Lindskold) • *Treecat Wars* (with Jane Lindskold)

EDITED BY DAVID WEBER

More than Honor • *Worlds of Honor* • *Changer of Worlds* • *The Service of the Sword* • *In Fire Forged* • *Beginnings*

House of Steel: The Honorverse Companion

ALSO BY DAVID WEBER WITH ERIC FLINT

1633 • *1634: The Baltic War*

A RISING THUNDER

DAVID WEBER

A RISING THUNDER

This is a work of fiction. All the characters and events portrayed in this book are fictional, and any resemblance to real people or incidents is purely coincidental.

A Baen Books Original

Baen Publishing Enterprises
P.O. Box 1403
Riverdale, NY 10471
www.baen.com

ISBN: 978-1-4767-3612-9

Cover art by David Mattingly

First Baen mass market paperback printing, January 2014
Second Baen mass market paperback printing, May 2014

Library of Congress Control Number: 2011045753

Distributed by Simon & Schuster
1230 Avenue of the Americas
New York, NY 10020

Pages by Joy Freeman (www.pagesbyjoy.com)
Printed in the United States of America

To Bruce, Treysa, Mackenzie,
and—especially—Indiana Graham.
The good fight is hard, but earthbound
mortals learn to fly by watching.
God Bless.

MARCH 1922 POST DIASPORA

"I'd rather not go there, but if we have to, we might as well go all the way."

—Queen Elizabeth III of Manticore

Chapter One

"GET YOUR GODDAMNED SHIPS the hell out of *my* space!"

The burly, dark-haired man on Commander Pang Yau-pau's com was red-faced and snarling, and Pang took a firm grip on his own temper.

"I'm afraid that's not possible, Commodore Chalker," he replied as courteously as the circumstances permitted. "My orders are to protect Manticoran vessels passing through this terminus on their way home to Manticoran space."

"I don't give a *damn* about your 'orders,' Commander!" Commodore Jeremy Chalker spat back. His six destroyers were 2.4 million kilometers—eight light-seconds—from Pang's cruiser, and one might have thought it would be difficult to maintain a properly infuriated conversation over such a distance, especially with the delays light-speed transmissions built into its exchanges. Chalker seemed able to manage it quite handily, however. "You're in violation of my star system's sovereignty, you've evicted Solarian Astro

3

Control personnel from their duty stations, and I want your ass *gone!*"

"Sir, it's not my intention to violate anyone's sovereignty," Pang replied, choosing to let the rather thornier question of the Solly traffic controllers lie. "My sole interest at this time is the protection of the Star Empire's merchant vessels."

Sixteen more seconds ticked past, and then—

"Shut your mouth, return control of this terminus to the personnel whose control stations you've illegally seized, and turn your ass around *now*, or I will by *God* open fire on the next fucking Manty freighter I see!"

Pang Yau-pau's normally mild brown eyes hardened, and he inhaled deeply.

"Skipper," a quiet voice said.

The single word couldn't have been more respectful, yet it was edged with warning, and Pang hit the mute button and glanced at the smaller screen deployed from the base of his command chair. Lieutenant Commander Myra Sadowski, his executive officer, looked back at him from it.

"I know he's a pain in the ass," she continued in that same quiet voice, "but we're supposed to do this without making any more waves than we have to. If you hand this guy his head the way you want to—the way he *deserves*, for that matter—I think it would probably come under the heading of at least a ripple or two."

Myra, Pang reflected, had a point. There was, however, a time and a place for everything. For that matter, the Admiralty hadn't sent Pang and HMS *Onyx* to the Nolan Terminus to let someone like Jeremy Chalker make that sort of threat.

No, they didn't, another corner of the commander's brain told him. *At the same time, I don't suppose it's too hard to understand why he's so pissed off. Not that it makes me like him any better.*

At the moment, *Onyx,* her sister ship *Smilodon,* the *Roland*-class destroyer *Tornado* and the much older destroyer *Othello* were over six hundred and fifty light-years from the Manticore Binary System and barely *two* hundred light-years from the Sol System. It was not a particularly huge force to have wandering around so deep in increasingly hostile territory, as Pang was only too well aware. In fact, Nolan was a protectorate system of the Solarian League, and Chalker was an SLN officer, the senior Frontier Fleet officer present. He looked old for his rank, which suggested a certain lack of familial connections within the SLN, although he must have at least some influence to have ended up with the Nolan command. The system's proximity to the Nolan Terminus of the Nolan-Katharina Hyper Bridge was what had brought it to the Office of Frontier Security's attention a hundred-odd T-years ago, and the local OFS and Frontier Fleet officers had been raking off a comfortable percentage of the terminus user fees ever since. Judging from the reaction of the SLN captain who'd commanded the OFS-installed terminus traffic-control staff when Pang ordered him to turn his control stations over to Manticoran personnel, another chunk of those fees had probably been finding its way into his pockets, as well. Precious little of that revenue had ended up in Nolan itself, at any rate.

Well, at least this time we can be pretty confident we're not hurting some innocent third-party star system's revenue stream, he thought. *And it's not like we're planning to* keep *the terminus...just now, anyway. We'll give it back to them when I'm sure we've gotten all our ships safely through it. And if someone like Chalker takes one in the bank account in the meantime, I'm sure I'll be able to live with my regret somehow.*

Of course, Pang never doubted that the rest of the Solarian League Navy was going to be just as infuriated as Chalker by Manticore's "arrogance" in seizing control of Solarian-claimed termini even temporarily. What was going to happen when Lacoön Two kicked in hardly bore thinking upon, although anyone who really thought *not* executing Lacoön Two was going to make one bit of difference to the Sollies was probably smoking things he shouldn't.

"I'm not the one making the waves," he told Sadowski out loud, then glanced across *Onyx's* command deck at Lieutenant Commander Jack Frazier, his tactical officer.

"I hope we're not going to have any business for *you*, Guns," he said. "If we do, I want to hold the damage to a minimum."

"You're thinking in terms of something more like what Admiral Gold Peak did at New Tuscany than what she did at Spindle, Sir?"

"Exactly." Pang smiled thinly. "Do you have Chalker's flagship IDed?"

"Yes, Sir." Frazier nodded with an answering smile. "I do. By the strangest coincidence, I've just this minute discovered that I've got her IDed, dialed in, and locked up, as a matter of fact."

"Good."

Pang paused a moment longer, taking an additional few seconds to make sure he had his own temper under control, then un-muted his audio pickup.

"Commodore Chalker," he said in a hard, flat voice quite different from the courteous one he'd employed so far, "allow me to point out two things to you. First, this terminus is, in fact, not in Nolan's territorial space. Unless my astrogation is badly off, it's five light-hours from Nolan, which puts it just a bit outside the twelve-minute limit. The Solarian League's claim to its possession rests solely on the SLN's supposed power to control the space about it. And, second, in regard to that supposed power, I respectfully suggest you consider the actual balance of force which obtains at this moment. Based on that balance, I submit that it would be unwise to issue such threats against Manticoran shipping... and even less wise to carry them out."

"Well, piss on you, *Commander!* You and the rest of your 'Star Empire' may think you can throw your weight around any way you like, but there's a cold dawn coming, and it's going to get here sooner than you think!"

"I have my orders, Commodore," Pang responded in that same flat voice, "and I don't intend to debate the question of who's responsible for the current state of tension between the Star Empire and the Solarian League. I fully intend to return control of this terminus to the League—and, obviously, to restore your personnel to their stations—as soon as I've satisfied myself, as my orders require, that all Manticoran merchant vessels in this vicinity have been given the opportunity to return to Manticoran space through it.

I regret"—neither his tone nor his expression was, in fact, particularly regretful—"any inconvenience this may cause for you or any other Solarian personnel or citizens. I *do*, however, intend to carry out *all* of my orders, and one of those orders is to use whatever level of force is necessary to protect Manticoran merchant shipping anywhere. And 'anywhere,' Commodore Chalker, includes Solarian space. So if you intend to fire on Manticoran freighters, why don't you just start with the ones right here under my protection? Go ahead—be my guest. But before you do, Commodore, I suggest you recall the Royal Navy's position where the protection of merchant shipping is concerned."

He sat waiting, watching his com for the sixteen seconds his words took to reach Chalker and for the signal to come back. Precisely on schedule, Chalker's face turned even darker.

"And what the fuck does *that* mean?" the Solarian snarled.

"It means my tactical officer has your flagship identified," Pang said, and his smile was a razor.

For another sixteen seconds, Chalker glared out of Pang's display. Then, abruptly, his facial muscles went absolutely rigid, as if some magic wand had turned his face to stone. He stayed that way for several seconds, then shook himself.

"Are you *threatening* me?" he demanded incredulously.

"Yes," Pang said simply. "I am."

Chalker stared at him, and Pang wondered what else the other man could have expected to happen.

"You think you can come waltzing into Solarian space and *threaten* Solarian citizens? Tell a *Solarian* warship you'll *open fire* on it?" Chalker said sixteen seconds later.

"It's not my wish to threaten anyone, Admiral. It is my intention to carry out my orders and to deal with any threat to the merchant shipping for which I'm responsible, and you've just announced your intention to fire on unarmed merchant vessels. Should you do so, I will fire on *you*, and I suggest you recall what happened to Admiral Byng at New Tuscany. If you actually intend to attack after doing that, go ahead and let's get it over with. Otherwise, Sir, I have rather more important matters which require my attention. Good day."

He punched the stud that cut the connection and sat back in his command chair, wondering if Chalker was furious enough—or stupid enough—to accept his challenge. If the Solly officer did anything of the sort, it would be the last mistake he ever made. There was no question about that in Pang's mind, although he was a bit less certain about the potential consequences for the future career of one Pang Yau-pau.

Better to be hung for a hexapuma than a housecat, he thought. *And it's not like I could've found some kind of magic formula to keep the jerk happy, no matter what I did! At least this way if he's stupid enough to pull the trigger, it won't be because he didn't know exactly how I'd respond.*

He watched his tactical repeater, waiting to see what Chalker would do. *Onyx* and *Smilodon* were both *Saganami-C*s, armed with Mark 16 multidrive missiles and mounting eight grasers in each broadside. At the moment, SLNS *Lancelot*, Chalker's antiquated *Rampart*-class destroyer flagship and her consorts were far outside the effective range of their own pathetic energy armament, and the situation was almost worse when it came to missiles. The Sollies *were* within their missiles' powered engagement range of Pang's command, but *Lancelot* was barely twenty percent *Onyx*'s size, with proportionately weaker sidewalls and a broadside of only five lasers and a matching number of missile tubes. If Chalker was foolish enough to carry out his threat, he could undoubtedly kill any merchant ship he fired upon. *Lancelot*'s chance of getting a laser head through *Onyx*'s antimissile defenses, on the other hand, much less burning through the cruiser's sidewalls, ranged from precious little to nonexistent.

Good thing Chalker wasn't on station when we arrived, *though, I suppose*, Pang thought. *God knows what he'd've done if he'd been inside energy range when we transited the terminus! And when you come right down to it, it's a good thing he's such a loud-mouthed idiot, too. It was only a matter of time until one of the incoming Solly merchies diverted to Nolan to let someone know what was going on out here. If the jackass had been willing to keep his mouth shut until he managed to get into energy range, this situation could've turned even stickier. In fact, it could have gone straight to hell in a handbasket if someone stupid enough to pull the trigger had managed to get that close before he did it.*

Without a clear demonstration of hostile intent, it would have been extraordinarily difficult for Pang to justify actually opening fire on units of the SLN. He would have had little choice—legally, at least—but to allow Chalker to approach all the way to the terminus threshold, and that could have turned really nasty.

Fortunately, Chalker had been unable to keep his mouth shut, and his open threat to fire on Manticoran merchant ships constituted plenty of justification for Pang to give him the Josef Byng treatment if he kept on closing.

Thank you, Commodore Chalker, he thought sardonically.

As a matter of fact, although Pang Yau-pau wasn't prepared to admit it to anyone, even Sadowski, he was only too aware of his own crushing responsibilities and the sheer vastness of the Solarian League. Nor was he going to admit how welcome he'd actually found Chalker's bellicosity under the circumstances. Any officer who commanded a Queen's starship knew sooner or later he was going to find himself out on a limb somewhere where he'd have to put his own judgment on the line, yet at this particular moment Commander Pang and his small command had crawled out to the end of a very, very long limb, indeed.

They were a mere three wormhole transits away from the Manticore Binary System, but it certainly didn't *feel* that way. The Dionigi System was only ninety-six light-years from Manticore, but it was connected to the Katharina System, over seven hundred and thirty light-years away, by the Dionigi-Katharina Hyper Bridge. And the Nolan-Katharina Bridge, in turn, was one of the longest ever surveyed, at nine hundred and fifteen light-years. Even allowing for the normal hyper-space leg between Manticore and Dionigi, he could be home in less than two weeks instead of the eighty days or so it would have taken his warships to get there on a direct voyage.

It would have taken a ship with a commercial-grade hyper generator and particle screening better than *seven months* to make the same trip through hyper, however, as opposed to only thirty days via Dionigi, which rather graphically demonstrated the time savings the wormhole networks made possible for interstellar commerce. And that, in turn, explained the sheer economic value of that same network . . . and Manticore's commanding position within it.

Which explains why the Sollies back in Old Chicago are going to be at least as pissed off as Chalker, Pang reflected grimly. *They've been mad enough for years about the size of our merchant marine, the way we dominate their carrying trade. Now they're about to find out just how bad it really is. Once we get all of our shipping out of Solly space, they're really going to be hurting, and we'll have done it by simply calling our own freighters home, without using a single commerce-raider or privateer. But when Lacoön Two activates and we start closing down as much as we can of the entire network, it's going to get even worse. They don't begin to have the hulls to take up the slack even if all the termini stayed open; with the termini closed, with every ton of cargo having to spend four or five times as long in transit, to boot . . .*

On the face of it, it was ridiculous, and Pang would be surprised if as much as five percent of the total Solarian population had a clue—yet—about just how vulnerable the League really was or how bad it was actually going to get. Something the size of the Solarian League's internal economy? With literally hundreds of star systems, system populations running into the tens of billions, and the mightiest industrial capacity in the history of mankind? That sort of titan couldn't possibly be brought to its knees by a "Star Empire" which consisted of no more than a couple of dozen inhabited planets!

But it could, if its pigmy opponent happened to control the bulk of the shipping which carried that economy's lifeblood. And especially if the pigmy in question was also in a position to shut down its arterial system, force its remaining shipping to rely solely on capillary action to keep itself fed. Even if Solarian shipyards got themselves fully mobilized and built enough ships to replace every single Manticoran hull pulled out of the League's trade, it *still* wouldn't be enough to maintain the shipping routes without the termini.

Of course, it's not going to do our economy any favors, either, Pang told himself. *Not an insignificant point, especially after the Yawata strike.*

He wondered if the Star Empire's continued possession of the termini would be a big enough economic crowbar to pry a few Solarian star systems free of the League's control. If the bait of access was trolled in front of system economies crippled or severely damaged by the termination of cargo service, would those systems switch allegiance—openly or unofficially—to Manticore instead of the League? He could think of quite a few in the Verge who'd do it in a second if they thought they could get away with it. For that matter, he could think of at least a handful of Shell systems that would probably jump at the chance.

Well, I guess time will tell on that one. And there's another good reason for us to make sure we're the ones who control the hyper bridges, isn't there? As long as we do, no one can launch naval strikes through them at us . . . and we can launch naval strikes through them at the League.

Attacking well-defended wormhole termini along the bridges between them was a losing proposition, but the tactical flexibility the network as a whole would confer upon light, fast Manticoran commerce-raiders would be devastating. For all intents and purposes, the Star Empire, despite its physical distance from the Sol System and the League's other core systems, would actually be inside the Sollies' communications loop. The League's limited domestic merchant marine would find itself under attack almost everywhere, whereas the Manticoran merchant marine would continue to travel via the termini, completely immune to attack between the star systems they linked.

No wonder Chalker was so livid. He might be so stupid he couldn't visualize the next step, couldn't see Lacoön Two coming, but he obviously did grasp the Manticoran mobility advantage which had brought Pang's squadron to Nolan. He might not have reasoned it out yet. Solarian arrogance might have blinded him to the possibility that Manticore might actually conduct *offensive* operations against the omnipotent League instead of huddling defensively in a frightened corner somewhere. But the mere presence of Pang's ships this deep into Solarian space would have been enough to push his blood pressure dangerously high, and Pang suspected that deep down inside, whether Chalker consciously realized it or not, the Solarian officer probably *was* aware of the implications of Manticoran mobility.

He glanced at the date-time display in the corner of the master plot. Over ten minutes since he'd bidden Chalker good day, he noticed. If the Solly had been infuriated—and stupid—enough to do anything hasty, he'd probably have already done it. The fact that he hadn't (yet) didn't mean stupidity and arrogance wouldn't eventually overpower common sense and self-preservation, but it seemed unlikely.

"Unlikely" wasn't exactly the same as "no way in hell," Pang reminded himself. All the same, it was time to let his people get a little rest . . . and it probably wouldn't hurt for him to display his own imperturbability, either. Confidence started at the top, after all, and he looked back down at his link to AuxCon.

"I think Commodore Chalker may have seen the error of his ways, Myra," he told Lieutenant Commander Sadowski. "We'll stand the squadron down to Readiness Two."

"Aye, aye, Sir," she acknowledged.

Readiness State Two, also known as "general quarters," was one step short of battle stations. Engineering and life-support systems would be fully manned, as would CIC, although Auxiliary Control would be reduced to a skeleton watch. The ship would maintain a full passive sensor watch, augmented by the remote FTL platforms they'd deployed as soon as they arrived, and the tactical department would be fully manned. Passive and active defenses would be enabled under computer control; electronic warfare systems and active sensors would be manned and available, although not emitting; and *Onyx*'s offensive weapons would be partially manned by their on-mount crews. Readiness Two was intended to be maintained for lengthy periods of time, so it included provision for rotating personnel in order to maintain sufficient crew at their duty stations while allowing the members of the ship's company to rest in turn. Which still wouldn't prevent it from exhausting Pang's people if they had to keep it up indefinitely.

"Let Percy take AuxCon while you head back over to the Bridge to relieve me," he continued to Sadowski. Lieutenant the Honorable Percival Quentin-Massengale, *Onyx*'s assistant tactical officer, was the senior of Sadowski's officers in Auxiliary Control. "We'll pull *Smilodon* and the tin cans back and let *Onyx* take point for the first twelve hours, or until our friend Chalker decides to take himself elsewhere. After that, *Smilodon* can have the duty for the next twelve hours. We'll let the cruisers swap off while the destroyers watch our backs."

And while we keep Othello *out of harm's way*, he added silently to himself. Unlike her more youthful consort, *Tornado*, the elderly destroyer *wasn't* armed with Mark 16s, and Pang had already decided to keep her as far to the rear as he could.

"Run a continually updated firing solution on him, Guns," the commander said out loud to Lieutenant Commander Frazier. "And have CIC keep a close eye on his emissions. Any sign of active targeting systems, and I want to hear about it."

"Aye, aye, Skipper."

Jack Frazier was normally a cheerful sort, fond of practical jokes and pranks, but no trace of his usual humor colored his response.

"Good." Pang nodded curtly, then looked back down at Sadowski. "You heard, Myra?"

"Yes, Sir."

"Well, I figure you already know this, but to make it official, if it should happen that Chalker is stupid enough to actually fire on us or one of the merchies, you're authorized to return fire immediately. And if that happens, I want him taken completely out. Clear?"

"I acknowledge your authorization to return fire if we're fired upon, Sir," Sadowski said a bit more formally, and Pang nodded again, then stood and looked back to Frazier.

"You have the deck until the XO gets here, Guns, and the same authorization applies to you," he said. "I'll be in my day cabin catching up on my paperwork."

"Like the old story about the mule, first you need to hit it between the eyes with a big enough club to get its attention."

—Hamish Alexander-Harrington,
Earl of White Haven

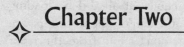

Chapter Two

"YOU CAN'T BE SERIOUS!"

Sharon Selkirk, Shadwell Corporation's senior shipping executive for the Mendelschon System, stared at her com display, and the man on it shook his head regretfully.

"I'm afraid I am," Captain Lev Wallenstein of the improbably named Manticoran freighter *Yellow Rose the Third* said. "I just got the dispatch."

"But...but—" Selkirk stopped sputtering and shook herself. "We've got a *contract*, Lev!"

"I understand that," Wallenstein said, running one hand through his unruly thatch of red hair. "And I'm sorry as hell. It wasn't my idea, Sharon! And don't think for one minute that the front office is going to be happy when I get home, either! Running *empty* all the way back to the Star Kingdom?" He shook his head. "I don't know whose brainstorm this was, but it's going to play merry hell, and that's the truth!"

"Lev, I've got one-point-six million tons of cargo that've been sitting in orbital warehouses for over two

T-months waiting for your arrival. One-point-six *million* tons—you understand that number? That's the next best thing to a *billion and a half* credits of inventory, and it's supposed to be in Josephine in less than four weeks. If you leave it sitting here, there's no way I can possibly get it there."

"I *understand*." Wallenstein shook his head help-lessly. "And if I had any choice at all, I'd be loading your cargo right now. But I *don't*. These orders are nondiscretionary, and they don't come from the front office, either. They come direct from the *Admiralty*, Sharon."

"But why?" Selkirk stared at him. "Why just...yank the carpet out from under me like this? Damn it, Lev, you've been on this run for over twelve T-years! There's *never* been a problem, not from either side!"

"Sharon, it doesn't have anything to do with you. Or with me." Wallenstein sat back in his chair aboard the *Yellow Rose*, gazing at the image of a woman who'd become a friend, not just another business contact. "You're right, there's never been a problem...not here in Mendelschon."

Selkirk had opened her mouth again, but she closed it once more and her eyes narrowed at his last four words. Or at the tone in which he'd spoken, to be more accurate.

"You mean this has to do with that business in, where was it, New Tuscany? And Spindle? *That's* what this is about?"

"No one's specifically said so," Wallenstein replied, "but if I had to guess, yeah, that's what it's about."

"But that's stupid!" She sat back in her own chair, throwing both hands up in frustration. "That's *seven hundred* light-years from Mendelschon! What possible bearing could it have on *us?*"

Despite his very real affection for her, Wallenstein found it difficult not to roll his eyes. Unlike the majority of people who found their way to her seniority in a Solarian multi-stellar, Sharon Selkirk had always been friendly and courteous in her dealings with the merchant-service officers who transported the Shadwell Corporation's goods between the stars. She'd never held the fact that Wallenstein wasn't a Solarian against him, either. In fact, that was the one thing about her which had always irritated him. She didn't even realize she was being condescending by *not* holding the fact that he wasn't a Solarian against him. Why, she was treating him just like a *real* person!

He was confident she'd never actually analyzed her own attitude, never realized how it could grate on anyone's nerves, because she was, frankly, too nice a person to treat someone that way if she'd ever realized she was doing it. But that was part of the problem. Solarian arrogance, that bone-deep assumption of superiority, was so deeply engraved into the Solarian League's DNA that Sollies never even thought about it.

"Look, Sharon," he said after a moment, "I agree that what happened in New Tuscany and what happened in Spindle don't have anything to do with you, or me, or Mendelschon. But they had one hell of a lot to do with the people who got killed in both those places, and you may not realize just how completely relations between the League and the Star Empire are going into the crapper. But they are, believe me. And looking at these orders, I think it's going to get a hell of a lot worse before it gets any better."

"But that's crazy." Selkirk shook her head. "I mean, I agree it's horrible all those people got killed. And I don't know what happened any more than you do. But surely nobody wants to get *more* people killed! They've got to settle this thing before that happens!"

"I agree with you, and I wish they would. But the truth is, it doesn't look like that's going to happen. And I'm guessing the government back home's decided it's time to get the Star Empire's merchant shipping out from under before it all comes apart."

"I can't believe this is happening." She shook her head again. "I'm sure that if your people would just sit down with our people we could work this out. There's *always* a way to work things out if people are just willing to be reasonable!"

"Unfortunately, that requires *both* sides to be reasonable," Wallenstein pointed out, and Selkirk's eyes widened in surprise. She started to say something back, quickly, but stopped herself in time, and Wallenstein smiled a bit grimly.

Almost said it, didn't you, Sharon? he thought. *Of course we're supposed to be reasonable. And I'm sure you meant what you just said about reasonable people working things out. Unfortunately, the Solarian view of "reasonable" is people "reasonably" agreeing to do things the* League's *way. The notion that the* League *might have to be reasonable doesn't even come into it, does it?*

"Well, of course it does," she said instead of what she'd been about to say, and she had the grace to look a little uncomfortable as she said it. But then she scowled.

"So you're just going to turn around and head back to Manticore? Just like that?"

"Actually, I'm going to turn around and head back

to *Beowulf*, and from there to Manticore," he said. "But, yeah, that's pretty much it."

"And our contract?"

"I'm afraid you're going to have to discuss that with the front office." He shrugged unhappily. "For that matter, you may end up discussing it with the foreign secretary's people before this is all over. Since the orders came from the government, I'm guessing the government's going to be responsible for any penalties the shippers collect."

"*If* they collect them, you mean, don't you?" she asked bitterly. She'd had more than one unhappy experience dealing with the Solarian government's bureaucracies.

"I don't know how it's going to work out. As far as I know, nobody knows how it's going to work out in the end. And I know you're unhappy, but you're not the only one. Don't forget, Sharon, I hold a reserve commission. When I get back to Manticore, I'm likely to find myself called to active duty. If this thing goes as badly as it could, I may just end up hauling something besides freight back into the Solarian League."

She looked at him blankly for a long moment, as if she simply couldn't comprehend what he was saying. Then she shook her head quickly.

"Oh, no, Lev! It's not going to come to that! I know your people are angry, and I would be, too, if what they think happened had happened to *my* navy. And I'm not saying it *didn't* happen!" she added even more quickly as Wallenstein's expression hardened. "But surely your Star Empire isn't crazy enough to actually go to war with the *League!* Why, that would be like . . . like . . ."

"Like David and Goliath?" Wallenstein provided a bit more sharply than he usually spoke to her, and her eyes widened. "I think that's probably the comparison you're looking for," he continued. "And I'll even grant that it's appropriate. But you might want to think about how that particular confrontation worked out in the end."

They looked at one another in silence for several endless seconds, and as he gazed into Selkirk's eyes, Lev Wallenstein saw understanding dawning at last. The understanding that Manticorans really weren't Solarians. That they truly could conceive of a galaxy in which the Solarian League wasn't the ultimate arbiter and dictator of terms. That they might actually be so lost to all reason that they truly were prepared to fight the Solarian juggernaut.

For the first time, Sharon Selkirk saw him as someone who truly believed he was her equal, whatever *she* thought, and he wondered if in the process she'd finally realized how unconsciously condescending she'd always been before. He was surprised and more than a little dismayed by the satisfaction that dawning awareness gave him, and he drew a deep breath and made himself smile at her.

"Of course I hope that's not going to happen," he told her as lightly as he could. Whatever else, she'd always been courteous, and he owed her a little gentleness in return. "In fact, I hope it all blows over and I'm back on my regular run ASAP. And if it happens, the front office may find itself cutting some special deals in order to earn back all the goodwill this is going to cost us. But whatever happens down the road, I don't have any choice but to follow the instructions I've been given. That's why I commed you in person. Like you say, we've known each other a long time, and we've always done right by each other, so I figured I owed you a personal explanation. Or as close to an explanation as I can give you with what *I* know. But either way, I'm supposed to be underway for Beowulf within six hours."

"There's going to be hell to pay for this, Lev. You know that, don't you?" Selkirk asked. "I'm not talking about between you and me. I mean, I understand it's not your idea and you don't have any choice, but my bosses aren't going to be happy about this. And their bosses aren't going to be happy about it. And eventually it's going to go all the way to the top, and members of the Assembly aren't going to be happy about it. For that matter, if Manticore's really recalling all of its merchant ships, this is going to *hammer* the interstellar economy. It's not just the transstellars that're going to be pissed off once that happens—it's going to be *everyone!*" She shook her head. "I don't know what your government *hopes* this is going to accomplish, but I can tell you what it's *really* going to do, and that's to squirt hydrogen right into the fire!"

"Maybe it is," Wallenstein conceded, "but that's a decision that's way above my pay grade, Sharon." He smiled again, a bit crookedly. "Take care of yourself, okay?"

"You, too, Lev," she said quietly.

"I'll try," he told her. "Clear."

❖   ❖   ❖

"I don't *care* what your damned orders say," Captain Freida Malachai said flatly. "I've got three and a half *million* tons of cargo aboard, and I'm supposed to deliver it in Klondike one T-month from today. Do you have any frigging idea what the nondelivery *penalty* on that's going to be?! Not to mention the question of piracy if I just sail off with it into the sunset!"

"I realize this is highly . . . inconvenient, Captain Malachai," Commander Jared Wu replied as reasonably as he could. "And it wasn't my idea in the first place. Nonetheless, I'm afraid the recall's nondiscretionary."

"The hell it is!" Malachai shot back. "I'm a free subject of the Crown, not a damned *slave!*"

"No one's trying to *enslave* anyone, Captain." Wu's voice was tighter and harder than it had been. "Under the Wartime Commerce Security Act, the Admiralty has the responsib—"

"Don't you go quoting the WCSA to me!" Malachai's blue eyes glittered with rage, and her short-cut blond hair seemed to bristle. "That thing's never been applied in the history of the Star Kingdom! And even if it had, we're not at *war!*"

Commander Wu sat back in his command chair and ordered himself to count to ninety by threes. It wasn't going to do any good—probably—to lose his own temper with her. He was tempted to try it anyway, but from what he'd seen of Captain Malachai of the good ship RMMS *Voortrekker*, a tantrum on his part would only make her dig in deeper. And the hell of it was that he sympathized with her.

Voortrekker didn't belong to one of the big shipping houses. The Candida Line owned only four ships, one of them *Voortrekker*, and Malachai was owner-aboard of her ship. She owned, in fact, a fifty percent share of the ship, which meant fifty percent of the profits belonged to her. But so did fifty percent of the expenses . . . and any penalties *Voortrekker* was forced to pay for breach of contract. The mere thought of how much the nondelivery penalty on close to four million tons of cargo could run was enough to make anyone wince. And that was assuming the admiralty courts didn't decide to tack on additional fees or fines for damages.

"Captain," he made himself say calmly after he reached ninety, "I truly understand what it will mean financially for you personally, not just Candida, if you find yourself liable for nondelivery of your cargo. I understand the numbers, and I know you're an owner-aboard. I sympathize with your concerns. But you know as well as I do that the WCSA gives the Admiralty the authority to issue a mandatory, nondiscretionary recall of all Manticoran-registry merchant vessels if the Crown determines that a state of war is *imminent*. Well, I'm here to tell you a state of war with the Solarian League is damned well as imminent as it gets! We've already destroyed or captured seventy Solarian super-dreadnoughts. You think Manticoran merchant ships wandering around inside the Solarian League aren't going to find themselves at risk if this continues?!"

Malachai glared at him, but she also made herself sit back visibly and drew a deep breath.

"You may understand the numbers, Commander," she said then, her nostrils flaring, "but whatever you think, you probably don't have a clue how bad the consequences would be. I've got a note coming due in six T-months. A big one. If I forfeit this charter, I'll probably come up short on the due date. If I get hit with a nondelivery penalty on top of that, I'll *certainly* come up short. And if I do, I lose my ship."

"You're right, I didn't know about that part of it," Wu said after a long, silent moment. "And I'm sorrier than I can say that you're facing that kind of a problem. But the order isn't discretionary—not for you, and not for me. You're required to obey it, and *I'm* required to enforce it . . . by whatever means are necessary."

"But Klondike isn't even a Solly system," Malachai pointed out, and there was a note of pleading in her voice—a note that obviously came hard for her. "We'd be in hyper the entire way there, and nobody could even *find* us there, much less touch us. I drop into Klondike, I off-load my cargo, and that's all there is. Then I'll come straight home, I promise!"

Wu stared into those angry, pleading, desperate blue eyes and hated himself and his orders. But they *were* orders, and he *was* responsible for enforcing them.

The government's got *to come up with some kind of compensatory arrangement*, he told himself. *They have to know what kind of economic hardship this kind of order's bound to inflict, and it's not the Crown's job to put honest merchant skippers out of work. Take away their* life savings!

Unfortunately, no requirement for compensation had been written into the Wartime Commerce Security Act when Parliament passed it over three hundred T-years earlier. Maybe nobody had thought of it at the time, but maybe someone *had*, too. Maybe somebody had realized just how stupendous the price tag might become, given the size the Manticoran merchant marine might attain in the next three T-centuries and declined to obligate the government to pay it. And even if they had, where was the government going to find the *cash* to pay it after the Yawata strike?

And especially if it was calling home the enormous merchant fleet which provided so much of its total revenue flow?

And then there was the minor question of just how the Star Empire of Manticore was going to manage to pay the bills for a war against something the size of the Solarian League. Even with a *healthy* tax base, that would've been a Herculean task. With what the Yawata strike had left behind and the inevitable loss of Solly traffic through the Junction on top of everything else...

If there is compensation, it's likely going to come slow, he thought grimly. *A hell of a lot too slow to pay off a note that's due in only six T-months. And it'll be cold comfort to Malachai if she finally gets a cash settlement—even assuming it's not discounted—when she's already lost everything she's worked for her entire life.*

"Captain," he said finally, "first, I don't see how you could possibly be accused of piracy. You're covered by the fact that you were ordered to return immediately to the Star Kingdom. Any accusations of piracy or theft on your part would fall legally at the government's door, not yours. Second, I think it's highly probable that the 'act of God or act of war' clause of your contract would protect you against any nondelivery penalty. Obviously, I can't guarantee that, because I frankly don't know how the courts are going to look at this after the dust settles. But my legal officer and I *have* discussed this, and that's her opinion."

"And if she's *wrong?*" Malachai demanded harshly.

"If she's wrong, she's wrong, and you're screwed, Captain," Wu admitted. "I'm sorry, but there it is."

"Even if I don't get hit with the nondelivery penalty, I'm going to come up short on the note, especially if I have to sit in a parking orbit somewhere in the home system between now and then," she pointed out. "A ship that's not moving is only a hole in space that people pour money into. It's sure as hell not a hole money comes *out* of!"

Well, that's *true enough,* Wu reflected. *And what are you going to do if she refuses?*

HMS *Cometary* was a mere light cruiser. Admittedly, she was an older ship, which meant she carried a larger Marine detachment than most current *battlecruisers* did, but he couldn't go peeling off details of his *Navy* personnel to take over the engine rooms and bridges of freighters and passenger liners. In theory, he could order his Marines to take control of *Voortrekker* and force Captain Malachai and her own crew to sail directly to Manticore, yet he shied away from the possibility. It wasn't the Royal Manticoran Navy's job to seize control of honest merchant ships, damn it! But if he didn't do *something* . . .

"Klondike, you said," he heard himself say and swore at himself silently when Malachai's eyes lit with sudden hope.

"Right, Klondike." She nodded vigorously. "I can be there in three and a half T-weeks. And from there to Beowulf's only another three T-weeks. Just six T-weeks—that's all I need."

"And it's only *two* T-weeks from *Hypatia* to Beowulf," he pointed out.

Her lips tightened, but she didn't say anything. She only looked back at him, blue eyes unaccustomed to asking for anything pleading with him to relent.

He looked back at her, wrestling with those eyes and his own temptation. He had no doubt the Admiralty would have quite a few choice things to say to him if he granted an exemption from a nondiscretionary order. Worse, once he started down that slippery slope, where did he stop? How did he justify letting *Voortrekker* slide if he wasn't going to grant exemptions to everyone *else* who asked as well? Hypatia wasn't a major traffic node, and it was unlikely he was going to see a lot more Manticoran ships before his own orders took him home again, but still . . .

You're a Queen's officer, Jared, he told himself. *You took an oath to obey all legal orders, and the shit's busy hitting the fan on a scale you never even dreamed of. It's not your job to go around second-guessing the Admiralty. Especially not at a time like this!*

All of that was true, but there was another side to the coin, as well. *Cometary* was only an old, obsolescent light cruiser, but she was still a Queen's ship, and Jared Wu was still her commanding officer. And that meant he was supposed to have the guts to do what his orders required him to do . . . and to be willing to put his own judgment on the line when it came to those selfsame orders.

"Captain Malachai," he said at last, "I have exactly zero authority to ignore the orders I've been given. You realize that?"

Malachai gave a single, choppy nod, her face grim, her eyes bleak once more. He let silence linger between them for two or three breaths, then squared his shoulders.

"I have no authority," he repeated, "but . . . I'm going to, anyway."

The last four words came out in more of a sigh of resignation than anything else, and he felt himself shaking his own head in disbelief as he said them. Malachai's eyes lit up like light-struck sapphires, though, and her face blossomed in an enormous smile.

"Understand me, Captain!" he said much more sharply, waving an index finger at the com pickup. "Straight to Klondike, unload your cargo, then straight to Beowulf and back to Manticore. I don't want to hear about any other charters you've got. I don't want you picking up any other cargoes. You're dropping off what you have aboard, and you're heading straight home. Is that perfectly clear?"

"Perfectly, Commander!" Malachai said, nodding hard.

"I hope to hell it is," he said, "because frankly, we're *both* going to be in a world of hurt if you don't do exactly that. I remind you that the WCSA's penalties for noncompliance are *ugly*, Captain."

"Don't worry, Commander," Malachai said, her voice far gentler than anything Wu had yet heard from her. "I owe you big-time for this." She shook her head. "I'm not going to do *anything* to screw you over, I swear."

Wu looked at her hard for several seconds, then smiled faintly.

"Glad to hear it. And I'm going to hold you *to* it, too, Captain!" Their eyes held for another heartbeat, and then he waved his right hand at the pickup. "Now, go on. Get out of here before I come to my senses and change my mind!"

◈ Chapter Three

"OH, *crap*."

The words were spoken quietly, almost prayerfully. For a moment or two, Lieutenant Aaron Tilborch, commanding officer of the Zunker Space Navy's light attack craft *Kipling*, didn't even realize he'd spoken them aloud, and they were hardly the considered, detached observation one might have expected from a trained professional. On the whole, however, they summed up the situation quite nicely.

"What do we do now, Sir?" Lieutenant Jannetje van Calcar, *Kipling*'s executive officer, sounded as nervous as Tilborch felt, and Tilborch thought it was an excellent question. Not that there was much *Kipling*'s small ship's company *could* do about the events preparing to unfold before them.

The ZSN wasn't much as navies went. There were several reasons for that, and one was that the Zunker System's nominal sovereignty had depended for the last T-decade and a half or so upon a delicate balancing act between the Star Kingdom of Manticore and the

35

Solarian League. The Office of Frontier Security's local commissioners had cast greedy eyes upon the Zunker System ever since the wormhole terminus associated with it had been discovered, but the terminus was the next best thing to six and a half light-hours from the system primary. That put it well outside Zunker's territorial space, which meant simply grabbing off the star system wouldn't necessarily have given OFS control of the terminus... especially since its other end lay in the Idaho System.

In point of fact, the "Zunker Terminus" had been discovered by a survey crew operating out of Idaho seventeen T-years earlier. And Idaho, unlike Zunker, lay only seventy-two light-years from the Manticore Binary System—three weeks' hyper flight for a merchant ship from the Manticoran Wormhole Junction. Actually, the survey ship had been Manticoran, not Idahoan, although it had been under charter to the Idaho government at the time. Prior to the discovery of the Idaho Hyper Bridge, Idaho had been a relative backwater, completely overshadowed by the bustling trade and massive economy of its Manticoran neighbor and fellow member of the Manticoran alliance.

For Zunker, whose existence had always been even more hand-to-mouth than that of many other Verge star systems, the consequences had been profound. The hyper bridge between it and Idaho was over four hundred light-years long, and the system lay roughly a hundred and ninety light-years from the Sol System and just over a hundred and fifty light-years from Beowulf. In fact, it lay almost directly between Beowulf and Asgerd, closing the gap between the Beowulf Terminus of the Manticore Wormhole Junction and the Andermani Empire's Asgerd-Durandel Hyper Bridge. That had turned both Zunker and Idaho into important feeder systems for the ever more heavily traveled Manticoran Wormhole Junction.

The sudden influx of so much traffic, and the kind of cash flow that went with it, dwarfed anything Zunker had ever imagined...and it had turned out to be a mixed blessing. The cascade of credits and the frenzied construction of shipping and support structures for the traffic that produced it had fueled an economic boom such as no Zunkeran had ever dreamed was possible. Over the last fifteen T-years, something like decent medical care, a proper educational system, and the beginning of true prosperity had sprouted in Lieutenant Tilborch's home star system. Yet that same abundance of cash had inevitably attracted the avarice of the Office of Frontier Security and its transstellar "friends."

Unfortunately for OFS, Idaho had no desire to do business with yet another tentacle of the OFS/corporate monstrosity. So when Frontier Security started sniffing around Zunker, Idaho mentioned the sudden upsurge in Solarian compassion and philanthropic urges to its neighbors (and allies) in Manticore. And those neighbors (and allies) in Manticore had intimated to Permanent Senior Undersecretary of the Treasury Brian Sullivan, Agatá Wodoslawski's immediate predecessor, that Solarian transit fees through any of the Manticoran Wormhole Junction's many termini might well experience an inexplicable upsurge if anything unfortunate were to happen to the Zunker System.

The result was an official Solarian consulate in Effingham, Zunker's capital city, an equally official

OFS observation post right next door to it, and a clear understanding that although the League would be permitted *influence* in Zunker, it would *not* be allowed the sort of puppetmaster control it exercised in so many other "independent" star systems. As a sort of quid pro quo for the League's . . . restraint, it was understood that Zunker fell ultimately under Solarian "protection," rather than Manticoran. The terminus itself, on the other hand, was granted Idahoan extraterritoriality, recognized by both Manticore and the League, although Prime Minister Cromarty of Manticore had insisted that the Zunker System government receive one third of all transit-fee revenues it generated.

All of which meant the Zunker Space Navy consisted of little more than a double handful of LACs, suitable for policing the traffic which flowed through the star system's freight-handling and servicing facilities. The ZSN certainly didn't possess anything remotely like a true warship, although it did assign a squadron of its LACs to Zunker Terminus Astro Control, where it worked in concert with a similar force of Idahoan vessels.

Which was how Lieutenant Tilborch and the crew of ZSNS *Kipling* came to have a ringside seat for what promised to be a most unhappy day in near-Zunker space.

"What do we do, Jannetje?" he asked now, never looking away from the display where a single Solarian merchant ship headed directly towards the terminus, escorted by six Solarian League Navy battlecruisers. "What *we* do is get the hell out of the way and com home to Effingham."

"But what about—?" van Calcar began.

"The Manties are the ones who announced they were closing the terminus to Solarian traffic, and Idaho backed them," Tilborch replied, cutting her off. "You know where my sympathies lie, but we've got no official business poking our noses in. Besides"—he smiled humorlessly—"it's not like *Kipling* was going to make any difference, is it?"

✧   ✧   ✧

Captain Hiram Ivanov watched his tactical display and frowned as he considered the odds and how they must look from the other side. His division of *Saganami-C*-class heavy cruisers was one ship understrength, leaving him only three to confront the oncoming Solarian battlecruisers. He also had four *Roland*-class destroyers, however, which actually gave him the numerical advantage, although destroyers and heavy cruisers were scarcely in the same league (nominally, at least) as battlecruisers. On the other hand, all of his ships had Mark 23-stuffed missile pods tractored to their hulls, which put rather a different complexion on traditional calculations of combat power. Unfortunately, it appeared these particular Sollies still hadn't worked through the implications of the Battle of Spindle.

"How do you want to handle it, Sir?" Commander Claudine Takoush asked softly from Ivanov's command-chair com display. Ivanov looked down at her image and raised his eyebrows, and she shrugged. "I know what we're supposed to *do*, Sir. I'm only wondering how much talking you plan to do first? I mean, this"—she twitched her head in the direction of her own tactical plot—"is just a bit more blatant than we expected."

"Blatant isn't precisely the word I'd choose, Claudine," Ivanov replied in a judicious tone. "In fact, on reflection, I believe '*stupid*' comes a lot closer to capturing the essence of my feelings at this moment. 'Arrogant' and 'pigheaded' probably belong somewhere in the mix, too, now that I think about it."

"Do you think it's the local Frontier Fleet CO's idea? Or that it represents orders from their admiralty?"

"I'm inclined to think it's the locals," Ivanov said. "Especially given Commissioner Floyd's attitude towards the Star Empire's 'interference' in his personal arrangements," he added, eyes drifting back to his own display.

The incoming icons had made their alpha translation the better part of fifty million kilometers from the terminus. That represented either pretty poor astrogation or else a deliberate decision to give any Manticoran warships plenty of time to see them coming. Ivanov suspected the latter. It was entirely likely that someone like Commissioner Floyd would figure the Manticorans' nerve would fail if they had to watch the slow, inexorable approach of the Solarian League Navy. Whether or not the Solly flag officer assigned to the mission would share that belief was another question, of course. Either way, it was going to take them a while to reach Ivanov's small force. The velocity they'd brought over the alpha wall into normal-space was barely a thousand kilometers per second, and their acceleration rate, held down by the 4,800,000-ton freighter at the core of their formation, was barely 2.037 KPS^2. At that rate, it would take them over two and a half hours to reach the terminus with a zero/zero velocity.

"It's only been a week since Idaho announced it was closing the terminus to Solly traffic," Ivanoff continued. "That's not enough time for the word to have reached Old Terra, much less for orders to deliberately create a provocation to've gotten all the way out here from Old Chicago. And this is a deliberate provocation if I've ever seen one." He snorted. "It's sure as hell not a case of a single merchie who simply hasn't gotten the word, anyway!" He shrugged. "I know Astro Control's transmission hasn't had time to reach them yet—they're still the better part of three light-minutes out—but I'll bet a dollar I know what they're going to say—or *not* say, more likely—when Captain Arredondo orders them off."

"No takers here, Skipper," Takoush said sourly.

"Well, until they get around to not saying it, there's not a lot we can do." Ivanov shrugged again. "We'll just have to wait and see if they really are stupid—and arrogant and pigheaded—enough to keep coming. And after they demonstrate that they are"—he showed his teeth—"we'll just have to see if we can't convince them to . . . reconsider their intransigence."

"You know, Skipper," Takoush observed, "I've always admired your way with the language."

✧   ✧   ✧

Although there was no way for Captain Ivanov to know it, Rear Admiral Liam Pyun, the commanding officer of Battlecruiser Division 3065.2 of the Solarian League Navy, rather agreed with the Manticoran officer's assessment of the orders he'd been given. Unfortunately, they *were* orders, legally issued by one Hirokichi Floyd, the Office of Frontier Security's commissioner for the Genovese Sector.

Floyd was one of the people who'd most resented OFS' failure to add Zunker (and the terminus associated with it) to its long list of unofficially annexed star systems. It affronted his sense of the way the universe was supposed to run ... and deprived him of his custom-hallowed rake-off from the terminus' lucrative use fees. To make matters worse, he'd been deprived by the then-Star Kingdom of Manticore, the most uppity of the neobarb star nations which were disinclined to grant the Solarian League the deference to which it was so obviously due. And, just for the frosting on Floyd's cake of discontent, the Star Kingdom had pulled no punches when the terminus was discovered. Despite (or perhaps *because* of) the fact that it was even then fighting for its life against the People's Republic of Haven in a war which had begun at a place called Hancock less than three months earlier, Manticore's explanation of why the League might choose to keep its fingers off Zunker had been presented rather more bluntly, one might almost say forcefully, than anyone *ever* spoke to the Solarian League, and Floyd had been a member of the delegation to which that "explanation" had been given.

Hirokichi Floyd was scarcely unique among Solarian bureaucrats in having personal reasons to loathe the Star Empire of Manticore and its intolerable insolence. Rear Admiral Pyun was only too well aware of that. Most of those bureaucrats, however, were far, far away from Liam Pyun, and he wished Floyd were equally far away.

"Sir," Lieutenant Commander Turner, Pyun's staff communications officer, said quietly, "we've received a transmission from Astro Control."

"Have we?" Pyun never turned away from the master display. There was silence on SLNS *Belle Poule*'s flag deck for several seconds. It was a rather uncomfortable silence, and Pyun's lips twitched humorlessly as he finally took pity on the com officer and looked over his shoulder at him.

"What sort of transmission, Ephram?" he asked.

"It's addressed to the senior officer present, Sir." Turner looked relieved by Pyun's even-toned response, but he clearly wasn't happy about the message itself. "Should I put it on your personal display, Sir?"

"No." Pyun shook his head. "Put it up on the master."

"Yes, Sir." Turner didn't—quite—shrug, but there was an undeniable, if respectful, element of "if you say so" in his body language. A moment later, the face of a dark-haired, bearded man appeared on the main communications display.

"I am Captain Fergus Arredondo, Zunker Terminus Astro Control Service." The bearded man spoke with a pronounced Manticoran accent, despite the fact that he wore the uniform of the nominally autonomous ZTACS. Not surprisingly, Pyun reflected. Idaho was a Manty ally, and most of the experienced personnel handling traffic through the Zunker Terminus were actually Manties "on loan" to ZTACS.

"You are hereby advised that, by order of the Royal Manticoran Navy, this terminus is closed to all Solarian warships and Solarian-registered merchant traffic," Arredondo continued. "Be aware that the Royal Manticoran Navy has issued instructions to Astro Control to inform all incoming shipping that vessels approaching this terminus are required to activate their transponders immediately upon receipt of this transmission. In addition, all Solarian vessels are prohibited from approaching within one light-minute of the terminus. The Star Empire of Manticore has declared this volume of space a prohibited zone and will act in accordance with international laws governing such zones. Arredondo, clear."

"Well, that's certainly clear enough, Sir," Steven Gilmore, Pyun's chief of staff said almost whimsically. "Arrogant, maybe, but clear."

"And not exactly a surprise," Pyun agreed. "Interesting that Idaho's telling us the terminus is closed 'by order of the Royal Manticoran Navy' rather than on its own authority, though, isn't it?" He smiled humorlessly. "There probably isn't anything Idaho could've done to *keep* the Manties from closing the terminus, whatever their own feelings might be. But this way they get to hide behind the Star Empire—'Look what they made us do!'—without *officially* doing anything to piss us off."

His eyes strayed to the single green light-bead of the *Zambezi Treasure*, the freighter Floyd had ordered his division to escort through the terminus, and wondered how Captain McKenzie had reacted to the transmission. He doubted, somehow, that McKenzie was any happier about it than he was.

Not that the Manties are likely to start right out shooting at him *if push comes to shove*, the rear admiral reflected.

"Any sign they've reinforced their picket, Josette?" he asked his operations officer, and Captain Josette Steinberg shook her head.

"No, Sir. I can't speak to what they might have lying doggo with its impellers down, but judging from the signatures we can see, it's still just the three cruisers and four of those big-assed destroyers of theirs."

"Seven-to-six odds, their favor," Gilmore observed. "In hulls, anyway. Of course, the *tonnage* ratio's in *our* favor."

Pyun nodded. His six battlecruisers were all *Indefatigable*-class ships, rather than Battle Fleet's newer *Nevadas*, but their combined mass was still over five million tons, whereas the Manty picket couldn't mass much over *two* million, despite the fact that the Manticoran "destroyers" were larger than most SLN light cruisers. By any traditional measure, his force advantage ought to be overwhelming.

One of the nagging little problems with traditions, however, was that they were subject to change.

I wonder how many missile pods they have? he thought. *Whatever Floyd thinks, they have to have some. I mean, Idaho's barely seventy light-years from their home system! No matter how much damage they've taken, they've got to have scraped up at least some additional firepower if they're going to count on only seven ships to cover the entire terminus.*

He would have been a lot happier if he'd had better information on what had happened in the Spindle System last month. He was sure the official version was on its way to Genovese from Old Terra, but Genovese was twenty light-years farther from Sol than Zunker. It took the better part of a T-month for anything from Old Terra to reach Genovese, as opposed to the one week of hyper travel between Zunker and Genovese, so at the moment all he—and Commissioner Floyd—had to go on were the reports which had come through from Idaho. Which meant all they really knew was what the Manties had told them. Well, what the Manties had told them and the fact that someone—and *not*, apparently, the SLN—had kicked the ever-loving hell out of the Manty home system shortly after whatever they'd done to Admiral Crandall at Spindle. Assuming, of course, that they'd actually done *anything* to Admiral Crandall at Spindle.

Commissioner Floyd was inclined to think they hadn't.

Rear Admiral Pyun was inclined to think Commissioner Floyd was an idiot.

"Anything from their picket commander, Ephram?" he asked out loud.

"No, Sir. Not yet, at least."

"I see."

Pyun turned his attention back to the master display.

✧　　✧　　✧

"I don't suppose we've heard anything back from our visitors, Justin?" Captain Ivanov asked. "No transponder signals? No snappy little comebacks to Captain Arredondo's instructions?"

"No, Sir," Lieutenant Justin Adenauer replied.

"Somehow I thought you would have mentioned it if we had," Ivanov said dryly, then looked down at the display screen connecting him to Auxiliary Control at the far end of HMS *Sloan Tompkins'* core hull from his own command deck.

"I guess it's time *we* got into the act, Claudine," he observed.

"Bound to get interesting when we do, Sir."

"There's a lot of that going around." Ivanov smiled grimly. "It seems we've been cursed to live in 'interesting times.'"

"True." Takoush nodded. "Of course, we can always try to make things more interesting for *others* than for us."

"My goal in life," Ivanov agreed, then turned back to Adenauer. "Record for transmission, Justin."

✧　　✧　　✧

"Admiral, we have another message," Ephram Turner announced. "This one's not from Astro Control."

"No?"

Pyun turned away from the master display and crossed to Turner's station. *Zambezi Treasure* (and his battlecruisers) had been in n-space for almost exactly ten minutes. During that time they'd covered almost a million kilometers and raised their closing velocity relative to the terminus to approximately 2,200 KPS. He'd wondered how long the picket-force commander was going to wait to contact him. In fact, he'd just won five credits on a side bet with Captain Steinberg on that very point.

"Go ahead and play it, Ephram," the rear admiral said, standing at Turner's shoulder and looking down at the com officer's console.

"Yes, Sir."

Turner touched a stud, and a brown-haired, green-eyed man in the uniform of a senior-grade RMN captain appeared on a small display.

"I am Captain Hiram Ivanov, Royal Manticoran Navy." Ivanov's voice was crisp and professional, and if he was dismayed by the disparity between Pyun's force and his own, there was no sign of it in those green eyes. "I'm aware that you've been instructed by Astro Control to activate your identification transponders and that no Solarian warships or Solarian-registry merchant vessels are allowed to approach within eighteen million kilometers of this terminus. Be informed at this time that while my Empress continues to desire a peaceful resolution to the current tensions between the Star Empire and the Solarian League, I have orders to enforce my government's directives concerning this terminus by force. Moreover, I also hereby inform you that I have no choice but to construe the presence of so many 'unidentified' battlecruisers in company with a single merchant ship as a deliberate effort on your part to defy those directives. Should you continue to approach this terminus without active transponders and close to a distance of less than thirty million kilometers, I will engage you. I would prefer to avoid that, but the choice is in your hands. Ivanov, clear."

Ivanov nodded almost courteously, and Turner's display blanked. Pyun stood gazing down at it for a heartbeat or so, then inhaled deeply.

"Thank you, Ephram." He patted the com officer on the shoulder and walked back across the flag bridge to Captain Gilmore.

"Well, that's clear enough, too," he observed dryly.

"Yes, Sir. And that thirty million-klick tripwire of his is consistent with what they say happened at Spindle, too."

"Agreed. On the other hand, it *would* be consistent, don't you think? Whether the 'Battle of Spindle' ever really happened or not."

Gilmore nodded, but his expression was unhappy, which pleased the rear admiral no end, since it indicated the presence of a functioning brain. Plenty of Frontier Fleet officers were just as wedded to the notion of Solarian invincibility as any Battle Fleet pain in the ass, but Pyun hadn't chosen his staff from among them. No one could ever reasonably call Steven Gilmore an alarmist, yet he was at least willing to admit the Manties might actually have learned a little something—or even developed a few new weapons systems—in the course of surviving a twenty-T-year war against the far larger People's Republic of Haven.

Of course, neither he nor Pyun had been anywhere near the Talbott Sector when that incomparable military genius Josef Byng managed to get his flagship blown away at New Tuscany. Nor had they been in the vicinity when Sandra Crandall set out to avenge her fellow genius, so there was no way they could have any firsthand impression of the weapons Manticore might have used. Unlike Gilmore, however, Pyun had enjoyed the dubious pleasure of actually meeting Crandall, and based on that, the Manties' version of what *she'd* done at Spindle carried a pronounced ring of truth. Which suggested the rest of their version of the Battle of Spindle was also at least reasonably accurate. Pyun might be willing to play devil's advocate with Gilmore, but he shared his ops officer's disinclination to simply dismiss the "preposterous" ranges which had been reported by at least some Solarian observers even before whatever happened to Crandall. Thirty million kilometers still sounded like too much to be true, but...

Pyun considered his orders once again. They were as clear as they were nondiscretionary, yet he hadn't earned flag rank in the Solarian Navy without discovering how much easier it was for people who were going to be far, far away at the critical moment to issue such unflinching directives.

Maybe it is, but he's still the commissioner, and you're still a Frontier Fleet officer assigned to his sector.

"Copy Captain Ivanov's message to Captain Zyndram, Ephram. Inform the Captain that I see no reason to alter our intentions at this time."

"Yes, Sir."

He folded his hands behind himself and stood gazing into the master display once more.

✧ ✧ ✧

"I don't suppose the Admiral actually replied to this, Vincent?" Captain Nereu Zyndram, CO of SLNS *Belle Poule*, asked.

"No, Sir," Lieutenant Vincent Würtz replied. The com officer started to say something else, but then he closed his mouth, and Zyndram smiled thinly.

Würtz was young, the flag captain thought. In fact, he was younger than he thought he was, prey to both the confidence and the trepidation of his youth. There was no way, in young Würtz's worldview, that any neo-barb navy could possibly stand up to the SLN. As far as the lieutenant was concerned, the Manty accounts of the Battle of Spindle could only be disinformation. No other possibility was admissible. Yet despite that, another part of the youngster was secretly afraid the Manty claims might contain at least a particle of truth, after all. And like the vast majority of *Belle Poule*'s company, Würtz had never seen actual combat. The possibility that he might see it very soon now had to be gnawing away inside him.

Fair enough, Zyndram thought. *You have seen combat, Nereu. And you've been around long enough to have a better feel than young Vincent for when someone's shooting you a line of shit, too. Which is why you're feeling a little nervous just this moment, yourself.*

Nereu Zyndram had felt profound reservations about this operation from the moment Rear Admiral Pyun shared their orders with him. Those reservations hadn't grown any smaller since, either. On the other hand, he'd known Pyun for a lot of years. There wasn't much chance the admiral was going to start ignoring orders just because he thought they were stupid.

❖   ❖   ❖

"He doesn't seem very impressed by my warning, does he?" Hiram Ivanov observed as the icons of the Solarian formation continued their remorseless, silent advance on the terminus.

"Typical pain-in-the-ass Solly response, Sir, if you don't mind my saying so," Lieutenant Commander Brian Brockhurst, *Sloan Tompkins'* tactical officer, replied, his voice harsh. "Or maybe I should say *lack* of response!"

"I don't mind your saying it, BB," Ivanov said in a rather milder tone. "On the other hand, let's not jump to any conclusions. We're a long way from Spindle, and there's no way this fellow could've gotten any detailed information from Old Terra yet. All he's got is whatever's come through from Idaho and trickled into his information net. So it's entirely possible he's basing his assessment of the opposing force levels on … flawed data, let's say." The captain's expression turned bleak. "He may be almost as ill-informed about our actual capabilities as we were about whoever ripped up the home system last month."

Brockhurst's own mouth tightened. His older brother, his sister, and their families had lived on a space station called *Hephaestus* prior to the attack on the Manticore Binary System, and a part of him wanted vengeance on someone—*anyone*. If he couldn't get at the people who'd actually launched "the Yawata strike," he'd settle for any legitimate target he *could* get at. Nor was he inclined to be any more sensitive to the Star Empire's enemies' perceptions, or the reasons for them, than he had to be.

"Closing velocity when they get to thirty million klicks?" Ivanov asked after a moment, and Brockhurst punched in the numbers.

"Just a shade under nine thousand KPS when they cross the line, Sir." He looked back up at his CO. "That'll add about another three-point-two million klicks to the powered envelope."

Ivanov nodded. He'd factored that into his calculations when he warned the Sollies not to approach within thirty million kilometers of the terminus. That was actually exceeding the letter of his orders, but the Royal Manticoran Navy's tradition was that an officer was expected to use his own judgment—and discretion—within the understood *intent* of his orders. Case Lacoön, the Royal Navy's long-standing contingency plan to close all termini normally under its control to Solarian shipping, didn't really apply to blowing Solarian battlecruisers out of space thirty million kilometers short of any of the termini in question. On the other hand, it was obvious the Navy was shortly going to move to full implementation of Lacoön *Two*. When that happened, Manticore would begin seizing control of every terminus it could, whoever those termini legally (or nominally, at least) belonged to, and closing all of *them* to the Sollies as well.

Whatever that took, and whatever the range at which the Navy found itself opening fire.

The fat is well and truly in the fire, no matter what happens, Hiram Ivanov thought grimly. *If those bastards in Old Chicago were going to do the reasonable thing, they'd already've done it. Since they haven't, things are going to get a hell of a lot worse before they get any better, and I think it's time to begin making that clear to the other side.*

"All right, BB," he told Brockhurst after a moment. "We'll go with Volley Alpha if our uncommunicative friends do cross the line."

Brockhurst looked as if he'd like to object. He hadn't been a huge fan of the Volley Alpha ops plan when Ivanov first trotted it out, and he still wasn't. But whether or not he wanted to object, what he actually did was nod.

"Volley Alpha, aye, Sir," he said. "I'll get it set up now."

❖   ❖   ❖

"Coming up on the thirty-million-kilometer mark in one minute, Admiral," Lieutenant Estelle Marker, Rear Admiral Pyun's staff astrogator, announced.

"Thank you, Estelle," Pyun acknowledged, and cocked his head at Josette Steinberg. "Status?" he asked.

"We're as ready as we're going to be, Sir." It wasn't the most formal readiness report Pyun had ever received, but Steinberg had been with him for almost three T-years. Unlike Battle Fleet, they'd actually accomplished something during that time, too.

"Halo is deployed and prepared for full activation," the ops officer continued. "Captain Zyndram reports all missile-defense systems are manned and ready. The rest of the division is green-board as well. I don't know what these people think they can hit us with at this range, Sir, but whatever it is, we're ready for it."

"Thank you," Pyun said, and returned to his contemplation of the master astro display. The distance to the terminus was as ridiculously high as Steinberg's readiness report implied, and he found himself wishing he shared the ops officer's dismissal of the range at which the Manties claimed to have devastated Sandra Crandall's command. For that matter, he was pretty sure *Steinberg* wished she really and truly disbelieved those claims.

Whatever else happens, at least the Solarian League Navy knows how to maintain a brave face, he thought.

The thought amused him, in a black-humor sort of way, yet he'd discovered he vastly preferred Steinberg's attitude to the panicky response he suspected the Manticoran reports had engendered elsewhere. Not that a *little* panic wouldn't do certain Battle Fleet officers he could think of a world of good. At the moment, though—

"Missile launch!" one of Steinberg's ratings suddenly announced. "CIC has multiple missile launches at three-zero million kilometers!"

❖   ❖   ❖

HMS *Sloan Tompkins*, like her sisters *Bristol Q. Yakolev* and *Cheetah*, was a *Saganami-C*-class heavy cruiser, and each of them mounted twenty launchers in each broadside. With the RMN's ability to fire off-bore missiles, that gave them the ability to fire forty-missile-strong double broadsides in a single launch, and they were armed with the internally launched Mark 16 dual-drive missile. Because of that, their tubes (and, just as importantly, their *fire control*) had been designed to take advantage of the Mark 16's drive flexibility and fire what were actually *quadruple* broadsides—salvos of eighty missiles each, not "just" forty—in order to "stack" their fire and saturate an opponent's missile defenses.

At the moment, Hiram Ivanov's ships had literally dozens of missile pods limpeted to their hulls as well, and those missile pods were loaded with full capability Mark 23 multidrive missiles, with even more endurance and powered range (and heavier laser heads) than the Mark 16. MDMs were in shorter supply than Mark 16s, though, and Ivanov had no intention of using them up unless he had to. So Volley Alpha used only the cruisers' internal tubes, and even the *Roland*-class destroyers attached to his force were mere spectators at the moment. They had barely a quarter of the cruisers' magazine capacity, and Ivanov had no more intention of wasting their limited ammunition than he did of wasting MDMs.

Which was why "only" two hundred and forty missiles, launch times and drive activations carefully staggered to bring all of them in as a single salvo, went howling towards Rear Admiral Liam Pyun's battlecruisers.

❖   ❖   ❖

"Two hundred-plus inbound," Josette Steinberg reported tersely. "Acceleration approximately four-five-one KPS-squared. Activate all Halo platforms now!"

"Activating Halo, aye, Ma'am!"

"Damn," Steven Gilmore said, so quietly only Pyun could possibly have heard him. "That's got to be a warning shot, Sir!"

"You think so?" Pyun's eyes were on the tac display now, watching the scarlet icons of the Manticoran missiles streak towards his command.

"*Has* to be, Sir." Gilmore shook his head. "Even assuming they've got the legs to reach us without going ballistic, their targeting solutions have to suck at this range."

"I imagine that's what Sandra Crandall thought, too." Pyun showed his teeth. "Assuming the Battle of Spindle really happened, of course."

Gilmore started to reply, but a fresh report from Steinberg cut him off.

"Admiral, assuming these drive numbers hold up, those things are going to be closing at better than a hundred and seventy thousand KPS when they get here." She looked over her shoulder at Pyun. "It looks like I may've been wrong about whether or not they can reach us, Sir."

"Time to attack range four minutes, Ma'am," one of her ratings told her, and she nodded.

"Halo active," another rating confirmed.

✧   ✧   ✧

"This is *not* good," Lieutenant Commander Austell Pouchard muttered under his breath.

"I think we could all agree with that, Lieutenant," Commander Hiacyntá Pocock, *Belle Poule*'s executive officer, observed caustically, and Pouchard grimaced as he realized he'd spoken more loudly than he'd meant to.

"Sorry, Ma'am," he said. "But if these numbers—"

He shook his head, and it was Pocock's turn to grimace. Pouchard was the flagship's senior tactical officer. As such, he, like Pocock, was assigned to Control Bravo, the SLN's equivalent of the Manticoran Navy's Auxiliary Control. Control Bravo was a complete duplicate of Captain Zyndram's command deck, tasked to take over if anything unfortunate happened to Control Alpha. Because of that, Control Bravo's personnel were supposed to be just as completely immersed in the tactical situation as anyone in Control Alpha, poised to assume command instantly in an emergency. In practice, though, there was a tendency for Control Bravo to be just a little detached. To stand back just a bit and watch the flow of a simulation or training exercise, looking for the patterns.

Except, of course, that this was no simulation.

Nonetheless, Pouchard had a point. If those incoming missiles could maintain their current acceleration numbers all the way in, stopping them was going to be a copper-plated bitch. And somehow she couldn't convince herself the Manties would have fired a "warning shot" quite so massive. Even with pods, three heavy cruisers couldn't have unlimited ammunition, and she couldn't see them expending that many missiles if they *didn't* have the legs to reach their targets with maneuver time still on their clocks.

In theory, a purely ballistic missile with the standoff range of a modern laser head was just as accurate as one which could still maneuver. Even an impeller-drive starship couldn't produce enough Delta V to change its predicted position sufficiently to get out of the laser head's effective range basket during the three minutes or so of the missile's flight. But theory had a tendency to come unglued when it ran headlong into the reality of that same impeller-drive starship's maneuverability *within* the range basket coupled with the impenetrability of its impeller wedge. The actual vulnerable aspects of a modern warship were remarkably narrow, unless one could attack the throat of its wedge, and a ship's ability to make radical maneuvers at four or five hundred gravities could do a lot to deny incoming missiles a favorable angle of attack. A missile which couldn't maneuver to pursue its target was unlikely, to say the least, to achieve that angle. Which didn't even consider a ballistic target's total vulnerability to defensive fire. No. Like an old pre-space wet-navy torpedo at the very end of its run, a missile which had exhausted its drive endurance before reaching attack range represented a negligible threat to any maneuvering target.

Which was why Hiacyntá Pocock was grimly certain those acceleration numbers were going to stand up.

❖   ❖   ❖

"Good telemetry on both the missiles and the Ghost Rider platforms, Sir," Lieutenant Commander Brockhurst reported. "Halo emissions match Admiral Gold Peak's reports almost perfectly."

Captain Ivanov only nodded. His attention was on his repeater plot.

❖   ❖   ❖

"Admiral, CIC's picking up something—"

Liam Pyun turned towards Captain Steinberg. The operations officer's eyes were on a side display; then she looked up at the rear admiral.

"It's coming up on the master plot now, Sir," she said, and Pyun's eyes darted back to the display. The new icons pulsed to draw the eye, help him separate them out of the clutter, and he frowned.

"What the hell *are* those?" he demanded as the absurdly low ranges registered. Those things were less than ten thousand kilometers clear of his flagship!

"We don't know, Sir," Steinberg admitted. "All we *do* know is that they seem to've been there all along. They just popped up a second ago when they cut their stealth."

"Cut their *stealth*?" Captain Gilmore repeated. "You mean the Manties got recon platforms that close to us without our ever even *seeing* them?"

"That's what it looks like," Steinberg grated harshly. "And I doubt they just dropped their stealth for no reason at all. They *want* us to know they're there."

"Ma'am," one of her assistants said, "we're picking up grav pulses all over the place. Dozens of point sources."

"Are these"—Pyun used a light pointer to jab at the new icons in the master plot—"some of those point sources, Chief Elliott?"

"Uh, yes, Sir. I think they are," the chief petty officer acknowledged.

"Oh, *shit*," Gilmore muttered.

We are so *going to get hammered*, a quiet little voice said in the back of Pyun's mind.

"How the *hell* did they fit FTL emitters into something that *small*?" Steinberg demanded almost plaintively.

The question was obviously rhetorical, which was probably just as well, since no answer suggested itself to Pyun. Not that it would have made any difference at the moment. What mattered was that the Manties had managed to do it. Unless he was badly mistaken, those had to be recon platforms—dozens of them, as Chief Elliott had just pointed out—and if they were capable of what the wilder theorists had proposed, they were feeding those Manty cruisers detailed tracking information at FTL speeds. Which meant their missile-control loop had just been cut in half, and the implications of that . . .

Belle Poule vibrated as counter-missiles began to

launch, but it was already evident to Pyun that his ships mounted far too few counter-missile tubes and point defense clusters to deal with *this* salvo.

❖   ❖   ❖

"Coming up on Point Alpha," Brockhurst announced.

"Execute as specified," Ivanov said formally.

"Aye, aye, Sir. Executing . . . now."

❖   ❖   ❖

There was little panic aboard SLNS *Belle Poule*, but only because her crew was too busy for that. There was no time for those who could actually see the displays, recognize what the readouts meant, to really consider what was happening, the stunning realization that they truly were as outclassed as the "preposterous" reports from Spindle had indicated.

And they *were* outclassed.

The Manticoran missiles came flashing in, still at that incredible—impossible—acceleration rate, and just before they entered the counter-missile zone, the electronic warfare platforms seeded among the attack birds spun up. Of the two hundred and forty missiles launched by Hiram Ivanov's three cruisers, fifty carried nothing but penetration aids, and they'd been carefully saved for this moment. Now "Dazzler" platforms blinded Solarian sensors even as their accompanying "Dragon's Teeth" suddenly proliferated, producing scores of false targets to confuse and saturate their targets' defenses. The Solarian battlecruiser crews had never seen, never imagined, anything like it. Ignorant of the energy budgets the RMN's mini-fusion plants allowed, they simply couldn't conceive of how such powerful jammers could be crammed into such tiny platforms. The threat totally surpassed the parameters their doctrine and their systems had been designed to cope with.

Pyun's battlecruisers managed to stop exactly seventeen of the incoming shipkillers in the outer zone. The other hundred and seventy-three streaked past every counter-missile the Solarians could throw with almost contemptuous ease.

❖   ❖   ❖

Liam Pyun watched his command's destruction ripping through his defenses. He'd always been more willing than most of his fellow officers to consider the possible accuracy of the outlandish reports coming back from the endless Manticore-Haven war. He'd had to be careful about admitting he was, given the contempt with which virtually all of those other officers greeted such "alarmist" rumors, but now he knew even the most bizarre of those reports had understated the true magnitude of the threat. No wonder the Manties had managed to punch out Byng's flagship so cleanly at New Tuscany!

His people were doing their best, fighting with frantic professionalism to overcome the fatal shortcomings of their doctrine and training in the fleeting minutes they had. They weren't going to succeed, and he knew it, but they weren't going to simply sit there, paralyzed by terror, either, and he felt bittersweet pride in them even as he cursed himself for having walked straight into this disaster.

But how could I have known? How could I really have known? And even if I had—

And then the Manticoran missiles burst past the inner edge of the counter-missile zone. They came driving in through the desperate, last-ditch, last-minute fire of the battlecruisers' point defense clusters, and the laser clusters were almost as useless in the face of the Manty EW as the counter-missiles had been. They managed to pick off another twelve missiles, but that still left a hundred and sixty-three shipkillers, and Pyun felt his belly knotting solid as his ships' executioners came boring in on the throats of their wedges. They were going to—

One hundred and sixty-three Mark 16 missiles, each with the better part of thirty seconds' time left on its drive, swerved suddenly, in a perfectly synchronized maneuver, and detonated as one.

✧   ✧   ✧

"Nicely done, BB," Hiram Ivanov said approvingly as the FTL reports came in from the Ghost Rider drones and *Sloan Tompkins'* CIC updated the master tactical plot. "Very nicely. In fact, I think that rates a 'well done' for your entire department."

✧   ✧   ✧

"They hit our wedges!" Steinberg blurted. "My God, they hit our *wedges!*"

Her tone was so disbelieving—and so affronted—that despite himself, Pyun actually felt his mouth twitch on the edge of a smile. The ops officer was staring incredulously at her displays as CIC's dispassionate computers updated them.

It was true. It had happened so quickly, the X-ray lasers had cascaded in such a massive tide, that it had taken Steinberg (and Pyun, for that matter) several endless seconds to grasp what had actually happened—to realize they were still alive—yet it was true.

The rear admiral would dearly have loved to believe Halo had succeeded in its decoy function. That the Manty missiles had been lured astray by his battlecruisers' sophisticated electronic warfare systems. But much as he would have preferred that, he knew differently. No defensive system in the galaxy could have caused *every single missile* in an attacking salvo to waste its fury on the roofs and floors of his ships' impeller wedges. No. The only way *that* could have happened was for the people who'd fired those missiles to have *arranged* for it to happen.

"*Christ!*" Captain Gilmore shook his head like a man who'd been hit one time too many. "How the hell—?" He stopped and gave his head another shake, then grimaced. "Sorry, Admiral."

Pyun only looked at him, then wheeled back towards Steinberg at the ops officer's inarticulate sound of disbelief. She looked up and saw the admiral's eyes on her.

"I—" It was her turn to shake her head. "Sir, according to CIC, *Retaliate* took one hit and *Impudent* took two. That's it. That's *all!*"

"Casualties?" Pyun heard his own voice asking.

"None reported so far, Sir."

"But that's ridic—" Gilmore began, then made himself stop.

"Ridiculous," Pyun agreed grimly. "Except for the minor fact that it happened. Which suggests it was what the Manties intended to happen all along. In fact, the hits on *Retaliate* and *Impudent* must've been unintentional." He smiled very, very thinly. "I suppose it's nice to know not even Manty fire control is *perfect.*"

Steinberg looked back up at him, and Gilmore inhaled deeply.

"Sir, are you suggesting they deliberately *targeted* our wedges?" the chief of staff asked very carefully. "That it was some kind of...of *demonstration?*"

"I don't have any better explanation for it, Steve. Do you?"

"I—"

"Excuse me, Captain," Lieutenant Turner interrupted respectfully, "but we're receiving a transmission I think the Admiral had better hear."

"What kind of transmission?" Pyun asked.

"It's from the Manties, Sir. But it's not a direct transmission from any of their ships. It's coming from . . . somewhere else."

"'Somewhere else'?"

"Yes, Sir." The communications officer seemed torn between relief at his continued existence and unhappiness at something else. "Sir, I think it's being relayed from another platform. From *several* other platforms, actually." Pyun only looked at him, and Turner sighed. "Sir, it looks to me as if they must have at least ten or fifteen relay platforms out there, and they're jumping the transmission between them to keep us from locking them up. And, Sir, I think they're transmitting to us in real time."

Pyun started to protest. They were still over a light-minute and a half from the Manties. There ought to be a ninety second-plus transmission lag. But then he remembered all those grav pulses, and his protest died.

"Very well," he said. "Put it on the main display."

"Yes, Sir."

The same brown-haired, green-eyed man appeared, and Pyun felt his jaw muscles tighten.

"I trust," Captain Ivanov said, "that you realize we just deliberately *didn't* destroy your ships. As I've already said, my Empress would prefer to resolve the differences between the Star Empire and the League without further bloodshed. That doesn't mean more blood won't be shed anyway, but I'd really prefer not to have it happen here, today. If you persist in approaching this terminus, however, I will have no choice but to continue this engagement, and the next salvo won't be targeted on your wedges. You have ten minutes to reverse acceleration or translate into hyper. If you've done neither at the end of those ten minutes, I *will* open fire once more, and this time we'll be firing for effect. Ivanov, clear."

It was very quiet on *Belle Poule*'s flag bridge. No one said a word. In fact, for several seconds, no one even breathed. All eyes were on Liam Pyun as he stood continuing to gaze at the blank display from which Hiram Ivanov had disappeared. Then the admiral squared his shoulders, drew a deep breath, and turned his back on the display.

"Captain Gilmore, instruct Captain Zyndram to reverse acceleration immediately. And tell him to get our hyper generators online."

Chapter Four

"THIS," YANA TRETIAKOVNA ANNOUNCED, "is booooooor-ing."

The tall, attractive, and very dangerous blonde flung herself backward into the threadbare armchair. She leaned back, crossed her arms, and glowered out the huge crystoplast wall at what any unbiased person would have to call the magnificent vista of Yamato's Nebula.

At the moment, she was less than impressed. On the other hand, she had a lot to not be impressed about. And she'd had a lot of time in which to be unimpressed, too.

"I'm sure you could find something to amuse yourself if you really wanted to," Anton Zilwicki said mildly, looking up from the chess problem on his minicomp. "This *is* one of the galaxy's biggest and most elaborate amusement parks, you know."

"This *was* one of the galaxy's biggest amusement parks," Yana shot back. "These days, it's one of the galaxy's biggest death traps. Not to mention being stuffed unnaturally full of Ballroom terrorists and Beowulfan commandos, not one of whom has a functioning sense of humor!"

"Well, if you hadn't dislocated that nice Beowulfan lieutenant's elbow arm wrestling with him, maybe you'd find out they had better senses of humor than you think they do."

"Yada, yada, yada." Yana scowled. "It's not even fun to tease *Victor* anymore!"

A deep basso chuckle rumbled around inside Zilwicki's massive chest. When Yana had first signed on to assist in his and Victor Cachat's high-risk mission to Mesa, she'd been at least half frightened (whether she would have admitted it to a living soul or not) of the Havenite secret agent. She'd agreed to come along—mostly out of a desire to avenge her friend Lara's death—and she was a hardy soul, was Yana. Still, the notion of playing the girlfriend (although the ancient term "moll" might actually have been a better one) of someone many people would have described as a stone-cold, crazed, sociopathic killer had obviously worried her more than she'd cared to admit. In fact, Zilwicki thought, Cachat had never struck him as either stone cold or crazed, but he could see where other people might form that impression, given his Havenite colleague's body count. As for sociopathy, well, Zilwicki's internal jury was still out on that one in some ways.

Not that he hadn't known some perfectly nice sociopaths. Besides, Zilwicki had observed that who was the sociopath and who was the defender of all that was right and decent often seemed to depend a great deal on the perspective of the observer.

And sometimes the cigar really is a cigar, of course, he reflected. *That's one of the things that makes life so interesting when Victor's around.*

Over the course of their lengthy mission on Mesa, Yana had gotten past most of her own uneasiness with the Havenite. And the four-month voyage from Mesa back to the Hainuwele System had finished it off. Of course, the trip shouldn't have taken anywhere near that long. The old, battered, and dilapidated freighter *Hali Sowle* their Erewhonese contacts had provided had been a smuggler in her time, and she'd been equipped with a military-grade hyper generator. It wasn't obvious, because her original owners had gone to considerable lengths to disguise it, and they hadn't tinkered with her commercial-grade impeller nodes and particle screening, but that had allowed her to climb as high as the Theta Bands, which made her far faster than the vast majority of merchant vessels. Unfortunately, the hyper generator in question had been less than perfectly maintained by the various owners through whose hands the ship had passed since it was first installed, and it had promptly failed after they managed to escape Mesa into hyper. They'd survived the experience, but it had taken Andrew Artlet what had seemed like an eternity to jury-rig the replacement component they'd required.

They'd drifted, effectively motionless on an interstellar scale, while he and Anton managed the repairs, and even after they'd gotten the generator back up, using the Mesa-Visigoth Hyper Bridge had been out of the question. They'd been better than nine hundred and sixty light-years from their base in Hainuwele (and well over a thousand light-years from Torch) but given the ... pyrotechnics which had accompanied their escape, they'd dared not return to the Mesa Terminus and take the shortcut that would have delivered them less than sixty light-years from Beowulf. Instead, they'd been forced to detour by way of the OFS-administered Syou-tang Terminus of the Syou-tang-Olivia Bridge, then cross the four hundred and eighty-odd light-years from the Olivia System to Hainuwele the hard way.

The trip had given them plenty of time to hone their cardplaying skills, and the same enforced confinement had given the coup de grace to any lingering fear Yana might have felt where Victor Cachat was concerned. It had also given Cachat and Zilwicki plenty of time to debrief Herlander Simões, the Mesan physicist who had defected from the Mesan Alignment. Well, "plenty of time" was probably putting it too strongly. They'd had *lots* of time, but properly mining the treasure trove Simões represented was going to take years, and it was, frankly, a task which required someone with a lot more physics background than Zilwicki possessed.

Enough had emerged from Simões' responses and from the maddeningly tantalizing fragments which had been proffered by Jack McBryde, the Mesan security officer who'd engineered Simões' defection, to tell them that everything everyone—even, or perhaps *especially*, the galaxy's best intelligence agencies—had always known about Mesa was wrong. That information was going to come as a particularly nasty shock to Beowulf intelligence, Zilwicki thought, but Beowulf was hardly going to be alone in that reaction. And as they'd managed to piece together more bits of the mosaic, discovered just how much no one else knew, their plodding progress homeward had become even more frustrating.

There'd been times—and quite a few of them—when Zilwicki had found himself passionately wishing they'd headed towards the Lynx Terminus of the Manticoran Wormhole Junction instead. Unfortunately, their evasive routing had been more or less forced upon them initially, and it would have taken even longer to backtrack to Lynx than to continue to Syou-tang. And there'd also been the rather delicate question of exactly what would happen to Victor Cachat if they should suddenly turn up in the Manticore Binary System, especially after the direct Havenite attack on the aforesaid star system, word of which had reached the Mesan news channels just over two T-months before their somewhat hurried departure. It had struck them as unlikely that one of Haven's top agents would be received with open arms and expressions of fond welcome, to say the least.

For that matter, exactly who had jurisdiction over Simões (and the priceless intelligence resource he represented) was also something of a delicate question. Their operation had been jointly sponsored by the Kingdom of Torch, the Republic of Haven (whether or not anyone in Nouveau Paris had known anything about it), the Audubon Ballroom, the Beowulf Biological Survey Corps, and Victor Cachat's Erewhonese contacts. There'd been absolutely no official *Manticoran* involvement, although Princess Ruth Winton's contributions hadn't exactly been insignificant. She'd been acting in her persona as Torch's intelligence chief, however, not in her persona as a member of the Star Empire of Manticore's ruling house.

Bearing all of that in mind, there'd never really been much chance of heading straight for Manticore. Instead, they'd made for Hainuwele, on the direct line to Torch. It was the closest safe harbor, given the available wormhole connections, and they'd hoped to find one of the BSC's disguised commando ships in-system and available for use as a messenger when they got there. They'd been disappointed in that respect, however; when they arrived, the only ship on station had been EMS *Custis*, an Erewhonese construction ship which had just about completed the conversion of Parmaley Station into a proper base for the BSC and the Ballroom to interdict the interstellar trade in genetic slaves.

Artlet and Zilwicki's repairs had been less than perfect, and *Hali Sowle* had limped into Hainuwele on what were obviously her hyper generator's last legs. *Custis'* captain been out of touch for two or three months himself while his construction crews worked on Parmaley Station, but he'd been able to confirm that as far as active operations between Haven and Manticore were concerned, a hiatus of mutual exhaustion had set in following the Battle of Manticore. Both Anton and Victor had been vastly relieved to discover that no one had been actively shooting at one another any longer, given what they'd learned on Mesa, but it had been obvious the good captain was less than delighted at the notion of finding himself involved in the sort of shenanigans which seemed to follow the team of Zilwicki and Cachat around. He'd apparently suspected that his Erewhonese employers wouldn't have approved of his stepping deeper into the morass he was pretty sure *Hali Sowle* and her passengers represented. They might have convinced him to change his mind if they'd told him what they'd discovered on Mesa, but they weren't about to break security on *that* at this point. Which meant the best he'd been willing to do was to take his own ship to Erewhon (which, to be fair, was the next best thing to twenty light-years closer to Hainuwele than Torch was) to fetch back a replacement generator for *Hali Sowle*. In the process, he was willing to take an encrypted dispatch from Victor to Sharon Justice, who'd been covering for him as the Republic's senior officer in the Erewhon Sector, but that was as far as he was prepared to go.

Zilwicki didn't try to pretend, even to himself, that he hadn't found the captain's attitude irritating. Fortunately, he was by nature a patient, methodical, analytical man. And there were at least some upsides to the situation. Neither he nor Cachat wanted Simões out of their sight, and while they had no particular reason to distrust *Custis'* captain or crew, they had no particular reason to *trust* them, either. If even a fraction of what Jack McBryde and Herlander Simões had told them proved true, it was going to shake the foundations of star nations all across explored space. They literally could not risk having anything happen to him until they'd had time for him to tell his tale—in detail—to their own star nations' intelligence services. Much as they might begrudge the month or so it would take *Custis* to make the trip to Erewhon, they preferred to stay right where they were until Justice could arrange secure transport to Torch. They'd both breathe an enormous sigh of relief once they had Simões safely squirreled away on Torch and could send discreet dispatches requesting that all of the relevant security agencies send senior representatives to Torch.

No one expected it to be easy, and he knew Cachat

was as worried as he was over the possibility that the Star Empire and the Republic might resume combat operations while they waited, but both of them were aware that they'd stumbled onto the sort of intelligence revelation that came along only once in centuries. Assuming it wasn't all part of some incredible, insane disinformation effort, the Mesan Alignment had been working on its master plan for the better part of *six hundred* T-years without *anyone's* having suspected what was happening. Under those circumstances, there were quite literally no lengths to which Victor Cachat and Anton Zilwicki wouldn't go to keep their sole source of information alive.

Which was why they were all still sitting here aboard Parmaley Station's moldering hulk while they awaited transportation elsewhere.

"You know," Yana said a bit plaintively, "nobody told me we were going to be gone on this little jaunt for an entire year."

"And we haven't been," Zilwicki pointed out. "Well, actually, I suppose we have, depending on the planetary year in question. But in terms of T-years, it's been less than one. Why, it's been barely ten T-months, when you come down to it!"

"And it was only *supposed* to be four," Yana retorted.

"We told you it might be five," Zilwicki corrected, and she snorted.

"You know, even Scrags can do simple arithmetic, Anton. And—"

The powered door giving access to the combination viewing gallery and sitting room was one part of Parmaley Station which had been thoroughly refurbished. Now it opened rather abruptly, interrupting Yana in mid-sentence, and a dark-haired man came through it. Compared to Zilwicki's massive musculature and shoulders, the newcomer looked almost callow, but he was actually a well-muscled young fellow.

"Ah, there you are!" he said. "Ganny El said she thought you were in here."

"And so we are, Victor," Zilwicki rumbled, and raised an eyebrow. "And since we are, and since you're here at the moment, may I ask who's babysitting our good friend Herlander? Unless I'm mistaken, it *is* your watch, isn't it?"

"I left Frank sitting outside his door with a flechette gun, Anton," Cachat replied in a patient tone, and Zilwicki grunted.

The sound represented at least grudging approval, although one had to know him well to recognize that fact. On the other hand, Frank Gillich was a capable fellow. He and June Mattes were both members of the Beowulf Biological Survey Corps, part of the original BSC team which had discovered the Butre Clan here on Parmaley Station and brokered the deal that left the Butres alive and turned the station into a BSC/Ballroom front. Most people (or most people who didn't know Victor Cachat, at least) would have considered Gillich and Mattes about as lethal as agents came, and Zilwicki was willing to concede that Gillich could probably be counted upon to keep Simões alive for the next fifteen or twenty minutes.

"I thought *I* was the hyper-suspicious, paranoid, obsessive-compulsive one," Cachat continued. "What is this? Are you trying to claim the title of Paranoiac in Chief?"

"Hah!" Yana snorted. "He's not trying to do anything.

He's just been hanging around *you* too long. That's enough to drive anyone—except Kaja...maybe—around the bend!"

"I don't see why the entire universe insists on thinking of me as some sort of crazed killer," Cachat said mildly. "It's not like I kill anyone who doesn't *need* killing."

He said it with a completely straight face, but Zilwicki thought it was probably a joke. *Probably.* One could never be entirely certain where Cachat was concerned, and the Havenite's idea of a sense of humor wasn't quite like most people's.

"May I assume there's a reason you left Frank playing babysitter and asked Ganny El where you might find us?" Zilwicki asked.

"Actually, yes," Cachat replied, dark brown-black eyes lighting. "I think I've finally found the argument to get you to agree to take Herlander straight to Nouveau Paris, Anton."

"Oh?" Zilwicki crossed tree-trunk arms and cocked his head, considering Cachat the way a skilled lumberjack might consider a particularly scrubby sapling. "And why should we suddenly depart from our agreed-on plan of parking him on Torch and inviting all the mountains to come to Mohammed?"

"Because," Cachat replied, "a dispatch boat just came in from Erewhon."

"A dispatch boat?" Zilwicki's eyes narrowed. "Why would anyone in Erewhon be sending a dispatch boat out here?"

"Apparently Sharon decided it would be a good idea to let anyone from the Ballroom or the BSC who checked in with Parmaley Station know what's going on," Cachat replied. He shrugged. "Obviously, she didn't know *I* was going to be here when she sent the boat—she sent it off about three weeks ago, and the earliest *Custis* could get to Erewhon is tomorrow."

"I'm perfectly well aware of *Custis'* schedule," Zilwicki rumbled. "So suppose you just go ahead and tell me 'what's going on' that's so important your minions are throwing dispatch boats around the galaxy?"

"Well, it happens that about three months ago, Duchess Harrington arrived in Haven orbit," Cachat said. "The news got sent out to all of our intelligence stations in the regular data dumps, but it still took over a month to get to Sharon, and she sent the dispatch boat out to distribute it to all our stations in the sector. It stopped off at Torch, too, according to its skipper. We were the last stop on the information chain." He shrugged again. "I imagine the only reason it got sent here at all was Sharon's usual thoroughness. But according to the summary she got from the home office, Duchess Harrington is in Nouveau Paris for the express purpose of negotiating a peace settlement between the Republic and the Star Empire."

Anyone who knew Anton Zilwicki would have testified that he was a hard man to surprise. This time, though, someone had managed it, and his eyes widened.

"A peace settlement? You mean a formal *treaty*?"

"Apparently that's exactly what she's there to get, and according to Sharon's summary, President Pritchart is just as determined as the Duchess. On the other hand, after twenty years of shooting at each other, I doubt they've already tied it all up in a neat bow. And since Duchess Harrington actually believed both of us before we ever set out for Mesa, I don't see any reason she wouldn't believe us if we turned up with Simões in tow. For that matter, she'll have her treecat with her, and he'll *know* whether or not we're telling the truth. Or whether or not Herlander is, when you come down to it."

"And if there's anyone in the Star Empire who could convince the Queen to listen to us, it's Harrington," Zilwicki agreed, nodding vigorously.

"Exactly. So my thought is that we leave the recordings of our interviews with Herlander here on our station to be picked up by the next BSC courier to come through and taken on to Torch. Redundancy is a beautiful thing, after all. In the meantime, though, you and I commandeer Sharon's dispatch boat, load Herlander on board, and head straight for Haven." Cachat grinned. "Do you think finding out about the Alignment's existence might have some small impact on the negotiations?"

Chapter Five

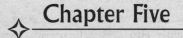

INNOKENTIY KOLOKOLTSOV ROSE as Astrid Wang formally ushered his visitor into his office. His secretary was more subdued than usual, and it was obvious to Kolokoltsov that she was on her best behavior.

Astrid always did have a good set of instincts, he thought. *Not that our manners are going to make very much difference this time around. Whatever else is going to happen, the Manties aren't the kind of neo-barbs we can* impress *into acknowledging the Solarian League's supremacy. The pain-in-the-ass bastards've made* that *clear enough!*

"Mr. Ambassador," he said, with a small, formal bow instead of extending a hand across his desk.

"Mr. Permanent Senior Undersecretary," Sir Lyman Carmichael responded in a pronounced Manticoran accent, with an even shallower bow.

"May we offer you refreshment, Mr. Ambassador?"

"No, thank you."

There was a distinct edge of frost in that reply, Kolokoltsov noted. Well, that wasn't unexpected. Lyman

Carmichael was a career diplomat, but he didn't really have the disposition for it, in Kolokoltsov's opinion. He felt things too deeply, without the professional detachment which ought to be brought to the task. No doubt there was a place for passion, for belief, even for anger, but it wasn't at the table where interstellar diplomats played for the highest stakes imaginable. That was a place for clearheadedness and dispassion, and a man who could be goaded into intemperance was a dangerous loose warhead for his own side.

"As you will."

Kolokoltsov inclined his head again, this time indicating the chair on the far side of his desk, and Carmichael's lips tightened ever so slightly. There was a much more comfortably and intimately arranged conversational nook in the angle of the palatial office's picture windows, looking out over the towers and canyons of Old Chicago. That was where Kolokoltsov met with visitors when he was prepared to pretend other star nations were truly the Solarian League's peers. It was particularly important to make the point that the Star Kingdom of Manticore was *not* the League's peer, however, and so he seated himself again behind his desk and folded his hands on the antique blotter.

"How may I be of service, Mr. Ambassador?" he asked with a pleasantness which fooled neither of them.

"I've been instructed by my government to deliver a formal note to Foreign Minister Roelas y Valiente."

Carmichael smiled thinly, and Kolokoltsov smiled back. Whatever the official flowchart of the Solarian League Foreign Ministry might indicate, Carmichael knew as well as Kolokoltsov that Roelas y Valiente was no more than a figurehead. Whoever the note might be addressed to, the Manticoran Ambassador was looking at its actual recipient.

"May I inquire as to the note's contents?" Kolokoltsov asked with a straight face.

"You may," Carmichael replied.

He didn't say anything else, however, and Kolokoltsov felt his jaw muscles tighten ever so slightly as the Manticoran simply sat there, smiling at him. Waiting.

"And those contents are?" he asked after a lengthy moment, keeping his voice even.

"As you're aware, Mr. Permanent Senior Undersecretary, my government is deeply concerned over the escalating series of . . . incidents between the Solarian League military and the Star Empire. We realize there's a difference of opinion between Landing and Old Chicago about precisely how those incidents occurred and who was responsible for them." His eyes met Kolokoltsov's coldly. "Regardless of who bears responsibility for those which have occurred in the past, however, my government is desirous of avoiding any additional incidents in the future."

"I'm sure that will come as very welcome news to Foreign Minister Roelas y Valiente," Kolokoltsov said when the Manticoran paused again.

"I hope it will," Carmichael continued. "However, in pursuit of that object, the Star Empire, as you may or may not be aware, Mr. Permanent Senior Undersecretary, has issued a general recall of its merchant shipping in the League."

Kolokoltsov stiffened. He'd only just begun receiving reports about disappearing Manticoran merchant vessels. Not enough of them had come in yet for any sort of pattern to reveal itself, but according to at least some of them, the merchant vessels in question had canceled charters and contractual commitments without explanation. He'd been inclined to discount those particular reports, given the hefty penalties the captains and shipowners in question would face, but if the Star Empire's government had issued a non-discretionary recall...

"In part," Carmichael said, "that recall represents an effort on our part to be sure none of the...unfortunate incidents which have so far involved only our military vessels spill over onto our civilian traffic. Obviously, we don't think a Solarian warship captain would lightly open fire on an unarmed merchant vessel in a fit of pique, but, then, we didn't think a fleet of battlecruisers would open fire on a handful of destroyers riding peacefully in orbit, either." He smiled again, a smile as cold as his eyes. "Accidents, it appears, do happen, don't they? So my government has decided to ensure that no more of them transpire. There is, however, another reason for the recall."

"And that reason would be exactly what, Mr. Ambassador?" Kolokoltsov's tone was level, its neutrality a deliberate emphasis of his decision to ignore the Manticoran's latest barb.

"You might think of it as an attempt to get the League's attention, Mr. Permanent Senior Undersecretary. We appear to have been singularly unsuccessful in our efforts to accomplish that so far, so my government has decided to resort to rather more direct measures."

"Are you implying that the recall of your merchant shipping should be viewed as an unfriendly act directed against the Solarian League?" Kolokoltsov asked in a voice he'd suddenly allowed to become frigid.

"I fail to see how simply withdrawing our shipping from Solarian shipping lanes could be construed as 'an unfriendly act,' Mr. Permanent Senior Undersecretary." Carmichael shrugged slightly. "On the other hand, I suppose it *will* have an unfortunate impact on the movement of the League's interstellar commerce."

Kolokoltsov sat rigidly in his chair, gazing across his folded hands at the Manticoran. He was no economist, no expert on international shipping, but the entire Solarian League was only too well aware of the extent to which the life's blood of its interstellar economy moved in Manticoran bottoms. It was one of the reasons so many Solarians so intensely resented and detested the Star Empire of Manticore. And it was also the reason—coupled with the Manties' control of the Manticoran Wormhole Junction and its commanding position among the warp bridges in general—that such a pissant little star nation had been able to... constrain Solarian foreign policy repeatedly over the last couple of T-centuries. But in all those years, Manticore had never threatened to actually withdraw its shipping from the League!

"I'm not an expert in interstellar commerce, Mr. Ambassador," he said after a few seconds. "It would appear to me, however, that the Star Empire's actions will result in the violation of numerous commercial agreements and contracts."

"That, unfortunately, is correct, Mr. Permanent Senior Undersecretary. It's regrettable, of course, but fortunately the majority of the shipping lines in question are bonded. In those instances where they aren't, the injured parties will of course be able to seek redress through the courts. With what degree of success"—Carmichael smiled thinly—"no one can say at this point. I suppose a great deal will depend upon whose court adjudicates the matter, don't you?"

"You're playing with the lives and livelihoods of millions of Solarian citizens, Mr. Ambassador," Kolokoltsov pointed out rather more sharply than he'd intended to.

"I suppose it could be interpreted that way. Considering the current—and apparently still deteriorating—relationship between the Star Empire and the Solarian League, however, my government believes it will be safest all around for our merchant vessels to remain in Manticoran space—or, at least, outside of *Solarian* space—until the matters under dispute between the Star Empire and the League have been satisfactorily resolved. At that time, of course, we would look forward to restoring our freighters and passenger liners to their normal runs."

Steel showed in Carmichael's smile this time, and despite his many years of experience, Kolokoltsov felt his own face darkening with anger.

"Some people," he said carefully, "might interpret the Star Empire's decision in this matter as an active economic war against the League."

"I suppose they might." Carmichael nodded, then stabbed the Solarian with his eyes. "And some people might consider what happened in New Tuscany and Spindle acts of war against the Star Empire, Mr. Permanent Senior Undersecretary. I suppose it would behoove both the Star Empire and the Solarian League to demonstrate to the rest of the galaxy that they wish to find an amicable resolution of all of the tensions and . . . disputed matters currently lying between them. That, as I'm sure Foreign Minister Roelas y Valiente has shared with you from our earlier notes, has been the Star Empire's view from the very beginning."

Kolokoltsov felt a very strong temptation to reach across the desk and strangle the man sitting on its other side.

"I'm sure all of those disputed matters *will* be settled in due time, Mr. Ambassador," he said instead.

"Oh, so am I, Mr. Permanent Senior Undersecretary. So am I." Carmichael smiled thinly.

"I'll pass your note to the Minister this very afternoon, Mr. Ambassador," Kolokoltsov promised curtly. "Was there anything else we should discuss?"

"Actually, there is one other small matter, Mr. Permanent Senior Undersecretary." The Manticoran's smile turned positively sharklike, and Kolokoltsov felt a stir of uneasiness.

"And what might that 'small matter' be?" he inquired.

"Well, it's occurred to the Star Empire that while removing its merchant shipping from Solarian space represents the best way to avoid the potential of incidents between them and Solarian warships, we would be derelict in our responsibilities if we didn't take measures to protect Solarian merchant shipping as well."

"Protect Solarian shipping?" Kolokoltsov repeated a bit blankly, and Carmichael nodded.

"Yes. It's unfortunately true that public opinion in the Star Empire at this particular moment is very... exercised where the Solarian League is concerned. I'm sure you've had reports from your own ambassadors and attachés in the Star Empire about demonstrations, even some minor vandalism, I'm afraid. It's all very sad, but understandable, I suppose."

His tone could have turned the Amazon Basin into a Sahara. His own embassy had been besieged literally for weeks by "spontaneous demonstrations" of Solarian citizens outraged by "Manticoran high-handedness" and demanding justice for Admiral Josef Byng and Fleet Admiral Sandra Crandall. Some of those demonstrations had turned even uglier than their organizers in the Ministry of Education and Information had intended.

"At any rate, as the authorities here in Old Chicago have pointed out to my staff, it's not always possible to constrain private citizens from acting on their anger and their outrage, however inappropriately placed those emotions may be and however hard the authorities try. Unhappily, that situation obtains in the Star Empire as well. More than that, my government has decided that it's absolutely imperative there be no further incidents until the current ones have been thoroughly investigated and resolved. While we don't believe that the Royal Manticoran Navy was the instigator of any of the . . . episodes which have so far occurred, we're aware that many in the Solarian League, including the Solarian League government, don't share our belief. In fact, many of them believe the RMN was the aggressor in all of these unfortunate cases. To date, our own investigation doesn't support that conclusion, but we aren't completely prepared to rule it out. So my government has decided it will be best to separate our warships from proximity with your own . . . and with your merchant vessels, as well."

"You're withdrawing all of your warships to Manticoran space?" Kolokoltsov said slowly.

"No, I'm afraid that would be quite impossible, Mr. Permanent Senior Undersecretary. The Royal Navy's responsibilities are far too widespread and demanding for us to do such a thing. Unhappily, that means our only alternative is to close all Manticoran warp termini to Solarian traffic, beginning immediately. Courier vessels and news-service dispatch vessels will be allowed passage regardless of registry, but all Solarian-registered freight carriers and passenger ships will, unfortunately, be denied passage until the current disputes are resolved."

"*What?!*"

The one-word question erupted from Kolokoltsov before he could stop himself. For the first time in decades, his carefully cultivated professional composure deserted him and he stared at the Manticoran incredulously.

"You can't be serious," he said in a marginally more controlled tone. "That would be illegal. It *would* constitute an act of war!"

"On the contrary, it's completely legal, Mr. Permanent Senior Undersecretary," Carmichael replied coolly.

"The Shingaine Convention on free passage mandates that all warp termini be open to all traffic," Kolokoltsov shot back.

"Does it?" Carmichael arched his eyebrows, then shrugged. "Well, I'm prepared to take your word for that, Mr. Permanent Senior Undersecretary. Unfortunately, the Star Empire of Manticore isn't a signatory of the Shingaine Convention." He smiled pleasantly. "Besides, it's my understanding that that particular provision of the Convention has been violated several times already."

Kolokoltsov's molars ground together. The Shingaine Convention had been sponsored by the Solarian League seventy T-years ago expressly as a means to pressure the then-Star *Kingdom* of Manticore. The Star Kingdom had already been beginning its preparations for its decades-long war against the People's Republic of Haven, and it had demonstrated that it was only too prepared to use its control of the Manticoran Wormhole Junction as a lever to pressure the League's foreign policy in its own favor if it decided that was necessary. The League wasn't used to dancing to anyone else's piping—*it* was supposed to provide the dance music in its relations with other star nations—so it had convened a meeting of "independent star nations" in the Shingaine System which had obediently produced the Shingaine Convention. The Solarian League had immediately recognized it as the basis of its "open door" policy, with the clear implication that it would enforce its interpretation of interstellar law by force if necessary.

But as Carmichael had pointed out, the Star Empire had never signed it and so, technically, wasn't bound by its provisions. Nor had Manticore ever shown any particular desire to kowtow to Solarian pressure on the matter. For that matter, as Carmichael had implied, the League would be on shaky ground if it did insist on enforcing those provisions, since the Office of Frontier Security had excluded independent Verge star systems from warp termini *it* controlled on several occasions over the last half-T-century or so as a means to pressure them into accepting OFS "protection."

"Whether or not the Star Empire considers itself bound by the terms of the Shingaine Convention," Kolokoltsov said coldly, "this high-handed, unilateral, hostile action is not going to pass unremarked in the League. However you may care to dress it up, it does constitute an act of economic warfare, as your government is perfectly well aware, Mr. Ambassador!"

"I suppose it could be described that way," Carmichael conceded judiciously. "On the other hand, it's far less destructive than a salvo of laser heads, Mr. Permanent Senior Undersecretary. My government has attempted from the very beginning to resolve the tensions between the Star Empire and the League without further bloodshed. Your government has steadfastly refused to meet us halfway. Or even a third of the way. Allow me to point out to you that however much damage your economy may suffer from the Star Empire's reasonable and prudent acts to defuse further incidents, it will suffer far less than it would in an all-out war against the Royal Manticoran Navy. You may not believe me, but my government is trying to *prevent* that all-out war. We've tried diplomacy. We've tried the exchange of notes. We've offered joint investigations. We've provided you with detailed sensor records of the incidents which have occurred. None of that appears to have moved the Solarian League in any way."

He looked levelly across the desk at Kolokoltsov, and his eyes could have frozen helium.

"The Star Empire of Manticore cannot dictate the Solarian League's foreign policy to it, Mr. Permanent Senior Undersecretary, nor will it attempt to. But it *will* pursue its *own* foreign policy, and if we cannot get you to listen to reason one way, we *will* seek another."

APRIL 1922 POST DIASPORA

"Everything *we've* ever seen out of the Manties suggests their first reaction to any threat, especially to their home system, is going to be to kill it."

—Assistant Director of Defense Justyná Miternowski-Zhyang, Beowulf Planetary Board of Directors

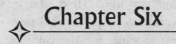

Chapter Six

"PERMANENT SENIOR UNDERSECRETARY KOLOKOLTSOV is here for his fifteen hundred, Mr. President."

"Ah! Excellent—excellent!" President Yeou Kun Chol, ostensibly the most powerful man in the entire Solarian League, beamed as Innokentiy Arsenovich Kolokoltsov (who arguably *was* the most powerful man in the entire League) followed Shania Lewis into his huge office. The president's desk was bigger than most people's beds, and he had to physically walk around it to get close enough to Kolokoltsov to offer his hand.

"Thank you, Shania," the president said to his personal secretary. "I think that will be all—unless there's anything *you* need, of course, Innokentiy?"

"No. No, thank you, Mr. President. I'm fine."

"Good. Good!" The president beamed some more and nodded to Lewis, who smiled politely, bestowed a slight bow on Kolokoltsov, and disappeared. "Sit, Innokentiy. Please," Yeou continued as the expensive, inlaid door closed silently behind her.

"Thank you, Mr. President."

Kolokoltsov obeyed the invitation, taking the comfortable biofeedback armchair facing the desk, and watched Yeou walk back around to his own throne-like chair. The president settled himself behind his desk once again, and the permanent senior undersecretary crooked a mental eyebrow.

Yeou Kun Chol, in Innokentiy Kolokoltsov's considered opinion, was pretty much an idiot. He'd attained his immensely prestigious (and utterly powerless) position because he knew when to smile for the cameras and because the true power brokers of the Solarian League knew he was a nonentity, the sort of person who would have been ineffectual even if his august office had retained a shadow of true power. There were other factors, of course. Including the fact that however ineffectual he might be, his *family* was immensely wealthy and wielded quite a lot of power behind the League's façade of representative government. Letting him play with the pretty bauble of the presidency kept them happy and him from interfering with anything truly important (like the family business), which had paid off quite a few quiet debts. And to give the man his due, Yeou was sufficiently aware of reality to realize his office's powers were far more ceremonial and symbolic than genuine.

That was one reason it was unheard of for the president to actually invite a permanent senior undersecretary to an audience. He didn't send "invitations" to them; *they* told *him* when they needed to see him for the sake of official appearances. And at any other meeting Kolokoltsov could think of, the president would have joined him, taking another of the palatial armchairs arranged in front of his desk to allow comfortably intimate conversations. He most definitely would *not* have reseated himself behind the desk, and Kolokoltsov wondered exactly where the unusual attempt to assert some sort of formality—possibly even authority, if the thought hadn't been too absurd for even Yeou to entertain—was headed.

"Thank you for coming so promptly, Innokentiy," Yeou said after a moment.

"You're welcome, of course, Mr. President." Kolokoltsov smiled. There was no point being impolite now that he was here. As long as Yeou didn't start meddling in things that were none of his affair, at least. "My time is yours, and your secretary indicated there was some urgency to your summons."

"Well, actually, there *is* some urgency to it, Innokentiy." The president tipped back in his chair, elbows on its armrests, and frowned ever so minutely at the permanent senior undersecretary for foreign affairs. "I just wanted to discuss with you—get your feeling about, as it were—this business with the Manties."

"I beg your pardon, Mr. President?" Kolokoltsov couldn't quite keep a trace of surprise out of his tone. "Ah, exactly which aspect of it, Sir?"

Kolokoltsov was aware that in most star nations a head of state would already have been thoroughly briefed about his nation's relationship with another star nation against whom it was very nearly in a state of war. Even for Kolokoltsov it was more an intellectual awareness than anything else, though. Yeou had received memos and reports from the permanent senior undersecretaries who were the League's true policymakers, but no one had ever so much as considered presenting him with any sort of genuine briefing. For that matter, even under the dead letter of the Constitution, the office of the president had been almost entirely symbolic. Had anyone been paying any attention to the Constitution, Prime Minister Shona Gyulay would have been the actual head of government, and any briefings would have gone to her, not to Yeou.

"I've read the reports, of course," Yeou told him now. "And I appreciate your efforts—both yours and your civilian colleagues', and Admiral Rajampet's—to clarify the...unfortunate events which have led to our current situation." The president's expression sobered. "Naturally, I can't pretend I'm happy thinking about all the people who have already lost their lives and where this all may be headed ultimately. But I must say I find myself particularly concerned at this moment about the Manticorans' decision to recall all of their merchant vessels." He shook his head, his expression even more sober. "It's a bad business all around, Innokentiy, but I'm worried about the immediate consequences for our economy. So I was hoping you could sort of bring me up to date on exactly what's been happening on that front."

❖   ❖   ❖

"*Yeou* asked you about that?"

Agatá Wodoslawski's gray eyes widened, then narrowed speculatively as Kolokoltsov nodded. The attractive, red-haired permanent senior undersecretary of the treasury's holo image sat directly across the virtual conference table from him. Actually, of course, she was seated behind her own desk in her own office, and now she sat back in her chair, shaking her head with the air of a woman who wondered what preposterous absurdity was going to happen next.

"So he's finally woken up to the fact that something's going on with the Manties, has he?" Malachai Abruzzi's holo image said sarcastically. The dark-haired, dark-eyed permanent senior undersecretary of information was a short, stocky man with powerful hands, one of which he now waved dismissively. "I'm dazzled by the force of his intellect."

"'Dazzled' may not be exactly the right word for it," Permanent Senior Undersecretary of Commerce Omosupe Quartermain said, "but when you've been looking into a completely dark closet long enough, even a candle can seem blinding. And let's face it, our beloved President is a very dark closet indeed," she added, and Kolokoltsov smiled sourly.

Between them, she, Abruzzi, Wodoslawski and Kolokoltsov represented four of what certain newsies—headed by that never-to-be-sufficiently-damned muckraker Audrey O'Hanrahan—had begun to call "the Five Mandarins." O'Hanrahan had been forced to explain the term's origin to her readership initially, but once she had, it caught on quickly. Abruzzi's publicity flaks were doing what they could to discourage its use, but it continued to spread with insidious inevitability. By now, even some of the tamer members of the Legislative Assembly were using it in news conferences and speeches.

It wasn't going to do them a lot of damage here on ancient, weary, cynical Old Terra. Old Terrans understood how the game was played, and they were far past the stage of expecting that ever to change. Besides, all politicians—and bureaucrats—were the same, really, weren't they? And that being the case, better to stay with the mandarins you knew rather than stir up all the turmoil of trying to change a system which had worked for seven T-centuries.

But there were other planets, other star systems, whose wells of cynicism weren't quite so deep. There were even places where people still believed the delegates they elected to the League Assembly were supposed to govern the League. Once O'Hanrahan's damned clever turn of phrase reached those star systems and *they* figured out what "mandarin" meant, the reprcussions might be much more severe than here on the League's capital planet.

"I can't fault your observation, Omosupe," Wodoslawski said, "but why do I have the feeling this particular glimmer didn't come from the force of *his* intellect at all?"

"Because unlike him, you have a measurable IQ," Kolokoltsov replied. "Although, to be honest, it did take me several minutes to realize I was basically talking to his family's ventriloquist's dummy."

"Ah!" Wodoslawski said. "The light dawns."

"Exactly." Kolokoltsov nodded. "Yeou Transstellar has a lot invested in President Yeou." *And in all of us, as well*, he carefully did not add out loud. "I'm inclined to think this is at least mostly a case of Kun Sang reminding us of that investment."

Quartermain and Abruzzi grimaced in understanding. Yeou Kun Sang was the president's younger brother. He also happened to be on Old Terra at the moment (officially on a "personal family visit" to his older brother which just happened to have been announced as soon as word of the New Tuscany incidents hit his homeworld's faxes) and the president and CEO of Yeou Transstellar Shipping. Yeou Transstellar was one of the Solarian League's dozen largest interstellar shippers, and, like most of those shippers, it actually owned very few freighters. Its business model—like its competitors'—relied on leasing cargo space from people who *did* own freighters ... which meant that whether the great commercial dynasties of the Solarian League *liked* Manticore or not, they did a great deal of business with it.

"I'm surprised Kun Sang didn't go directly to you, Omosupe," Abruzzi said after a moment.

"So was I, at first," Quartermain agreed. "But now that I think about it, Kun Sang's always been inclined to stay out of the day-to-day details of managing the clan's business with Commerce or Interior. And the Yeou family's *really* old money, you know. They've been one of the first families of Sebastopol for the better part of a thousand years, and they like to pretend all that sordid business of trade is beneath them."

"Yeah. *Sure* it is." Abruzzi rolled his eyes.

"Well, part of the pretense is that everyone knows it's *only* a pretense," Quartermain pointed out. "And the fact that Kun Sang started out as a mere planetary manager and worked his way to the top tends to make it a bit more threadbare in the Yeous' case. Still, now that he's *at* the top, he's more or less required by tradition to work through the interface of professional managers. The 'hired hands' that do all of those sordid, business-related things the aristocratic family doesn't sully its own digits dealing with, especially where politics are concerned."

"Exactly," Kolokoltsov agreed. "Which I think is part of the point he's making, assuming I'm reading the situation accurately. He still keeping his thumbs out of the soup, but at the same time he's letting us know—indirectly, at least—that he's sufficiently concerned to be on the brink of coming into the open."

"Which, for a family that's spent so much time operating in the Sebastopol mode, indicates a *lot* of concern," Quartermain said soberly.

"Exactly," Kolokoltsov repeated. "I'm pretty sure Kun Chol was reading from a prepared script, and what it all came down to was finding out how much worse we expect this to get and how long we expect it to last."

"If we had the answer to either of those questions—" Abruzzi began, then cut himself off, shaking his head grimly.

"I notice neither Rajampet nor Nathan has joined our little tête-à-tête," Quartermain observed.

"No, they haven't, have they?" Kolokoltsov showed his teeth for a moment.

Nathan MacArtney, the permanent senior undersecretary of the interior, was the fifth "Mandarin," and Fleet Admiral Rajampet Kaushal Rajani was the Solarian League's chief of naval operations.

"Is there a reason they haven't?" Wodoslawski asked.

"Nathan's out of the office at the moment," Kolokoltsov replied. "He's on his way out to Elysium—family business, I think—and I don't really trust the security of his communications equipment until he gets there. Besides, he's already out beyond Mars orbit. The light-speed delay would be almost a minute and a half." The permanent senior undersecretary of state shrugged. "I'll see to it that he gets a complete transcript, of course."

"Of course." Quartermain nodded. "And Rajampet?"

"And I think we all already know what Rajampet's contribution would be." Kolokoltsov's colleagues *all* grimaced at that one, and he shrugged. "Under the circumstances, I thought we could just take his excuses and posturing as a given and get on with business."

Quartermain nodded again, more slowly this time. The permanent senior undersecretary of commerce was a striking woman, with gunmetal-gray hair and blue eyes that contrasted sharply with her very dark, almost black skin, but at the moment those blue eyes were narrowed in speculation. She had no doubt Nathan MacArtney was exactly where Kolokoltsov had said he was, but she wasn't exactly blind to the fact that as much as MacArtney personally despised Fleet Admiral Rajampet Kaushal Rajani, he was also the closest thing to an ally Rajampet had among the civilian permanent senior undersecretaries who actually ruled the Solarian League. That was inevitable, really, given the fact that the Office of Frontier Security belonged to the Interior Ministry, which meant MacArtney's personal empire was even more directly threatened than most by the specter of a successful "neobarb" star nation's resistance to OFS's plans. Not to mention the fact that Frontier Security's entire position depended on the perceived omnipotence of the Solarian League Navy.

"So what, exactly, is the point of this meeting, Innokentiy?" Wodoslawski asked.

"I realize there's not a lot we can do about the Manties' shipping movements," Kolokoltsov replied just a bit obliquely. "At the same time, I feel pretty confident that while Yeou Kun Sang may have been one of the first to ask those questions of his, he's damned well not going to be the last. Under the circumstances, I think we ought to be thinking about how we want to respond—not just in private, Malachai, but publicly, with the newsies—when those other people start asking. And I'd appreciate it if you and Omosupe could give us a better feel for how bad this is really going to be, Agatá."

"Exactly what do you think we've been *trying* to do? Especially since your little tête-à-tête with that son-of-a-bitch Carmichael?" Wodoslawski demanded tartly, and he shrugged.

"I know you've been warning us we were headed for trouble," Kolokoltsov said in a slightly apologetic tone. "And I may not've been paying as much attention as I should have. I've known it would be bad, but I haven't really tried to conceptualize the numbers for myself, because it's not my area of competence and I know it. I know they're huge, but I've been a lot more focused on finding ways to prevent it from ever happening than on trying to really grasp numbers that big. I'm trying now, though, so could you go ahead and give it another try, please? What I'm looking for isn't the reams of numbers and detailed alternate contingency estimates and analyses in all of those reports of yours but more of a broad overview. Something even an economic ignoramus can grasp. In those terms, just how bad is this really likely to get?"

"That depends on how far the Manties are prepared to push it, now, doesn't it?" Wodoslawski snorted. "We can give you a pretty fair estimate, I think, for what happens if they settle for simply recalling all their own shipping, though." She raised her eyebrows at Quartermain as she spoke, then returned her attention to Kolokoltsov when the permanent senior undersecretary of commerce nodded. "And the short answer to that part of your question is that it will really, really suck."

"I'm not precisely sure what that technical term means," Kolokoltsov told her with an off-center smile.

"It means Felicia Hadley has a point," Wodoslawski replied without any answering smile at all, and Kolokoltsov scowled.

Felicia Hadley was the senior member of the Beowulf Delegation in the Legislative Assembly. That gelded body had exercised no real power in centuries, but it still existed, and Beowulf, unlike most of the League's member systems, still took it seriously enough to send delegates who could seal their own shoes without printed instructions. Hadley was a prime example of that, and ever since the current crisis had begun, she'd been a persistent (and vociferous) critic of the government's policies. She'd even formally moved that the Assembly empanel a special commission of its own to investigate exactly how those policies had come to be put into place! Fortunately, there'd been too few delegates present for a quorum when she made the motion, and Jasmine Neng, the Assembly Speaker (who, unlike Hadley, understood which side of her personal bread was buttered), had killed it on procedural grounds and removed it from the vote queue before most of the other delegates (or any of the 'faxes) even realized it was there.

It was equally fortunate the newsies knew as well as anyone that the Assembly possessed no real power, because God only knew what would have happened if they'd actually bothered to cover its sessions. If any of their stringers had been there to report Hadley's passionate address to the empty seats of Assembly Hall, the public might actually have believed what she was saying—might even have started insisting someone in a real policymaking position listen to her! Of course, there was no mechanism for that to happen, but a lot of the Solarian electorate didn't realize that.

Hadley had also been warning anyone who would listen from the beginning that the League was playing with economic fire. She'd actually produced numbers to support her allegations, although Kolokoltsov hadn't paid a lot of attention to them. He hadn't needed her to tell him it would be bad, and as he'd just admitted, *he* wasn't a number-cruncher, anyway. He'd accepted Wodoslawski and Quartermain's warnings that the situation was potentially serious, but he'd left that side up to them while he concentrated on trying to control the *non*-economic aspects of the crisis. After all, if he'd only been able to convince the Manties to see sense, they wouldn't have pushed things to this point in the first place. The way he'd seen it, all he really needed to know was that there would be serious consequences if he *couldn't* make the Manties recognize reality, and to be honest, he hadn't wanted the distraction of dealing with hard potential numbers like the ones Hadley had been throwing around. Now, though . . .

"So, how *good* a point does she have?"

"A *damned* good one, and if you'd actually read the reports my staff's been generating for the last couple of T-months, you'd already know that," Wodoslawski said bluntly. "Better than *two-thirds* of our total interstellar commerce—the percentage is higher for freight, lower for passengers and information—travels in Manticore-registered bottoms at some point in the transport cycle, Innokentiy. Almost thirty percent of it travels in Manty ships all the way from point of origin to final destination; another twenty-seven percent travels in Manty bottoms for between thirty and fifty percent of the total voyage. And another ten or fifteen percent of it travels in Manty bottoms for up to a quarter of the total transit." Her expression was that of someone smelling something which had been dead for several days. "As you can see, simply pulling their own shipping out of the loop will reduce our available interstellar lift by better than half."

Kolokoltsov looked profoundly unhappy, and Quartermain made a sound halfway between a snort of amusement and a grunt of disgust.

"Agatá and I have been telling and *telling* all of you the Manties are in a position to inflict plenty of grief on us," she pointed out. "And I have to add that the figure she just gave you is what we're looking at if the Manties simply decide to go home and take their ships with them. Now that they're closing their termini to *our* shipping, it's not just the reduction in the number of hulls available to us—it's how much longer those hulls are going to take to reach their destinations. If transit times double, effective lift gets cut in half, which means things are going to get worse. A lot worse. Unfortunately, how *much* worse is impossible to predict at this point, to be honest. The shipping networks have always been incredibly complex and fluid, and I don't think anyone could give us hard numbers on just how badly simply taking the Manty-controlled termini out of it is going to extend shipping times. I can tell you it's going to be bad, though. And that assumes they stop at closing just *their* termini."

Kolokoltsov lips tightened at her last sentence.

Reports of withdrawing Manticoran shipping had been trickling into news accounts for weeks. Although Lyman Carmichael had officially told Old Chicago of the Star Empire's decision to recall all its freighters and passenger liners only the week before, it was obvious the order must have gone out at least a couple of T-months earlier than that—probably as soon as word of the Battle of Spindle reached Manticore. It had taken people a while to notice what was going on, mostly because the delay in transmitting instructions across such vast distances, even with Manticore's commanding position in the wormhole network, meant the recall had reached its recipients piecemeal. By this time, though, the trickle of withdrawing Manticoran merchant vessels had become a flood. More newsies than just O'Hanrahan had picked up on it now, and Kolokoltsov wondered how those newsies were going to react once it finally leaked out that the Star Empire had officially notified the League of its intention to close all Manticoran wormhole termini to Solarian-registry vessels.

Rajampet, predictably, had waved off the threat. It was only to be expected, he'd pointed out, and while it might be an inconvenience for the League, the impact on the Manties themselves would be even worse, given how huge a percentage of their total economy depended on servicing Solarian shipping needs. Besides, it would only be temporary—just until the SLN got around to pinning back the Manties' ears and taking control of the wormhole network for itself.

Funny how the man in command of the navy responsible for protecting Solarian commerce can be so blasé about watching that commerce go right down the crapper, Kolokoltsov thought bitterly. *I guess he doesn't see what's happening as the Navy's fault. After all, no one's actively* raiding *our shipping, now, are they? Although exactly what else we should be calling what happened at Zunker eludes me.*

The reports from Zunker and Nolan had arrived, almost simultaneously, over the weekend, and the newsies hadn't yet picked up on them. That wasn't going to last, though, and it was hard for Kolokoltsov to decide which incident would ultimately prove more infuriating to the Solarian public. The Zunker Terminus was officially the territory of a Manticoran ally, so closing it to Solarian traffic presented no gray areas. The Idahoans hadn't signed the Shingaine Convention either, which meant they were arguably within their rights under interstellar law to deny terminus access to anyone they chose. And they were also within their rights to request the Royal Manticoran Navy's assistance in enforcing that decision. The fact that the local Manty commander had actually fired on Solarian battlecruisers showed just how far the Star Empire was prepared to escalate things, however, and the "insult" was going to arouse a passionate fury in at least some of the League's citizens, especially those with whom Abruzzi's propaganda had been most successful. Unfortunately, other members of that same citizenry were going to realize it wouldn't have happened if that fool Floyd hadn't pushed things. Even more unfortunately, some of them were going to figure out the Manty commander had deliberately *not* blown

Admiral Pyun's battlecruisers out of space. When they recognized the implications of *that* . . .

As far as public opinion was concerned, though, what had happened at Nolan might be even worse. Unlike Zunker, the Nolan Terminus was claimed by the Solarian League, not by the Manties or one of their allies. And when the terminus astro-control staff—all of them Solarians—had refused transit to the Manticoran freighters queuing up to return home (he made a mental note to remind Abruzzi to play down any references to the Shingaine Convention when he spun *that* one), the Manty naval commander had marched them to their personal quarters almost literally at pulser point and put his own people aboard the command platforms. And then he'd offered to blow away the local Frontier Fleet detachment if it tried to intervene! Kolokoltsov could already hear how the 'faxes were going to play up that "blatant act of aggression" in *Solarian* space!

"How much of the League's gross product are we talking about here, Omosupe?" Abruzzi asked, and Kolokoltsov felt a flicker of surprise as he realized he'd never asked the same question.

"Damned near twenty percent of our total gross product depends *entirely* on our interstellar commerce," Quartermain said in a flat tone. "Another fifteen percent will, at the very least, be seriously impacted."

"*And*," Wodoslawski added grimly, "something Rajampet seems to have failed to keep in mind is that seventy percent of all federal revenue derives directly or indirectly from shipping duties and tariffs. The other thirty percent derives primarily from protectorate service fees."

Which meant, as her listeners understood perfectly

well, the tribute extracted from OFS's empire of protectorate star systems. That particular revenue stream was scarcely what anyone might have called enormous compared to the League's overall economy, but it was stupendous in absolute terms, and it belonged *entirely* to the League's bureaucracies. That was one reason—indeed, *the* reason, really—Frontier Security had been allowed to build its empire in the first place. And, of course, it was also the primary reason *nothing* could be permitted to undermine the League's grip on the protectorates, which had been the entire reason for the belligerent policy which had gotten them into this mess in the first place.

Unbelievable, Kolokoltsov thought for far from the first time. *Unbelievable that the monumental stupidity of just* two *people could set something like this in motion!*

Of course, a small corner of his brain reminded him, not even Josef Byng and Sandra Crandall could have brought the League to such a pass without the help of Kolokoltsov and his fellow Mandarins.

Damn it, now I'm *starting to use the word!* he thought disgustedly.

"So you're telling us we're in a position to lose up to thirty percent of the entire League's gross product?" Abruzzi asked incredulously.

"We're telling you we're already *losing* a big chunk of that *thirty-five* percent," Quartermain replied. "Exactly how big a chunk we won't know until the dust settles and we see how much damage the Manties have actually done us. But I don't want anyone thinking that's all that's going to happen. There'll be a ripple effect across our entire economy, one that's going to lead to a *significant* drop in activity in almost every sector if it lasts more than a very short time. And, as Agatá's just pointed out, even in a best-case scenario, this is going to *hammer* federal revenues. Most of the *system* governments won't be hurt all that badly at first, thank God, but if this goes on for two or three quarters, that's going to change."

"*Shit*," Abruzzi muttered.

"There are a couple of brighter spots buried in all this," Quartermain said after a moment. "As Rajampet's pointed out often enough, what's going to hurt us badly will hurt the Manties themselves worse. In a lot of ways, this really is a case of their having cut off their noses to spite their faces, as my momma used to say. And that's just looking at the *immediate* economic and financial impact. If they throw us back on our own shipping resources, and if they close the wormholes so that we need more shipping than ever to meet our requirements, it's got to lead to a huge upsurge in our own shipbuilding. Eventually, our merchant marine will have to expand to fill the vacuum, and once that happens, it'll be difficult for Manticore to ever maneuver itself into a similar stranglehold position again."

"Assuming there's still a Manticore to *do* any maneuvering," Wodoslawski added.

"Exactly," Kolokoltsov said bleakly. He surveyed his colleagues' faces for several moments, then sighed.

"Assuming Rajani's strategy with Filareta works, all of this becomes a moot point. Assuming it *doesn't* work, things are going to get a lot uglier before they get any better. In fact, my greatest concern right now is that if the Manties basically tell Filareta to pound sand—and, worse, if it turns out Rajani was wrong about their ability to make that stick—we're going to find it difficult to revert to that 'short of war' diplomatic stance."

Heads nodded in glum agreement, and Kolokoltsov castigated himself again for allowing Rajampet's opportunism to seduce him into accepting the CNO's strategy. He should have known better than to listen! Yet given what had happened to the Manties' home system, the temptation to double down had been overwhelming. Surely their morale had to crack under the one-two punch of such a devastating assault and the realization that the League wasn't going to back off! It *had* to be that way, didn't it?

And it still may *be. Sure, they're recalling their freighters and closing their termini, but they're doing all that with no idea Filareta's close enough to hit them this quickly. When he turns up in their own backyard, things could change in a hurry.*

Unfortunately . . .

"If the Manties don't cave, and if we're looking at this kind of nosedive in revenues, can we go back to that position at all?" Abruzzi's question put Kolokoltsov's own thoughts into words.

"I don't know," the permanent senior undersecretary of state said frankly, and Abruzzi scowled.

Kolokoltsov didn't blame him. *He* still wasn't positive his own proposed strategy—buying time by negotiating "more in sorrow than in anger" until the Navy acquired weapons capable of offsetting the Manties' tactical advantages—would have worked, when all was said. Patience was not a Solarian virtue, especially where "neobarbs" were concerned. That was one reason he'd been convinced to back Rajampet's new strategy, despite its potential to restrict his future options. But until this moment, he hadn't fully realized how *badly* a failure by Filareta would restrict them.

If the Manties defeated Filareta—and especially if they also turned the economic screws Wodoslawski and Quartermain were describing—it would be impossible to convince the public that a return to diplomacy stemmed from anything but fear of still worse to come. It would be seen as an admission of impotence. Of ineffectuality. And that was the kiss of death. If the people running the League couldn't demonstrate they were doing something *effective*, the electorate might start listening to loose warheads like Hadley and demanding changes. Even completely leaving aside personal consequences, the potential for political and constitutional disaster *that* represented was terrifying.

"I don't know," he repeated. "I do know that if Rajani's brainstorm turns into a spectacular failure—*another* spectacular failure, I should say—the situation isn't going to *improve!* In fact, we may find ourselves essentially forced to do what Rajani wanted to do in the first place."

"Whoa!" Wodoslawski stared at him. "I thought we were all in agreement that just serving up the Navy as target practice for Manty missiles was what they call a losing proposition, Innokentiy!"

"We still are. But whatever else may have happened, the Manties have to've lost a lot of their missile-manufacturing capacity. Rajani has to be right about that, even if he's wrong about everything else! So the odds are that they'd have to stand on the defensive, rather than coming after us, at least until they're able to regenerate their industrial base. And as we've just been saying, they'll be trying to do that at a time when they've cut off the lion's share of their own interstellar cash flow."

"And this helps us exactly how?" Abruzzi asked.

"It means they can't reach just down our throats and rip out our lungs," Kolokoltsov said flatly. "Not right away, at least. It gives us time to work on ways to negate their combat advantages. For that matter, it gives us time to see if *their* economy can survive, especially after so much of their home system got clear-cut. And if we spin it right, we can use what they've done to our shipping routes to explain why we're not yet in a position to take the war to them. Why we have to 'hold the line' until our economy and naval logistics recover from their 'treacherous blow.' And—"

"And at the same time we focus the anger over the economic meltdown on *them*, not us!" Abruzzi interjected, and Kolokoltsov nodded.

"That's still going to be tough to pull off," Quartermain pointed out, blue eyes narrow.

"No question," Kolokoltsov acknowledged. "And I can think of a few of our member systems who won't do a thing to make it any easier."

Quartermain's mouth tightened, her eyes glittering with more than a hint of anger, and Kolokoltsov snorted.

"We always knew that was at least a possibility, Omosupe. And I've been thinking about ways to, ah, *rectify* the situation."

"Oh?" Quartermain cocked her head. "And have any solutions suggested themselves to you?"

"As a matter of fact, one or two *have* reared their heads," Kolokoltsov said. "In fact, one of them came from Rajani, although I rather doubt he's been thinking about it the same way I have. Let me explain..."

Chapter Seven

"EXCUSE ME, SIR, but an Admiral Simpson is on the com. She's asking for a priority appointment with you."

"Admiral Simpson?"

Gabriel Caddell-Markham, the Director of Defense for the Beowulf Planetary Board of Directors, arched an eyebrow at Timothy Sung, his personal aide, whose holo image floated above the director's desktop com. It had taken Caddell-Markham years to master the art of moving only one eyebrow while the other remained motionless. Despite his wife Joanna's more or less tolerant amusement at the affectation (the acquisition of which she ascribed to his many, many years in starship commands with no *useful* skills to spend his time mastering), he'd actually found it quite handy since he'd resigned from the Beowulf System Defense Force to pursue a political career.

"Yes, Sir," Sung replied in answer to his question.

The dark-haired, brown-eyed Sung's rather pale complexion contrasted sharply with his boss's very black skin, yet there was an oddly familial resemblance between them. Probably because the defense director's aide had been with him for the better part of eleven T-years. Given that Sung was only forty, that meant he'd been young and malleable enough to be influenced by older, more evil examples. That was Sung's own explanation, anyway. Some senior government officials might have taken that explanation amiss, but given that the theory had originally been propounded by Joanna Markham-Caddell, Caddell-Markham wasn't in the best of positions to do that. Besides, the younger man's insouciance was one of the main reasons the director had chosen him as an aide in the first place. Sung had performed his own military service in the Biological Survey Corps, which was scarcely renowned for its spit-and-polish attitude, and the arched eyebrow was usually good for a snort when Caddell-Markham used it on him. Today, he seemed not even to have noticed.

"She's not one of our officers," Sung continued. "In fact, I understand she's on Admiral Kingsford's staff."

Caddell-Markham's eyebrow came down and his face tightened ever so slightly. It would have taken someone who knew him as well as Sung did to notice, but his aide nodded.

"Yes, Sir. She obviously doesn't want to get specific with me, but from her attitude, I think she has to be here about Filareta."

Timothy Sung was thoroughly briefed in on a vast assortment of highly classified information, which was why he knew about the plan to send Massimo Filareta to attack the Manticore Binary System, despite the plan's Utter-Top-Secret, Burn-Before-Reading-and-Then-Self-Terminate Classification. And, like his boss, he thought it was the stupidest, most arrogant excuse for a strategy he'd ever heard of.

What Sung *wasn't* aware of—yet—was that the Beowulf System government had very quietly used an extremely "black" communications channel to warn Manticore Filareta was coming.

"Since you say you *think* she's here about Filareta, I assume she hasn't said anything specific about the reason she wants to see me?"

"No, Sir. As I said, she obviously doesn't want to get specific with an underling." Sung grimaced. "She was pretty emphatic about the urgency of her need to speak to you as soon as possible, though. And she *did* say it was something she didn't want to discuss—with you, presumably, since she was 'discussing' damn-all with *me*—over the com."

"I see."

Caddell-Markham pursed his lips, then shrugged.

"I further assume that as the skilled bureaucrat and politician-minder you've become, you haven't told her I'm *immediately* available?"

"No, Sir." This time, Sung smiled slightly. "In fact, I told her you were out of the office and that I'd see if I could contact you. I'm afraid I may have implied you were closeted with some of the other Directors at the moment and it might not be possible to 'disturb' you."

"So sad to see a stalwart military officer descending to such depths of chicanery," Caddell-Markham observed with a smile of his own. Then the smile vanished, and he shrugged. "In that case, tell her I'm afraid I won't be able to see her until sometime fairly late this afternoon. Go ahead and feel free to 'imply' that I'm out of the city at the moment—I'm probably in Grendel, in fact, now that I think about it. At any rate, I'll be happy to meet with her absolutely as soon as I can get back to Columbia. And as soon as you've finished 'implying' that to her and scheduling the meeting, please be good enough to get the CEO, Secretary Pinder-Swun, Director Longacre, and Director Mikulin on a secure conference link."

❖   ❖   ❖

"So, has anyone ever actually met this Admiral Simpson?"

Chyang Benton-Ramirez, the Chairman and CEO of the Planetary Board of Directors, was about eight centimeters taller than Caddell-Markham's hundred and seventy-five centimeters. He also had dark hair which was turning white, despite the fact that he was barely seventy-five T-years old. Personally, Caddell-Markham suspected Benton-Ramirez preferred things that way, on the theory that it gave him an interestingly distinguished look in a society accustomed to prolong's extended youthfulness. And the snowiness of his hair made a nicely distinctive visual contrast with the darkness of his bushy mustache. The political cartoonists just loved it, regardless of their own political persuasions, at any rate.

His Board colleagues looked around at one another's images, then turned back to him with various combinations of shrugs and head shakes.

"Marvelous," he said dryly.

"I've never met her, Chyang," Director at Large Fedosei Demianovich Mikulin said, "but I did have a chance to give her dossier a quick once-over before the conference."

Despite the fact that he was the Board of Directors' oldest member by the better part of two decades, the blond-haired, blue-eyed Mikulin actually looked younger than Benton-Ramirez. He was almost thirteen centimeters taller, as well. A physician by training, he'd been a member of the Board for over thirty T-years, always as a director at large rather than heading any specific planetary directorate. His colleagues in the Chamber of Shareholders and Chamber of Professions had returned him so persistently to the Board because of his demonstrated ability as an all-around troubleshooter, and Benton-Ramirez, like his last two predecessors, had learned to rely on Mikulin's advice . . . especially in intelligence matters.

"And her dossier told you what, Fedosei?" the CEO asked now.

"She's Kingsford's operations officer," Mikulin replied. "She's also some sort of cousin of his, and she's connected by marriage to Rajampet, as well. Despite that, she's only a *rear* admiral, and according to her dossier her last shipboard command was as the captain of a superdreadnought. As far as we know, she's never commanded a fleet or a task force or even a squadron in space. She does have a reputation as an operational planner, but that's an *SLN* reputation, so I'd take it with a grain of salt, especially when someone with her family connections hasn't been promoted beyond junior flag rank. She's obviously trusted by her superiors when it comes to politics and bureaucratic infighting, though. As nearly as I can tell, Kingsford—or Jennings, at least—has used her as go-between on some fairly gray operations that no one wanted officially on the record."

Benton-Ramirez nodded. Fleet Admiral Winston Seth Kingsford was the commanding officer of the Solarian League Navy's Battle Fleet. That made him Rajampet's heir apparent as chief of naval operations, and Admiral Willis Jennings was Kingsford's chief of staff. Neither was any stranger to the internecine warfare of the League bureaucracy.

"I think we can safely assume, then," the CEO said, "that none of us are going to be too happy about any minor gray areas she may have been sent to go between in our case."

"Probably not," Director of State Jukka Longacre agreed. "The thing I have to wonder is how *un*happy we're going to be?"

The director of state's amethyst eyes narrowed. Those eyes were his most striking feature—especially against his dark complexion and depilated scalp—but his powerful, hooked nose ran them a close second. Caddell-Markham had always thought that with the possible addition of a golden earring, Longacre would have made a wonderful HD pirate. In fact, he'd been Chairman of Interstellar Politics at the University of Columbia before his election to the Board seven T-years earlier.

"You're wondering if something's leaked about our warning to Manticore?" Benton-Ramirez's tone made the question a statement, and Longacre nodded.

"I doubt it," Secretary Joshua Pinder-Swun said.

Although his official title was simply Secretary of the Planetary Board of Directors, the red-haired, blue-eyed Pinder-Swun was actually the Vice Chairman and CEO of the system government. He was a little unusual for someone of his exalted political position in that he'd come late to politics, and then through the Chamber of Professions, rather than the Chamber of Shareholders. One of Beowulf's leading physicists before his "temporary" election to the Chamber of Professions some twenty T-years before, he still cherished the illusion that he would someday be allowed to return to his beloved research. Everyone else knew that wasn't going to happen.

"I doubt it," Pinder-Swun repeated when everyone's eyes swivelled to him, and shrugged. "First, from all I've seen, no one has a clue our conduit to Manticore even exists. Second, if anyone on Old Terra had figured out we'd warned Manticore, they would've sent someone a lot more senior—and probably a lot more official—to . . . remonstrate with us." He shook his head. "No, this has something to do with Filareta, all right, but I don't think it's anything to do with our having alerted the Manties."

"I think Joshua has a point," Caddell-Markham said. "The problem is that if she's not here to break our heads over our little security faux pas—and Joshua's *definitely* right about that; if that was what they wanted, they would've sent someone more senior— that means Rajampet's had another brainstorm. One that involves us. And given the fact that we're two T-months from Manticore through hyper-space even for a dispatch boat, and that Filareta's supposed to be leaving Tasmania (assuming he manages to make Kingsford's schedule) in less than two weeks, whatever brilliant inspiration he might've had has to concern our terminus of the Junction."

Faces tightened, and Mikulin nodded grimly.

"I can't see anything else that would cause the *Navy*

to send us a personal representative," he agreed. "If it were a purely political matter, we wouldn't be looking at someone from the military, and they would've come to call on you, Jukka, not Gabriel. Or if they'd wanted to handle it at a higher level, on you or Joshua, Chyang. And Gabriel's right about the Junction. It's a bit late in the day for them to suddenly decide to ask us if we have any insight into Manticoran capabilities which might have somehow eluded their own inspired analysts." Mikulin's contempt was withering. "Which means some ass in Kingsford's or Rajampet's office has decided there's some way to use the Junction against Manticore."

"I realize we're not talking about mental giants," Pinder-Swun observed, "but surely they have to realize any sort of attack through the Junction would be suicide!"

"You'd think so, wouldn't you?" Caddell-Markham said. "On the other hand, calling the geniuses running the SLN—and the rest of the League, for that matter—'imbeciles' would be a gross slander on imbeciles."

"Are you positive this is coming out of Rajampet or Kingsford?" Longacre asked.

"No, but who else would be sending Kingsford's ops officer as his messenger girl?" Caddell-Markham asked.

"That depends on what it is they're really after," Longacre countered. "I'll grant that Kolokoltsov and his apparatchiks have been acting as if they don't have two brain cells amongst them, but as far as gaming the system he understands is concerned, he's right there in Machiavelli's league. The problem is that he doesn't seem to grasp the possibility that there's any universe *outside* the system he understands. Or, at least, that he failed to grasp it in time to avoid our current debacle."

"And?" Caddell-Markham knew he looked skeptical, and he twitched his head apologetically. "I'm not disagreeing with your analysis of Kolokoltsov and the Mandarins, Jukka. I just don't understand why he'd send someone from the military to deliver a *political* message."

"That's because you grew up as a straightforward military officer!" Longacre snorted.

"Maybe he did," Mikulin said, "but I still think it's a valid question."

"Of course it is. But think about this." Longacre looked around the other faces, ice-blue eyes more intent than ever. "We're agreed Kolokoltsov and the others—probably especially MacArtney—stumbled into this because they were too arrogant and full of their own omnipotence to realize where it was headed. By now, though, Kolokoltsov, at least, has to've realized he's looking down the barrel of a pulser at a full-fledged political and constitutional crisis. Rajampet's twisting Article Seven like a pretzel to cover what he's already done, far less what he *plans* on doing. In the end, that pretzel may break. If it does—*when* it does—the shit's going to hit the fan in a way the Solarian League's never seen. And even if none of the Mandarins suspect we've already warned Manticore what's coming, they all know how close our relations with the Star Kingdom—Empire, I mean—are."

He paused, and Caddell-Markham nodded.

The Star Empire of Manticore was far and away Beowulf's biggest trading partner. Given that fact and Manticore's unwavering support of Beowulf's crusade against the genetic slave trade, it had been one of Beowulf's closer allies for over three T-centuries. Indeed, unlike any other Solarian military organization, the Beowulf System Defense Force had a tradition of close cooperation with the RMN and carried out frequent joint exercises in defense of the Beowulf Terminus. More than that, Manticorans and Beowulfers had been intermarrying (among other things) ever since the Junction's discovery in 1585 PD. At least four members of the Planetary Board of Directors, including its CEO, had relatives in Manticore. For that matter, quite a few Beowulfers (again, including members of the Board) had lost family members in the Yawata strike. Even the masterminds responsible for the Solarian League's foreign policy had to grasp what that was going to mean where Beowulf's attitude was concerned.

As far as that goes, the director of defense reminded himself, *by now it sure as hell ought to have occurred to someone in Kingsford's shop that we must've known a lot more about Manticore's capabilities than we ever shared with the Navy. It couldn't be any other way, given all those joint exercises. So by this time, somebody's got to be asking himself why we never mentioned those multi-drive missiles. Of course, no one ever* asked *us about them, but still . . .*

"Well," Longacre continued, "suppose it's occurred to them that we're not going to be happy when we find out about the attack on Manticore we're not supposed to know anything about at the moment. And suppose it's also occurred to them that if it comes down to a genuine debate over a formal declaration of war, we're certain to exercise our veto to prevent it. What do you think they might want to do about that?"

"I don't think there's anything they *can* do," Caddell-Markham replied. "I think they're in so deep they figure the only thing they can do is keep bashing straight ahead and hope for the best."

"Probably so, but that's not going to keep someone like Kolokoltsov from trying to shove an ace or two up his sleeve, Gabriel." Longacre shook his head. "No, he's going to be looking for some way to change the equation. And one way to do that might be to get us involved in the attack. If we *help* them attack Manticore, we'll be right in the same boat with them when it comes to defending our actions."

"But no one with even half a brain could believe we *would* help them," Pinder-Swun objected. "Not only do we have obvious commercial and cultural ties with Manticore, but our Assembly delegates've been calling for moderation ever since the Monica Incident. Not to mention Hadley's motion! And we've been steadfast in rejecting the hysteria about the Green Pines bombing, as well. They have to realize how Manticore's allegations of Mesan involvement in everything that's happened to the Star Empire are going to play with our citizens!"

The secretary had *that* right, Caddell-Markham reflected. Indeed, Pinder-Swun himself was an outstanding example of why that was true, since his mother had been a liberated genetic slave. Liberated, in fact, if memory served, by a cruiser of the Royal *Manticoran* Navy.

"Of course Kolokoltsov's perfectly well aware of that, Joshua," Longacre agreed. "But if he's taking the long view—trying to position his little quintet for an actual war, or at least a protracted crisis—then what he may want is to discredit us with the rest of the League.

"Try this scenario. The Navy wants our assistance in carrying out its attack on Manticore. Maybe they want the BSDF to participate actively, or maybe they just want to use the Junction to threaten Manticore from the rear and expect us to help with the necessary ship movements. Anyway, whatever they want, they tell us about it, and we turn them down. Under Article Five of the Constitution, we can refuse to place the System-Defense Force under federal control unless the League's formally at war, and the Beowulf Terminus of the Junction is outside the twelve-minute limit, which means it's not 'our' property to dispose of, anyway. They might not want to buy that interpretation, especially given our treaty with Manticore, but *technically* Beowulf Astro Control is a chartered private company, not an official organ of our government, and it *leases* the terminus from its Manticoran discoverers. So we've got plenty of wiggle room to keep the lawyers happy for the odd decade or two if they try to push it. Which means that if we do turn them down, refuse to cooperate, we can legitimately argue we're within our rights under the Constitution.

"From their perspective, though, one of two things is going to happen when Filareta reaches Manticore. Either he succeeds and the Manties back down without a fight—which every one of us knows perfectly well *isn't* going to happen—or else there's going to be a battle. Kolokoltsov and the others may actually believe Filareta can win, given how badly Manticore's been damaged. Of course, if any of their so-called *analysts* think anything of the sort after what happened to Crandall, I'd like to distribute a few kilos of whatever they're snorting at my next fundraiser! At any rate, either Filareta wins, in which case our refusal to cooperate doesn't hurt anything since the crisis is over, or else Filareta gets hammered . . . in which case, they blame his defeat on our lack of cooperation. You can bet your bottom credit that when the official report gets presented, *we'll* be the reason Filareta got blown out of space, which will undercut our credibility as opponents to any post-Filareta hard-line position."

"You really think they'd believe they could get away with that?" Caddell-Markham wished his own tone sounded more incredulous.

"I'm pretty sure they would," Longacre replied. "*Believe* they could get away with it, at any rate. I think they'd probably be wrong, but let's be honest, Gabriel. It wouldn't be any rawer than a lot of other 'facts' they and Abruzzi's shills at Education and Information have sold the public, now would it? I doubt any of them think they could count on brushing us permanently out of their way—even in the League, the truth has an annoying tendency of coming out eventually. But if there's any basis to my suspicions, then what they're after is a tactical objective, rather than a strategic one. If Filareta's operation blows up in their faces, the Mandarins want us neutralized during any immediate public debate over exactly how that happened or who's to blame for the resultant bloodbath.

"In the longer term, they'll hardly be heartbroken if they can keep us sidelined long enough to get the entire League committed to their policy vis-à-vis Manticore. We all know from personal experience that once a policy's been set, it's a lot harder to change it than it ever would have been to nip it in the bud. And they probably figure that if the Assembly's signed off—even passively—on whatever policy they choose, it's a lot less likely anyone's going to be able to generate any effective resistance to that policy."

The director of state leaned back in his office chair, folding his arms across his chest, and the other participants in the holo conference looked at one another's images. Caddell-Markham was pretty sure most of the others were thinking the same thing he was. Unfortunately, what Longacre had just suggested sounded entirely too likely for comfort.

"All right," Benton-Ramirez said after a moment. "Personally, I hope you're being excessively paranoid, Jukka. I'm not prepared to bet against you, though. So the question before us becomes how we respond to whatever 'request' this Simpson is here to make."

"You want my honest, off-the-cuff, immediate reaction to it, Chyang?" Pinder-Swun asked.

The CEO nodded, and the secretary gave a harsh, barking laugh. It sounded like the hunting cry of some forest predator, and Pinder-Swun's always ruddy complexion was about half a shade darker than usual.

"Okay," he said. "What I'd really like to do is point them at the terminus and invite them to go right ahead!"

He smiled nastily, and Caddell-Markham winced.

The ceiling on any simultaneous mass transit of the Manticoran Wormhole Junction was around two hundred million tons. That meant the largest force the SLN could throw through the Beowulf Terminus in a single wave would be about thirty of its *Scientist*-class superdreadnoughts, after which the terminus would be destabilized and useless for over seventeen hours. That sounded like a lot of ships...until one reflected that a single missile salvo from a force composed solely of cruisers and battlecruisers had completely destroyed twenty-three units of the same class in the Battle of Spindle. What the Manticoran Home Fleet's ships-of-the-wall—or even just the Junction forts—could do would make Spindle look like a love tap.

"While I'll admit to a certain vengefulness of my own, Joshua," Benton-Ramirez said after a moment, his tone mild, "we might want to bear in mind that the spacers aboard those ships wouldn't be the ones who decided to attack Manticore in the first place. Not to mention the fact that they're our fellow Solarians . . . and somebody's husbands, wives, sons, or daughters."

"I said it was my *immediate* reaction," Pinder-Swun replied. "You're right, though, of course. Although when I think about how often the Navy's sat on its collective ass and watched slavers go trundling past, my sense of empathy becomes oddly deadened. Despite that, I agree we shouldn't be encouraging Rajampet and Kingsford to get job lots of Navy personnel killed in one-sided massacres."

"So what *do* we do?" Benton-Ramirez looked around his colleagues' faces once more. "Suggestions, anyone?"

❖   ❖   ❖

"Thank you for agreeing to meet with me so promptly, Director," Rear Admiral Marjorie Simpson said, reaching across the desk to shake Caddell-Markham's proffered hand. Her smile actually looked genuine.

"I'm sorry I wasn't available when you first screened, Admiral," Caddell-Markham replied with an equally warm (and false) smile. "According to Mr. Sung's message, though, it sounded fairly urgent, so I cleared space on my calendar as quickly as I could."

"I appreciate that," Simpson told him, but she also cocked her head at the fair-haired, gray-eyed woman who'd risen from one of the armchairs in front of Caddell-Markham's desk. The rear admiral's expression was politely inquiring, and Caddell-Markham released her hand and gestured at the other woman.

"Allow me to introduce Assistant Director of Defense Justyná Miternowski-Zhyang," he said. "Justyná is the assistant director for the BSDF's naval component." He smiled. "Given your own naval rank, it seemed likely your errand here on Beowulf was going to involve Justyná's bailiwick. Assuming it does, it seemed simplest and most efficient to have her here at the outset."

"I see. And I appreciate your forethought," Simpson said, although her own smile seemed just a little forced as she reached out to shake Miternowski-Zhyang's hand in turn.

"Please," Caddell-Markham said then, waving at the waiting armchairs. "Let's all have seats and get down to whatever brings you to Beowulf, Admiral. Can I offer any refreshment?"

"I'm fine, Director," Simpson demurred, shaking her head. "Perhaps later."

"Fine." The director of defense tipped back slightly in his own chair and waved one hand in an inviting "go-ahead" gesture.

Simpson paused for a moment, as if making certain her mental note cards were properly arranged, and he took advantage of the opportunity to study her unobtrusively. She wasn't a particularly tall woman, although she was solidly if compactly put together. According to the dossier Mikulin had shared with him, she was in her early seventies, but her hair was still dark, without a hint of gray, and her brown eyes were commendably open and mild. Earnest. Even guileless, one might almost have said. Which, given her position and duties, had to be deceptive.

"What I'm about to discuss with you," she said finally, "is top-secret, level-seven classified material."

She paused again, briefly, as if for emphasis. In the Solarian classification system, there was only one level above that, and Caddell-Markham reminded himself to look suitably impressed.

"I'm sure you and Assistant Director Miternowski-Zhyang have been fully briefed on what happened to Admiral Crandall's task force at Spindle," she resumed. "Obviously that came as a shock to all of us in the Navy. We're not convinced by any means that the Manties' version of what happened is accurate, of course. In particular, given what we know of Admiral Crandall's standing orders, it seems unlikely her actions and attitudes were actually as provocative as they've been portrayed. It does seem probable that she . . . mismanaged the situation badly, but some of our analysts believe the com records the Manties sent us have been skillfully edited. Be that as it may, however—whatever actually happened and whoever really fired the first shot—we're all left facing the consequences of Manticore's actions."

She paused again, as if inviting a response to what she'd just said. Particularly, Caddell-Markham suspected, to her version of just whose actions were responsible for the consequences in question. Both Beowulfers had their expressions as thoroughly under control as her own, however.

"Clearly," she continued with an air of candor when

neither of them rose to the bait, "what happened to Admiral Crandall indicates we in the Navy have badly underestimated Manticoran military capabilities. Our analysts are firmly of the opinion that the missile performance we observed at Spindle never came from anything that could be launched from cruiser or battlecruiser missile tubes, whatever they may be claiming or seeking to imply. But even with that caveat—even assuming what they actually used were heavy system-defense missiles—their capabilities were, frankly, little short of terrifying. It's painfully evident that at the moment, at least, the Manty navy has a significant technological edge.

"At the same time, however, the Solarian League has a tremendous quantitative advantage. There's simply no way anything the size of the Manties' 'Star Empire' could possibly match our productivity and available manpower. In the end, those advantages have to prove decisive.

"Unfortunately, despite the fact that their defeat would be ultimately certain, God only knows how many of our own people would get killed along the way." She shook her head, expression grave. "Even completely ignoring our moral responsibility not to throw away lives unnecessarily, those sorts of casualty levels would inevitably—and rightly—lead to universal repugnance in the League. Bearing all of that in mind, it seemed evident to everyone on Admiral Kingsford's staff—and to Admiral Rajampet and *his* staff, for that matter—that Assemblywoman Hadley had a point. Even if not everyone agreed with her logic, the ultimate conclusion was effectively the same: despite the Navy's understandable fury and desire for vengeance, any sort of precipitous operations against Manticore were out of the question. At the very least, every diplomatic avenue had to be explored first."

She paused again, and this time Caddell-Markham allowed himself to nod in sober agreement, despite his quick lick of anger at Simpson's clumsy effort to suggest some sort of agreement with Felicia Hadley.

"Unfortunately," the admiral went on, "it's become evident to Foreign Minister Roelas y Valiente and to Permanent Senior Undersecretary Kolokoltsov that Manticore has no intention of negotiating in good faith." She sighed. "Whatever Assemblywoman Hadley and those who share her concerns may think, the Manties' diplomatic correspondence—not to mention the obvious duplicity of the way in which they misrepresented the Republic of Haven's diplomacy in the resumption of their long-standing war against Haven; the shameless, cynical imperialism of coldbloodedly partitioning a sovereign star nation in the Silesian Confederacy's case; the unilateral decision to close not just their own Junction but every other termius they control against Solarian traffic; and their questionable actions in the Talbott Sector—all make it clear they have every intention of pressing their current military advantage for all it's worth."

That wasn't, Caddell-Markham reflected, the way *he* would have described the Star Empire's diplomatic exchanges with the League. Or any of the rest of its foreign policy over the last, oh, fifty T-years or so. As fantasies went, though, it stuck together fairly well, he supposed. Or would have, assuming anyone with the IQ of a gnat had been prepared to believe a single word that came out of the Office of Frontier Security.

And isn't it interesting that she never even mentioned *Green Pines?* he thought sardonically.

"That was the unpalatable situation in the immediate aftermath of the New Tuscany and Spindle incidents," Simpson said. "More recently, however, that situation has changed radically. I'm sure you here in Beowulf have an even better appreciation than most for just how badly the Mantics were damaged by that attack on their home system."

For just a moment, despite her obviously formidable self-control, those brown eyes hardened. Obviously she and her superiors suspected Beowulf really did have a far better "appreciation" for events in Manticore than it had chosen to share with them. Caddell-Markham and Miternowski-Zhyang only nodded courteously, however. Her lips thinned ever so briefly, but then she shrugged and actually smiled.

"We don't know who was responsible for that attack. I assure you, the Office of Naval Intelligence is working overtime to figure out who it could have been! The obvious fact that at least one other navy also has capabilities we can't match at the moment doesn't make any of us very happy. At the same time, it's clear this mysterious third party has managed to significantly prune back Manty capabilities. In fact, our analysis suggests the Manticoran heavy industrial structure's been effectively destroyed, with obvious consequences for their ability to support sustained operations. None of which has done anything to mitigate Manty ambitions, unfortunately. To be honest, they seem to have become even more ambitious—or aggressive, at any rate—judging by their actions where the wormhole network is concerned. In fact, we have reports—unconfirmed at this time, but from usually reliable sources—that they've begun to go beyond shutting down their own termini by actually seizing control of any other termini they can reach, regardless of who they may belong to, to close *them* against us as well.

"Given the Manticorans' clear, unwavering intention to hold to the aggressive course they've set, Prime Minister Gyulay concurs with Admiral Rajampet's view that it would be criminally negligent to give them the gift of time to rebuild their military. Ultimately, that would almost certainly result in an unconscionable death toll for our own military. For that matter, it would result ultimately in a staggering death toll for the *Manties*, once we fully mobilized against them. So, the Navy intends to move quickly, taking advantage of this window of opportunity. We happen to have a force of approximately four hundred ships-of-the-wall either already at or within a very few days' hyper travel of the Tasmania System. Within the next two or three weeks, those ships, reinforced by everything we've been able to get to them, will advance on Manticore under Fleet Admiral Filareta. They should reach Manticore no later than the middle of June."

Simpson's voice had become deeper and more measured, and this time the Beowulfers allowed their own eyes to widen in surprise leavened by more than a hint of trepidation.

"Admiral Rajampet fully realizes the grave risks of the operation he's instructed Admiral Kingsford to mount. Obviously, we hope the combination of the damage the Manties have already suffered and the speed with which Admiral Filareta can reach their home system will convince them to see reason. Failing that, we believe their defensive capabilities will have been sufficiently reduced for Admiral Filareta to succeed in defeating their remaining forces with a minimum of casualties. Nonetheless, the possibility does exist that he'll take severe losses if it turns out their defensive canopy hasn't been quite so badly eroded as our current analyses suggest. Which is what brings me to Beowulf."

She stopped speaking almost abruptly and sat back in her own chair, gazing at Caddell-Markham levelly.

"I beg your pardon?" he said. "I'm afraid I don't quite understand how Admiral—Filareta, you said?— and his operations affect us here in Beowulf, Admiral Simpson."

"It's actually fairly simple, Director," Simpson replied. "In an ideal universe the *psychological* aspects of this operation will allow Admiral Filareta to succeed without firing a single shot. The idea is to demonstrate to the Manties that whatever their present, transitory advantages, they can't ultimately hope to defeat something with the size and staying power of the Solarian League and the Solarian League Navy. To help push that lesson home, we need to apply pressure from as many directions as possible, as closely to simultaneously as possible."

"Wait a minute," Caddell-Markham said (after all, it wouldn't do to appear *too* obtuse). "I do hope you're not proposing to launch a second prong of this attack through the Beowulf Terminus, Admiral Simpson!"

"That's exactly what we're proposing, Sir."

"Well, I'm afraid I can't agree that it's a very good idea," he told her flatly.

"Why not?" If Simpson was dismayed (or surprised) by his response, her tone gave no indication of it.

"Several reasons occur to me right offhand. First and foremost, there's the question of pre-transit intelligence." Caddell-Markham shook his head, his expression sober. "I'm sure you realize how much Manticore's closure of the Junction is hurting us here in Beowulf. They've shut it down from their end, not ours, but with Manty merchant traffic all heading for home or already there and the Junction closed to all *Solarian* traffic, one of our major revenue producers is effectively completely off-line. I'm sure Admiral Kingsford and Admiral Rajampet were aware of that when they sent you to make this proposal to us, and no doubt there are some people right here on Beowulf who want to see our terminus reopened just as badly as anyone in Old Chicago might. But whether that's true or not, the fact that it's currently closed to Solarian traffic—including ours—means we don't have a clear idea of what's currently happening in and around the Junction. Everything we *have* heard and been able to piece together, however, suggests they've concentrated their defenses to cover the Junction from their side more throughly than at any time since the Star Kingdom took Trevor's Star away from the People's Republic. At the very least, the forces they already had in place have to be at a very high level of alert.

"Even leaving that consideration aside, though, there's the problem of coordinating our own forces. Manticore may be only a single wormhole transit from Beowulf, but it's light-centuries away in n-space. Trying to coordinate simultaneous assaults between two forces which are literally months apart in terms of communications time strikes me as a recipe for disaster. Especially when, if I understand what you said earlier correctly, there won't be time to get a dispatch boat to Admiral Filareta with the news that your second force is even coming!"

"You're right," Simpson conceded, "and we've considered that. We can't communicate directly with Admiral Filareta, of course, but we've already infiltrated one of our own dispatch boats into the Manticore System. It's covered as a news-service vessel, since the Manties are so 'graciously' allowing even Solarian courier and dispatch vessels passage, and we've arranged to rotate additional couriers through the Junction under similar covers throughout the entire operational window. The Manties' own movements should make it evident to everyone in the system when Filareta arrives, at which point our dispatch boat transits to Beowulf and another thirty or so of our SDs transit directly into the Junction. The sudden arrival of another task force that powerful in their rear should certainly drive home to the Manties the sheer disparity between our resources and theirs."

"Even assuming your courier boat's allowed to make transit—which it might well not be, once Filareta arrives and the system goes to a high state of military alert," Miternowski-Zhyang said, speaking for the first time, "what makes you think the Manties will *let* you make transit with that many wallers?" The assistant director of defense wasn't making any particular effort to disguise her own incredulity. "I'm assuming from the number you've just given us that you're talking about a simultaneous transit, but whether you plan on a simultaneous transit or a phased transit, those ships are still going to be emerging suddenly, without clearance, when the Manties are already facing the open arrival of *four hundred* Solarian wallers. As Director Caddell-Markham just pointed out, all our sources indicate their Junction defense forces are at a strength and readiness level we haven't seen in years. And, to be blunt, whoever's in command of those forces is going to shoot first and worry about IDs later."

"That's clearly a possibility." Simpson nodded. "Fleet Admiral Bernard and the Office of Strategy and Planning feel the odds are in favor of their standing down—or being momentarily paralyzed, at least—in the face of such a sudden multiplication of threat axes, however."

"'The odds are *in favor*' of their standing down?" Miternowski-Zhyang sounded as if she couldn't believe her own ears. "You're talking about sending better than thirty ships-of-the-wall with—what? A hundred and eighty thousand men and women aboard?—into a situation from which they can't possibly retreat, because the odds 'are *in favor*' of the Manties not pulling the trigger?" She shook her head. "Fleet Admiral Bernard does understand Manticore's been at war effectively continuously for *twenty T-years*, doesn't she?"

"Of course she does." Simpson's tone had become a bit testy at last. "I would submit, however, Assistant Director, that there's a vast difference between fighting something as ramshackle as the People's Republic of Haven and fighting the *Solarian League*. And that has to be especially true after they just got their entire system-defense force royally reamed by whoever got through to their industrial platforms!"

Miternowski-Zhyang shoved herself farther back in her chair, shaking her head yet again.

"I'm sure there *is* a 'vast difference,' Admiral," she said with a noticeable edge of frost. "At the same time,

I think we've probably seen a bit more of Manticore here than the Office of Strategy and Planning's seen in Old Chicago. I'm not trying to cast any aspersions on the analysts and planners in question"—there might, Caddell-Markham thought, have been just a *hint* of insincerity in that last little bit—"but everything *we've* ever seen out of the Manties suggests their first reaction to any threat, especially to their home system, is going to be to kill it. And whatever they may have used at Spindle, I think we can safely assume they have even heavier weapons defending the home system."

"Which someone else has already cleared a path through for us," Simpson pointed out. "And which the damage to their industrial capacity will prevent them from replacing."

"Assuming they hadn't taken the elementary military precaution of having more of them stockpiled in secure areas, well away from their industrial platforms," Miternowski-Zhyang shot back. She shook her head yet again, more sharply than ever. "I'm sorry, Admiral Simpson. I realize this isn't your plan, that you're simply in the position of describing it to us. But speaking as someone who's spent the last thirty or forty T-years helping manage the naval side of our own system-defense force, there's no way *I* could possibly sign off on such a high-risk, no-fallback operational plan."

"And if Justyná *could* sign off on it, Admiral," Caddell-Markham put in, "I'm afraid neither Chairman Benton-Ramirez nor I could."

"I see."

Simpson sat for a moment, looking back and forth between the two Beowulfers. Then she shrugged.

"I'm sorry to hear that. We'd hoped the BSDF

would help flesh out the secondary force. In fact, I'm afraid my instructions are to officially request that of the Planetary Board of Directors, even if Chairman Benton-Ramirez is as likely to reject our request as you're suggesting. Fortunately, we should be able to make up the necessary numbers out of SLN units, although without Beowulfan support we won't have the redundancy to follow up once the terminus stabilizes again. I hope the Chairman will at least consider the ... advisability of providing that minimal level of support to an operation of such obviously critical importance."

Well, score one for Jukka's "paranoid" analysis, Caddell-Markham thought. *Although, to be honest, I find it difficult to believe anyone even in Rajampet's office is crazy enough to think something like this could possibly succeed!*

"If you intend to make a formal request for BSDF support, I will of course present it to Chairman Benton-Ramirez," he said. "And while I understand your viewpoint, I'm afraid my own recommendation will be that he turn it down. I'm sorry, Admiral, but I fully share the Assistant Director's view of the probable outcome of any such operation. Under the circumstances, I can't recommend anything which might be construed as approval of it."

"Obviously, that's your privilege, Sir," Simpson said more than a little coldly.

"I see it not as a 'privilege,' but as a moral *duty,* Admiral," Caddell-Markham said equally coldly. "In fact, to be frank, my initial reaction is that this entire plan is based on overly optimistic and extremely problematic assumptions which rest on completely unverified—and unveri*fiable*—estimates of the Manties' current vulnerability. I'm perfectly prepared to review any intelligence analyses which would appear to support those assumptions and estimates, but all of the intelligence available to us here in Beowulf, right on the other side of the terminus, suggests that Justyná's view of the Manties' probable response is unfortunately accurate. Indeed, I suspect the Planetary Board will officially go on record as opposing the entire operation as hasty, ill-conceived, and likely to result in extraordinarily heavy casualties."

Chapter Eight

"I DON'T KNOW, LUIS."

Governor Oravil Barregos paused and took a sip of the really nice Mayan burgundy Admiral Luis Roszak had chosen to accompany dinner. It wasn't actually very much like Old Terran burgundy, despite the name. Fermented from the Mayan golden plum, not grapes, it reminded Roszak more of a rich, fruity port, but no one had consulted him when it was named, and it was one of Barregos' favored vintages. The governor's expression was not that of a man savoring a special treat, however, and he sighed as he lowered the glass.

"I don't know," he repeated, gazing down into its tawny heart. "After the way you got hammered at Congo and given how that maniac Rajampet seems to be calling the shots, I have to admit I'm feeling at least a minor case of... cold feet, let's say."

Roszak sat back, nursing his own wineglass, and studied the Maya Sector Governor across his small kitchen table. He'd known Oravil Barregos a long time, and "cold feet" were something he'd never before associated with the other man. Especially not where the "Sepoy Option" was concerned.

Then again, the admiral thought, *we've never been this close to actually pulling it off, and none of our calculations considered the possibility of an outright shooting war between the League and someone like the Manties. Throw in "mystery raiders" with invisible starships, and I suppose even Alexander of Macedon might experience the odd moment of trepidation. And Oravil, bless his Machiavellian little heart, never believed he was a demigod to begin with!*

"I agree we got hammered," he said after a moment. "And when it comes right down to it, it's *my* fault we did."

He made the admission unflinchingly and raised his free hand in a silencing motion when Barregos started to contest his self-indictment.

"I'm not saying I made wrong decisions based on what I thought I knew," he said. "I *am* saying I was too damned complacent about thinking that what we all thought we knew was accurate. Or, rather, that we understood all its implications, let's say." He shrugged. "We knew Mesa was using Luft and his people as deniable mercenaries, and we assumed—on the basis of what happened at Monica with the Manties—that they might reinforce them with heavy Solarian-built units, which is exactly what they did. Our mistake— *my* mistake—was to assume that if they were using Solarian-built units, they'd be using SLN *missiles*, too. I built all my tactics around the assumption my opponents would be range-limited, unable to reply effectively." He shrugged again, dark eyes bitter with memory. "I was wrong."

"If you were wrong, so was everyone else," Barregos pointed out. "Edie Habib and Watanapongse both thought the same thing."

"Of course they did. They're no more mind readers than I am, and it was a logical assumption. And there was no sign they had any missile pods on tow, either, since they didn't. If they *had* been towing pods, though—if we'd seen something like that—even I might have remembered those long-ranged missiles Technodyne provided for Monica and at least considered the possibility that Mesa had given something similar to Luft.

"My point, Oravil, is that I was the commanding officer. There's an old saying, one I think too many officers and politicians routinely ignore: 'The buck stops here.' I was the commander; the responsibility was mine. And what made it my fault we got hammered was that if I'd thought about it at all, I didn't have to close as far as I did. Even with those 'cataphract' missiles, we had them outranged. But I wanted to get right in on the edge of their powered envelope, get the best accuracy I could while staying too far away for them to fire effectively on us. If I'd been more cautious, settled for poorer firing solutions and just accepted that I was going to expend more ammunition, they wouldn't have been able to hurt us anywhere near as badly as they did. In fact, we probably wouldn't've gotten hurt *at all*."

"I still say it's not your fault." Barregos shook his head stubbornly. "You have to go with the information you've got when you plan something like a battle. I may not be an admiral, but I know that much! And no plan survives contact with the enemy. I don't know how many times I've heard you say that, and it's as true in politics as it is in the military. It works both ways, too. They may have surprised you with the range of their missiles, but you surprised the hell out of *them*, too! And your deployment gave you the reserve to run the table once you'd taken out their battlecruisers." The governor shrugged. "You got hurt a lot worse than we ever anticipated, but you still won the battle—decisively—because you were prepared to deal with Murphy when he turned up."

"All right, I'll give you that." Roszak nodded. Then he smiled, and his eyes narrowed. "And where I was headed, using the strategy of the indirect approach, was to point out that *you* do a pretty good job of disaster-proofing your plans, too. We always knew we were going to have to make a lot of it up as we went along when the token finally dropped, Oravil. You've laid your groundwork; despite all the people I managed to get killed at Congo, we've still got most of our critical senior personnel in position, and I can't really think of something closer to producing the conditions Sepoy envisioned than what's going on with the Manties now. We just have to be ready to improvise and adapt when Murphy starts throwing crap at us on the political front as well."

Barregos gazed at the admiral for several seconds, then snorted in harsh amusement.

"'Indirect approach,' is it? All right, you got me. But this is a little different from defending Torch against an Eridani violation, Luis. If I push the button on Sepoy, it's for all the marbles. We have to come out into the open, and that's going to put *us* up against Frontier Fleet, maybe even Battle Fleet, and we're nowhere near the Manties' size and weight!"

"I think your plans for staying in the shadows a bit longer will hold up," Roszak demurred. "Oh, there's a risk they won't, but don't forget the rumblings we're getting from other Frontier Security sectors. I think the situation's going to go a lot further south on Kolokoltsov and Rajampet than they ever imagined. It's going to happen a lot faster than even you and I assumed it would, too, and this confrontation with the Manties is what's driving it, because it's destroying the League's perceived omnipotence among the independent Verge systems. I'm sure the fear of where that's going to lead is a big part of what's driving Kolokoltsov to back MacArtney and Rajampet, but they don't seem to've considered that a lot of the more restive *protectorates* may have read the evidence the same way as the independent systems. I think they're in for a rude awakening on that front sometime really soon now, and when the shitstorm hits, they're going to be so busy worrying about outbreaks closer to home that we're going to sort of disappear into the general chaos, at least at first. They aren't going to be sending any major fleets out here while they're dealing with forest fires in the Core's front yard. Especially when we keep explaining that we're really good, loyal OFS thugs just doing what we have to to maintain order in the League's benevolent name."

Barregos frowned thoughtfully, his eyes focused on something only he could see. He stayed that way for a while, then inhaled deeply and refocused on his host across the table.

"All right, I'll give you that," he said, deliberately reusing Roszak's own words. "And you're right about where their attention's likely to be focused...assuming they don't just go ahead and steamroller the Manties after all. But that could still happen, especially after the Yawata strike."

Roszak nodded soberly. No one in the Maya Sector was yet clear on exactly how much damage the Manties had taken from that surprise attack. It had happened barely five weeks ago, and the Maya System was ten days from the Manticore Binary System by dispatch boat even using the shortcut from the Manticoran Wormhole Junction via Hennessy, Terre Haute, and Erewhon. What they *did* know, though, was that casualties—*civilian* casualties this time, unlike those suffered in the Battle of Manticore—had been horrific, and it sounded as if Manticore's industrial capabilities had taken a major blow. That had to have serious implications in any conflict with the League, and the absence of any evidence as to who'd actually attacked the Manties increased the uncertainty quotient exponentially.

"I'm not going to say the Manties aren't in a deep crack," the admiral said. "We don't know how deep it is, but it's not someplace *I'd* like to be. On the other hand, they've been in cracks before, and it's usually worked out worse for the other side than for them, so I'm not prepared to write them off. And even if they do go down, they're not going easy. Old Chicago's still going to be concentrating primarily on them for at least a while, and the fact that Erewhon's no longer part of the Manticoran Alliance works for us, too. No one on Old Terra's looking in Erewhon's direction at the moment, and if our reports go on stressing how our investment in the system is giving us additional clout to suck them deeper into the League's pocket, we can keep it that way for quite a while."

"Probably," Barregos conceded with a nod. That had been part of his own core planning from the outset, after all.

"Well, new construction's already more than replaced everything I lost at Congo," Roszak pointed out. "We're two and a half T-years into our master building program, too, and the Carlucci Group's actually a bit ahead of schedule on the wallers. Not a lot— we're still looking at somewhere around two more T-years before we'll be able to put the first SD into commission—but the light units will be ready a lot sooner than that. They're already starting to supply us with all-up multidrive missiles for our arsenal ships as well, and however long the podnoughts are going to take, we should have the first pod *battlecruisers* in another ten months or so. Call it mid-October for the first units' builder's trials. Whatever happens with the Manties, I'm pretty damn sure they'll last at least that long against anything a thumb-fingered 'strategist' like Rajampet can throw at them, if only because of the transit times involved! And, like I say, Kolokoltsov and MacArtney are going to be a lot more occupied with the unrest that's headed for them out in the open than by our own discreet activities. On that basis, I'd say we're almost certain to get at least a few squadrons of wallers ready for service before Rajampet decides we're another nail that needs hammering."

Barregos nodded again. It wasn't as if Roszak were telling him anything he didn't already know. And as the admiral had also suggested, Oravil Barregos had known from the beginning that his plans were going to require fancy footwork. He'd seen this storm coming long ago, even if he'd never counted on actual hostilities between the League and someone like the Star Empire. The cataclysm poised to demolish the League's arrogant complacency was going to come as an even greater shock to the men and women who thought of themselves as its masters than his original plans had dared anticipate, but to reach his destination he'd have to embrace the storm, *use* its downdrafts and savage crosscurrents.

And skydiving in a thunderstorm never was the safest hobby, was it, Oravil? he asked himself dryly. *I guess it's time you find out whether you've got the intestinal fortitude to really do this after all.*

He took another sip of wine, thinking about all the years of effort and careful planning, of cautious recruitment and trust-building, which had led him to this point. And as he did, he realized that however nervous he might feel, what he felt most strongly of all was eagerness.

No one who'd ever met Oravil Barregos could have doubted for a moment that he was intensely ambitious. He knew it himself, and he'd accepted that he was the sort of man who was never truly happy unless *he* was the one wielding authority. Making decisions. *Proving* he was smarter, better, more qualified for the power he possessed than anyone else. Nor, he admitted, was he averse to wealth and all that came with it.

That, in many ways, was the perfect profile of an Office of Frontier Security commissioner or sector governor, and it explained a great deal about how he'd risen to his present position. But it didn't explain *all* of it, and that was important, because the bureaucrats who'd accepted him as one of their own had made a fatal mistake. They'd failed to recognize that unlike them, Barregos actually *cared* about the people he governed. That he'd recognized the rot, seen the corrosion, realized the reaction Frontier Security's abuse of the protectorates must inevitably provoke.

Whether or not he and Luis Roszak and the other men and women committed to the Sepoy Option succeeded, the storm was coming, and the League's confrontation with the Star Empire of Manticore could only speed the day its winds swept over the explored galaxy. And that was really the point, wasn't it? When that storm broke, the chaos and confusion, the warlordism and the violence, which followed the shipwreck of any empire, were going to sweep across the protectorates as well. They were going to sweep across the Maya Sector, and Maya's wealth could only make it even more attractive to brigands and pirates and potential warlords.

That wasn't going to happen to the people Oravil Barregos was responsible for. On oh-so-many levels, it *wasn't* going to happen. And for him to prevent it, he and Roszak had to build the strength to stand against the hurricane.

To stop the warlords, they had to *become* warlords... and the biggest, nastiest warlords on the block, at that.

"You're right, Luis," he said, setting the glass down with a snap. He looked across the table at the admiral who was not simply his accomplice in treason but his closest friend, and smiled. "You're right. So let's just consider my cold feet warmed up."

Roszak smiled back at him and raised his own glass.

"I'll drink to that," he said.

Chapter Nine

"I DON'T SUPPOSE we've received any updates on those damned missile ships?"

Fleet Admiral Massimo Filareta's hundred and ninety centimeters, broad shoulders, close-cropped beard, strong chin, and dark eyes gave him an undeniably commanding physical presence. When he was angry, that presence tended to become actively intimidating, and at the moment, Admiral John Burrows, his chief of staff, estimated, he was somewhere well north of "irritated" and closing rapidly on "irate." The rest of his staffers were busy finding other places to park their gazes, and quite a few seemed to have discovered that the wallpaper on their personal computers had become downright fascinating.

"No, Sir, we haven't," the short, fair-haired Burrows said calmly.

He'd been with Filareta long enough to develop a certain deftness at managing the fleet admiral, and to Filareta's credit, he realized he *needed* a manager. He hadn't risen to his present rank without family connections, but in Burrows' opinion he was also one of a handful of truly senior officers who were actually competent. He was hardworking, levelheaded, and paid attention to the details all too many other flag officers simply ignored or shoveled onto their overworked staffs. At the same time, though, he was a man of passions, unruly emotions, and huge appetites, and he needed someone like Burrows to keep him balanced... or at least focused. Which was one reason John Burrows routinely faced an irritated Filareta with a confidence which filled lesser staffers with the sort of admiration normally reserved for counter-grav-free skydivers, alligator wrestlers, and similar adrenaline junkies.

"Of course we haven't!" Filareta more than half snarled, and this time Burrows simply nodded, since he and Filareta were both aware the fleet admiral had known the answer before he ever asked the question.

Filareta clamped his teeth hard on his frustrated anger and turned to the briefing room's smart-wall bulkhead and the distant, fiery spark of the star named Tasmania. He clamped his hands equally tightly behind him and concentrated on fighting his temper under control.

What he *really* wanted to do was to turn that temper loose. A good old-fashioned, red-in-the-face-and-screaming tantrum might relieve at least some of the anger, frustration, and (little though he cared to admit it even to himself) fear swirling around inside him. Unfortunately, any relief would have been purely temporary, and he didn't need to be displaying his own reservations in front of his staff.

Especially not on the eve of the biggest combat

deployment in the eight-hundred-year history of the Solarian League Navy.

"All right," he said, once he was fairly confident he'd locked down his temper. "Since we're stuck here, twiddling our thumbs until they *do* deign to arrive, I suppose we should look at the results of yesterday's exercise." He looked over his shoulder at Admiral William Daniels, his operations officer. "Suppose you start the ball rolling, Bill."

"Yes, Sir."

The brown-haired, brown-eyed Daniels had been with Filareta almost as long as Burrows, but he wasn't as good at fleet admiral-managing, and he couldn't hide his relief as the meeting turned to something less inflammatory than the ammunition ships' much-discussed tardiness.

"First, Sir," he continued, "I'd like to observe that Admiral Haverty's task force did particularly well in the missile-defense role. We all know ONI's current opinion is that whoever leveled the Manties' home system has to've blown a huge hole in their missile umbrella, and I know we all hope that's true. If it isn't, though, we're going to need the kind of performance Haverty's people turned in. In particular"—he activated his previously prepared report, and a stop-motion hologram of a detailed tactical plot appeared above the briefing-room conference table—"I'd like to direct everyone's attention to this missile salvo here." A flight of missile icons blinked scarlet on the plot. "As you can see, we adjusted the simulation's parameters to reflect the reports of extended ranges we've been receiving. As of this time, we still don't know what their *actual* ranges are, of course, but this simulation assigned them a fifty percent increase in powered envelope, and we didn't warn anyone it was coming ahead of time. Despite that, though, if you watch what happens when Admiral Haverty's task force detects them incoming"—he entered a command and the missile icons began moving steadily across the holographic plot—"you'll see that..."

✧   ✧   ✧

"What did you think of Daniels' analysis of Haverty's performance?" Filareta asked Burrows some hours later.

The two of them sat in Filareta's dining cabin, forming a small island of humanity at the enormous compartment's center, with the remnants of a sumptuous lunch on the table between them. Burrows was always a little astonished Filareta could eat as heartily as he did without ever appearing to gain a single gram. Of course, the fleet admiral did work out regularly, and there *were* those...other interests of his.

"I thought he was pretty much on the mark, Sir." The chief of staff sipped from his wineglass. "I think we probably need to push the simulator parameters farther out—I agree with you there, entirely—but he was right about how well Haverty did within the *existing* parameters. And, frankly, there's at least some question in my mind about how far we want to go in simulating Manticoran range advantages."

Not many officers would have admitted that so frankly, Filareta reflected, but Burrows had a point. If they started putting their fleet through simulations which assumed the Royal Manticoran Navy's effective missile ranges really were as extreme as some reports claimed, it would devastate their own morale.

And if the bastards do *have that kind of range—and accuracy—there's no point training to fight them, anyway. We'll be dead meat no matter what we do!*

It wasn't a thought he was prepared to share even with Burrows, although he suspected the chief of staff had reached the same conclusion. On the other hand, Burrows continued to believe—probably correctly, Filareta thought—that the Manty missiles at Spindle must have come out of system-defense pods, not shipboard launchers. No matter what else, missiles that long-ranged had to be *huge*, which meant no mobile unit could carry them in the numbers which had been reported. And if they *had* come out of system-defense pods, then even that incomparable military genius Rajampet was probably right about how the January attack on the Manties' home system had depleted their supply of them.

Unfortunately, that attack had occurred at least six T-months before Filareta could possibly get there to exploit it. He wasn't as confident as Rajampet that the Manties wouldn't be able to make a lot of that damage good in the meantime. And, even more unfortunately, there were a few things Burrows didn't know and Filareta was in no position to tell him.

The fleet admiral picked up his own wineglass, sipping with less than his usual appreciation while his mind flowed down internal pathways which had become entirely too well worn over the two T-weeks since he'd received his orders for Operation Raging Justice. Actually, they'd started wearing their way into his cortex the instant he heard about Sandra Crandall's debacle. Or, at least, the instant he first heard the Manticorans' analysis of how Crandall had come to be aimed at them in the first place.

Burrows, he knew, put zero credence in Manty claims that Manpower and/or other Mesa-based transstellars had deliberately fomented the incidents in the Talbott Sector. The chief of staff was no innocent virgin where corporate influence on naval policies was involved, but it was preposterous to suggest that any transstellar, however powerful, could actually control major fleet movements! That was the stuff of paranoid conspiracy theories, as far as Burrows was concerned.

It might not have been if he'd known what Massimo Filareta knew.

Filareta couldn't be positive Crandall had been influenced by Manpower, but he knew for damned certain that *he* had. He knew all about his own reputation as a hard-partying fellow, and he knew there were rumors about certain other of his more . . . esoteric tastes. As far as he knew, though, no one knew about his most deeply hidden cravings. No one, at least, but his "friends" at Manpower, who'd long since fallen into the habit of providing for those cravings. Those same "friends" had eased his way in other fashions as well, and he'd always known that someday they'd want payback. But he'd been all right with that; it was the way the system worked, even if his particular set of incentives would have been regarded as beyond the pale even by jaded Solarian standards.

So he hadn't been surprised when one of his "friends" explained why they wanted him in command of the task force to be deployed to Tasmania. They wanted a Solarian naval presence close to the Manties—close enough to discourage them from diverting strength to Talbott to respond forcefully to Manpower's proxies—and they wanted its CO to be someone they could trust to make that point to Manticore if the need arose.

And you just can't quite brush off the suspicion that they may have sent Crandall out to Talbott with exactly the same "you're just a diversion" explanation, can you, Massimo? Especially when you're sitting here waiting for the damned missile colliers.

That was the final element which had him considering the sort of "paranoid conspiracy theories" with which Burrows had so little patience. The order to prepare to receive a massive influx of reinforcements had arrived on April the eleventh, with instructions to sortie no later than the twenty-fifth. Obviously, the reinforcements he was to expect had already been put into motion, and although the timetable had been tight, he'd felt reasonably confident of making the ordered departure date. Except that two days *later* he'd received orders to await a convoy of ammunition ships loaded with the latest Technodyne ship-to-ship and system defense missile variants. As a follow-up dispatch had explained, it would delay the operation by no more than forty-eight hours, assuming the missile colliers experienced no delays of their own.

He'd been surprised Technodyne was supplying anything, given the legal firestorm still swirling around the huge arms manufacturer. But then he'd examined the new order a bit more closely and discovered that the "Technodyne" shipment had actually originated in the Mesa System.

Which was odd, since there was no Technodyne manufacturing facility in that star system.

Technodyne did have a corporate headquarters on Mesa, so it might have made sense for shipping *orders* to originate there, but there was no way the missiles themselves should be coming from that star system. Not if they'd actually been built by Technodyne, at least. Unless, perhaps, they were coming out of ammunition stockpiles already amassed by someone—someone other than the Solarian League Navy—in the aforesaid system.

As far as Filareta knew, not even Burrows had noticed that discrepancy. Nor had the chief of staff looked at the transit times involved. Oh, if anyone did look, they'd probably find that the colliers had been "diverted in transit" from some other, reasonably innocent destination, just like quite a few of his reinforcing superdreadnought squadrons. Massimo Filareta wasn't "anyone," however. He was as certain as a man could be that the missiles in question had actually left Mesa *before* his orders to sortie had been written on Old Terra, and they hadn't been "diverted in transit," either. They'd been intended for Tasmania from the outset...which, in turn, suggested that the same *someone* in the Mesa System from whose stockpiles they'd been drawn had calculated that Filareta's command was going to receive exactly the orders it had received.

And those orders had been written only as a consequence of what had happened to Sandra Crandall.

Given all that, the Manties' "preposterous" claims about Mesa began to seem a lot less preposterous. And the fact that "Technodyne" just *happened* to have been developing a longer-ranged, tube-launched shipkiller missile at the very moment the analysts back home in

Old Chicago had finally become aware of *Manticoran* missile ranges was another of those "coincidences" Filareta found difficult to swallow.

No, he thought now, lowering his glass and staring down into the wine. *No, you're a pulser dart aimed at Manticore by your "friends," Massimo. And so was Crandall. And someone else—someone back in the Sol System itself—has to be in on this, too. It's the only way those oh-so-fortuitously available missiles could have been slipped into the order queue so smoothly. It could be Kingsford, I suppose. He's spent long enough learning to punch Rajampet's buttons. Or it could be Rajampet himself. I never would've thought he was* smart *enough to make a good conspirator, but someone else could be calling the shots for him the same way they were for Crandall . . . or me, for that matter. And when you come down to it, it doesn't really have to've been someone at the top. Someone in the right position in Logistics could've stage-managed the whole thing, at least as far as the missiles are concerned. Not that it really matters how they managed that part. No, what* matters is *whether they pre-positioned me just in case I'd be needed, or because they figured all along that Crandall was going to get reamed? Because if they deliberately set her up to get wasted, they could be doing exactly the same thing to* me.

On the face of it, he couldn't see any advantage for anyone in the Mesa System in getting another three or four hundred Solarian ships-of-the-wall killed. On the other hand, he was damned if he could see what advantage they'd gotten out of what had happened to Crandall. So either they'd miscalculated in her case, or else *they* saw an advantage he couldn't.

It was odd how neither of those possibilities reassured him.

✧　　✧　　✧

The bored-looking electronics tech swiped her ID and presented a palm to the scanner before stepping onto SLNS *Philip Oppenheimer*'s flag bridge. The scanner considered the card's biometric data, comparing it briefly but thoroughly to the DNA of the proffered hand. Then it blinked a green light, and the officer of the watch glanced in the newcomer's direction with a raised eyebrow.

"Permission to enter Flag Bridge, Ma'am?" the tech asked with a salute which might have been a bit sharper.

"Do we have a fault I don't know about, PO... Harder?" the officer of the watch responded, checking the readout from the ID for the tech's name before acknowledging her salute.

"I don't think so, Ma'am," Harder replied. "Just a routine, scheduled maintenance check somebody forgot to make. Or forgot to log, anyway."

Harder's tone made it clear she didn't appreciate having been sent to tidy up someone else's mistake.

"The Chief Engineer sent me to make sure it's done and done right," she continued. "Everything's probably fine, really, but Captain Hershberger wants to be certain it really is, under the circumstances."

"Well, I'm not about to argue with that," the officer of the watch agreed, and nodded for Harder to get on with it.

The noncom pulled up her minicomp work order, then doublechecked the command-station number to be certain before she headed across the bridge. She pulled the access panel on the back of Admiral Daniels' console, laid out her tool kit, flopped down on the decksole, and slid under the complex collection of molecular circuitry with her testing equipment.

✧ ✧ ✧

"Well, *there's* a thing," Anton Zilwicki said mildly.

He sat at the communications officer's station on the Havenite dispatch boat's cramped bridge. Such bare-bones craft couldn't begin to match the sensor reach of a real warship, and their much simpler sensor suites had no dedicated plot, either. Instead, they used the main com screen to display such data as they managed to collect, and it was customary for the com officer to be responsible for them. As it happened, the dispatch boat's official com officer— who seemed to be about twelve, anyway—was in sickbay with, of all ridiculous things, an impacted wisdom tooth.

The situation, Zilwicki thought, said volumes about just how poor medical care, and especially preventative medical care, had been under the People's Republic of Haven. The restored Republic was working hard to get the backlog of completely preventable complaints—like dental problems—under control, but it hadn't caught up yet.

Fortunately for Lieutenant Dahmer, the boat's skipper, Anton Zilwicki had forgotten more about sensor systems and communications equipment than his ailing com officer had yet learned. Which explained why Zilwicki was monitoring the display as the small vessel accelerated towards the planet of Haven. Now he leaned forward, fiddling with the controls and frowning at the icons before him.

"What?" Victor Cachat demanded after a moment, and Zilwicki looked up over his shoulder.

"What 'what'?"

"You said, and I quote, 'Well, there's a thing.'"

"Did I?" Zilwicki raised both eyebrows and sighed. "A bad sign, Victor. Talking to myself, I mean." He shook his head. "I hope you avoid this kind of mental disintegration when *you* get to be my age."

The Havenite glowered at him. Victor Cachat was extraordinarily capable, even gifted, in certain very specific, very narrow types of human endeavor. You needed someone killed? Victor Cachat was your man. A lock picked, an extortionist shown the error of his ways, a counterespionage sting run with consummate artistry, a planetary régime destabilized? Pish-tush! Mere bagatelles! Any of those minor challenges, and he was quite literally in a league of his own.

Step outside those...call them his "core competencies," however, and his expertise disappeared rapidly. When it came to electronics (other than those specifically associated with explosions, arson, and general mayhem, at least), he was not, to put it charitably, at his best. Indeed, Thandi Palane had been known to observe that he was the only man in the universe who could make a standard wrist chrono explode... accidentally. Zilwicki, on the other hand, was one of the galaxy's top handful of hackers, cyberneticists, and mollycirc wizards. Worse, at the moment, he was a trained naval officer, fully at home on the bridge and (unlike Cachat) able to absorb and interpret its displays as naturally as breathing.

"You know," Cachat said now, "it would be a tragedy if the working relationship you and I have developed should come to a catastrophic end due to the sudden, unanticipated demise of one half of that relationship."

"Really?" Zilwicki's tone remained grave, but there might have been the merest hint of the twinkle in those dark eyes, and his lips twitched ever so slightly. "Are you feeling ill, Victor? *You* don't have a bad tooth, do you?"

"Oh, no." Cachat smiled sweetly. "*I'm* feeling just fine."

"Oh, stop it, you two!" Yana said from behind them. Both men looked at her, and she shook her head, her expression disgusted. "I swear, I've known *three*-year-olds with higher maturity quotients than either of you!"

"Hey, *he* started it!" Cachat said virtuously, jabbing a finger in Zilwicki's direction.

"Did not."

"Did too!"

"Didn't!"

"Did!"

"Stop it!" Yana thwacked Cachat on the back of the head, then shook an index finger under Zilwicki's nose. "Victor isn't the only one you're teasing, Anton, so don't think I'm going to let you keep this up."

"Just as a matter of idle curiosity, what do you propose to do about it?" he inquired mildly.

"*Me?* Nothing." Yana's smile was even sweeter than Cachat's had been. "Not directly, anyway. No, I'll just mention your behavior to Her Majesty. I'm sure you don't want Berry taking you to task for picking on Victor this way, do you?"

Zilwicki regarded her thoughtfully, then shrugged. His daughter was unlikely to "take him to task," but that didn't mean she couldn't find ways to demonstrate her disapproval. And Yana had a point. Berry did have an especially warm spot in her heart for Victor Cachat, galaxy-renowed assassin, ice-cold killer, and general purveyor of doom, chaos, and despair. Besides...

"All right," he said. "There's good news, and there's bad news. The bad news is that there's no sign of Eighth Fleet. The *good* news is that the star system's still intact. So we're not likely to find Duchess Harrington on-planet, but it doesn't look like the talks could've collapsed *too* disastrously."

"Are you sure you'd be able to find Eighth Fleet if it was still here?" Cachat asked. Zilwicki looked at him, and he shrugged. "You're the one who told me our sensors were crappy, Anton, and everybody knows Manty stealth is better than anyone else's."

"That's true," Zilwicki acknowledged. "On the other hand, according to your friend Justice, Eighth Fleet wasn't making any effort to hide. First, I imagine, because the whole point was for the Pritchart administration to be well aware—*painfully* well aware, if I may be so bold—of the iron fist inside Duchess Harrington's velvet glove. And, second, because sitting there with its stealth and EW online for such extended periods would give your Navy entirely too good a look at their capabilities under what would amount to laboratory conditions. In other words, if they were still here, we'd be able to see them even with this one-eyed bastard."

He jerked his head at the display pretending to be a plot, and Cachat nodded. It would have taken someone who knew the Havenite spy as well as Zilwicki did to recognize the worry in his expression.

"Hey, it's not the end of the world, Victor," Zilwicki

said more gently. "Like I said, the system's still here. For that matter, I'm picking up Capital Fleet's transponder beacons. If the talks had come apart spectacularly, there'd be a lot fewer ships and a lot more wreckage."

"True enough, I suppose." Cachat nodded brusquely, then gave himself a mental shake. "I could wish Duchess Harrington were still here, for a lot of reasons. But all we can do is the best we can do. Are we close enough for me to call in?"

"You'll still be looking at a twenty-five-minute two-way lag," Zilwicki told him. "Do you want to send a one-way burst, or are we going to have to go through some kind of challenge-response validation?"

"Burst, I think," Cachat said after a moment's reflection. "We can at least get the ball started rolling."

"Fine. In that case, you'd better get started recording it."

❖   ❖   ❖

The officer of the watch looked up from her own paperwork as Petty Officer Harder finished resecuring the access panel and started folding up her tool kit once more.

"Any problems, PO?"

"No, Ma'am." Harder smiled wryly. "Matter of fact, it looks like they *did* catch up on the last inspection and just forgot to log it. Everything's fine."

"Good." The officer smiled back and shook her head. "Sorry you had to come all the way down for something that was already done, but Captain Hershberger's right. Everything has to be four-oh on this one."

"You got that one right, Ma'am," Harder agreed and headed for the flag-bridge hatch.

❖   ❖   ❖

The uniformed four-man escort waiting dirtside for the shuttle seemed unable to decide whether its passengers were honored guests, prisoners, or homicidal maniacs. Since the escort was meeting Victor Cachat, Zilwicki thought that wasn't an unreasonable attitude on its part.

"Officer Cachat," the senior man said, looking at Cachat.

"Yes," Cachat replied tersely.

"And this would be Captain Zilwicki, then?"

"Yes, and this is Yana Tretiakovna." Cachat's tone had taken on a certain dangerous patience, Zilwicki noted.

"Thank you, Sir. But I don't believe anyone's told me who *this* is," the escort commander said, twitching his head in Herlander Simões' direction.

"No, they haven't, have they?"

"Sir, I'm afraid I'm going to have to insist on some identification."

"No," Cachat said flatly.

"Officer Cachat, I realize you're senior to me, but I'm still going to have to insist. My orders are to escort you directly to Péricard Tower, and I ,don't think Presidential Security's going to be happy about admitting someone they don't even have a *name* for!"

"Then they're just going to have to be unhappy," Cachat told him. "I'm not simply posturing, Officer . . . Bourchier," he went on, reading the other man's nameplate. "This man's identity—for that matter, the very fact of his existence—is strictly need-to-know. Frankly, I'd be a lot happier if you'd never even seen him. But the only four people who have the authority to decide *you* have a need-to-know who he is are Director Trajan, Director Usher, Attorney General LePic, or

President Pritchart. Now, do you want to get one of them on a secure com to get that kind of clearance, or do you want to just take my word for it?"

"Believe me," Yana said in an exaggerated stage whisper, one hand cupped beside her mouth. "You want to just take his word for it."

Bourchier looked at all of them for a long moment, then inhaled deeply. Obviously he'd heard the stories about Victor Cachat.

"Fine," he said. "Have it your way. But if Agent Thiessen shoots him on sight, nobody better blame *me* for it."

❖   ❖   ❖

Approximately ninety minutes later, Cachat, Simões, and Zilwicki were escorted into a maximum-security briefing room. Yana had declined Cachat's invitation when she found out who else was going to be present. Apparently there were limits to her insouciance, after all.

Actually, Zilwicki didn't really blame her as he surveyed the briefing room's occupants. President Eloise Pritchart, Secretary of War Admiral Thomas Theisman, Attorney General Denis LePic, Vice Admiral Linda Trenis of the Bureau of Planning, and Rear Admiral Victor Lewis, the CO of the Office of Operational Research, sat waiting for them, along with three members of the President's security detail. All of whom, Zilwicki noted, looked just as unhappy as Officer Bourchier had suggested they might.

Well, that was fine with him. He wasn't especially happy himself. To Bourchier's credit, he'd refused to allow even Victor Cachat to simply steamroller him. Instead, he'd flatly insisted on clearing Simões' presence with some higher authority before he'd go any farther. Wilhelm Trajan, the Director of the Foreign

Intelligence Service, hadn't been available—he was off-planet at the moment—so Bourchier had gone directly to LePic. Who, not unreasonably, had insisted on meeting Simões himself before he'd even consider authorizing his admittance into Pritchart's presence.

Zilwicki had no problem with that. What he did have a problem with was that their interview with the attorney general had been the first any of them had heard about what had happened—or, at least, what Mesa *claimed* had happened—in Green Pines. Discovering that he'd been branded as the worst mass murderer in recent memory tended to be just a tad upsetting.

And thinking about how the people he loved must have responded to that lie was even more so.

"So, our wandering boy returns, I see," Pritchart murmured. She regarded all of them for a moment, then looked directly at Zilwicki.

"I'm afraid the galaxy at large thinks you're, well, *dead*, Captain Zilwicki," she said. "I'm pleased to see the reports were in error. Although I'm sure quite a few people in Manticore are going to be just as curious to know where *you've* been for the last several months as we are about Officer Cachat's whereabouts."

"I'm sure they are, too, Madam President. Unfortunately, we had a little, um, engine trouble on the way home. It took us several months to make repairs." Zilwicki grimaced. "We played a lot of cards," he added.

"I imagine so." The President cocked her head. "And I imagine you've also discovered there have been a few developments since whatever happened—and I do trust you're going to tell us what it was that *did* happen—in Green Pines?"

"I'm sure that will be covered, Ma'am," Zilwicki

said grimly. "It wasn't much like the 'official version' I've just heard, but it was bad enough."

Pritchart gazed at him for a moment, then nodded slowly and looked at Simões.

"But I don't believe I know who this gentleman is," she continued.

"No, Madam President, you don't—yet," Cachat replied. "This is Dr. Herlander Simões. Of the planet Mesa."

Pritchart's spectacular topaz eyes narrowed slightly. The first-class brain behind those eyes was obviously running at top speed, but all she did was sit back in her chair.

"I see," she said after a moment, gazing speculatively at the Mesan. "May I assume Dr. Simões is the reason you've been...out of touch, let's say, for the last, oh, six or seven T-months?"

"He's one of the reasons, Ma'am."

"Then by all means be seated," she invited, waving a hand at the empty chairs on the other side of the table, "and let's hear what you—and Dr. Simões, of course—have to tell us."

❖   ❖   ❖

"Readiness reports complete, Sir," Admiral Daniels reported. "All squadron and task-group commanders report ready to proceed as ordered."

"Thank you, Bill," Fleet Admiral Filareta acknowledged.

He stood on the flag bridge of SLNS *Philip Oppenheimer*, flagship of the Solarian League Navy's newly designated Eleventh Fleet, gazing at the endless rows of status reports and thinking. The missile ships had taken a few days longer than expected to join him, which had given just enough time for a last set of dispatches from the Sol System to reach Tasmania. Which, in his opinion, was very much a mixed blessing.

The news that the Manties were closing wormhole termini to Solarian traffic was *not* something he'd wanted to hear. Whatever else it might indicate, it hardly sounded like the action of a star nation reeling from a surprise attack and terrified for its very life. One might have expected people in that position to be looking for ways to *avoid* infuriating something the size of the Solarian League, which didn't appear to have even crossed the Star Empire's mind. That was a disconcerting thought, and the fact that neither Rajampet nor his civilian masters seemed to share it was even more unpleasant. Judging from their amendment of his original mission orders, however, the only "thinking" they appeared to have done was to fasten on it as yet another Manty "provocation" to justify their own actions. They certainly hadn't been dissuaded by it, at any rate!

They probably think the Manties are just running a bluff, trying to convince us to back down, he reflected. *And maybe they are. But maybe they* aren't, *too. Maybe it's an indication they're genuinely that confident they can stand up to us, instead, and I sort of wish at least someone in Old Chicago was willing to at least consider the possibility. That'd be asking too much, though, I guess, since it would require a brain bigger than a pea!*

He shook his head mentally. It was far too late to be worrying about the blindness—or desperation—of the people behind his orders. It was too late to be worrying even about how large a hand Manpower might have had in drafting those orders in the first place, and at least four hundred and twenty-seven of the four hundred and thirty-one ships-of-the-wall which had been ordered to join him had actually arrived. That was a phenomenal accomplishment, by SLN peacetime readiness standards. In fact, he suspected the status reports on a half dozen or so of his SDs had been fudged by captains who had no intention of being caught short at a moment like this, but as long as they weren't covering up *fundamental* problems, that was fine with him.

The more the merrier, he thought sardonically, yet not even his cynicism was proof against commanding the most powerful armada the Solarian League had ever launched. As he looked at those status reports, at the glittering sea of icons, he was aware of the true size and power of the Solarian League Navy in a new and different way. His concerns about Manticoran weapons hadn't magically disappeared, by any means, yet despite those concerns, what he felt at this moment was the ponderous, unstoppable power of all those millions upon millions of tons of starships.

Four hundred and twenty-seven ships-of-the-wall. Thirty-two battlecruisers, thirty light cruisers, and forty-eight destroyers to screen the battle squadrons and provide the scouts they'd probably need. And fifty fast freighters (and personnel transports), all with military-grade hyper generators and particle screening. All told, his command counted almost six hundred starships, massing over three billion tons. Indeed, his wallers alone massed 2.9 billion tons, and counting the freighter and transport crews, he commanded over 2.7 million naval personnel, which didn't even count the transports' 421,000 Marines and support personnel. By any meter stick, it was an enormous force, and fifty percent of the missiles in his SDs' magazines were the new dual-drive Technodyne Cataphract-Bs. He would have preferred a heavier warhead, but that was what the five thousand pods loaded with Cataphract-Cs were for. At over sixteen million kilometers, their powered envelope was better than twice that of the Trebuchet capital missiles they'd replaced.

He was still a long way from truly leveling the playing field, assuming there was any truth in the Manty accounts of Spindle. As it happened, he was convinced there was quite a lot of truth in those accounts, but almost despite himself, he'd been deeply impressed when he saw the Cataphracts' performance numbers. Whether they'd come from Technodyne or the tooth fairy was far less important than how enormously his fleet's effective reach had been increased. He was going to be outranged by any surviving Manty system-defense missile pods, but he should at least come close to matching their *shipboard* missiles. If there was any validity at all to the Office of Strategy and Planning's assessment of the Star Empire's morale, that ought to be enough to convince them that no qualitative advantage could ultimately offset the sheer quantitative edge of the Solarian League.

Sure it will, he told himself. *You go right on thinking that way. But don't get your ass so wedded to the concept that you end up getting yourself and a couple of million other people killed!*

"Very well," he said at last, then drew a deep breath and turned to face Daniels once more.

"I believe we have a date with the Manties, Bill. Let's get this show on the road."

MAY 1922 POST DIASPORA

"What the hell. I've always liked a challenge."

—Queen Elizabeth III of Manticore

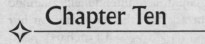

Chapter Ten

"MORE COFFEE, YOUR MAJESTY?"

Elizabeth Winton looked up at the murmured question, then smiled and extended her cup. James MacGuiness poured, smiled back at her, and moved on around the table, refilling other cups, and she watched him go before she sipped. It was, as always, delicious, and she thought yet again what a pity it was that MacGuiness made such splendid coffee when Honor couldn't stand the beverage.

The familiar reflection trickled through her brain, and she set the cup back down and gave herself a mental shake. No doubt her staff back at Mount Royal Palace had its hands full covering for her absence, but they were just going to have to go on coping for a while longer. Despite the grinding fatigue of far too many hours, far too much adrenaline, and far too many shocks to the universe she'd thought she understood, she knew she and Eloise Pritchart were still far from finished.

She looked across the table in the admiral's dining

cabin aboard HMS *Imperator* at the president of the Republic of Haven, who had just finished a serving of MacGuiness' trademark eggs Benedict and picked up her own coffee cup. Despite a sleepless night, following a day even longer than Elizabeth's had been, the other woman still looked improbably beautiful. And still radiated that formidable presence as well. Elizabeth doubted anyone could have intentionally planned a greater physical contrast than the one between her own mahogany skin and dark eyes and Pritchart's platinum and topaz, and they'd been produced by political and social systems which were at least as different as their appearances. Yet over the last day or so she'd come—unwillingly, almost kicking and screaming—to the conclusion that the two of them were very much alike under the surface.

I wonder if I would have had the sheer nerve to sail straight into my worst enemy's home system— especially after what those "mystery raiders" did to us—and admit my secretary of state doctored the correspondence that sent us back to war? After so long, so many deaths, because I got played, maneuvered into doing exactly what someone else wanted? Even having Simões' story to back me up, selling that to someone with my reputation for carrying grudges to the grave and back again took more plain old-fashioned gall and guts than any three women ought to have. Especially after I'd proven this "Alignment" could play me just as thoroughly as it ever played her.

Elizabeth's mind flicked back over the last two Manticoran days. Even her formidable intelligence was having difficulty coping with the tectonic shock which had just rumbled through her entire known universe. It seemed impossible, preposterous on the very face of things, that a mere two days could have changed everything she'd thought she knew about two *decades* of bitter warfare and millions of deaths, yet it had. And it explained so much.

"So," she said, sitting back from the table she shared with only Honor, Pritchart, and Thomas Theisman, "is Simões telling the truth or not, Honor?"

The two Havenites looked at Honor with slightly surprised expressions, and Honor smiled. Nimitz was sound asleep on his perch, and after the night which had just passed, she saw no point in waking him up.

"There's a reason Her Majesty's asking me, instead of Nimitz or Ariel," she told her guests. "As it happens, I've been hanging around with treecats long enough to have caught at least some of their abilities. I can't read minds, but I can read emotions, and I know when someone's lying."

It was astonishingly easy for her to make that admission to the leaders of the star nation she'd fought her entire adult life.

Pritchart blinked at her; then those topaz eyes narrowed in thought, and the President began nodding—slowly, at first, then more rapidly.

"So *that's* why you make such a fiendishly effective diplomat!" she said with something very like an air of triumph. "I couldn't believe how well a total novice was reading us. Now I know—you were *cheating!*"

The last word came out in something very like a laugh, and Honor nodded back.

"Where diplomacy's concerned, according to my mentors in the Foreign Office, there *is* no such thing as 'cheating,' Madam President. In fact, one of those mentors quoted an old axiom to me. Where diplomacy is involved, he said, if you aren't cheating, you aren't trying hard enough."

Elizabeth snorted in amusement, and Theisman shook his head.

"In this instance, however," Honor continued more seriously, "what Her Majesty is asking me is whether or not I can tell if Dr. Simões is telling the truth. I already informed her"—she looked directly at Pritchart—"that I knew *you* were, Madam President. On the other hand, I also assumed you would have expected from the beginning that Nimitz would have been able to tell me and that I would have passed his observations on to Her Majesty, so I didn't feel any particular scruples about that."

Pritchart nodded again, and Honor shrugged.

"What I can tell you about Simões is that his anger—his outrage—at this 'Alignment' is absolutely genuine. The *pain* inside that man is incredible."

She closed her eyes for a moment, and her nostrils flared.

"Everything I can 'taste' about his 'mind-glow' tells me he's telling us the truth, insofar as he knows the truth. Whether or not McBryde might have been passing along disinformation is more than I can say, of course. But, on balance, I think he was telling the truth as well. It all fits together too well with what we've already seen, and with what Simões can tell us about their hardware."

"And there are still so *damned* many holes in it," Elizabeth half snarled.

"Yes, there are," Honor agreed. "On the other hand, I'd say the Star Empire knows infinitely more than we knew yesterday, Elizabeth . . . given that we didn't know *anything* at that point."

Elizabeth nodded slowly, then looked at Pritchart.

"So, I guess what it comes down to," she said slowly, "it's where we go from here. Whatever happens, I want you to know I'm enormously grateful for the information you've provided us. And I think we can both agree that the war between Haven and Manticore is over."

She shook her head, as if, even now, she couldn't quite believe what she'd just said. Not because she didn't want to, but because it seemed impossible, like something which couldn't possibly be true because of how badly everyone *wanted* it to be true.

"Mind you," she continued, "I don't expect everybody to be delighted about that. For that matter, a few days ago, I probably would have been one of the people who wasn't delighted myself," she admitted.

"Trust me, there's the odd couple of billion Havenites who probably feel exactly the same way," Pritchard said dryly.

"And that's the sticking point, isn't it?" Elizabeth asked softly. "Stopping shooting at each other—that much I'm sure we can manage. But it's not enough. Not if Simões and McBryde's story is true after all."

"No, it's not," Pritchart agreed quietly.

"Well," Elizabeth said and smiled with very little humor, "at least I can feel confident now that you'll keep the Republican Navy off our backs long enough for us to deal with this Admiral Filareta."

"Actually," Pritchard said, "I had something else in mind."

"Something else?" Elizabeth's eyebrows rose.

"Your Majesty—Elizabeth—the Mesan Alignment wants both of us destroyed, starting with the Star Empire. I don't know if it honestly believes the SLN can do the job where you're concerned, or if it was anticipating *we'd* do it when we recognized the opportunity it had given us. But it doesn't really matter. What *matters* is that the Solarian attack on you is simply one more step in a strategy directed against *both* of us. So I think something a bit more pointed than simply stopping shooting at each other might be in order."

"Such as?" Elizabeth asked slowly, eyes slitted in concentration.

"I understand your missile production facilities have been taken off-line," Pritchard said. "Tom here tells me you've undoubtedly got enough of those ungodly super missiles in your magazines to thoroughly kick the ass of this Filareta if he really insists on following his orders. But that's going to cut into your reserves, and given that the Alignment managed to rip the hell out of your home system, I think it would be a good idea for you to conserve as much ammunition as you can in hopes we'll find someone a bit better suited to playing the role of target."

"And?" Elizabeth's eyes were opening wider in speculation.

"Well, it just happens that Thomas here has a modest little fleet—two or three hundred of the wall, I believe—waiting approximately eight hours from Trevor's Star in hyper. If you're willing to trust us in Manticoran space, perhaps we could help you encourage Filareta to see reason. And while I'm well aware our hardware isn't as good as *yours*, every indication I've seen is that it's one hell of a lot better than anything the *Sollies* have."

"Are you offering me a *military alliance* against the *Solarian League?*" Elizabeth asked very carefully.

"If McBryde was right, there isn't going to be much of a Solarian League very much longer," Pritchart replied grimly. "And given the fact that the same bunch of murderous bastards who shot up your home system is also directly responsible for you and I having killed a couple of million of our own people, I think we could say we have a certain commonality of interest where they're concerned. And it's not a case of selfless altruism on my part, you know. We're *both* on the Alignment's list. Don't you think it would be sort of stupid for either of us to let the other one go down and leave us all alone?"

Brown eyes and topaz met across the table littered with the remnants of breakfast, and it was very, very quiet.

"We're still going to have those problems, you know," Elizabeth said almost conversationally after a moment. "All those people on both sides who don't like each other. All that legacy of suspicion."

"Of course." Pritchart nodded.

"And then there's the little matter of figuring out where this Alignment's real headquarters is, and who else is fronting for it, and what other weapons it has, and where else it has programmed assassins tucked away, and exactly what it's got in mind for the Republic once the Star Empire's been polished off."

"True."

"And, now that I think about it, there's the question of how we're going to rebuild our capabilities here, and how much technology sharing we can convince our separate navies and our allies to put up with—and how quickly. You know there's going to be heel-dragging and tantrum-throwing the minute I start suggesting anything like that!"

"I'm sure there will be."

The two women looked at one another, and then, slowly, both of them began to smile.

"What the hell," Elizabeth Winton said. "I've always liked a challenge."

She extended her hand across the table.

Pritchart took it.

◆ ◆ ◆

"You're joking!"

Chairman Chyang Benton-Ramirez looked incredulously at Fedosei Mikulin and Jacques Benton-Ramirez y Chou. The three men sat face-to-face in the Chairman's high-security private briefing room, buried under the roots of the West Tower of the Executive Building in downtown Columbia. Benton-Ramirez had been more than a little irked when Mikulin insisted on meeting in person, rather than com-conferencing. He had plenty of other things he could spend time doing besides hiking clear over here and then taking the lift shaft down five hundred meters, but Mikulin was his most trusted advisor. That was why in addition to his at-large directorship he was Commissioner of Central Intelligence for the Republic of Beowulf.

And why Benton-Ramirez had accepted his "invitation" to join him here despite the inconvenience.

Benton-Ramirez y Chou, Third Director at Large of the Planetary Board of Directors (and one of the Chairman's cousins), on the other hand, enjoyed a carefully ill-defined relationship with Central Intelligence. That was because he was also the Planetary Board's unofficial (*very* unofficial) liaison to the Audubon Ballroom. It would never have done for the Board (or—especially!— its intelligence services) to admit overt contact with the Ballroom, even here on Beowulf. If anyone had wondered why, the way Manticore had been hammered over the Green Pines incident made the reasons crystal clear. Despite which, everyone knew that contact existed, and most people were pretty sure Benton-Ramirez y Chou, as the ex-chairman and current vice-chairman of the Anti-Slavery League, did the contacting. It was one of those "don't ask, don't tell" situations, and the fact that the customarily aggressive Beowulfan newsies had never once asked the question said volumes about how Beowulf in general regarded the genetic slave trade.

That wasn't why Benton-Ramirez y Chou was here today, though. No, he was here because another of the Chairman's cousins was deeply involved in what Mikulin had just reported.

"I'm absolutely *not* joking, Chyang," Mikulin said now. "I realize we're not supposed to spy on our friends, but everyone does, and I doubt anyone in Manticore smart enough to seal his own shoes doesn't know we do. Although, to be fair, I'm not sure how happy they'd be to find out just how highly placed some of our . . . assets actually are."

"Your niece wouldn't happen to be one of them, would she, Jacques?"

"No, she would not." Benton-Ramirez y Chou's voice was considerably colder than the one in which he normally addressed the Chairman. Benton-Ramirez y Chou was a small man, with dark hair and sandalwood skin. He also had almond eyes, which he shared with his sister . . . and his rather more famous (or infamous) niece. "And if I'd ever been stupid enough to ask her to become any such thing, she would have told me to piss up a rope," he added succinctly.

"Oh, I doubt she would've put it that way," Benton-Ramirez said with a chuckle which was oddly apologetic. "I'm sure Duchess Harrington would have been considerably less, um, earthy."

"Not if I'd asked her to spy on Elizabeth, she wouldn't have been," Benton-Ramirez y Chou smiled tartly. "In fact, what she'd probably have done is rip off my head for a soccer ball!"

"All right, point taken," the Chairman acknowledged. "But I assume from what you're telling me, Fedosei, that whoever our informant *is*, we can place significant confidence in this report?"

"Yes," Mikulin said flatly.

"Damn." Benton-Ramirez shook his head. "I know we were hoping they'd at least stop shooting at each other, especially after we warned both of them Filareta was coming, but I never expected *this!*"

"None of us did," Mikulin agreed. "But, to be honest, the fact that Elizabeth and Pritchart have decided to bury the hatchet is actually a hell of a lot less important than the *reason* they decided to bury it."

There was something very odd about his voice, and the Chairman glanced at Benton-Ramirez y Chou. The other man's expression was an interesting mix of agreement and something that looked like lingering shock, all backed by a white-hot, blazing fury. Despite the self-control he'd learned over the decades, Jacques Benton-Ramirez y Chou had always been a passionate man, yet Benton-Ramirez was more than a little taken aback by the deadly glitter in those dark-brown eyes.

"What do you mean?" The Chairman sat back, eyes narrowed. The fact that Eloise Pritchart had gone unannounced to the Manticore Binary System and apparently agreed to some sort of alliance against the *Solarian League*, especially after how savagely the Star Empire had been weakened, struck him as one of the more fundamental power shifts in the history of mankind. So if Mikulin found something else even *more* significant...

"I think the notion of a Manticore-Haven military *alliance* is going to be interesting enough to the rest of the universe, Fedosei," he observed.

"I'm sure it is," Mikulin said grimly, "but what's even more 'interesting' to me—and to the rest of Beowulf, I'm pretty damn sure—is that the reason Pritchart made this trip to Manticore is that Zilwicki and Cachat have resurfaced. And it turns out that where they've been all this time was either on the planet Mesa or on their way back from it."

Benton-Ramirez's narrowed eyes widened, and Mikulin shrugged.

"We only have very a preliminary report at this point, Chyang," he pointed out, "and our source hasn't been able to give us *everything*. Or even come *close* to everything, for that matter. But from the little bit we do have, it seems Zilwicki and Cachat were in Green Pines—*both* of them were there, together—about the time the explosions went off. And it sounds like they *were* involved, albeit peripherally, as well. Hopefully we'll have better intelligence on that pretty soon, but the key point is that they brought out a Mesan with them, and the Mesan in question is providing all kinds of information. Information that, frankly, contradicts almost everything we've thought we knew about Mesa."

"I beg your pardon?"

Benton-Ramirez's tone sounded preposterously calm, but it wasn't really his fault. It was simply that no one could process information like that without the equivalent of a massive mental hiccup. If there was a single star system in the entire galaxy upon which Beowulfan intelligence had expended more effort than Mesa, or about which it was better informed, he couldn't imagine which one it might be. Ever since Leonard Detweiler and his malcontents had relocated to Mesa, the system had been Beowulf's dark twin. The source of one of the galaxy's most malignant cancers, and the undying shame of the society from which its founders had sprung.

The possibility of errors in Beowulf's intelligence appreciations of Mesa was one thing. In fact, Benton-Ramirez had always assumed there had to be such errors, since Mesa was painfully well aware of Beowulf's interest in it and had always taken steps to blunt Central Intelligence's operations there. But Mikulin clearly wasn't suggesting mere "errors"—not in that tone of voice, or with that expression.

"If what we've heard so far is any indication, most of what we thought we knew about Mesa isn't just mistaken, it's a deliberate fabrication on Mesa's part," Mikulin said now, his voice harsh. "I'm not ready to sign off on the reliability of what we're hearing at this point. To be honest, there's a big part of me that doesn't want to admit even the possibility that we might have been that far off, and the meeting between Elizabeth and Pritchart took place less than forty hours ago. All of this is still pretty damned preliminary, and God only knows how many holes there could be in it. But, assuming there's any validity to it at all, Mesa's had its own plans—plans that go a hell of a lot deeper than just making money off the genetic slave trade or even rubbing our collective nose in how much contempt they have for the Beowulf Code—literally for centuries. Not only that, but the Manties have been right all along in saying it's behind what's been happening in Talbott, and the Yawata strike, as well. And not just because Talbott brought the Star Empire's borders too close to the Mesa System, either. Apparently, they've got plans of their own where the entire *human race* is involved, and I think we can be pretty sure that if they had plans for the Star Empire and the Republic of Haven, they've got to have a page or two for dealing with *us* as well."

Chapter Eleven

"WHAT ARE THE ODDS *your* people will actually ratify this, do you think?" Elizabeth Winton asked almost whimsically.

"Not as good as they would have been once upon a time," Eloise Pritchart admitted from the other side of the small Mount Royal Palace conference table. "I've used up a lot of credit with Congress—and the voters, for that matter—in the last three T-years. And admitting *our* Secretary of State doctored the correspondence in the first place isn't going to make our firebrands any happier."

"That's what I thought, too. Pity. I was hoping you'd have a better chance with your legislative branch than I'm going to have with mine."

Elizabeth pursed her lips, looking at the document on the display in front of her. As treaty proposals went, it was about as bare bones as things got, she reflected. Neither she nor Pritchart had traded away their star nations' sovereignty for a handful of beads, but she was sure critics and partisans on both sides were going to carry on as if they had. And little though she liked to admit it, there was still plenty of wiggle room. They hadn't tried to nail things down in fully finished, set-in-stone form. Instead, they'd roughed out a list of absolutely essential points to be submitted to the Havenite Congress and Elizabeth's own Parliament, coupled with a specific provision that other treaties would deal with the still-outstanding points a little thing like twenty years of bitter warfare were likely to have created.

Still, if someone had told her she and Pritchart could accomplish this much, *agree* to this much, in only seven days, she would have suggested they be confined in a nice, safe cell. Yes, there were still huge gray areas, but what they'd gotten down in written form proved that knowing one was about to be hanged (or invaded by the Solarian League) truly did concentrate one's mind wonderfully. This treaty, rough as it was, created an alliance between the Star Empire of Manticore and the Republic of Haven which committed each of them to the defense of the other. There hadn't been time—with one exception—to consult with the Star Empire's allies, but Eloise had been careful to bring every one of those allies' ambassadors on board, and most of them had initialed the draft on their governments' behalfs. The Andermani ambassador hadn't, yet that was hardly surprising, given the traditional Andermani *realpolitik*. By the same token (and for the same reasons), he hadn't voiced any official *opposition* to it, either, though, and the Andermani Empire was an "associated power" rather than a full member of the Manticoran Alliance, anyway.

The one ally there *had* been time to actually consult

was the Protectorate of Grayson, three and a half T-days from the Manticore Binary System by dispatch boat. Elizabeth had sent Benjamin Mayhew word of Pritchart's totally unexpected visit the day the president arrived, and Benjamin Mayhew, with a decisiveness and speed unusual even for him, had needed only hours to decide where *he* stood. He'd sent back his enthusiastic support ... and his only brother as his personal envoy.

Michael Mayhew had arrived yesterday, just in time to put his own signature on the draft as Grayson's plenipotentiary. Which, given most Manticorans' attitude towards their most constant ally, could only be a major plus. Not to mention demonstrating to all the Star Empire's allies as conclusively as humanly possible that William Alexander and his government were *not* Michael Janvier and *his* government.

So now all they had to do was submit it for the approval of the Manticoran Parliament and the Havenite Senate.

"*All,*" she thought glumly. *As in "all we have to do is find the philosopher's stone and we can turn as much lead into gold as we want." We can ask both of them to expedite on an emergency basis and point out that there's no time to be sending drafts back and forth for revision, but how much good is that really going to do? However big the crisis, we're talking about* politicians, *and that means any number of wannabe cooks can be counted on to shove their spoons in and start stirring, damn it.*

"Actually, I think you're both being overly pessimistic," another voice said, and two pairs of eyes, one brown and one topaz, swiveled towards the speaker.

"I hate to point this out, Admiral," Pritchart said with a lopsided smile, "but I suspect you've had a bit less experience dealing with legislative idiots than Her Majesty and I have."

"I wouldn't be too sure about that, actually, Eloise," Elizabeth said, and grimaced when Pritchart looked back at her. "Don't forget, she's a steadholder. I realize steadholders have the sort of absolute power you and I only fantasize about, but she still has her own Chamber of Steaders to deal with, and she's been pretty hands-on about the job. Whenever we've let her out of uniform, at least. For that matter, she's a sitting member of the Conclave of Steadholders on Grayson *and* our House of Lords. She's spent her time in the trenches, and she was front and center of the Opposition during our delightful interlude with that ass, High Ridge. She knows a lot more about how it works than that innocent demeanor of hers might suggest."

"I suppose that's true." Pritchart cocked her head. "It's hard to remember just how many hats you've worn, Your Grace."

"Her Majesty's comments aside, I won't pretend I've had as much legislative experience as you two," Honor replied. "On the other hand, she's right that I'm not a complete stranger to ugly political fights, and both of you are just about dead on your feet. My feeling is that both of you are so worn out from working on this thing that it'd be a miracle if you *didn't* feel pessimistic. In fact, if I'd thought it would've done any good, I'd've chased you off to bed every night to make sure you got at least eight solid hours."

Pritchart considered her thoughtfully and decided

she wasn't really joking. And while the President of the Republic of Haven wasn't accustomed to being "chased off to bed," she rather suspected Honor Alexander-Harrington could manage it if she put her mind to it.

"Interesting you should say that, Honor," Elizabeth observed. "My beloved spouse was saying something rather similar last night. Or was it the night before?"

"Probably the night before. Justin's a lot better at *making* you rest than you are at *remembering* to rest."

"I don't doubt he is," Pritchart said. She kept her voice light, although she knew Honor, at least, had sensed the spike of pain which went through her as she remembered nights Javier Giscard had made *her* rest. "At the moment, though, I'm more interested in why you think our estimate is overly pessimistic, Admiral. I don't doubt you're right about how tired we both are, and I know how fatigue and worry affect people's judgment, but that doesn't necessarily mean we're wrong and you're right."

"Of course not, Madam President." Honor leaned back, sipping from a stein of Old Tillman, and shrugged. "Despite that, though, I think you're both underestimating the selling power of what each of you have gotten out of the other. Your offer to help us deal with Filareta when you didn't have to do anything of the sort—when you had every reason *not* to, in fact—is going to buy you a *lot* of goodwill in the Star Empire. And Elizabeth's renunciation of any reparations will smooth a lot of ruffled feathers in Nouveau Paris . . . not to mention cutting the legs right out from under that snot, Younger."

She smiled almost dreamily at the thought.

"Your own suggestion that we hand all of Second

Fleet's units back to the Republic won't hurt, either, Honor," Elizabeth pointed out, and this time Pritchart nodded.

"It certainly won't. And neither will Admiral Tourville's glowing report on how well his people were treated after surrendering," she agreed, then sighed. "I've always regretted ordering that attack, and the number of people who got killed—on both sides—because I did is always going to haunt me. But at least *something* good may come out of it in the end."

It was Honor's turn to nod, although the good Pritchart was referring to hadn't come solely out of the Battle of Manticore. Thomas Theisman's determination that any prisoners *his* Republic took would be decently treated had gone a long way towards washing the taste of StateSec's barbarisms out of the Star Empire's mouth. And for that matter—

"Your decision to bring all the tech people Admiral Griffith captured at Grendelsbane along with you is going to do even more from our side," she said quietly. "Especially the fact that you brought them all home—made their repatriation a unilateral concession—without knowing whether or not we were even going to talk to you."

"That *was* a masterstroke," Elizabeth put in, her voice equally quiet, and shrugged when Pritchart looked back to her. "I'm not trying to suggest it was all political calculation, and neither is Honor. But once it sinks in that you'd decided to repatriate forty-two thousand Manticorans without any preconditions—and forty-two thousand trained and experienced *shipyard workers*, at that—one hell of a lot of entrenched ill feeling is going to take a shot on the chin. Especially given how desperately we need people like that after the Yawata strike."

Pritchart shrugged a little uncomfortably.

"Well, we'll find out soon enough whether we're being too pessimistic or Duchess Harrington's being too optimistic, I suppose," she said. "Especially when we go public about my presence here in the Star Empire."

She still wasn't positive that was the best idea. They couldn't keep her arrival a secret forever, of course—in fact, she was amazed it hadn't already leaked, given the number of ambassadors who'd been consulted—but once Elizabeth handed the treaty over to Parliament, that little secret was going to be as thoroughly outed as any in the history of humanity. Nor was she blind to the PR advantages in publicizing her "daring mission." Yet she was still the woman who'd ordered the resumption of hostilities almost three T-years ago...and the one who'd ordered Thomas Theisman to launch Operation Beatrice against this very star system.

"Oh, I'm not worried about *that*." Elizabeth waved one hand.

She and Pritchart had discussed the president's concerns in detail, and the empress was convinced the other woman was worrying unduly. Yes, the Battle of Manticore had killed an enormous number of people, but far fewer than the Yawata strike, and all of them had been *military* casualties. Unlike the people behind the Yawata strike, the Republic had scrupulously avoided preventable civilian casualties. After fifteen T-years fighting the *People's* Republic, even the most anti-Havenite Manticoran had been only too well aware of what a change *that* represented, and the contrast with the slaughter of the Yawata strike only underscored the difference. Say what the most bigoted Manticoran might, the restored Republic had fought *its* war with honor, and the majority of Manticorans knew it.

"To be honest, I'm more concerned about Simões," Elizabeth went on. "We've got to go public with most of what Cachat and Zilwicki brought back from Mesa, or we're never going to sell this to your Congress, Eloise. For that matter, there are enough die-hard Haven-haters in the Star Empire to make it a hard sell *here* without that, even with Filareta bearing down on us! But the bottom line is that it's still awfully thin for anyone who's inclined to be skeptical about what we've been saying about Mesa—or Manpower, at least. And, frankly, with the best will in the universe, there's only so much Simões can confirm."

Pritchart sighed heavily in agreement. Then she surprised both of the Manticorans—and herself—with a sudden snort of amusement.

"What?" Elizabeth asked after a moment.

"I was just thinking about a conversation Tom Theisman and I had on that very subject," the President replied, and cocked her head at Honor. "I believe you've met Admiral Foraker, Your Grace?"

"Yes, I have," Honor agreed. "Why?"

"Because I've turned out to be even more prophetic than I expected. Right after Cachat and Zilwicki brought Simões in, we were discussing the intelligence windfall he represented, and Tom was waxing pretty enthusiastic . . . until I asked how valuable an intelligence source he thought Shannon Foraker would have been outside her own specialty."

"Oh, my." Honor gazed at her for a moment, then

shook her head. "I hadn't really thought of that comparison, but it does fit, doesn't it?"

"Too well, actually."

Pritchart smiled tartly, but the unfortunate truth was that Herlander Simões really was a male version of Shannon Foraker... and in more ways than one. Like Foraker, he'd been so immersed in his tightly focused researcher's world that he'd been almost totally oblivious to the "big picture." For that matter, the people responsible for the Mesan Alignment's security had obviously taken pains to encourage his tunnel vision. Also like Foraker, however, his apolitical disinterest in the system in which he'd lived had been shattered. Foraker's awakening had led directly to the destruction of twenty-four State Security superdreadnoughts in a star system called Lovat, and while it was unlikely Simões was going to inflict anything that overtly dramatic upon the Alignment, the long-term effects of his defection were likely to be far worse, eventually. But that was the problem, because "eventually" might not offer a great deal of short-term benefit when it came to getting the draft treaty ratified.

No one was ever going to get Simões back into obliviousness again, yet his fierce determination to do anything he could to smash the Alignment didn't change the fact that he could offer virtually nothing concrete about the Alignment's master strategy, its military resources, or exactly how the Mesa System's open power structure fitted into the Alignment's *covert* structure. None of those things had mattered to him before Francesca Simões' death, and he hadn't exactly been taking notes for a future defection after his daughter's termination, either.

The president thought once more of the tragedy of Jack McBryde's death. Most of what they "knew" about the Alignment came from the information he'd produced to convince Victor Cachat and Anton Zilwicki to help him and Simões defect. Kevin Usher's Federal Investigation Agency had turned up forensic evidence which strongly corroborated at least some of McBryde's allegations, and Pritchart was thankful they had even that much, but without McBryde himself to be debriefed in detail (and trotted out to testify before Congress and Parliament), they still had far more questions than answers. Questions whose answers almost certainly would have helped enormously with the ratification fight she expected.

And let's face it, Eloise, she told herself, *McBryde would've been a lot more convincing than Simões as a "talking head" in front of the media, too. I believe everything Simões has told us, and God knows the man's got motivation by the megaton! But he simply doesn't* know *enough—not firsthand, not in the areas that really matter—to sell a determined skeptic our version of The Truth. And, bless him, but the man is a geek of truly Forakerian proportions.*

She shuddered at the memory of the last time Foraker had testified before the Senate Naval Affairs Committee. Even today, her inability to translate her own technical expertise into political-speak was awesome to behold. In the end, Theisman had been forced to trot out Linda Trenis to interpret for his pet tech witch.

"You know a lot of people, and not just Mesans or Sollies, are going to say this whole thing is one huge fabrication," she went on.

"Of course they are, even if no one with a functional cortex is going to be able to come up with a reason *why* we fabricated it." Elizabeth's voice was a growl of disgust. "I mean, obviously it's hugely to the Republic's advantage to make it all up as a way to justify stepping into the ring against something the size of the Solarian League beside the star nation it's been fighting for the last twenty years! The fact that *I* can't imagine why you did that isn't going to keep idiots from figuring there *has* to be a reason. Not that *they're* going to be able to suggest one that holds water, either!"

"Well, at least the 'cats will vouch for Simões' truthfulness," Honor pointed out, stroking Nimitz, who lay curled in her lap. The treecat raised his head with an unmistakably complacent purr, and Ariel added a bleeking laugh of his own from the back of Elizabeth's chair. The two of them looked so smug Honor laughed and gave one of Nimitz's ears a tug.

"As I was saying," she continued, "and at the risk of overinflating—*further* overinflating, I should say—two unnamed furry egos, the 'cats can confirm he's telling the truth, and a lot of people here on Manticore will trust their judgment. That may not cut much ice anywhere else, but nothing we could say would convince someone like Kolokoltsov to just take our word for it, anyway. And while I could wish he'd been involved in developing this 'spider drive' of theirs, instead of the 'streak drive,' the stuff he's already given Admiral Hemphill makes it obvious he knows what he's talking about. And what he does know about the 'spider drive' dovetails entirely too neatly with what happened to us for him to be some delusional nut. Not to mention"—her voice hardened—"pretty thoroughly demonstrating that Mesa *must* have been behind the attack, since no one *else* could've gotten close enough to hit us that way."

Something icy flickered in her eyes, and Nimitz's purr cut off abruptly as he half rose with a sudden snarl. It was very quiet for a heartbeat or two, but then she gave herself a shake, touched the back of the 'cat's head gently, and smiled apologetically at the other two women.

"You're right about all of that, of course, Admiral," Pritchart agreed in a tone which diplomatically failed to notice the anger and pain which were seldom far from Honor's surface these days. "And it may convince *us*, and probably even Congress or your Parliament. But it isn't going to change the woman in the street's mind if she's not already inclined to go along with it. And no conspiracy theorist worth her paranoia badge is going to buy it for a heartbeat."

"The best we can do is the best we can do, Madam President," Honor replied in something much closer to a normal tone. She smiled her thanks for the Havenite head of state's tact, then glanced at her chrono. "And assuming the news got released on schedule, we'll be finding out in the next couple of hours just how the Manticoran public, at least, is going to react."

❖   ❖   ❖

"—most ridiculous thing I've ever heard, Patrick!" Kiefer Mallory snorted several hours later. The tall, handsome political columnist was one of the Star Empire's more sought-after talking heads, and he knew it. Now his dark eyes glittered as he waved both hands in a gesture of frustration. "Mind you, we're all aware of the threat the Star Empire in general—and this star system in particular—faces. And I won't pretend I wouldn't be *delighted* to find someone prepared to support us. But really—!" He shook his head. "I know I'm not the only one who finds all of this suspiciously convenient for the people who got us into this mess in the first place!"

"Oh?" Jephthah Alverson, a longtime Liberal MP who'd thrown his allegiance to Catherine Montaigne following the High Ridge Government's implosion, leaned forward to look down the HD set's conference table and raise a sardonic eyebrow. "Let me see, now . . . That would be Baron High Ridge and Elaine Descroix, wouldn't it?"

Mallory, who'd been associated with the Progressive Party for at least three decades (and who'd served as one of the now-vanished Descroix's public spokesmen, before her spectacular downfall), flushed angrily.

✧   ✧   ✧

"My, he didn't take that one well, did he?" Emily Alexander-Harrington observed.

"No, he didn't," Honor agreed. Which, she thought, stretched out on the comfortable couch in Emily's private suite, was remarkably foolish of him. Nimitz was comfortably ensconced on her chest, and she tasted his agreement. Even a complete novice should've seen *that* one coming!

"That's because, despite any surface slickness, he comes from the shallow—*very* shallow, in his case— end of the gene pool . . . intellectually speaking, that is," Emily replied from the life-support chair parked at the head of the couch. She'd followed Honor's thought almost as easily as the 'cat, and the two of them glanced at each other with matching smiles.

Hamish was stuck in Landing, submerged in the latest deluge of Admiralty business, but Honor had decided she deserved at least one day at home at White Haven after her participation in the Elizabeth-Pritchart political marathon. She'd spent most of that day with her parents and her younger brother and sister, and her family's still sharp-edged grief, especially her father's, had taken their toll on her and Nimitz. At least Alfred Harrington was finally beginning to develop the emotional scar tissue he needed to survive, yet Honor was grateful to have this time with Emily to herself. She *needed* the older woman's serenity at moments like this, and there wasn't a more insightful political strategist in the entire Star Empire.

Which may be even more useful than usual over the next few weeks, she thought, watching the broadcast as Mallory responded to Alverson.

❖   ❖   ❖

"There's a limit to how long the Grantville Government can go on blaming High Ridge for its own current problems." Mallory's tone could have melted lead, but at least he'd paused long enough to be sure he had his temper on a tight leash. "No one's trying to pretend mistakes weren't made on High Ridge's watch, although some of us continue to question the wisdom of sentencing an ex-prime minister to prison for the actions of his government. I know that's not a popular position, but the precedent of criminalizing political opponents is likely to produce all kinds of ugly fallout down the road. And dragging out the 'usual suspects' to wave like some red herring whenever someone criticizes the current government's policies is scarcely a reasoned response to the criticism, Mr. Alverson!"

"Really?" Madeleine Richter asked. "I was under the impression he was convicted of bribery, vote-buying, perjury, extortion, and obstruction of justice, not the actions of his *government*. Did I read the news accounts incorrectly, Kiefer?" She smiled brightly. "As for Jephthah's point, while I'll agree it's not an extraordinarily *polished* response, in this instance it does have the virtue of cutting to the heart of the matter. And it's not like your criticism was exactly nuanced and carefully thought out, either."

Mallory's flush darkened, and Rosalinda Davidson shook her head. Richter, the sitting MP for East Tannerton, was a senior member of the Centrist Party. As such, her support of the Grantville Government was as much a given as Mallory's opposition to it. Davidson, on the other hand, had been a Liberal Party MP until she got washed out of office in the post-High Ridge tsunami. Since then, she'd earned her living as a columnist and lecturer, and although she and Mallory weren't exactly bosom buddies, they were united in their distaste for the current government.

"You know," she said, a bit pointedly, "bashing people for past or present political affiliations isn't the reason we're here tonight, Madeline. Or I was under the impression it wasn't, at any rate. Minerva?"

She turned to Minerva Prince, who, with Patrick DuCain, co-hosted the awesomely popular and long-running *Into the Fire*. The syndicated show was only one of the flood of programs trying to cope with the bombshell revelation of Eloise Pritchart's presence in the Manticore Binary System, but it had the highest viewership of them all.

"You're right, of course, Rosalinda," Prince replied.

"On the other hand, you know Patrick and I usually let our guests have at least some voice in where the discussion goes."

❖   ❖   ❖

"That's true enough," Emily agreed, smiling more broadly at Honor. "All that blood in the water's just what their ratings need!"

"I remember," Honor said feelingly, recalling her own *Into the Fire* appearance, when she'd been beached by the Janacek Admiralty. "And they're not above steering their guests' 'voices' when the water isn't sufficiently chummed, either."

❖   ❖   ❖

"At the risk of undermining my own reputation as a troublemaker," Abraham Spencer said from the HD, "I suggest we all hang up our partisan political axes for the moment and concentrate on our official topic." The photogenic (and incredibly wealthy) financier smiled charmingly. "I know no one's really going to believe I'm not hiding in the underbrush to bash someone over the head myself when the moment's ripe, but in the meantime, there *is* this little matter of the Empress's proposed treaty with Haven. And that other minor revelation about the 'Mesan Alignment.'"

"You mean that *so-called* revelation, don't you?" Mallory snorted. "It's not as if anyone's offering the kind of evidence we could take to court!"

"Whether the allegations are accurate or not, there's not much question about their explosiveness, Kiefer," DuCain pointed out.

"Assuming anyone in the entire galaxy—outside the Star Empire, at least—is going to believe in this vast interstellar conspiracy for a moment," Davidson riposted. She gave Alverson a scathing look. "Especially given the open ties between certain members of Parliament and the Audubon Ballroom."

It was Alverson's eyes' turn to narrow dangerously at the obvious shot at Catherine Montaigne, but Richter intervened before he could fire back.

"You might be surprised how many people will believe it, Rosalinda," she said coldly, reaching up to stroke her dark blue hair. That hair hadn't been dyed or artificially colored; it was the legacy of a grandparent who'd been designed to the special order of a wealthy Solarian with idiosyncratic tastes in "body servants."

"I won't say the devil is beyond blackening," she continued, "but I will say that anyone who looks at Mesa with an open mind has to admit the entire star system, not just Manpower, has never given a single, solitary damn what the rest of 'the entire explored galaxy' thinks of it."

"You know my own feelings where the Ballroom is concerned, Rosalinda," Spencer put in, his expression turning hard. "No matter how much I sympathize with genetic slaves and detest the entire loathsome institution, I've never sanctioned the sort of outright terrorism to which the Ballroom's resorted far too often. I've never made any secret of my feelings on that subject. Indeed, you may recall that little spat Klaus Hauptman and I had on the subject following the liberation of Torch."

One or two of the guests snorted out loud at that. The "little spat" had taken place right here on *Into the Fire*, and the clash of two such powerful (and wealthy) titans had assumed epic proportions.

"But having said that," he continued, "and even

conceding that this information appears to have reached us at least partially through the Ballroom's auspices, *I* believe it. A lot of odd mysteries and unexplained 'coincidences' suddenly make a lot more sense. And as Madeline says, if any star system in the galaxy is corrupt enough to have given birth to something like this, it's sure as hell Mesa!"

"And on that basis we're supposed to believe there's some kind of centuries-long conspiracy aimed at us and the *Republic of Haven* out there?" Davidson rolled her eyes. "*Please*, Abraham! I'm entirely prepared to admit the Mesans are terrible people and genetic slavery is a horrible perversion, but they're basically nothing more than examples of the evils of unbridled capitalism. And, no, I'm not saying capitalism *automatically* produces evil ends. I'm simply saying that where Manpower is concerned—and looking at all the other transstellars headquartered in Mesa with it—we're talking about something that makes the worst robber barons of Old Terra's history seem like pikers. People like that don't try to destabilize something like the Solarian League when they're doing so well swimming around in the corruption of its sewers!"

"Then why do *you* think President Pritchart made this unprecedented, dramatic voyage to Manticore?" Prince asked, and Davidson turned back to the hostess with a shrug.

"There could be any number of reasons. It's even possible—however unlikely *I* think it is—that she genuinely believes Mesa is after both of us. On the other hand, I think it's also possible she and her intelligence types, possibly with the cooperation of the Audubon Ballroom and its . . . allies"—she pointedly avoided looking in Alverson's direction—"concocted the entire story. Or least *embroidered* it, shall we say?"

"For what possible reason?" Spencer demanded. Davidson looked at him, and it was his turn to shrug. "As Kiefer himself pointed out a moment ago, the Republic's standing with us against the *Solarian League*. Could you possibly suggest any logical motive for people we've been fighting for twenty years to suddenly decide, completely out of the blue, to get between us and something the size of the Sollies at a moment when we're more vulnerable than we've been in over a decade? Forgive me if I seem obtuse, Rosalinda, but for the life of me, I can't figure out why any Machiavellian worth his—or in this case, *her*—'I am devious' Evil Overlord's badge would do something that stupid!"

❖   ❖   ❖

"I believe Abraham, to use Hamish's delightful phrase, is about ready to rip someone a new anal orifice," Emily observed.

"Odd," Honor said, "I don't seem to recall his using those two words."

"That's because he doesn't," Emily replied with a smile, then elevated her nose with a sniff. "*I*, on the other hand, am far more genteel than he is."

"That's one way to describe it."

"Hush!" Emily smacked Honor on the head with her working hand. "I want to see if Rosalinda has a stroke on system-wide HD."

"You *wish*," Honor muttered.

❖   ❖   ❖

"I just acknowledged that Pritchart might genuinely believe all this," Davidson told Spencer tightly. "I think there are other possibilities, as well—convincing us we're both on someone else's 'hit list' in order to extort such favorable peace terms out of us comes to mind, for example—but of course she could really believe it. Which doesn't mean someone else hasn't sold her a fabricated bill of goods and used her to sell it to *us*. You just mentioned the Ballroom. Surely if it would benefit anyone in the galaxy for us and the Republic to turn on the Mesa System with everything we've got, it would *have* to be the Ballroom and its ideological allies, don't you think?"

"That's the most paranoid thing I've ever heard!" Alverson snapped. "And I can't *believe* the mental hoops you're willing to jump through to avoid admitting even the possibility that this McBryde might conceivably've been telling the truth! For that matter, the treecats verify that Dr. Simões, at least, definitely *is* telling the truth. Which means—"

"*If* you're prepared to take the treecats' word," Mallory interrupted. Several of the others looked at him incredulously, and he scowled. "What I mean is that we've had plenty of experience with people who've been brainwashed—or simply *misled*—into genuinely believing something that's demonstrably false. So far as I'm aware, not even the treecats' most fervent champions have claimed they can know when that's the case. Suppose for a moment Rosalinda's right about someone like the Ballroom wanting to fabricate a story like this. I'm not saying that's necessarily what happened; I'm just asking you to consider the possibility. In that case, knowing you were going to have to sell your story to the Star Empire, wouldn't it make sense to brainwash your 'star witness' into absolutely—and *honestly*—believing what you've primed him to tell us?"

"Oh, for the love of—!" Richter began.

"And, on that note, we have to go to break," Prince interrupted, smiling brightly at the camera while DuCain struggled mightily not to laugh. "Don't go away! *Into the Fire* will be back in just a few moments to continue this . . . lively exchange."

JUNE 1922 POST DIASPORA

"I want him hammered so hard even *Sollies*
have to get the message that this...is
a *war—their* war—and that wars have
consequences!"

—Admiral Lady Dame
 Honor Alexander-Harrington,
 Steadholder and Duchess
 Harrington

✧ Chapter Twelve

"WELL, *this* IS UNEXPECTED."

Admiral Stephania Grimm, Manticoran Astro Control Service, looked at Captain Christopher Dombroski and cocked her head.

"Since this is all you're showing me," she continued, without looking away from him as she twitched a thumb at the terse message he'd relayed to her display, "and since you're a reasonably competent sort, I assume you queried them for additional details and they declined to provide them?"

"That's about right, Ma'am. They were polite, but they wouldn't say a word about who they're sending. They just repeated that they'll be inserting 'an unscheduled diplomatic courier' into the queue. They *did* apologize for any 'inconvenience,' but that's about it. Given everything that's been happening, I thought I should call it to your attention."

"I see." Grimm looked back at her display. A little explanation would have been nice, she reflected, but it was hardly his fault he didn't have one.

Dombroski's official title on the Junction Astro Control Service's organizational chart was Senior Officer, Traffic Management Division. That made him responsible for imposing order upon thousands of Junction transits, and his usual, unflappable composure had begun to fray. Grimm wasn't even tempted to hold that against him given how hectic his task had become. First there'd been the torrent of recalled merchantmen. Then, as Lacoön *Two* hit its stride, there'd been the scores of Solarian-registry vessels—most with indescribably irate skippers—who'd suddenly discovered they were going to have to make it home the long way. And as if *that* hadn't been enough, there'd been the need to accommodate the movement of all the warships and mobile repair platforms the Navy was juggling in the Yawata strike's wake.

No, it was no wonder Dombroski looked a little stressed these days.

She frowned, trying to parse the message's officialese. On the face of it, it was simple enough, but there'd just about been time for news of Eloise Pritchart's presence on Manticore—and of the bombshell she'd brought with her—to get back through the Junction to the people who'd sent it.

And that *suggests it's anything* but *'simple,'* she thought.

"All right, Chris," she said finally, "I'll see Mount Royal's informed. At least they gave us a couple of hours' warning before they jumped the queue." She shrugged philosophically. "I know it'll complicate things, but it shouldn't make *too* many waves."

"Ma'am, they're supposed to tell us about this kind of thing a hell of a lot further ahead of time." There was a lot of irritation in Dombroski's voice. "They *know* that, and I doubt it just slipped their minds."

"I'm aware of that, Chris," Grimm said patiently, reminding herself of the strain under which he'd labored of late. "There's no legal *requirement* for them to warn us, though, whatever the customary procedures may be."

She gave him a pointed look. If he wanted some official protest, he wasn't going to get one, however much she sympathized. She held his eyes until she was sure he'd gotten the message. Then she shrugged again.

"I admit it's a violation of good manners," she told him a bit wryly, "but we have to assume they have their reasons. And even if they don't, Beowulf does happen to be a sovereign star nation."

❖   ❖   ❖

"I don't understand why *I* have to be here," Honor Alexander-Harrington complained. "I've been away from Trevor's Star way too long already." She crossed restlessly to a window, gazing out across the landscaped Mount Royal grounds. "Alice is on top of things, but I shudder to think about everything that can still go wrong on that front. And Hamish's delightful phrase about excreting bricks is probably a pretty fair description of how ACS is going to react when Theisman starts bringing two or three hundred *Republican* podnoughts through the Junction!"

She heard the plaintiveness (it would never have done to call it *petulance*) in her own voice and grimaced. Alice Truman, the CO of Task Force 81, and Eighth Fleet's second in command, was fully capable of handling things in her absence, and she knew it. In fact, if she'd wanted to be honest, what *really* ticked her off was that she'd far rather be at White Haven than here in Landing. Not that she had any intention of admitting that to a living soul.

"If I could tell you why you're here, I would." There was a certain tartness in Elizabeth Winton's response. "Unfortunately, I've already told you everything I know. Beowulf's specifically requested your presence, but their note's remarkably short on details. It doesn't say why. It doesn't even say who. It just requests you be here to meet this 'special embassy.'" The empress's eyes narrowed. "If I were a betting woman, I'd be willing to wager it has something to do with relatives of yours, but that's solely a guess, Honor."

Honor grimaced again and rested both hands on the windowsill, leaning closer to the crystoplast. For her, that was the equivalent of fidgeting violently, and Nimitz crooned softly in her ear. She glanced at him, and his fingers flickered.

<Worried about more bad news,> those agile fingers signed. <Worse, worried whatever this is will darken Deep Roots' mind glow again.>

Honor looked at him, then, almost against her will, nodded. Ever since she'd learned her father's treecat name, she'd thought it was even more appropriate than most. His roots truly did run deep, and he'd been the towering crown oak which had sheltered her more times than she could count during her childhood. But those roots of his, the thing which anchored him so securely against life's tempests and undergirded so much of who and what he was, had been his sense of family. His awareness of who he was, where he came from, and everyone who'd gone before him.

That was the rich, sustaining soil from which he'd

drawn his strength, and too much of it was gone now, seared away by the Yawata strike. His roots were beginning to recover, but *healing* was another matter entirely, one she was far from certain could ever be accomplished.

And Stinker's right, too, she thought. *It doesn't make sense on any rational level, but what I really am is* afraid. *Afraid some message from Uncle Al or somebody else on Beowulf is going to start him bleeding all over again. Which is pretty stupid, when you come down to it. I sort of doubt the Board of Directors would've sent an official diplomatic mission—especially under such mysterious circumstances—just to deliver a family message.* She shook her head. *Am I really that fragile, myself? Running scared enough to jump at that kind of imagined shadow?*

"You're right," she admitted out loud, leaning forward until her cheek touched the treecat's nose. "And I guess it *is* pretty silly. It's just—"

"Just that you're human," Elizabeth said quietly. Honor looked at her, and the empress shrugged, stroking Ariel's ears as he lay across her lap. "I can read sign, too, you know. And I know you both well enough to follow the subtext." She smiled sadly. "You're not the only person who's been hit hard enough to be a little illogical, either. Sometimes I think the smarter we are, the better we are at finding ways to hammer ourselves with imagined disasters ahead of time."

"I don't know about smarter," Honor said, walking back across the room to the couch facing Elizabeth's armchair. "I do think people with more *imagination* do a better job of putting themselves through the wringer, though."

"All right, I'll grant that." Elizabeth's smile turned mischievous. "But if I do, then *you* have to grant—"

A discreet, musical chime interrupted the empress, and she glanced at the small com unit on the coffee table between them.

"Ah, our mystery guests have arrived!" she said. "I wonder if Ellen and Spencer are going to let them join us without demanding some ID?"

She smiled whimsically, and Honor chuckled.

"I doubt it," she said, shaking her head. "Ellen's the only person I know who's even more paranoid than Spencer. Now, at least."

Her voice dropped and her eyes darkened with the last three words, and Elizabeth looked at her sharply. The empress started to open her mouth, but Honor shook her head quickly. The memory of Andrew LaFollet's protectiveness—of all the years he'd served her and of how he'd died when she wasn't even there—could still ambush her with no warning at all. But it was getting better, she told herself firmly. It was getting better.

"Anyway," she went on in a determinedly brighter tone, "if one of them doesn't insist on complete identification, you *know* the other one will. And Ellen isn't about to let anyone into your presence without a complete briefing on—"

The door opened and Colonel Ellen Shemais, who'd headed the empress' personal security detachment since she'd been a little girl, appeared as if the mention of her name had summoned her. Elizabeth looked at her, eyebrows raised, but the colonel only bowed to her.

"Your Majesty, Your Grace"—she angled her bow subtly in Honor's direction—"the . . . special embassy from Beowulf."

Elizabeth darted a surprised glance at Honor. All joking about their security personnel aside, the last thing the empress had expected was for the mysterious envoy to be shown straight into her presence. But Honor was just as perplexed as she was. All she could do was shrug at the empress, and the two of them stood, facing the small presence chamber's door.

Perhaps a dozen people filed through it, and Honor felt her eyes go wide as she recognized most of them.

"Your Majesty," Chyang Benton-Ramirez, Chairman and Chief Executive Officer of the Beowulf Planetary Board of Directors, said with a small bow, the sort heads of state bestowed upon one another, "I apologize for the unorthodoxy of this visit, but there are a few things we need to discuss privately. *Very* privately."

✧   ✧   ✧

"I guess," Elizabeth Winton said several hours later, in tones of profound understatement, "that I should be getting accustomed to having foreign heads of state drop in with no warning, but I keep thinking we ought to get a little . . . I don't know, *regularity*, I suppose, into this sort of thing."

"Regularity?" William Alexander, Baron Grantville and Prime Minister of the Star Empire of Manticore, shook his head. "At this point, I'd settle for *rationality*! Does it occur to you, Your Majesty, that we've somehow stumbled through the looking glass?"

"It does seem that way," she acknowledged. "I guess the real question is whether or not the good surprises outnumber the bad ones. I remember my father saying true leadership isn't the ability to accomplish the things you *plan* on; it's the ability to cope with the things you never in a thousand years saw coming."

She smiled a bit raggedly. "I seem to've been getting a lot of practice at that lately."

"All of us have, Your Majesty," Sir Anthony Langtry, the Star Empire's Foreign Secretary, agreed wryly. "My people are supposed to have at least some vague notion of how other star nations are thinking—especially the ones we're on *good* terms with!—but this blindsided us completely."

"There's been a lot of that happening lately, Tony." Baroness Morncreek's tone was desert dry. She and portly, fair-haired Bruce Wijenberg were the only other two members of Grantville's Cabinet at the table. Hamish Alexander-Harrington *had* been present, but he and Sir Thomas Caparelli were currently closeted in a separate meeting with Gabriel Caddell-Markham and Justyná Miternowski-Zhyang.

Honor was no longer in Landing. She'd tried to stay, but Elizabeth and Hamish had put their joint foot firmly down. It had been a pretty near thing, even so, but the CEO of Beowulf's support had turned the trick.

"Francine's right, Tony." Wijenberg nodded in wry agreement with Morncreek. "And I doubt you're any more surprised than she and I are! The Exchequer and Ministry of Trade do have our own high-level contacts in Beowulf, and we never saw it coming, either."

"Well, now that we've all expressed our surprise, what do we do about it?" Elizabeth asked.

"Your Majesty, forgive me, but that's a no-brainer," Grantville said. "If anyone at this table can think of anything more valuable than adding Beowulf to our list of 'associated powers,' please tell me now what it is!"

❖   ❖   ❖

"Jacques!"

One of the things Honor always associated with her mother was her ability to take surprises in stride. There was nothing phlegmatic about Dr. Allison Harrington. Indeed, what most impressed people who met her were her wicked sense of humor (there was a reason the treecats called her "Laugh Dancer") and enthusiasm. Her ability to focus with total intensity upon whatever her current project might be while still bounding effortlessly from one focus to another. She wasn't *erratic*; she simply multitasked with a joyous abandon any AI could only have envied. Yet under all that zest, there was a calm balance, a treecat-like sense of composure which met even the most unexpected events without missing a beat.

But not today.

She took one look at the small, almond-eyed man who'd followed her daughter from the air limo in Harrington Steading's colors, then flung herself into his arms, and her daughter could taste the incredible brilliance of her sorrow-burnished joy and astonishment.

"Hello, Alley." Jacques Benton-Ramirez y Chou's voice was husky as he hugged his twin sister fiercely. She put her head on his shoulder, and he nestled his cheek against her. "It's good to see you, too."

❖   ❖   ❖

"I'm sorry I didn't get here sooner," Jacques said some time later.

He looked down at the glass in his hand, then raised his head and leaned back. He sat with his sister, his brother-in-law, and his niece on the terrace overlooking the White Haven swimming pool. The sun was setting, and this late in the local year (and this far north) evenings were chill, even on Manticore. Wisps of steam rose from the heated pool, gleaming gold in the sun's slanting rays, and he was grateful for his light jacket.

"I'm sorry," he repeated, looking into Alfred Harrington's eyes, "but with so much pure hell breaking loose, I just couldn't justify taking personal time." He shook his head. "Al told me how bad it was, but I knew you and Alley had each other, and I figured, well..."

His voice trailed off into silence, and Alfred shrugged.

"We got your letters, Jacques. It's not like we didn't know you were thinking about us. And I figured you probably had your hands full back home. Besides"—his tone darkened, despite his very best efforts—"like you say, Alley and I had each other. And the twins. And Honor, once she got back from Nouveau Paris, for that matter."

Jacques started to say something more, then stopped. It wouldn't have done any good...and there was no need to actually *say* it, anyway. He and Alfred had been friends for almost eighty T-years. In fact, it had been Jacques who (much to the surprise of the rest of his all-too-prominent family) had introduced the towering young Manticoran naval officer, yeoman, and ex-Marine sergeant to his younger sister.

Technically, Jacques and Allison were fraternal twins, although he'd been born five T-years before she had. Their parents had filed for a single-birth pregnancy, only to discover they'd conceived twins. The second child could have been placed for adoption, of course, but they'd known they wanted a fourth child after they packed their eldest off to college and qualified for another. So the second embryo had been held in cryo until that day, and Jacques had ended up with a younger sister as well as a twin.

He'd always adored her, and he'd developed a fiercely protective streak where she was concerned as they both grew older. There'd been times when she'd cut him down to size with bloody efficiency for "interfering" in her life, but he hadn't let that faze him. It wasn't easy being a Benton-Ramirez y Chou, and he'd known how much Allison hated the thought of being squeezed and molded into one of the roles expected out of her family. He hadn't wanted her forced to be anyone she didn't want to be, and he'd been damned if he'd let anyone do that to her, even if his "nosiness" and "rock-headedness" had pissed her off upon occasion. And he'd been picky as hell about who he encouraged to get close to her, too. Yet he'd never had a single qualm about introducing her to Alfred Harrington . . . and he'd stood as Alfred's best man at the wedding.

There'd never been a moment in all the years since when he'd felt the least trace of regret, either. Jacques Benton-Ramirez y Chou had two birth brothers, and he loved both of them (although Anthony could *really* piss him off; not all sibling rivalries died with the mere passage of time), yet the truth was that he was closer to Alfred than to either of them.

God, he looks awful, he thought now, *and the frigging strike was three damned* months *ago! He must've been a basket case, right after it, and I let my goddamned "responsibilities" get in the way? Christ! Four fucking days. That's how long it would have taken. I could have given him the* four days *to at least come out here and tell him in person that I—*

Tell him what? The question cut Jacques off in mid-thought. He couldn't have told Alfred one thing he didn't already know. Couldn't have accomplished anything Allison and his daughters and son couldn't. Yet he knew he would never forgive himself for not somehow accomplishing something anyway.

"Daddy's right, Uncle Jacques," Honor said now. "We knew what you'd have said. You *did* say it, in your letters. And it's not like we're the only family—here or on Beowulf—who's had to deal with the same thing. We're . . . handling it as well as anyone else, I think."

"I can see that," Jacques replied. But he and Honor had always been close, and he knew she saw the question behind his lie. *If you're handling it that well, why are all of you still* here *and not home on Sphinx?* He saw the awareness in her eyes, but she only looked back steadily.

"At any rate, I'm here now," he said more briskly, "and it looks like I'm going to be able to stay for at least a while."

"Really?" Allison looked across the lawn table at him, and he heard the happiness in her voice. "How long?"

"At least—" he began, then paused and quirked an eyebrow at Honor. "What, another T-week or so, you think, Honor?"

"About that." She smiled crookedly. "Maybe a day or two longer."

Allison and Alfred both looked sharply at their elder daughter, and Honor tasted their emotions as they did the math. It didn't take long; every Manticoran knew when the Solly attack was due to reach Manticore.

"Well, we'll be delighted to have you," Allison said after a moment. "On the other hand, if you're going to be here that long, maybe we should go ahead and reopen Harrington House, Honor?" She gave her daughter a half-humorous, half-resigned look. "He wouldn't be staying so long if it weren't official, and if that's the case, he probably needs to be close to Landing. Besides, your father and I have been imposing on your and Emily and Hamish's hospitality long enough."

"You know perfectly well that you haven't been imposing on anyone, Mother. But if you want the house, of course you're welcome to it. For that matter, I've told you before—it's yours and Daddy's now. I spend every minute I can here at White Haven, anyway, and it makes a lot more sense for you and the twins to use the house than for it to just stand empty."

She shrugged, although "stand empty" was a highly inaccurate description of her Jason Bay mansion's normal state. It was fully staffed at all times, whether she herself was in residence or not. For that matter, it was Harrington Steading's embassy on Manticore, and its official functions never shut down. But the true reason *she'd* avoided the cliff-top mansion since coming home from Haven were all the memories it held of Andrew and Miranda LaFollet, of Farragut, and of Sergeant Jeremiah Tennard. Eventually she'd have to return, she knew, but she wasn't prepared to confront all those reminders just yet.

And Mother knows that, too, she thought. *But if she thinks* Daddy's *healed enough to go home—as far as Landing, at least, even if he's not ready for the freehold yet—that's got to be a good sign. And she's right, having Uncle Jacques along will help a lot. Besides, it really* is *more home for them than it is for me. That'd be true even if I hadn't married Hamish and Emily, given how much time I spend completely off-world.*

"That's settled, then," Allison said. "I'll screen M— I mean, I'll have *Mac* screen the staff to warn them we're coming home."

It was such a brief pause, and so quickly corrected, that only Honor and Nimitz caught the way she'd almost slipped and said "Miranda."

"Well, it would appear it's a good thing the two of you have finished settling my fate," Jacques said with a smile. "I see we're about to be descended upon by what I believe is technically called a thundering herd."

He pointed to the small group of people (or perhaps not so small as all that, actually) spilling out of the house's French doors, and Honor tasted the way the alertness of the posse of armsmen (and one arms*woman*) scattered around the terrace spiked, as they, too, noticed the newcomers.

They were more focused than ever, those guardians, after the Yawata strike and Anton Zilwicki's briefings about nano-programmed assassins, and she tasted her uncle's cold, grim approval of their alertness.

Once, she knew, he'd found watching her learn to put up with her personal armsmen amusing, even though he'd understood (better than her parents, really) why that sort of security was necessary. Yet today she sensed no amusement in Jacques Benton-Ramirez y Chou's mind-glow as he gazed at that protective, green-uniformed cordon.

And Mother and Daddy have changed their *attitudes, too,* she thought sadly.

There'd been a time when her parents had put up

with the twins' personal armsmen only because Grayson law required them to. They'd realized Jeremiah Tennard and Luke Blackett kept a watchful eye on *them*, as well, but they'd regarded it as a necessary (if rather touching) nuisance in their own case. One to be evaded whenever possible.

Not since the Yawata strike. Not since Allison Harrington and her grandson had lived only because two of those armsmen had died for them.

They hadn't raised even a token objection when Honor informed them, firmly, that from now on they had their own personal armsmen. And despite an initial standoffishness—a defensive reaction born of the hurt of LaFollet's and Tennard's deaths—they'd adjusted better than she'd been afraid they might. Not that she hadn't put some careful consideration into picking the proper guardians.

First, she'd decided, any candidates had to be prolong recipients. None of her own original armsmen had received the antiaging therapies. She *knew* how that felt, and she wasn't about to have her parents watch someone that close to them grow old and die before their eyes. Yet that had been only the first (and least difficult) of the qualifications she'd considered when she and Spencer Hawke started reviewing dossiers.

Sergeant Isaiah Matlock, her father's armsman, was a very rare bird: the son of a forestry ranger on a planet whose wilderness didn't precisely welcome human intruders. The hearty souls who ventured out into it anyway were regarded as dangerous crackpots by their stay-at-home friends and neighbors, but Matlock's family had been involved in managing Grayson's forests for three hundred T-years. They had a love for those forests which was possibly even deeper than that of a Sphinxian like Alfred Harrington, probably precisely because their homeworld's wilderness did its level best to kill them every day. Honor expected Isaiah to embrace Sphinx joyfully, despite its gravity, and she was pleased with the compatibility already apparent between him and Dr. Harrington. If anyone was likely to understand her father's need for an occasional fishing or hunting foray, it was going to be Isaiah . . . who would undoubtedly help browbeat the rest of the security detail into submission.

She'd expected choosing her mother's guardian to be more difficult, however. Allison's Beowulf upbringing made it still harder for her to accept the notion that she needed to be protected against people she'd never even met. She could grasp it intellectually, but even after multiple attempts to assassinate her elder daughter, she found it emotionally incomprehensible that complete strangers might wish *her* harm. Besides, any Beowulfer was bound to have a few problems with the notion of a personal retainer prepared to die in her defense. On top of which, and also as a product of that Beowulf upbringing, she . . . took a little getting used to for even the most liberal-minded Grayson armsman imaginable.

Honor had been painfully aware of the Herculean task she faced finding some way to deal with all of *that*, which was why she'd been so delighted by how quickly she'd discovered Corporal Anastasia Yanakov, the very first Grayson woman to complete the harsh, demanding armsman's training course.

A double handful of additional women had followed her since, and more than half of them had ended up in the Harrington Steadholder's Guard. About half the others had been snapped up by the Mayhew Guard and Palace Security, and the remainder were scattered about in the guards of some of Grayson's more progressive steadholders.

The real dinosaurs were going to resist such a bizarre notion to the last ditch, but their loss (and stupidity) was Honor's gain, and Anastasia (a fourth cousin of High Admiral Judah Yanakov) was the perfect example of why. Her deplorably radical father had sent her off-world to Manticore for her schooling, where she'd completed a master's degree in criminology and law enforcement (and captained her college pistol team) before going home and fighting her way into the armsman's program. She'd graduated third in her class as well, and there was no question she was headed for officer's rank. All armsman officers rose from the ranks, however. Every one of them started as a simple armsman, and while any woman intruding into that traditionally male preserve was likely to find the climb more difficult than her X-chromosome-challenged fellows, Anastasia clearly had a head for heights.

In the meantime, she was very much the product of two worlds. She was the perfect interface for someone like Allison Harrington, and while she possessed a sly sense of mischief, she was enough *unlike* Miranda LaFollet to avoid reminding Allison (or Honor) of another Grayson woman who'd learned to straddle both of her steadholder's worlds.

At the moment, Matlock and Yanakov were stationed with her own trio of personal armsmen. The five of them had spread out far enough to allow Honor and her family an island of privacy, but they formed an alert ring around the terrace's perimeter as they watched the newcomers finish trooping out the doors.

Emily's life-support chair led the parade, accompanied by *her* personal armsman, Jefferson McClure. Faith and James Harrington walked on either side of her chair, and Honor felt a fresh pang as she gazed at her sister.

Jeremiah Tennard's death had devastated Faith. Death was always hard to understand when you weren't quite nine, and it wasn't as if Faith hadn't lost enough family— enough uncles and aunts and cousins—on that same dreadful day to darken any childhood. But Jeremiah had watched over her literally since birth as protector, guardian, friend, and big brother, all in one. It hadn't really penetrated that he was there specifically to die, if that was what it took to keep her safe, yet she'd recognized his fierce devotion, the love that went beyond mere duty, and she'd given him the uncomplicated, uncompromising love of childhood in return.

She and James had both clung to Luke Blackett since the Yawata strike, and Honor had realized it would be the next thing to impossible to find someone to replace Jeremiah. Someone the twins would allow close to them after the brutal amputation of so many others they'd loved. They were smart, sensitive kids; they weren't going to expose themselves to that sort of loss again if they could help it.

Honor understood that, and because she did, she'd known she'd have to cheat. Which she had, and she allowed herself a sense of sorrow-tinged triumph as she considered the tall—quite tall, for a Grayson— auburn-haired armsman behind Faith. Corporal Micah LaFollet had finished his training less than two T-years ago, and some sticklers might consider him a bit junior for his new position, but Faith had known Andrew and Miranda LaFollet's younger brother for her entire life. Micah was already inside her defensive shell. In fact, she'd spent most of the day after the Yawata strike weeping into his shoulder over his brother's and sister's deaths.

And it's what Micah *needed, too,* Honor thought now. *He loves Faith and James to pieces, and I don't think I could have found an assignment that would've meant more to him.*

Except one, perhaps, she reflected, looking at the young woman guiding the counter-grav double stroller.

Quick-heal had repaired Lindsey Phillips' broken collarbone, but she was no more immune than any other member of Honor's family to the devastating losses they'd all suffered. The same shadow had touched her, and she'd dealt with it by investing herself even more deeply in Raoul and Katherine. Honor was grateful for that, yet it was the towering young armsman behind the nanny who drew her eye.

Lieutenant Vincent Clinkscales had drawn the impossible duty of filling Andrew LaFollet's place as Raoul Alfred Alistair Alexander-Harrington's personal armsman. No one could ever truly *replace* Andrew. Honor knew it was unfair to feel that way, yet she also knew it was true. Inevitable. Andrew LaFollet had been with her through too much, given too much, for it to be any other way. In many ways, she would have preferred to allow Micah to step into his older brother's place, but Micah was simply too young, too inexperienced. The Conclave of Steadholders would have pitched a collective tantrum at the very notion. They wouldn't have been able to stop her, but that wouldn't have kept them from trying. And little though she cared to admit it, they probably would have had a point.

That was why she'd stolen Clinkscales from Protector's Palace Security. A nephew of Howard Clinkscales and the older brother of Commander Carson Clinkscales, he was several years older than Micah. In fact, he was old enough to have been restricted to first-generation prolong, which would make him look reassuringly mature to Honor's fellow steadholders in another few T-years. And the Clinkscales Clan was officially sept to the Harrington Clan, which made Vincent legally Honor's nephew. Not even the stodgiest steadholder could argue with *that* qualification, and he'd amply demonstrated both his ability and his loyalty.

And if I still don't know him as well as I knew Andrew, that's true of every other member of the Guard, she thought sadly. *They're all gone, now. Every one of my original armsmen.*

Oh, don't be so maudlin, *Honor!* she scolded herself a moment later. *Vincent's a perfectly wonderful young man, or you wouldn't have picked him in the first place. And if he's not Andrew, neither is anyone else. So isn't it about time you stopped dwelling on that and let him be whoever he* has *to be to take care of Raoul?*

Nimitz made a soft sound of mingled sympathy and scolding from his perch beside her, and she smiled at him.

"I'm working on it, Stinker," she said softly, touching the tip of his nose with her index finger. "I'm working on it."

He caught her finger in one true-hand and squeezed,

and she tasted his approval. Then she looked back at the approaching group and found herself smiling in amusement as she counted noses.

It really is like watching an army, she thought. *It's a pity Mac didn't come along with them; Emily would've had an even dozen if he had! And it's a good thing the terrace is as big as it is, too.*

"Hi, Emily," she called as the cavalcade came closer. "Did Mac send you to fetch us for supper?"

"Not yet," Emily replied wryly. "In fact, I decided it was time to demonstrate my independence by coming to get you on my own. I figure I beat *his* summons by a clear two minutes. Maybe even three."

"Always mistress of your own fate, I see," Honor observed.

"Huh! *You're* a fine one to talk! You think I haven't figured out whose whim of steel *really* rules your menagerie?"

"Nonsense." Honor elevated her nose. "He's simply developed a keen appreciation for what I want to be doing anyway. It just *happens* that what I choose is what Mac thinks I ought to be doing at any given moment. I'm always perfectly free to change my mind or refuse to go along with him."

"*Sure* you are." Emily's chair reached them, and Faith and James swarmed forward. They were too big now to climb into their uncle's lap, but he wrapped his arms around them, and Emily smiled at him. "Was Honor this mendacious as a child?"

"Mendacious?" Benton-Ramirez y Chou repeated thoughtfully after depositing welcoming kisses on his niece and nephew. He cocked his head, considering the word, then shrugged. "I wouldn't say *mendacious* so much as able to . . . creatively reconstruct her world at need, let's say."

"Yes, and she got it from her uncle," Allison Harrington interjected.

"Well, from someone with the same genetic package, at least." Benton-Ramirez y Chou smiled sweetly at his twin. "For that matter, Alley, you're the geneticist. You know nurture trumps nature in cases like this. So, much as I'd like to, I don't really think I can honestly claim the credit."

"Oh, stop it, both of you." Honor shook her head. "Whatever my faults may be—and I'm sure they're legion—I don't think either of *you* is brave enough to let Mac's dinner get cold, either. So why don't we all just head back and let the two of you finish threshing out who's to blame for the dreadful way I turned out over supper?"

"My goodness, you really *are* a superior strategist, aren't you?" her uncle replied. "Who would've thought it?"

Chapter Thirteen

THE BEDSIDE COM'S rippling attention signal was quiet and discreet, almost apologetic, yet Honor's eyes opened instantly.

It was still dark outside the bedroom windows, but just the faintest edge of dawn gilded the horizon. It brought back memories, that knife-edge of light. Memories of sleepy Sphinxian dawns, before the Queen's Navy had gifted her with that instantaneous transition between sleep and awareness. Memories of a younger Honor Harrington who now seemed incredibly far away . . . and far more innocent than the woman looking out those windows this predawn morning. For just an instant, as she saw that glow kiss the eastern sky, she wished she were still that teenaged girl looking out her bedroom window at the four-hundred-year-old greenhouse and the ancient, ninety-meter crown oak, its bark carved with Stephanie Harrington's initials and the name "Lionheart." The girl who'd never worn the uniform, who had no blood upon her hands, no burden of beloved dead, and for whom the universe was a new, unstained promise on the horizon.

That edge of grief, that flare of loss, flashed through her, sharper than a razor and crueler than winter, in the instant the chimes roused her. It struck her in that first moment, before her defenses were back in place, and she clenched internally. But then, almost before the razor had cut, she felt another presence. *Two* more presences: the loving glow from the sleeping 'cat on his bedside perch, and the warm, deeply breathing presence at her back, arms wrapped protectively about her even in sleep.

They were there with her, Nimitz and Hamish. They were there *for* her, just as they always would be, reminders that the universe was filled with even more love than loss.

Then the chimes sang again, and she patted the hand on her ribs.

"Um?" a voice uttered indistinctly.

Unlike Honor, Hamish Alexander-Harrington seldom woke without a struggle. Or, rather, he had an ability (which Honor frequently envied but had never managed to acquire) to turn the Navy's hardwired "Wake Up *Now*" switch off and then on again as needed. At the moment, he clearly had it in the "off" position, and she patted his hand again, harder.

"Wh' zat?"

He didn't sound any clearer, so she jabbed with a reasonably gentle elbow.

"Urruuff!"

That got his attention, and she smothered a giggle as he twitched awake.

"One of us has to take that call," she observed,

still gazing out the windows as the com chimed yet again.

"So?" His voice was still soft-edged with sleep, but she tasted his amusement an instant before his lips nuzzled under her braid to nibble the nape of her neck with slow, teasing thoroughness. "And you're telling *me* this exactly why?" he inquired between gentle nips.

"Because the com is on *your* side of the bed," she told him severely. "And because—*stop* that!"

"Stop what?" he asked innocently, and she sighed as the hand she'd patted earlier cupped her breast. "Oh. You mean stop *this?*"

"No...I mean, *yes!*"

She laughed and twisted in his arms, turning to face him and putting her own arms around him. She kissed him thoroughly while the com continued patiently (and with steadily rising volume) to chime for their attention.

"I don't think you really *do* mean that," he told her.

"That's because you're a wicked, evil fellow who knows me entirely too well." The severity of her tone was somewhat undermined when she paused in mid-sentence to kiss him again, and she felt Nimitz's and Samantha's silent laughter as they roused on their perches.

"And it's also because *I'm* a weak, easily distracted person who hasn't had nearly enough time to do this sort of thing in the last few months," she continued. "But Mac or Spencer wouldn't let calls through at this ungodly hour—especially not since they both *know* I'm a weak, easily distracted person who hasn't had nearly enough time to do this sort of thing in the last few months—if it weren't important. So"—she drew back languorously, then poked suddenly with a rigid forefinger—"answer the com!"

"You realize you're going to pay for that later," Hamish said as he sat up, rubbing his rib cage.

"I'm looking forward to it," she told him with a smile, then reached out to touch the side of his face. "And thank you," she said softly.

"Thank me?" He raised a quizzical eyebrow. "Thank me for *what*?"

"For being you . . . and for being here."

His blue eyes softened, and he cupped a palm over the hand still on his cheek.

"You're welcome, Your Grace. And it works both ways, you know."

She nodded, wishing he could taste her emotions as clearly as she tasted his.

You know, that's sort of unreasonable of you, she told herself as he punched the "audio only" accept key. *How many people are lucky enough to have what you already have with him and Emily? I know it's human nature to always want more, but let's not get too greedy, okay?*

"Yes?" Hamish said.

"I'm sorry to disturb you, Milord," James MacGuiness' voice responded.

"That's all right, Mac. I think we were about to get up anyway." Hamish gave Honor a wicked, laughing look, then glanced at the time and grimaced. "For that matter, I've got that early meeting at Admiralty House, and I need to be in the air in the next couple of hours."

"I know, Milord. In fact, that's one reason I went ahead and woke you. Dr. Arif's on the com for Her

Grace, FTL from Sphinx. And I think Her Grace should probably take the call before you leave, Milord."

"I beg your pardon?" Hamish frowned at Honor, who shrugged.

She had no idea why Adelina Arif might screen her this early, or why MacGuiness thought Hamish should be part of the conversation, but...

"Ask her to hold a few more seconds, please, Mac," she said, raising her voice.

"Of course, Your Grace," he replied, and Hamish muted the com.

"I think we should go ahead and get decent," Honor continued, giving her husband one more peck on the cheek before she rolled out of bed.

"Some people," he returned, surveying her with obvious approval, "*wake up* decent because they wear pajamas, you know."

"No, really?" She laughed and stretched luxuriously, arching her spine and savoring the sharp, bright flicker of desire flowing through his emotions, then scooped up her kimono and slipped into it. "Doesn't that waste a lot of time?" she asked innocently.

"And you called *me* a wicked, evil fellow! A case of the pot and the kettle, don't you think?"

"Certainly not." She sniffed virtuously. "*I'm* not a 'fellow'!"

"No, you're not, thank God," he conceded fervently.

"I'm glad you approve. Now get your butt out of bed and into a robe!"

"Yes, Your Grace. At once, Your Grace. As you command, Your Grace," he said obsequiously, and ducked as she hurled a pillow at him.

❖   ❖   ❖

"All right, Mac," she said a few minutes later, seated at her workstation in their suite's comfortable sitting room. Hamish sat beside her, casually dressed in a pullover shirt and slacks. "Please put Dr. Arif through."

"Yes, Ma'am."

The display blanked briefly. Then an attractive, dark-complexioned woman looked out of it at her.

"Adelina," Honor said. "It's good to see you."

"And you, too, Your Grace." The woman who'd taught the treecats to sign smiled after a brief lag. Despite the fact that she was several light-minutes away, in her office on Sphinx, the delay was little more than ten seconds. "I apologize for screening so early, though." Her smile turned a bit sheepish. "Actually, I hadn't realized it was quite *this* early for you. I counted the time zones wrong."

"That's all right," Honor assured her, and glanced at Hamish. "We needed to get up early this morning, anyway."

"I hope you're not just saying that to make me feel better," Arif chuckled a handful of seconds later. "Anyway, though, the reason I'm disturbing you this early is that something came up about thirty-five minutes ago, and I thought you ought to hear about it ASAP."

Honor cocked her head and frowned. If she had the numbers right, the time in Arif's office in the Sphinxian town of Green Bottom was just past Compensate, the "midnight hour" (thirty-seven minutes, actually) inserted into the middle of Sphinx's night to "round out" the twenty-five standard-hour planetary day.

"You're up kind of late, aren't you, Adelina?"

"I think everybody's working strange hours lately, Your Grace," Arif replied. "Although, when I realized I'd dragged Mac out of bed, I started to tell him not to disturb you. But he mentioned it was about time for him to be getting you up. Besides"—she shrugged with something that wasn't quite a grin—"the 'cats are sort of insistent about talking right now. They, ah, don't seem quite as obsessed with clocks as humans are."

"You've got that one right!" Honor snorted. "It took a couple of years for Nimitz to catch on that two-legs really cared exactly when they got around to doing something." She smiled. "Actually, it came in kind of handy for a while. I got to be late and blame it on him...until Mom and Daddy figured out who was *really* to blame, anyway."

Nimitz made an amused sound, and Arif chuckled.

"I can believe that. And most of the 'cats I've been working with are still 'wild,' of course. They haven't had the advantage of Nimitz's earlier training."

"No, but they're probably less *stubborn* than him, too," Honor said, reaching up to stroke Nimitz's ears.

"Far be it from me to agree with you about that," Arif said a bit primly, and Nimitz bleeked a laugh as Samantha nodded vigorously from the back of Hamish's chair.

"Anyway," Arif went on, her expression more serious, "earlier this evening, I was discussing today's progress with Song Shadow when she suddenly stopped in mid-sign. She just sat there for several seconds, obviously 'listening' to someone else. It's not like her to just stop like that, without at least warning me, and whoever she was talking to, the conversation went on a long time for a 'cat. When it was over, she asked me to send an air car to Bright Water Clan."

Honor felt herself frowning. She wasn't going to interrupt with questions—even with the grav-pulse com, interplanetary conversations quickly disintegrated if people started breaking in on one another—but her curiosity burned brightly as she wondered where the linguist was going.

She'd never met Song Shadow, but from her name, she was obviously a "memory singer." Arif was still exploring exactly what memory singers were, but she'd already learned enough to recognize they were absolutely central to treecat society, as its historians and teachers. From what Arif had so far discovered, a memory singer could literally "record" and play back the actual experiences of another treecat. In fact, they could play back *centuries'* worth of those experiences.

Honor doubted any human—even she, who'd developed her own version of the treecats' empathy—would ever truly grasp what that meant, appreciate the continuity "mind songs" bestowed upon a telepathic species who could literally "hear" the mind-voices and experience the very emotions of treecats who'd died centuries before their own birth. But the fact that *Samantha* was a memory singer had been critical to Arif's success in teaching the 'cats to sign, because once *she'd* learned how, she'd been able to "teach" any other treecat the same thing.

"I sent the car, of course," Arif continued. "It took an hour or so to get to Bright Water's range, and the SFC ranger had to wait a while for all his passengers to arrive. Then they had to fly all the way to Green Bottom."

She grimaced, and Honor nodded. Green Bottom was halfway around Sphinx from Bright Water Clan's home range. And, she thought more grimly, from the ruins of Yawata Crossing as well.

"Thanks to all the delays, they only got here about an hour ago, and I was more than a little surprised by who Song Shadow had sent a ride for." Arif shook her head. "It was seven other memory singers."

Honor felt her eyes widen. One thing they *had* learned about memory singers was that they virtually never left their clans' ranges. Which, of course, raised the question of exactly what a memory singer by the name of Samantha was doing bonded to a human. Honor had the impression that neither Nimitz nor Samantha was being as forthcoming about that as they could have, although it was obvious Samantha wasn't exactly your *typical* memory singer.

Obviously, there'd always been some exceptions (besides Samantha), especially recently, since memory singers had been involved with Dr. Arif's efforts from the beginning. But Honor didn't think there'd ever been more than two or three of them in Green Bottom at any one time before.

"I know I don't have to tell you how surprised I was when the ranger opened the car door and seven *memory singers* piled out!" Arif said wryly. "I'd met three of them before: Wind of Memory, Songstress, and Echo of Time." Honor pursed her lips in a silent whistle as Arif named all three of Bright Water Clan's senior memory singers. "Song Shadow introduced the others once they got to my office. Songkeeper and Clear Song are the senior and second singers of Laughing River Clan. Winter Voice is the senior singer of Moonlight Dancing Clan. And then"—Arif's eyes darkened and her voice dropped—"there's Sorrow Singer." The linguist swallowed. "She's the only surviving memory singer of Black Rock Clan, Honor."

Samantha and Nimitz keened softly, and Honor inhaled sharply.

"I didn't know any of them had survived," she said, voice soft, when Arif paused. "I thought the entire clan had been killed."

"As far as Sorrow Singer knows, she's not just Black Rock's surviving singer," Arif said a few seconds later. "She's the only survivor, period. And the only reason she's alive is that she was visiting Moonlight Dancing Clan. One of her litter brothers had married into Moonlight Dancing, and their central range was just far enough away to be outside the blast area and firestorm." The linguist shook her head slowly. "Moonlight Dancing was close enough its memory singers *felt* Black Rock die...and so did she."

Honor felt her hand press her lips, felt Hamish's arm encircle her, felt Nimitz pressing against the back of her neck, and all she could think of was the horror of a telempath—a *memory singer*—actually *experiencing,* all at once, the deaths of everyone she'd ever known and loved.

"I don't know how they kept her from suiciding." Arif's voice was softer than Honor's had been. "I... have the impression it wasn't easy."

Her eyes met Honor's from the display, and Honor nodded. Treecats who'd adopted almost never survived the deaths of their human partners. Before prolong, that had been *the* great tragedy of the bonds, for treecats normally lived over two hundred T-years, and their humans' deaths had deprived them of all those additional years. Honor could think of only two 'cats in her own lifetime who'd survived their humans' deaths: Prince Consort Justin's companion, Monroe, and Samantha herself. What it must have been like when every single person in Sorrow Singer's clan was ripped away from her in one brutal instant . . .

"It must have been terrible for all the clans in range," Arif went on starkly, "and Moonlight Dancing was closest of all. The SFC says they've lost over a dozen 'cats since the strike, and others don't look good. Which made me wonder why in God's name the clan's two senior memory singers were traipsing off to visit me at a time like this."

Stillness hovered. Then, finally, Honor cleared her throat.

"Why—" She paused, her soprano husky, and cleared her throat again. "Why *had* they come, Adelina?"

"I know Nimitz and Samantha were off-world when it happened," Arif said a bit obliquely, "but from what Song Shadow and the others say, every 'cat who *wasn't* off-world felt it. The more distant clans felt it less strongly, thank God, but even our crew here at Green Bottom got hammered. Trust me, it was . . . bad. *Really* bad.

"I don't know if they understand exactly how it happened even now, but they know it was the result of a human attack. Personally, I wouldn't have blamed them for turning their backs on all humans, but that's not the way treecats' heads work. Apparently they've been passing around Nimitz's experiences with you, and especially what happened with Lieutenant Mears, for some time now. And, according to Song Shadow, they've overheard at least part of the newscasts about President Pritchart and Dr. Simões; some of the SFC rangers were viewing the news channels during a medical visit to Moonlight Dancing. They've figured out

Nimitz and Samantha must've actually met Simões, and the clans want them to come home for the memory singers to get their first-hand experience with his mind-glow, but I think that's just a formality. They figure that if he was lying, or if he was crazy, Nimitz would already've told you. For that matter, they know *you* can sense emotions. So there's not much question in their minds that Simões is telling the truth...or that Mesa is behind everything that's happened."

"I'm glad they don't blame *us* for it, although God knows *I* sometimes do," Honor said somberly. "I still don't understand why they wanted to come see you in person, though. For that matter, I don't see how Song Shadow got the word all the way from Bright Water that they did! Nothing I've ever seen has suggested they've got enough range to reach halfway around a planet."

"I'm pretty sure they relayed from clan to clan," Arif said. "And the reason they wanted to see me is that Sorrow Singer has a proposal."

"A 'proposal'?" Honor's eyes narrowed. "What sort of 'proposal'?"

"She wants to tell you herself," Arif replied, and a slender, dappled brown and white form jumped into her lap and into her com's field of view. The treecat sat up on her rearmost limbs, facing the com, her eyes and body language somber. She looked so *small*, so fragile, Honor thought, feeling the tears at the back of her own eyes.

"Sorrow Singer?" she asked softly, and the treecat nodded.

Honor wanted to reach out and hug that distant 'cat. To share with her the depth of her own grief for what had happened to Sorrow Singer's clan. Her sense of guilt that humans—*any* humans—could have caused such an atrocity. But she couldn't, and so she simply bent her head in a small half bow of acknowledgment.

Sorrow Singer inclined her own head in response. Then her hands rose, and she began to sign with a flowing grace that somehow communicated a bottomless sea of sadness.

<I know of you, Dances on Clouds,> those graceful fingers said. <I have tasted your mind-glow in the songs from Laughs Brightly. And since the Day of Sorrow, Wind of Memory and Echo of Time have sung the songs of all those who came before you, as well. I have tasted them all, even Death Fang's Bane herself. I *know* your clan.>

Her hands emphasized the verb, and as Honor looked into those bottomless green eyes, she realized what Sorrow Singer meant. That for the treecats, the mind-glows of all who'd gone before were still available, still *there*, as long as the chain of singers was unbroken. In a very real sense, Sorrow Singer had actually *met* Stephanie Harrington, Honor's own ancestor, the very first human ever adopted by a treecat, and Honor felt a strange, powerful envy.

"I wish I could share those memories with you," she heard herself say. "I've always wished I could have known her."

<You would have liked her,> Sorrow Singer signed. <Indeed, I think she was much like you in many ways. But in all the years since she and Climbs Quickly bonded, Death Fang's Bane's Clan has been the People's friend and protector. We know what your clan has done for us. We know what *you* have done for us. And now, it is time for us to protect *you*.>

For a moment, Honor was certain she must have misread those flowing fingers. Protect her? Protect *her*, when humans had destroyed Sorrow Singer's entire clan?

"Nimitz has already protected me many times," she said. "And I've done my best to protect him. That's what you do when you love someone."

<I know that,> Sorrow Singer replied, and her tail flirted as if in a sad laugh. <I could not have tasted the Bright Water memory songs without tasting your love for Laughs Brightly and his love for you, Dances on Clouds. But that was not what I meant.>

"Then, forgive me, but what *do* you mean?"

<The evildoers who destroyed my clan, who have destroyed so much of Death Fang's Bane's Clan, who have brought such sorrow to the People and to our two-legs, cannot be allowed to do still more evil.> Now Sorrow Singer's fingers moved with a flat, somehow terrible emphasis. <We know—*I* know, from your mind-glow—that you will die to prevent that. That your friends among the two-legs, even those we have never met or tasted, will do the same. That you will *stop* their evil, whatever the cost, however long it may take. And we know from the stories we have heard over the "HD">—she signed the obviously unfamiliar term carefully—<that the evildoers who slew my clan have tried to slay you, as well. That they forced one you loved to attack you against his will. I have tasted that, too, in Bright Water's memory songs. And it seems likely that if they have tried once, they will try again. And again. Not to slay only you, but also Soul of Steel or others of your great elders.>

She paused again, and Honor nodded.

"I'm afraid you're right," she said soberly. "And we don't know how they're doing it. How to stop them."

<Nor do the People,> Sorrow Singer said. <But unlike two-legs—*other* two-legs, at least—the People can taste mind-glows. We do not know how the evildoers make others do their bidding, but we *can* recognize the moment when it happens. From Laughs Brightly's memories, we know now what to look for. I believe we could taste it even sooner with that knowledge . . . and give other two-legs at least some warning.>

Honor inhaled sharply. She looked at Sorrow Singer for several seconds, then spoke very carefully.

"We've thought—*I've* thought—about that possibility," she admitted. "As you say, Nimitz recognized the same fear, the same desperation, I saw in Tim that day. And from the security footage of the attempt to assassinate Berry Zilwicki, Judson Van Hale and Genghis recognized those same things in the killer they sent after her. So, yes, I've thought about it. But Genghis was bonded to Van Hale just like Nimitz is bonded to me. They tried to protect each other because they loved each other, just like Nimitz and I love each other. And Genghis *died*, Sorrow Singer, just like Nimitz could have died trying to stop Timothy." She shook her head. "Like I said, you protect the ones you love."

<And you would not have the People risk themselves for those they do *not* love,> Sorrow Singer signed and gave a slow, human-style nod. <That is what I would have expected from you, Dances on Clouds. But this choice is for the People, and we have made it. Speaks from Silence>—she nodded again, this time in Arif's direction—<has labored long to help us find ways we

may become true partners with our two-leg neighbors, as Golden Voice urged. Now we have found one, and one which will allow us in at least some small way to strike back against the slayers of my clan.>

The small, dappled creature gazed into Honor's eyes once more.

<The People know how to deal with those who would slay us,> her implacable fingers said with iron determination. <We know how to deal with those who would slay those we love. Do not forget how Death Fang's Bane and Climbs Quickly first met. They fought, and they bled, and each almost *died* for the other. Now it is our turn, and we wish you to go to Soul of Steel and Truth Seeker. Tell them the People—*all* the People of this entire world—know who would protect them and who would slay them. We know how you and your clan have always loved and protected and shielded us from harm, Dances on Clouds. But the time has come for that to change, and we do not choose to be kittens forever. If you would guard us, then *we* will guard *you*, and if we die as Far Climber did, as Climbs Quickly almost did, as Laughs Brightly has almost died for you and you for him, then we will die. But we will not hide. We will not be children. If you will fight for all this world, for all of us, then *we* will fight for *you*.>

Chapter Fourteen

INNOKENTIY KOLOKOLTSOV considered the message on his display.

Well, it's hardly a surprise, he thought. *And I thought I was ready for it. But I don't suppose anyone could really be ready for something like this. And the Manties are capitalizing on it, damn them.*

He didn't know how the newsies had first gotten wind of "Operation Raging Justice," but any secret had a limited shelf life. Sooner or later, somebody always "outed" it, either for some advantage they might gain or simply for the ego stroking newsies gave those "unnamed sources." And it didn't matter what the secret was. It could be that some political or bureaucratic rival was maintaining a clandestine love nest on the taxpayers' credit, or it could be a literally life-or-death operation like Raging Justice. It was all grist for the mill, as far as the leakers were concerned.

So however much he'd hated the thought of telling the Manties what was coming, it had scarcely been a surprise. And neither had their response.

By this time, he had a sizable file of messages from Sir Lyman Carmichael, Manticore's ambassador to the Solarian League. The first dozen or so had maintained the diplomatic fiction that the League and the Star Empire weren't yet actually at war and simply requested "clarification" of "unconfirmed news reports" of SLN fleet movements. Over the next week or so, though, as Kolokoltsov systematically ignored them, they'd segued from "requests" into forthright demands.

By now, Carmichael wasn't even pretending Manticore didn't know what was headed its way, and his communications had become increasingly blunt. Like the present one.

Kolokoltsov pressed the button, starting Carmichael in mid-sentence.

"—done our best to convince you and your colleagues to see reason, Mr. Permanent Senior Undersecretary," the Manticoran said flatly, pointedly jettisoning the fiction that he was actually addressing Foreign Minister Roelas y Valiente. "You, however, have steadfastly ignored our warnings, rejected any attempt to reach a diplomatic resolution of the crisis provoked entirely by your military's actions, and continued to prepare additional military operations against the Star Empire. We've endeavored through nonmilitary responses to indicate at least some of the potential costs of your actions. Obviously, the interruptions and damage your interstellar commerce is already suffering as a consequence of your intransigence have failed to get through to you. Now, with all the hyena-like 'courage' we've come to associate with Admiral Rajampet and his navy of gallant murderers, you're clearly preparing to take advantage of the catastrophic damage inflicted upon the Old Star Kingdom in February.

"I've warned you repeatedly, on behalf of my Empress and my Government, of the extraordinary risks you run in pursuing such a policy. I warn you again, now, formally, that your obvious belief that our defenses have been crippled by what's become known as the Yawata strike is in error. If Fleet Admiral Filareta attacks the Manticore Binary System, he won't simply be defeated as Admiral Crandall was in her attack on Spindle. He will be *destroyed*, and if the reported number of superdreadnoughts assigned to him is accurate, the loss of life among Solarian naval personnel will be unconscionable. We have no desire to kill hundreds of thousands of men and women whose only 'crime' will be obedience to the lawful orders of superiors too arrogant to recognize reality when they see it. It would appear, however, that you and your colleagues intend to leave us no choice.

"The Star Empire of Manticore therefore formally demands that you immediately dispatch to the Manticore Binary System via the Beowulf Terminus of the Junction an officer with sufficient authority to order Fleet Admiral Filareta to stand down. Assuming press reports of this operation's timing are as accurate as I have reason to believe they are, there's still time—if only barely—for those orders to reach Manticore before Fleet Admiral Filareta. *We* cannot order him to disregard orders he was given by lawful superiors; *you* can. If you decline to do so, the responsibility for whatever happens will lie squarely on your shoulders, and the Star Empire will be prepared to produce copies of my correspondence with you, in its entirety, in any future dispute over who bears responsibility for any consequences of your most recent unilateral aggression against a sovereign star nation. Moreover, under the circumstances, Her

Majesty's Government will not consider itself bound
to maintain the confidentiality of our correspondence
where the press is concerned."

He paused, obviously giving that last sentence time
to sink in, then continued in the same flat, uncompromising tone.

"It's not yet too late to prevent a disaster of staggering dimensions. We will do all we can to minimize
the catastrophic consequences of this confrontation. We
invite you—we *implore* you, in the name of your own
military personnel—to stop this *now*. If you decline
this opportunity, if you refuse to act, be certain history
will know exactly where to assign the blood guilt for
the massacre which will most certainly ensue."

I suppose that's about as blunt as it comes, Kolokoltsov thought, and shook his head. Even now, he
couldn't quite believe anyone would address the *Solarian
League* like that. Despite everything—despite Crandall's
devastating defeat, despite the Manties' provocative
closure of wormhole bridges and junctions—he still
couldn't quite believe it deep down inside.

*Which is stupid of me. If I haven't figured out
anything else by now, I should at least have realized that whatever else Manties may be, they* sure
*as hell aren't impressed by the League's reputation!
Not anymore. It may be ultimately suicidal, given the
difference in our resources and populations, but that
doesn't change the way they feel.*

Of course, even if they were actually terrified, they'd
be sending him exactly this sort of correspondence.
Diplomatic threats cost nothing, and the temptation
to run a bluff, to convince Kolokoltsov they could do
to Filareta what they'd done to Crandall—especially

if they really *couldn't*—had to be overwhelming. If they could frighten him into calling Filareta off, they ran the table without having to fire a single missile. Which would also just happen to save them if they didn't have any missiles left *to* fire.

Which is all well and good, but doesn't change the fact that they may actually be able to do exactly *what Carmichael's threatening. And if they* are, *and if they really are prepared to hand all their notes to someone like O'Hanrahan...*

His expression turned bleak as he contemplated just how damaging the publication of Carmichael's correspondence could prove if things went to hell on Filareta. Yet it would be almost as damaging to take the ambassador's "advice." Sending the stand-down orders Manticore was demanding could only be seen as a sign of weakness. It would damage the League's prestige still further, and that could only worsen the consequences they all feared in the Verge and the Shell, which didn't even consider the *personal* consequences to him and his colleagues. Or, for that matter, the potential constitutional train wreck when everyone began assigning blame and, in the process, revealed just how threadbare the pretense of representative government in the Solarian League truly was.

But if we don't *order him to stand down, and it turns out remotely as badly as Carmichael's warning us it will, we'll have all of those consequences* plus *the deaths of thousands of our own spacers!*

He considered calling yet another meeting to discuss Carmichael's latest message, but what could it accomplish? The others would argue, they'd worry, try to weasel around into a position which heaped the blame on everyone else, and in the end decide to do what he and, perhaps, MacArtney suggested. And the truth was, God help him, that he couldn't see any choice but to continue backing Rajampet's strategy.

It was simply too late to make any other decision.

Besides, everything I've been able to dig up on Filareta suggests he's at least four or five times as smart as Crandall was. And he knows what happened at Spindle. If the Manties really are *in a position to chew him up and spit him out, he's smart enough to stand down on his own rather than get his fleet killed for nothing. That'd be bad enough, but a hell of a lot* less b*ad than actually getting himself blown out of space!*

And relying on Filareta to be smart enough also just happened to avoid the consequences of caving in to Carmichael's demands without even trying to find out if they were a bluff.

❖　　❖　　❖

"I'm afraid there's been some misunderstanding, Admiral," the dark-skinned man on Fleet Admiral Imogene Tsang's display said. "The Beowulf government has clearly stated its opposition to your proposed movement. In fact, we've informed both Fleet Admiral Rajampet and Prime Minister Gyulay that the Planetary Board of Directors declines to authorize or permit the transit of Solarian naval vessels through this terminus at this time. If that information wasn't transmitted to you prior to your departure for Beowulf, I'm officially informing you of it now."

"I'm not privy to your system government's communications with the Prime Minister or the Admiralty, Director Caddell-Markham," Tsang replied in a reasonably courteous but firm tone. "I do, however, have orders to transit this terminus with my task force to support Eleventh Fleet's operations. Those orders aren't discretionary, nor are they preconditioned on anyone's permission or *lack* of permission. For myself, I'll simply observe that my understanding of the Constitution is that federal authority is paramount in circumstances such as these. I'll also concede that I may be mistaken in that understanding, and if I am, I sincerely apologize for anything which may seem to overstep my authority. Nonetheless, I remain bound by the orders I've received from my lawful superiors."

"I suggest you consider that very carefully, Admiral." Gabriel Caddell-Markham's voice was considerably colder than Tsang's had been. "The confrontation between the League and the Star Empire has the potential to become the most disastrous collision in human history. It's the belief of the Beowulf government that the situation is being manipulated by forces inimical to both the League and the Star Empire and that we would be derelict in our duty—and our responsibility to the human race in general, not simply to the citizens of the Beowulf System—if we contributed to that disaster. We have no intention of doing so, and with all due deference to your understanding of the Constitution, it's *our* opinion that the federal government grossly overstepped its power by issuing your orders. There's been no declaration of war, and Article Five of the Constitution specifically denies the federal government authority to dictate to system governments in time of *peace*. As a consequence, the Beowulf System's government is under no requirement to assist you in this movement, and our personnel and citizens will *not* assist you.

"The Beowulf Terminus is administered and controlled by the Beowulf Terminus Corporation, a civilian corporation based in Beowulf, but the Terminus' actual sovereignty rests with Manticore, as its discoverer. Whether or not we would have the legal authority to allow you passage against Manticore's will, even if we wished to, is a question complex enough to keep battalions of lawyers busy for decades. But the bottom line is that neither we nor the BTC have any desire to assist you in this madness to begin with and that virtually all the personnel manning the traffic-control platforms on the terminus are Beowulfan citizens. *Solarian* citizens— civilians—over whom the Solarian military has no jurisdiction in time of peace. For that matter, the Solarian military has no jurisdiction over Solarian civilians even in time of *war* unless a legitimate declaration of martial law has first been issued. None has. Since that's the case, the Beowulf System Defense Force would be morally, legally, and constitutionally justified in protecting our citizens against illegal coercion by whatever means may be necessary. And in case I haven't been sufficiently clear, 'whatever means may be necessary' *does* include the use of deadly force."

"Mr. Director, are you actually threatening to fire on the *Solarian League Navy?*" Tsang demanded, brown eyes widening.

"I'm telling you as an official representative of the Beowulf Planetary Board of Directors that we will not assist you in making transit, that BTC's astro-control personnel will refuse your orders to do so, and that should you attempt to unlawfully coerce them into doing so, we will resist. If you persist despite that warning—if shots are fired and blood is spilled—it will be a consequence of the *unconstitutional* actions of the federal government, and Beowulf will not be responsible for the potential consequences for the League's stability which will undoubtedly follow. I don't know how I can be any clearer than that. And since I've been as clear as I know how to be, I see no point in continuing this conversation. Good day, Admiral."

The display blanked, and Tsang sat looking at it for several seconds, grappling with the fact that Caddell-Markham had literally hung up on a senior flag officer of the Solarian Navy. As far as she knew, nothing like that had ever happened in the SLN's entire previous seven and a half centuries.

Finally, she shook herself and looked up at the officer across the briefing room table. Admiral Pierre Takeuchi, Task Force 11.6's chief of staff, looked just as astonished as she was (and, she thought, even more outraged) by Caddell-Markham's peremptory departure.

"Are these people as crazy as those Manty lunatics?" Tsang demanded rhetorically. She shook her head. "Where the hell does a cabinet minister of any system government—and I don't care if it *is* a frigging Core World government—come off talking to the *federal government* that way?!"

"I don't know, but somebody clearly needs his ass kicked up between his ears, Ma'am!" Takeuchi replied harshly. "And, frankly, a part of me wishes his damn system-defense force really *would* try to stop us."

Tsang grunted in agreement, but her brain was busy with the potential ramifications. And with that secret clause of her orders. She hadn't liked it when she'd seen it, but she'd comforted herself that it was going to remain a moot point. Now it looked like it might not, and the potential consequences of the Beowulfers' position appalled her.

Her task force consisted of just over a hundred superdreadnoughts, accompanied by two dozen supply ships and transports and screened by twenty-five cruisers and forty destroyers. That was a hell of a lot more tonnage than she could possibly fit through the Beowulf Terminus in a simultaneous transit, but the ops plan called for her to provide additional reinforcements for the main body of Eleventh Fleet after the Manties' surrender. And it was also the next best thing to three times the total combat strength of the Beowulf System Defense Force's *thirty-six* superdreadnoughts. If the Beowulfers were stupid enough to provoke a shooting incident, it would be a very short and—from their perspective—very ugly affair.

That's probably what Crandall was thinking before Spindle, a corner of her brain suggested, but then she scowled.

Maybe so, she told that corner, *but Crandall was going up against Manties, and whatever new designs the* Manties *may've come up with, we* know *what Beowulf has. Oh, they might have a couple of little wrinkles we don't know about, but they sure as hell don't have the Manties' new damned designs! If they did, we'd know about it already.*

"They've got to be bluffing, Ma'am," Takeuchi said. "They can't *really* want to get thousands of their people killed just to protect a bunch of neobarbs against their fellow Solarians!"

"You're probably right," Tsang agreed. "At the same time, let's not let ourselves invest too much confidence in that theory."

"Are you—forgive me, Ma'am, but are you *serious?*" Takeuchi demanded, and she barked an unhappy laugh.

"I don't know," she admitted. "But this is *Beowulf*, Pierre. The rest of the League may see the Manties as neobarbs, but Beowulf's right on the other side of their Junction. Beowulfers have been marrying Manties for centuries, and they do one hell of a lot of business with each other. That's bound to shape how they see Manticore. Worse, they're probably the only people in the explored galaxy who're even more paranoid about Mesa than Manticore is! You know they've rejected Mesa's version of Green Pines, and from what Caddell-Markham just said, their government officially buys this Manty fantasy about some kind of plot coming out of Mesa. So, yeah, I think it *is* possible—remotely possible—they might order their wallers to fire on us if we try to carry out our orders."

"If you say so, Ma'am." It was obvious from Takeuchi's tone that he found it difficult to wrap his mind around the possibility that she might have a point. "If they do, though, what do *we* do?" he asked.

"Well," she said, thinking about that secret clause yet again . . . and of the catastrophic consequences to the career of any flag officer who failed to carry out Fleet Admiral Rajampet Rajani's orders at this juncture in the Solarian League Navy's history, "given the disparity in combat power between the task force and the BSDF, there's no way in hell they could actually stop us. They have to know that as well as we do. So if it looks like they're genuinely contemplating forcible resistance, we'll give them their choices: stand down or be fired upon. And if they choose not to stand down, then we *will* fire on them."

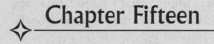

Chapter Fifteen

"YOU KNOW," ELIZABETH WINTON SAID conversationally, "just the other day I was saying to Willie, 'Willie,' I said, 'we need to get some regularization into this business of visiting heads of state.'" She shook her head. "Somehow I suspect we're still behind the curve on that."

"No! You think?" Honor replied with a grin.

She and the Empress stood watching a sting ship–escorted shuttle drop towards the Mount Royal Palace pad, and her smile faded as she brought up her artificial left eye's telescopic function and zoomed in on the shuttle's boldly emblazoned Bible and crossed swords. It was the first time that blazonry had ever been seen outside the Yeltsin System.

"Fair's fair," she said after a moment, turning back to Elizabeth. "At least *this* head of state didn't just turn up totally unannounced."

"Oh, heavens, no! Why, we had an entire day's notice!" The empress rolled her eyes, but then her tone turned more serious. "Actually, I really do wish all these high-powered visitors would give us at least a little more warning, if only for security reasons. I hate to think how Grayson would react if we let *anything* happen to Benjamin and his family, Honor!"

"I agree that would come under the heading of a really bad thing," Honor acknowledged. "Still, he obviously thought it was important for him to get here in person as quickly as possible. He must've put this together completely on the fly—I hate to think about the Keys' reaction to the very notion!—but even though he's enough of a schoolboy to enjoy teasing his security people, he knows how hard their job is. He's not going to run any unnecessary chances, especially with Katherine, Elaine, and three of the kids along. And let's face it, landing directly at Mount Royal is about the most secure thing he could do. He *knows* you have to've already ramped up Palace Security, when you've got Eloise Pritchart and her delegation as houseguests. And last but not least—"

She waved at the discreet weather domes which simultaneously protected the powerful weapon emplacements around the Winton family's official home from the elements and concealed them from the casual eye.

"Short of a planetary invasion, no one's likely to crash this particular party," she pointed out dryly.

"No," Elizabeth agreed, watching the shuttle settle the last few meters. "And if I were really worried, I wouldn't be standing here joking about it. But you do have to admit this is turning into the highest voltage summit meeting in the Star Kingdom's—much less the Star *Empire's*—history, and we're making the entire thing up as we go along. We heads of state really prefer to have some sort of an agenda *before* we sit down at the high-stakes table, you know. All bad novelists notwithstanding, surprise and improvisation are *not* the best basis for successful diplomacy!"

"Oh, trust me, I do know," Honor said. "Although organizationally speaking, at least, you've got it easier than *some* of the people involved, Elizabeth. Poor Arethea looks just about ready to drop!"

"I know!" Elizabeth chuckled, smiling fondly.

Dame Arethea Hart, Countess Middlehill, was Elizabeth's senior seneschal. As such, she was responsible for the planning and execution of all major state functions under Lord Chamberlain Jacob Wundt's general direction, and she'd taken on a distinctly harried look.

"I agree we're wearing her out," Elizabeth continued, "but she's having the time of her life, too, Honor. And now she gets to manage the Protector of Grayson's first ever extra-system state visit?" The two women looked at each other. "The only thing she's looking forward to more than this is Roger and Rivka's wedding, and you know it!"

"All right, I'll grant that. But I still say she looks worn to a frazzle."

Elizabeth started to respond, then stopped as the shuttle's hatch slid open.

The pad was surrounded by Palace Security and the Queen's Own Regiment of the Royal Manticoran Army. In addition, Grayson Palace Security and the Protector's Guard were heavily represented as well. The Grayson advance party, preceding Benjamin's shuttle by six hours, had linked up smoothly with Colonel Shemais' personnel. Now, as the hatch opened, a square-shouldered, weathered-looking major with graying red hair stepped out. He looked around quickly, taking in every detail of the security arrangements, then moved to one side and came to attention.

Benjamin Mayhew stepped past the major, followed by Katherine and Elaine Mayhew, and Elizabeth felt a sudden pang. It was only seven T-years since her state visit to Grayson, yet Benjamin was perceptibly grayer. He stood just as straight as she remembered, but there were more lines on his face, and she wondered if it was only her imagination that he moved a bit more slowly.

He's six years younger than I am, she thought. *Thirteen years younger than Honor. But he looks older than either of us.*

It was true. In fact, looking at Benjamin and Honor side by side, anyone from a pre-prolong society would have thought the age differential was reversed... and twice what it actually was.

For a moment, as she was brought face-to-face with the awareness that Benjamin Mayhew had never received prolong, she felt a presentiment of loss to come. The loss not simply of a valuable political ally, of a trusted military ally, but of someone who'd become a personal friend. Somehow, despite the regular messages they exchanged, despite the exchanged Christmas and birthday gifts, the personal recordings which had nothing at all to do with state occasions, her inner image of him hadn't really changed until she saw him here, on these familiar grounds, in person.

Oh, stop that! she told herself. *Yes, you're going to lose him... eventually. And you've always known— you've both always known—you were. But it's not going to happen tomorrow, and the last thing he needs—the last thing either of you need—is you getting all maudlin! Besides,* she glanced sideways, quickly, at Honor, *there are people who're going to miss him even more than you are when that finally happens*.

Honor seemed unaware of that quick scrutiny, although Elizabeth knew better.

"I think we should go meet our guests, Your Grace," she said.

"I think that's an excellent idea, Your Majesty," Honor agreed.

✧   ✧   ✧

"And just who's minding the store back home while you gallivant around the galaxy?" Elizabeth asked the better part of an hour later.

"Floyd has things under control, I'm sure," Benjamin replied, waving his iced-tea glass cheerfully. "I won't say he was delighted with my decision to go traipsing off, but the way I see it, it's good practice for him."

Elizabeth hadn't personally met Floyd Kellerman, the Chancellor of Grayson, but she'd exchanged quite a few messages with him, and William Alexander *had* met him. On that basis, she suspected Benjamin was rather understating Kellerman's reaction. The Protector had chosen him as chancellor because of his native ability, but he wasn't quite forty yet, and some of Grayson's more senior steadholders tried to bully him into doing things their way . . . especially if they thought Benjamin might not notice.

"Saying Floyd wasn't 'delighted' is something of an understatement, dear," Katherine Mayhew pointed out dryly, confirming Elizabeth's suspicions. "I think he was of the odd opinion that things like negotiating treaties with allies is the reason you have a foreign minister."

"Such a stodgy, conventional attitude." Benjamin shook his head mournfully. "Besides, Uriah's busy."

"Oh?" Elizabeth cocked her head. She *had* met Brother Uriah Madison, the Grayson priest Reverend Jeremiah Sullivan had personally recommended to Benjamin when Lord Berilynko, the previous foreign minister, retired, and she'd been impressed with him. "I wondered why you sent Michael to initial the draft agreements instead of Brother Madison. Is this one of those things another head of state can ask about, or should I remain tactfully incurious?"

"Actually," Benjamin said, "I sent Michael instead of Uriah for two reasons. One was that given the potential objections some of the more recalcitrant Keys are bound to nurse about concluding peace with someone we've been fighting for so long, I wanted a Mayhew personally involved in the treaty process. We're still a very traditional people, Elizabeth, and the Mayhew name carries weight. With Mike's signature on the treaty, it's going to take a particularly hardy steadholder to oppose ratification."

"I can see that." Elizabeth nodded. The Winton Dynasty had been known to use family members as plenipotentiaries for much the same reasons. For that matter, that was precisely what she'd done, in a way, by sending Honor to negotiate with Haven.

"And, secondly," Benjamin continued, "given the, um, *rapidity* with which events seem to be moving, I needed Uriah to talk to someone else." His eyes met Elizabeth's. "From a few 'purely exploratory' feelers which have been extended my way, I think Walter Imbessi might like to mend some fences. And since we appear to be in the process of fence-mending in general, I thought it might not be a bad idea to see just what he had in mind." He smiled faintly. "Which, of course, puts everyone involved in what I suppose we might call a delicate position."

"I can see where you could put it that way," Elizabeth said dryly.

She sat back, frowning thoughtfully while she considered her response. Walter Imbesi was not, to put it mildly, universally beloved in the Star Empire, given his role in the Republic of Erewhon's withdrawal from the Manticoran Alliance. Not to mention the mutual-defense treaty Erewhon had then signed with the Republic of Haven...just in time for the war between Manticore and Haven to start up again. No Manticoran (including Elizabeth Winton) doubted that the technical exchanges which had accompanied that defense treaty explained quite a bit of Haven's technological improvements since the shooting had resumed, which was the reason Manticore had hammered the Erewhonese with massive trade penalties. At the same time, the Star Empire *had* permitted Erewhon (which had declared neutrality during the current hostilities, since Haven had reinitiated them without being attacked first) to continue using the Junction and even trading with the Star Empire itself.

Which, she admitted, *was mainly to keep the door open a crack. A point of which anyone as sharp as Imbesi has to've been aware.*

"So, you really think he wants to—how did you put it?—'mend fences'?" she asked.

"I think he never really wanted them in such disrepair in the first place, actually." Mayhew's tone was serious. "Let's face it, Elizabeth. From Erewhon's perspective, and especially without knowing hostilities were about to resume..."

He shrugged, and Elizabeth nodded.

"I know." She sighed. "I never blamed Erewhon as much as a lot of other Manticorans did. It was High Ridge's fault, and I know you were warning Descroix the whole time about where their so-called foreign policy was leading. So was *I*, for that matter! I even know Imbesi was pissed off as hell when Pritchart went back to shooting at us. That still isn't going to make it easy for Erewhon and the Star Empire to do some kind of sweetness-and-light kiss-and-make-up!"

"Granted. And unless I'm mistaken, that's not what Imbesi has in mind, exactly, either."

"No?" She raised an eyebrow. "Then what does he have in mind?"

"Obviously, there wasn't much time for back-and-forth exchanges before I climbed aboard ship to come visit you," Benjamin pointed out. "You, know Havlicek, Hall, and Fuentes have been using Imbesi as their theoretically unofficial point man with both Haven and Congo, though. My impression is that someone in Haven—or possibly Congo—dropped a partial summary of what Captain Zilwicki and Agent Cachat brought back from Mesa on their friends in Maytag, and I think the Triumvirate's concluded that this corner of the galaxy's about to get a lot lonelier and more dangerous. They don't want to be caught out in the cold, so they've reached for their 'unofficial' go-to guy to do something about that."

"I said I don't blame them as much as a lot of Manticorans do. That doesn't mean I'm feeling especially *fond* of them. On a personal level, at least, the thought of their catching a chill doesn't exactly break my heart."

"Trust me, the same thought crossed *my* mind." Benjamin smiled thinly. As Manticore's major military ally, the Grayson Space Navy had taken its own losses at the hands of improved Havenite combat capabilities. "As you say, though, that was on a *personal* level."

"I know." Elizabeth grimaced. "And we've had our own unofficial interface with them through Congo and Torch all along. It's not as if we don't have any common ground anymore. That's why I proposed Torch as the site for that summit meeting Eloise and I were going to have before the assassination attempt. For that matter, Erewhon's backing for Torch is bound to attract this Alignment's attention in its direction, isn't it?"

"True. And then"—Benjamin glanced casually around, as if reassuring himself even here that no one but Katherine was close enough to overhear them—"there's Smoking Frog."

Elizabeth looked at him for a moment, then nodded.

"Point taken," she said quietly. "And I won't pretend I wouldn't like . . . a little more insight into Barregos' plans, let's say. Not to mention the fact that an, ah, *understanding* with the Maya Sector would do quite a bit for our own security on that flank. For that matter, Maya has to be even higher on Mesa's list than Erewhon, after the Battle of Congo!"

"Exactly what I was thinking. And I don't doubt Imbesi's thinking the same way. Among other things, the man's almost terminally pragmatic. He'd have to see the possibility of brokering a relationship between us and Maya as a way of getting back onto acceptable terms with all of us."

Benjamin had that right, Elizabeth reflected. When

it came down to it, no one in the galaxy was more pragmatic than the Erewhonese. Except, of course, that all the pragmatism in the universe didn't change that inflexible Erewhonese view that a deal was a deal—the very attitude which had led to so much anger on Erewhon's part when the High Ridge Government chose to effectively ignore its responsibilities to its allies.

"When they sign on, they do have a tendency to stay signed, don't they?" she said, and Benjamin nodded.

"More than some star nations I could mention, anyway," he said. "Speaking of which, how are the Andermani taking all of this?"

Elizabeth gave him a pained look.

"That wasn't the most diplomatic segue in the history of statesmanship, Benjamin."

"That's the sort of thing I keep professionals like Uriah around for," he replied. "And you'll notice I'm asking you personally, not any members of the formal diplomatic corps."

"Yes, I did notice." She eyed him repressively for another second or two, then smiled crookedly. "Obviously I haven't had time for a formal exchange of views with Gustav, but judging from his ambassador's reaction and that of the Andermani officers still attached to Eighth Fleet, I think he's a lot less likely to bolt the Alliance than he would have been before we told him about this killer nanotech. All our analyses of New Potsdam's internal dynamic suggest Prince Huang and Herzog von Rabenstrange have been the closest thing the Andermani court has to Manticoran partisans. In Huang's case it was always a more pragmatic and tactical stance than any great love for us, of course. In fact, I'm inclined to think it was more the intensity of his abolitionist leanings than his pro-Manticore tendencies that got him onto the Mesan hit list. Still, I doubt the notion that Mesa tried to kill him—and did manage to kill his younger son—is going to make him any *less* pro-Ballroom! And while Gustav's never been as intensely opposed to genetic slavery as Huang, he's not the sort to take kindly to the murder of his nephew, either."

"None of which is to say our pragmatic friends are going to be eager to stand up to the Solarian juggernaut with us, no matter how pissed off they may be at Mesa," Benjamin observed.

"No," Elizabeth agreed, and smiled very coldly. "But if this Filareta gets hammered, someone like Gustav's going to be thinking about the desirability of being on the winning side. Personally, I've never really had any imperial ambitions. In fact, I'd just as soon never have embarked on something that's almost certain to change the entire character of the Old Star Kingdom the way this sudden expansion is going to. But I'm not a descendant of Gustav Anderman, either, and the Andermani *do* think in imperial terms."

"I know," Benjamin said soberly. "That's why I have to wonder how Gustav's going to feel about finding himself squeezed between the Star Empire's lobes in Silesia and the Talbott Quadrant."

"Hopefully, that's not going to be an issue anytime soon. Not that it isn't damned well going to become one *sometime*." Elizabeth sighed. "I'd really like things to be simple and straightforward without automatically involving all sorts of future repercussions. Just once, at least."

"Would be nice, wouldn't it?" Benjamin grinned and

shook his head. "Not going to happen, though. Trust me. You young whippersnapper monarchy-come-latelies have no idea! Four and a half centuries—ha!" He snapped his fingers. "Wait until you've been around for a *thousand* T-years, like us Mayhews. You'll be *amazed* by all the chances you'll have had to screw up by forgetting about those 'future repercussions' at inconvenient moments!"

✧ Chapter Sixteen

"INCOMING MESSAGE FROM ADMIRAL TRUMAN, Your Grace!" Lieutenant Commander Harper Brantley announced.

"Throw it on Display Two," Honor said without ever taking her eyes from the main plot.

Nimitz pressed his nose against her cheek with a confident, buzzing purr, but the icons on that plot were getting decidedly complicated. Her Ghost Rider platforms updated the data on the intruding Solarian fleet, and she frowned at the hurricane of MDMs which had erupted from Eighth Fleet's missile pods eighteen seconds ago. The massive salvo streaked towards the glaring red codes of the enemy, and her frown deepened as Admiral Filareta's ships spawned an answering cloud of tiny ruby chips.

"Yes, Alice?" she said as Truman's larger-than-life, golden-haired image appeared on the display which had just opened in the plot's upper quadrant.

"My advanced LACs and the recon platforms all confirm the bastards are towing *pods*, Honor," she said without preamble, her expression somewhere between irritated, exasperated, and just plain pissed off.

"Yes, CIC just put them up on the plot." Honor's tone was considerably calmer than Truman's. "And they just launched from them," she continued. "Which I doubt they'd be doing at twenty million kilometers if they didn't have the range for it."

"Enemy launch at one-point-three light-minutes!" Captain Andrea Jaruwalski, Honor's operations officer, reported crisply, as if to confirm Honor's statement. Jaruwalski was looking at her own displays. "Acceleration approximately forty-eight thousand KPS, Your Grace. Assuming constant acceleration, time of flight is five-point-two minutes. CIC makes their closing velocity at the inner defense perimeter approximately point-four-niner cee!"

That was actually a bit better—about 2,000 KPS better, in fact—than the RMN's own Mark 23 could do, Honor reflected. Obviously, the same thought had occurred to Truman, as well.

"Damn it, that's ridiculous!" the other admiral snapped.

"Which doesn't mean it isn't happening," Honor pointed out.

"But—" Truman stopped herself, then gave her head a shake.

"Point taken," she conceded more calmly.

Honor smiled, but it was a thin smile, and her eyes had already moved back to the plot. Five minutes wasn't much time to be making changes, yet if the Sollies' missile acceleration exceeded projections by this much, there was no telling how much better their targeting systems and penaids might be as well.

I think "a lot" is probably a pretty fair estimate, she thought tartly. *Which suggests—*

"It looks like we're going to have leakers, Andrea. Get the Loreleis deployed. It seems we're going to find out how well they work after all."

"Deploying Lorelei, aye, Your Grace!"

"As soon as you've done that, go to Tango-Two."

"Tango-Two, aye," Jaruwalski acknowledged, and Honor turned back to Truman.

"Alice, push your perimeter squadrons out on the threat axis."

"How far out do you want them?"

"As far as you can get them." Honor smiled crookedly. "One way or the other, this isn't going to last long, so you're not going to get them as far out as either of us would like. Choose your own deployment package."

"Consider it done."

Truman disappeared from the display, and Honor turned to Commodore Mercedes Brigham.

"Alice's LACs will give the defense zone a little depth, but there's a pretty good chance we're still going to get hammered. Get on the horn. Request release of the system-defense pods." She showed her teeth. "We may just need a bigger hammer of our own."

"Yes, Your Grace!" her chief of staff acknowledged, and Honor turned to the display tied permanently to HMS *Imperator*'s command deck.

"I assume you heard all that, Rafe?"

"Yes, Your Grace," Captain Rafael Cardones replied.

"We can hope the Loreleis will take at least some of the sting out, but I'm afraid your damage-control parties are about to get busy." Cardones nodded quickly, and she shrugged. "Fight your ship, Rafe."

"Yes, Your Grace."

Honor returned her attention to the master plot.

At such ranges, even MDMs seemed to crawl, but the Solarian fire swept remorselessly towards Eighth Fleet, and there was a *lot* of it—at least three times ONI's estimate of Filareta's firepower. The LACs assigned to the fleet's perimeter accelerated to meet that incoming tide, adjusting their own formation as they went, and the Grayson-designed *Katanas*, with their potent missile armaments and heavy loads of Viper missiles, led.

Manticoran doctrine had hardened in favor of using LACs as the wall of battle's primary screen. They were strictly sublight, but that wasn't a significant factor inside a star's hyper limit, and very few engagements took place *outside* a hyper limit. And while even a Manticoran LAC had far less long-range offensive firepower than, say, a *Roland*, the *Katanas*, especially, had nearly as much anti-missile capability. They couldn't take as much damage, but the laser heads carried by multidrive missiles made that pretty much a moot point. Destroyers couldn't survive more than a hit or two from weapons that powerful, either, and they were far easier to hit in the first place than something as agile as a LAC.

While Truman's bantamweights headed out, the rest of Eighth Fleet turned away and began to shift into Formation Tango-Two. No one on Honor's staff had really anticipated Solarian MDMs or such a heavy weight of fire, but the RMN believed in being prepared. That was why she and her task-force and task-group commanders had brainstormed situations very like this one in their planning sessions. And, after analyzing the tactical data from every engagement against the Republic of Haven and interpolating the data from Michelle Henke's engagements in the Talbott Quadrant, Honor and her staff had evolved a new defensive doctrine.

Traditional missile defense wove every platform into a single, tight-knit pattern designed to bring every defensive system to bear on the threat axis. In order to focus that concentration of defensive fire, the units of a task force or fleet maintained a close, unflinching formation with every squadron meticulously slotted into the most advantageous position. That sort of precision maneuvering even in the heart of furious combat required highly experienced, steel-nerved personnel, and it had been a hallmark of the Royal Manticoran Navy for generations.

But the massive weight of pod-launched MDM salvos placed unprecedented strains on that doctrine. When the threat was measured in tens of thousands of laser heads, instead of scores or hundreds, not even the most precise stationkeeping was enough to stave off disaster. As the threat grew progressively worse, Manticore had countered by increasing the density, power, and accuracy of its anti-missile armaments, yet many of the RMN's tacticians had come to the conclusion that, absent some significant improvement in the available defensive systems, simply packing in more point defense clusters and counter-missile tubes had reached a point of diminishing returns.

Honor was one of the tacticians who suspected that was the case. She had cautiously optimistic hopes for the new Lorelei platforms, which represented an entirely new generation of highly capable decoys, and she'd strongly supported the decision to massively upgrade the Keyhole platforms' defensive armament. Despite that, she'd been forced to the conclusion that the Navy owed its survival to date at least as much to the inherent inaccuracy of extremely long-range missile fire as to any improvements in its defenses. Worse, it had never been anything more than a matter of time before someone as inventive as the Republic of Haven's navy had become under Thomas Theisman and Shannon Foraker managed to duplicate—or at least approximate—Apollo's long-range accuracy. At which point, things were going to get ugly.

Ultimately, if ships-of-the-wall weren't going to become simply very expensive target drones, they needed to begin intercepting missiles farther out, expand the fleet's active interception envelope beyond the roughly 3.6 million-kilometer reach of the current Mark 31 counter-missile. The problem was how to accomplish that. Pushing the perimeter LACS farther out, getting those screening platforms deeper into the threat zone, was one approach, but what Honor really wanted was an organic capability for the wallers to extend their *own* intercept range. She and her staff had a few thoughts on how that might be accomplished, and she knew Sonja Hemphill was looking at the question as well, but for now, she had to fight with what she had, not what she'd *like* to have, which was why Eighth Fleet's formation wasn't quite what The Book envisioned.

Given the nature of the threat and the expansion of each ship's defensive field of fire courtesy of Keyhole, she'd decided to *loosen* Eighth Fleet's formation rather than seeking to tighten it still further. Since her Keyhole-equipped units had more "reach" than they'd ever had before, she'd reasoned, they could target threats across a greater volume, provide mutual support without maintaining such close, rigid station on one another. There were trade-offs, of course—there always were—and the greater distance between subunits inevitably decreased the accuracy of the support they could offer one another. But what they lost in pinpoint precision they got back (hopefully) by broadening and deepening the total defensive basket. Each defensive shot had an individually lower probability of a kill, but there were more *of* them, and allowing squadrons to maneuver more independently also permitted their individual units to interpose their impeller wedges against incoming fire most effectively and with far less risk of the accidental wedge-on-wedge fratricide that would destroy the most powerful superdreadnought.

Andrea Jaruwalski and the rest of Eighth Fleet's operations and tactical officers had spent hours tweaking both software and doctrine to put it all together. Honor was delighted by how well they'd run with her concepts, and they'd come up with a few wrinkles all their own. At Jaruwalski's suggestion, for example, they'd detached half of Eighth Fleet's total LAC strength from the perimeter force and tasked the reassigned groups to operate not between the wall and the threat but *inside* the wall, maneuvering in close coordination with individually assigned squadrons of capital ships to cover the expanded gaps between those squadrons.

Well, that's the theory, *anyway*, Honor thought now, reaching up to stroke Nimitz's ears while she watched the plot.

"Lorelei platforms active, Your Grace," Jaruwalski reported.

"Thank you," Honor replied as scores of small blue starbursts suddenly spangled the plot. Lorelei was the latest addition to the Ghost Rider stable...the last one the R&D staff on HMSS *Weyland* had produced before the space station's destruction. Given how recently it had gone into production (and how quickly destruction of the production lines had followed), the RMN had a lot fewer of the new platforms than anyone would have liked, and she hated the thought of expending so many of them.

You'd hate expending your wallers even worse, Honor, she told herself tartly. *Of course, if they don't work the way we expect them to, you may just have expended* both *of them. Wouldn't* that *be fun?*

Her lips twitched ever so slightly, but her eyes were intent. She'd launched her own shipkillers first. That meant her massive attack was going to reach its target fifteen seconds before Filareta's reached her, despite the Solarian missiles' unanticipated performance. Unfortunately, the Solarians, without Apollo, would have cut their telemetry links long before that, and their missiles would follow their seekers into the targets they'd been ordered to attack, whatever had happened to the humans who'd given those orders. If they lost lock on *those* targets, they'd be forced to quest around for replacements on their own, strictly limited initiative, but either way, they'd already have switched to autonomous mode, and not even the total destruction of the ships which had launched them would make any difference at all.

Which wasn't the case for *her* missiles.

"Enemy ECM is within projections, Your Grace," Jaruwalski reported, monitoring the FTL telemetry coming back from the Mark 23-E control missiles which were the heart of the Apollo system. "Halo platforms are active, and from the density of their counter-missile targeting systems, CIC estimates they may have fewer Aegis upgrades than we'd anticipated."

"Nice to find out we got *something* right, Your Grace," Brigham muttered, and Honor snorted.

"Now, Mercedes! You don't really think this is *ONI*'s fault, do you?"

Brigham's answering snort was considerably more sour than Honor's had been, but she nodded.

"Looks like they've done some Halo tweaking," Jaruwalski continued, "but the filter upgrades seem to be coping."

Honor nodded. Michelle Henke had sent back working examples of Halo EW platforms from Sandra Crandall's surrendered ships, and Solarian security protocols left a bit to be desired. BuWeaps had been able to analyze them literally down to the molecular level, and Sonja Hemphill's people had not been impressed.

From a manufacturing standard, the decoys were as good as anything Manticore could have produced, but they'd never been designed to confront this sort of threat environment. They'd been designed to face a *Solarian*-style missile threat—one with single-drive missiles, less capable sensors, and enormously less capable fire control, and one without the massive density of pod-launched salvos. They were also range-limited, because they had to stay close enough to their motherships to receive broadcast power. And the same restriction also meant they could operate only in the plane of those ships' own fields of fire, since no broadcast power transmission could be driven through an impeller wedge.

Within those limitations, they were actually a well-thought-out, workmanlike proposition. Which, unfortunately for the Solarian League Navy, was nowhere near good enough.

The same thing was true of the Aegis program, the SLN's effort to thicken its counter-missile launchers. Within the limitations of the missile threat its designers had visualized, Aegis represented a significant upgrade by increasing the number of CMs its wall could control. In an MDM-dominated environment, however, all Aegis actually accomplished was to increase the density of its defensive fire from total futility to something which was merely hopelessly inadequate.

And then there were Ghost Rider and Apollo.

"Estimate twenty seconds to their missile defense perimeter, Your Grace," Jaruwalski said. "Attack profile EW coming up in fifteen seconds. Ten. Five . . . four . . . three . . . two . . . one . . . *now*."

Eighth Fleet's missiles—13.2 million kilometers downrange and traveling at .36 c—were still 9.8 million kilometers short of their targets, but the maximum powered endurance of Solarian counter-missiles was just under 1.8 million kilometers before their overpowered drives burned out and the impeller wedges they used to "sweep up" incoming missiles disappeared. Given the attack's geometry, that worked out to a range at launch of 9.2 million kilometers . . . which the still-accelerating Manticoran MDM would reach in approximately another five seconds.

Which was why the electronic warfare platforms seeded thoughout that massive salvo had come online now.

The Solarian missile defense officers had been

tracking the incoming tide of destruction, allocating their counter-missiles, refining their tracking data, for the better part of four full minutes. At their velocity, the MDMs would cross the entire counter-missile engagement zone in barely twelve seconds, which meant there would be no time for a second wave of CMs. Aware that one launch was all they were going to get, the SLN officers were totally focused on making it as effective as possible.

Then the Dazzler platforms suddenly activated, radiating huge, blinding spikes of jamming. Tracking systems shuddered in electronic shock under the brutal assault, and the humans and computers behind those tracking systems were just as shocked. They did their best, but they had only sixty seconds in which to react, and at the same moment, the Dragon's Teeth came online as well, radiating hundreds—*thousands*—of false targets.

Given more time, the defenders might have differentiated between the true threats and the counterfeits. Or if their targeting systems hadn't been driven back in confusion by the Dazzlers, they might have been able to keep track of the genuine shipkillers they'd already identified, ignore the masqueraders. But they *had* no more time, and their targeting systems *had* been driven back in confusion.

A defense which would have been grossly inadequate under the best of circumstances had just become irrelevant, instead.

Eighth Fleet's MDMs ripped through the pathetic scatter of counter-missiles and smashed into the final, desperate inner perimeter of laser clusters at forty-nine percent of the speed of light, and those laser clusters' fire control was just as confused, just as befuddled, as the CMs had been. The Solarians managed to stop perhaps two percent of the incoming fire; all the rest of the shipkillers reached attack range, under the direction of Mark 23-Es' AIs with complete updates from the ships which had launched them which were barely five seconds old.

The crimson icons didn't vanish from Honor's plot with anything so gentle as "metronome precision." No, they disappeared—completely blotted away as the ships they represented were ripped to pieces or transformed into the purple icons of broken, technically still intact wrecks—in one cataclysmic instant. Their killers were upon them, then through them, in less time than it would have taken to cough twice. The Ghost Rider recon platforms brought the hideous wash of detonating laser heads, the seemingly solid carpet of nuclear fire, to HMS *Imperator*'s visual displays with dreadful clarity and at faster-than-light speeds, but no merely human brain could possibly have sorted out the details.

Honor had almost ten seconds to absorb the destruction of the Solarian fleet . . . and then those slaughtered superdreadnoughts' fire crashed into her own command.

There were almost as many missiles in the Solarian launch as there'd been in Eighth Fleet's, and their closing velocity was actually a bit higher. Yet there was no comparison between the outcomes of the two attacks.

Alice Truman's perimeter LACs met the incoming salvo first. The *Katanas*' rotary launchers punched out Viper missiles at maximum-rate fire, and the Vipers (with exactly the same drive and oversized wedge as the Mark 31) ripped holes in the wave of Solarian shipkillers.

Some of those shipkillers locked on to LACs (or tried to, at any rate) when the LACs' impeller signatures blocked their lines of sight to their original targets. At their enormous velocity, their new victims had only seconds to defend themselves, and point defense clusters spat coherent light with frantic speed. Fortunately for the *Katanas* and *Shrikes*, current-generation Manticoran and Grayson LACs were extraordinarily difficult targets, and "only" sixty-three were destroyed. Their surviving consorts spun, yawing through a hundred and eighty degrees to bring their laser clusters and the *Shrikes'* energy armaments to bear. Anti-ship missiles' terminal attack maneuvers were designed to use their wedges to protect them from their targets' energy weapons as they scorched in on their final attack runs. The SLN had given virtually no thought to evading fire coming from *astern*, however, and in the handful of seconds before they swept out of the LACs' range, another thousand shipkillers were blown out of space.

The survivors burst past the light attack craft, roaring down on the ships-of-the-wall they'd come to kill, but the majority had lost sight—briefly, at least—of Eighth Fleet's wallers. They still knew where to look to reacquire their targets, of course. Unfortunately, when they did, there were far too *many* of those targets.

Conceptually, Lorelei was light-years beyond Halo. Powered with the same onboard fusion technology the RMN had developed for Ghost Rider, the Mark 23, and the Mark 16, the Lorelei platforms had independent energy budgets beyond the dreams of any Solarian designer. They needed no line of sight for broadcast power to drive their powerful EW systems, and their onboard AI was even better than the Mark 23-E's.

Halo provided false targets to confuse an incoming missile, but those lures had to be relatively close to the missile's actual target, and even with broadcast power available, Halo's false targets were significantly weaker—dimmer—than a ship-of-the-wall's actual emissions.

Lorelei didn't need to be in close proximity to anyone, and its emitters were much more powerful than Halo's. The false targets Lorelei generated were still far weaker than those of genuine superdreadnoughts, but they could be interposed *between* those superdreadnoughts and the threat. More, they could be physically separated from the ships they were trying to protect . . . and the signatures they generated had been artfully camouflaged. Yes, they were weaker and dimmer than a true starship might have produced, but what they looked like was an all-up starship using its own EW systems to *make* its signature as weak and dim as possible.

And, as a final touch, over a third of Andrea Jaruwalski's Loreleis had been deployed to keep formation on one another as complete, false squadrons of ships-of-the-wall. Squadrons which maneuvered in perfect synchronization with Eighth Fleet's *real* squadrons but lay on the threat axis, deliberately exposed to the incoming tsunami of Solarian missiles.

Those missiles took the targets they'd been offered.

Not *all* of them were spoofed. Not even Lorelei was *that* good. But where multiple thousands of Manticoran laser heads had ravaged Filareta's fleet, no more than seven hundred actually reached Honor's, and they were no match for the defensive fire of her dispersed squadrons and their attached close-defense LACs. Seventeen of her superdreadnoughts took hits; only two took significant damage.

Honor looked at the main plot's damage sidebar and felt her eyebrows rise. When she'd seen the initial acceleration rates on the Solarian missiles, she'd anticipated severe losses of her own. Instead—

"Simulation concluded," a voice announced, and the displays froze. "I can see we're going to have to go back to the drawing board to make you people work for it, Your Grace."

"Thank you, Captain Emerson," she said to the smiling senior-grade captain whose image had just replaced her "tactical plot." She nodded to him, then looked at her staff.

"Good work, people," she told them. "That was *solid*. Dinner at Harrington House tonight, down on the beach. The beer's on me; the surf forecast looks good; my dad's already basting the barbecue; and Mac's got something special planned for desert. So don't be late—and bring friends, if you've got them!"

"All right!" Brigham responded, and Honor smiled as the others whistled and applauded enthusiastically.

"I hope it doesn't take you very long to touch up those scuff marks on your paintwork," another, closer voice said dryly under cover of the staffers' obvious pleasure.

"Oh, I think we can probably manage our repairs fairly promptly," she replied, still smiling as she turned to face Thomas Theisman.

The two of them stood in the Advanced Tactical

Course Center's main tactical simulator. It was far from Honor's first visit—she'd commanded ATC after her return from Cerberus—but Theisman had been obviously impressed by the facility even before the simulation had begun. Now he looked around the enormous room and shook his head.

"That was scary," he admitted frankly, turning back to Honor. "I knew we were screwed as soon as you people got Apollo deployed, but I genuinely hadn't realized how *badly* screwed we'd have been if you hadn't convinced the Empress to negotiate with us."

"I was scarcely the only one who 'convinced' Elizabeth, Tom. And by now you realize as well as I do that however good she may be at holding grudges, she really doesn't like killing people."

"Neither do I." Theisman's tone was light, and he grinned, but Honor tasted the emotions behind his words and realized yet again why Nimitz had assigned Thomas Theisman the name "Dreams of Peace."

"Neither do I," he repeated, "and I especially don't like killing my own people by sending them out to face that kind of combat differential. So if it's all the same to you, I'm just *delighted* I'm not going to be doing that again anytime soon."

She nodded, and the two of them started across the huge room towards the exit while Brigham oversaw the simulation's formal shutdown.

"Did you know they were going to throw MDMs at you?" Theisman asked, and she shook her head.

"No, somehow that managed to slip Captain Emerson's mind when he was describing the mission parameters," she said dryly.

"I suspected that might've been the case, given

Admiral Truman's reaction," Theisman said, and she chuckled.

"I'm not certain, but I suspect that that particular wrinkle may have come from a suggestion on the part of my beloved husband."

"Having faced your 'beloved husband,' I can believe that." Theisman's voice was equally dry. "Both of you always did have that nasty tendency to think outside the box."

"We weren't the only ones." Honor gave him a level look. "Once you got rid of Saint-Just and State Security, you turned up a *bunch* of capable COs. In some ways, though, I'd really never realized just how good you were until we finally got a look at just how *bad* the Sollies are!"

"Please!" Theisman grimaced in mock pain. "I'd like to think you could find someone better than *that* to compare us to!"

Honor chuckled again and Nimitz bleeked a laugh as they stepped through the exit. Spencer Hawke, Clifford McGraw, and Joshua Atkins fell in behind them, and Waldemar Tümmel, who'd been promoted to lieutenant commander following their return from Nouveau Paris, had been waiting with her personal armsmen. She smiled at him, and he smiled back, although the dark memory of the parents, brother, and sister he'd lost with *Hephaestus* was still there, behind the smile.

"How far ahead of schedule are we, Waldemar?" she asked.

"Almost an hour, Your Grace," the flag lieutenant who was no longer a lieutenant replied, and his smile got a bit broader. "I don't think the umpires expected you to polish them off quite that quickly."

"Well, let's not get too carried away patting ourselves on the back," she said. She was speaking to Tümmel, but she met Theisman's eyes as she spoke. "All something like this can really tell us is how well we're likely to perform against the threats we think we know about, and Filareta seems to be several cuts above the Sollies we've seen in Talbott. If it turns out someone with a working brain has something we *didn't* know about..."

The Havenite nodded soberly. They'd both had enough unpleasant experience with that sort of discovery.

Honor nodded back. She'd always liked Theisman, and the better she got to know him, the more strongly he reminded her of Alistair McKeon. Although—her lips twitched in a faint, fond smile of memory—he was *definitely* less inclined than Alistair had been to simply head for the nearest enemy and start slugging.

Ever since Beowulf's initial warning, however, Honor had studied everything Pat Givens' ONI had on Massimo Filareta, and Theisman had joined the effort from the moment Pritchart and her delegation arrived. Admittedly, Haven hadn't had a lot to add to ONI's meager bio on Filareta, but there'd been enough for her to be cautiously confident that she and Theisman had a feel for his basic personality. He was clearly very different from the late Sandra Crandall, and he had her horrible example to make him even less like her. Whatever the rest of the Solarian League Navy might think, Filareta was unlikely to reject reports of Manticoran technological superiority out of hand. Perhaps he might have, once, but despite some hints in ONI's dossier about objectionable personal habits, he was obviously too smart to do that after the Battle of Spindle.

"I take your point," Theisman said. "That's one reason I'm so happy—now, at any rate—to see you people base your training on the assumption that the other side's better than it really is."

"If you don't push your own systems and doctrine to the max, all you're doing is practicing things you already know how to do." Honor shrugged. "And that's the best-case scenario. The *worst*-case scenario is that you get fat, happy, and dumb. If I had a dollar for every spacer some stupid, overconfident flag officer's gotten killed—"

She cut herself short, and Theisman nodded again.

"Been there, seen that," he agreed.

They were silent for a moment as they continued down a hallway towards the lifts. Then Theisman gave himself a little shake.

"I have to say the look inside your hardware's been even more fascinating than watching the way you set up simulations," he said. "We've never had the opportunity to examine Apollo, of course, and I'm afraid your security arrangements have worked a lot better in general than we really would've preferred. Shannon's been especially frustrated. We've managed to recover enough to give us a leg up in quite a few areas, but they've mainly been matters of gross engineering."

Honor nodded. Like every other navy, the Royal Manticoran Navy routinely incorporated security protocols into its sensitive technology. There wasn't a lot they could do to disguise things like mini-fusion plants or improvements in laser-head grav lenses, but computers and molecular circuitry were another matter. Without the proper authorization codes, efforts to access, study, or analyze those triggered nanotech security protocols that reconfigured them into so much useless, inert junk. Trying to find ways to crack, spoof, acquire, or otherwise evade those codes was part of the never-ending cycle of cyber warfare, and she'd been pleased by the confirmation that Manticore had stayed in front of Haven in that contest.

"To be honest," Theisman continued, "the most useful things we recovered right after Thunderbolt were some of your tech manuals." He did not, Honor noted, mention the fact that far more tech manuals had come into Havenite hands from their Erewhonese allies *before* Thunderbolt. Tactful of him. "But those weren't much help when your new-generation technology started coming online, and by then, you were the ones capturing most of the tech that got captured, anyway. All of which"—he turned his head to look at her sharply—"is my way of segueing tactfully into the question of shared hardware."

"You know my position, Tom," Honor replied. "That's Elizabeth and Hamish's position, too, and as nearly as I can tell, Sonja Hemphill's firmly on board, as well. So there's no doubt in my mind that it's going to happen. The question is how soon, and I think that's going to depend on how soon we get formal ratification of the treaties."

She looked at him as sharply as he'd looked at her, and he shrugged.

"You've seen the political calculus back in Nouveau Paris, Honor," he said. "I don't even want to *think* about how Younger and McGwire must've reacted when the draft terms got home and they found out where their President and two thirds of Capital Fleet had wandered off to!" He shook his head. "I'm sure a lot of Eloise's political opponents must be screaming bloody murder about now, and I imagine Tullingham and Younger are making all kinds of veiled—or not so veiled—comments about people exceeding their constitutional authority. But the truth is that she *isn't* exceeding her authority, and your own diplomatic mission had significantly changed public opinion even before the Yawata strike and Simões."

"Really?" she raised an eyebrow as they reached the lifts, and Theisman chuckled.

"Most Havenites, whether they'd admit it or not, have always felt a sneaking admiration for you. Even when that pyschopath Ransom was in charge of Pierre's propaganda. Of course, there was a lot of 'bogeyman' about it, too. You had this really irritating habit of kicking the shit out of us."

"I never—"

Honor broke off, unsure how to respond, and he laughed out loud.

"I didn't say you were the only Manty who managed that. You were just the most . . . noticeable. Let's face it, even the Sollies figured you made good copy, and it didn't hurt that you were reasonably photogenic, unlike your humble servant."

"Yeah, sure!" She rolled her eyes.

"I did compare you to *me*," he pointed out. Then his smile faded.

"But all joking aside, you had a pretty damned towering reputation in the Republic, and a big part of that was the fact that you were an honorable enemy. That's the real reason StateSec and Public Information went to such lengths to blacken your name when they decided to hang you."

His smile vanished, and she tasted the bleakness of remembered shame as he relived his own helplessness in the face of Cordelia Ransom's determination to have Honor judicially murdered.

"Anyway"—he twitched his shoulders—"you were already pretty visible, let's say, in the Republic even before they gave you Eighth Fleet and turned you loose on our rear areas. And then there was that little business of the Battle of Manticore. For better or worse, you'd become the personification of the Star Kingdom as far as our public opinion was concerned.

"Then you turned up in Haven itself. Not to attack the system when everyone knew you could've trashed it. No, you were there to negotiate a *peace settlement* . . . and since we got rid of Saint-Just, we've never tried to deny our people access to the Star Empire's news services. It didn't take long for most people to figure out you were there to do the negotiating because you *wanted* to be there. It was your own idea."

The two of them stepped into the lift, followed by Tümmel and Honor's armsmen, and the door closed behind them.

"I doubt you have any idea, even now, how much goodwill you've built up for yourself," Theisman said very seriously. "Trust me, though: there's a lot of it. And, frankly, Eloise's notion of proposing an actual military alliance, not just a peace treaty, was a stroke of genius." He shook his head. "Talk about resolving the 'reparations issue'! And it gets her—and all of us—out from under the stigma of caving in. Even under the most magnanimous terms you could've offered before the Yawata strike, we'd still have been *surrendering*. On far better terms than we could ever have demanded, given the balance of power, maybe, but still surrendering. Now we're not. I doubt anyone like Younger or McGwire's going to be able to get much traction against that!"

Honor nodded slowly. Theisman's analysis matched her own, although she was inclined to think he was probably overestimating her stature among his fellow Havenites.

"I don't much like politics," he continued as the lift car moved upward, "but I've seen enough of it to figure out how it works. I'm not saying there won't be some people screaming not just 'No,' but '*Hell*, no!' I'm just saying there won't be nearly enough of them to slow ratification up appreciably. Especially not if Filareta's smart enough to back down. Manticore and Haven, standing shoulder to shoulder to face down the *Solarian League*? Talk about your public relations bonanzas!"

He shook his head, and Honor nodded again.

"Well," she said, "assuming this masterly summation of yours bears some nodding acquaintance to reality, I imagine the first technical mission to Bolthole—and I do hope you intend to tell us just where that is"—she gave him a speaking look—"is going to be heading your way sometime very soon now. And I don't think Mesa's going to be a *bit* happy about that!"

Chapter Seventeen

"*What* DID YOU SAY?"

Albrecht Detweiler stared at his oldest son, and the consternation in his expression would have shocked any of the relatively small number of people who'd ever met him.

"I said our analysis of what happened at Green Pines seems to have been a little in error," Benjamin Detweiler said flatly. "That bastard McBryde wasn't the only one trying to defect." Benjamin had had at least a little time to digest the information during his flight from the planetary capital of Mendel, and if there was less consternation in his expression, it was also grimmer and far more frightening than his father's. "And the way the Manties are telling it, the son-of-a-bitch sure as hell wasn't trying to *stop* Cachat and Zilwicki. They haven't said so, but he must've deliberately suicided to cover up what he'd done!"

Albrecht stared at him for several more seconds. Then he shook himself and inhaled deeply.

"Go on," he grated. "I'm sure there's more and better yet to come."

"Zilwicki and Cachat are still alive," Benjamin told him. "I'm not sure where the hell they've been. We don't have anything like the whole story yet, but apparently they spent most of the last few months getting home. The bastards aren't letting out any more operational details than they have to, but I wouldn't be surprised if McBryde's cyber attack is the only reason they managed to get out in the first place.

"According to the best info we've got, though, they headed toward Haven, not Manticore, when they left, which probably helps explain why they were off the grid so long. I'm not sure about the reasoning behind that, either. But whatever they were thinking, what they accomplished was to get Eloise Pritchart—in person!—to Manticore, and she's apparently negotiated some kind of damned *peace treaty* with Elizabeth."

"With *Elizabeth?*"

"We've always known she's not really crazy, whatever we may've sold the Sollies," Benjamin pointed out. "Inflexible as hell sometimes, sure, but she's way too pragmatic to turn down something like that. For that matter, she'd sent Harrington to Haven to do exactly the same thing before Oyster Bay! And Pritchart brought along an argument to sweeten the deal, too, in the form of one Herlander Simões. *Dr.* Herlander Simões...who once upon a time worked in the Gamma Center on the streak drive."

"Oh, *shit*," Albrecht said with quiet, heartfelt intensity.

"Oh, it gets better, Father," Benjamin said harshly. "I don't know how much information McBryde actually handed Zilwicki and Cachat, or how much substantiation they've got for it, but they got one hell of a lot more than *we'd* want them to have! They're talking about virus-based nanotech assassinations, the streak drive, *and* the spider drive, and they're naming names about something called 'the Mesan Alignment.' In fact, they're busy telling the Manty Parliament—and, I'm sure, the Havenite Congress and all the *rest* of the fucking galaxy!—all about the Mesan plan to conquer the known universe. In fact, you'll be astonished to know that Secretary of State Arnold Giancola was in the nefarious Alignment's pay when he deliberately maneuvered Haven back into shooting at the Manties!"

"What?" Albrecht blinked in surprise. "We didn't have anything to do with that!"

"Of course not. But fair's fair; we did know he was fiddling the correspondence. Only after the fact, maybe, when he enlisted Nesbitt to help cover his tracks, but we did know. And apparently giving Nesbitt the nanotech to get rid of Grosclaude was a tactical error. It sounds like Usher got at least a sniff of it, and even if he hadn't, the similarities between Grosclaude's suicide and the Webster assassination—and the attempt on Harrington—are pretty obvious once someone starts looking. So the theory is that if we're the only ones with the nanotech, and if Giancola used nanotech to get rid of Grosclaude, he must've been working for us all along. At least they don't seem to have put Nesbitt into the middle of it all—yet, anyway—but their reconstruction actually makes sense, given what they think they know at this point."

"Wonderful," Albrecht said bitterly.

"Well, it isn't going to get any better, Father, and that's a fact. Apparently, it's all over the Manties' news services and sites, and even some of the Solly newsies are starting to pick up on it. It hasn't had time to actually hit Old Terra yet, but it's going to be there in the next day or so. There's no telling what's going to happen when it does, either, but it's already all over *Beowulf*, and I'll just let you imagine for yourself how *they're* responding to it."

Albrecht's mouth tightened as he contemplated the full, horrendous extent of the security breach. Just discovering Zilwicki and Cachat were still alive to dispute the Alignment's version of Green Pines would have been bad enough. The rest...!

"Thank you," he said after a moment, his tone poison-dry. "I think my imagination's up to the task of visualizing how *those* bastards will eat this up." He twitched a savage smile. "I suppose the best we can hope for is that finding out how completely we've played their so-called intelligence agencies for the last several centuries will shake their confidence. I'd *love* to see that bastard Benton Ramirez y Chou's reaction, for instance. Unfortunately, whatever we may hope for, what we can *count* on is for them to line up behind the Manties. For that matter, I wouldn't be surprised to see them actively sign up with the Manticoran Alliance . . . especially if Haven's already on board with it."

"Despite the Manties' confrontation with the League?" The words were a question, but Benjamin's tone made it clear he was following his father's logic only too well.

"Hell, we're the ones who've been setting things up so the League came unglued in the first place, Ben! You really think someone like *Beowulf* gives a single good goddamn about those fucking apparatchiks in Old Chicago?" Albrecht snorted contemptuously. "I may hate the bastards, and I'll do my damnedest to cut their throats, but whatever else they may be, they're not stupid or gutless enough to let Kolokoltsov and his miserable crew browbeat them into doing one damned thing they don't *want* to do."

"You're probably right about that," Benjamin agreed glumly, then shook his head. "No, you *are* right about that."

"Unfortunately, it's not going to stop there," Albrecht went on. "Just having Haven stop shooting at Manticore's going to be bad enough, but Gold Peak is entirely too close to us for my peace of mind. She thinks too much, and she's too damned good at her job. She probably hasn't heard about any of this yet, given transit times, but she's going to soon enough. And if she's feeling adventurous—or if Elizabeth is—we could have a frigging Manty fleet right here in Mesa in a handful of T-weeks. One that'll run over anything Mesa has without even noticing it. And then there's the delightful possibility that Haven could come after us right along with Gold Peak, if they end up signing on as active military allies!"

"The same thought had occurred to me," Benjamin said grimly. As the commander of the Alignment's navy, he was only too well aware of what the only navies with operational pod-laying ships-of-the-wall and multidrive missiles could do if they were *allied* instead of shooting at one another.

"What do you think the Andies are going to do?" he asked after a moment, and his father grated a laugh.

"Isabel was always against using that nanotech anywhere we didn't have to. It looks like I should've listened." He shook his head. "I still think all the arguments for getting rid of Huang were valid, even if we didn't get him in the end, but if the Manties know about the nanotech and share that with Gustav, I think his usual 'realpolitik' will go right out the airlock. We didn't just go after his family, Benjamin—we went after the *succession*, too, and the Anderman dynasty hasn't lasted this long putting up with that kind of crap. Trust me. If he thinks the Manties are telling the truth, he's likely to come after us himself! For that matter, the Manties might deliberately strip him off from their Alliance. In fact, if they're smart, that's what they ought to do. Get Gustav out of the Sollies' line of fire and let him take care of us. It's not like they're going to need his pod-layers to kick the SLN's ass! And we just happen to have left the Andies' support structure completely intact, haven't we? That means they've got plenty of MDMs, and if Gustav comes after us while staying out of the confrontation with the League, do you really think any of our 'friends' in Old Chicago'll do one damned thing to stop him? Especially when they finally figure out what the Manties are really in a position to do to them?"

"No," Benjamin agreed bitterly. "Not in a million years."

There was silence for several seconds as father and son contemplated the shattering upheaval in the Mesan Alignment's carefully laid plans.

"All right," Albrecht said finally. "None of this is anyone's fault. Or, at least, if it *is* anyone's fault, it's mine and not anyone else's. You and Collin gave me your best estimate of what really went down at Green Pines, and I agreed with your assessment. For that matter, the fact that Cachat and Zilwicki didn't surface before this pretty much seemed to confirm it. And given the fact that none of our internal reports mentioned this 'Simões' by name—or if they did, I certainly don't remember it, anyway—I imagine I should take it all our investigators assumed he was one of the people killed by the Green Pines bombs?"

"Yes." Benjamin grimaced. "As a matter of fact, the Gamma Center records which 'mysteriously' survived McBryde's cyberbomb showed Simões as on-site when the suicide charge went off." He sighed. "I should've wondered why those records managed to survive when so much of the rest of our secure files got wiped."

"You weren't the only one who didn't think about that," his father pointed out harshly. "It did disappear him pretty neatly, though, didn't it? And no wonder we were willing to assume he'd just been vaporized! God knows enough other people were." He shook his head. "And I still think we did the right thing to use the whole mess to undercut Manticore with the League, given what we knew. But that's sort of the point, I suppose. What's that old saying? 'It's not what you don't know that hurts you; it's what you *think* you know that isn't so.' It's sure as hell true in *this* case, anyway!"

"I think we could safely agree on that, Father."

They sat silent once more for several moments. Then Albrecht shrugged.

"Well, it's not the end of the universe. And at least we've had time to get Houdini up and running."

"But we're not far enough along with it," Benjamin pointed out. "Not if the Manties—or the Andies—move as quickly as they could. And if the *Sollies* believe this, the time window's going to get even tighter."

"Tell me something I don't know." His father's tone was decidedly testy this time, but then he shook his head and raised one hand in an apologetic gesture. "Sorry, Ben. No point taking out my pissed-offedness on you. And you're right, of course. But it's not as if we never had a plan in place to deal with something like this." He paused and barked a harsh laugh. "Well, not something like *this*, so much, since we never saw this coming in our worst nightmares, but you know what I mean."

Benjamin nodded, and Albrecht tipped back in his chair, fingers drumming on its arms.

"I think we have to assume McBryde and this Simões between them have managed to compromise us almost completely, insofar as anything either of them had access to is concerned," he said after a moment. "Frankly, I doubt they have, but I'm not about to make any optimistic—any *more* optimistic—assumptions at this point. On the other hand, we're too heavily compartmentalized for even someone like McBryde to've known about anything close to *all* the irons we have in the fire. And if Simões was in the Gamma Center, he doesn't know crap about the operational side. You and Collin—and Isabel—saw to that. In particular, nobody in the Gamma Center, including McBryde, had been briefed about Houdini before Oyster Bay. So unless we want to assume Zilwicki and Cachat have added mind reading to their repertoire, that's still secure."

"Probably," Benjamin agreed.

"Even so, we're going to have to accelerate the process. Worse, we never figured we'd have to execute Houdini under this kind of time pressure. We're going to have to figure out how to hide a hell of a lot of disappearances in a really tight time window, and that's going to be a pain in the ass." Albrecht frowned, his expression thoughtful as he regained his mental balance. "There's a limit to how many convenient air-car accidents we can arrange. On the other hand, we can probably bury a good many of them in the Green Pines casualty total. Not the really visible ones, of course, but a good percentage of the second tier live in Green Pines. We can probably get away with adding a lot of them to the casualty lists, at least as long as we're not leaving any immediate family or close friends behind."

"Collin and I will get on that as soon as he gets here," Benjamin agreed. "You've probably just put your finger on why we won't be able to hide as many of them that way as we'd like, though. A lot of those family and friends *are* going to be left behind under Houdini, and if we start expanding the Houdini lists all of a sudden..."

"Point taken." Albrecht nodded. "Look into it, though. Anyone we can hide that way will help. For the rest, we're just going to have to be more inventive."

He rocked his chair from side to side, thinking hard. Then he smiled suddenly, and there was actually some genuine amusement in the expression. Bitter, biting amusement, perhaps, but amusement.

"What?" Benjamin asked.

"I think it's time to make use of the Ballroom again."

"I'm not sure I'm following you."

"I don't care who the Manties are able to trot out to the newsies," Albrecht replied. "Unless they physically invade Mesa and get their hands on a solid chunk of the onion core, a bunch of Sollies—most of them, maybe—are still going to think they're lying. Especially where the Ballroom's concerned. God knows we've spent enough time, effort, and money convincing the League at large that the entire Ballroom consists of nothing but homicidal maniacs! For that matter, they've done a lot of the convincing for us, because they *are* homicidal maniacs! So I think it's time, now that these preposterous rumors about some deeply hidden, centuries-long Mesan conspiracy have been aired, for the Ballroom to decide to take vengeance. The reports are a complete fabrication, of course. At best, they're a gross, self-serving misrepresentation, anyway, so any murderous response they provoke out of the Ballroom will be entirely the Manties' fault, not that they'll ever admit their culpability. And, alas, our security here is going to turn out to be more porous than we thought it was."

Benjamin looked at him for another moment, then began to smile himself.

"Do you think we can get away with its having been 'porous' enough for them to have gotten their hands on additional nukes?"

"Well, we know from our own interrogation of that seccy bastard who was working with Zilwicki and Cachat that it was the *seccies* who brought them the nuke that went off in the park," Albrecht pointed out. "Assuming anyone on their side's concerned with telling the truth—which, admittedly, *I* wouldn't be, in their place—that little fact may just become public knowledge. In fact, now that I think about it, if Cachat and Zilwicki are telling their side of what happened, they'll probably want to stress that they certainly didn't bring any nukes to Mesa with them. So, yes,

I think it's possible some of those deeply embittered fanatics, driven to new heights of violence by the Manties' vicious lies, will inflict yet more terroristic nuclear attacks upon us. And if they're going to do that, it's only reasonable—if I can apply that term to such sociopathic butchers—that they'd be going after the upper echelons of Mesan society."

"That could very well work," Benjamin said, eyes distant as he nodded thoughtfully. Then those eyes refocused on his father, and his own smile disappeared. "If we go that way, though, it's going to push the collateral damage way up. Houdini never visualized *that*, Father."

"I know it didn't." Albrecht's expression matched his son's. "And I don't like it, either. For that matter, a lot of the people on the Houdini list aren't going to like it. But messy as it's going to be, I don't think we have any choice but to look at this option closely, Ben. We can't afford to leave any kind of breadcrumb trail.

"McBryde had to know a lot about our military R&D, given his position, but he was never briefed in on Darius, and he was at least officially outside any of the compartments that knew anything about Mannerheim or the other members of the Factor. It's possible he'd gotten some hint about the Factor, though, and he was obviously smart enough to've figured out we had to have something like Darius. For that matter, there are a hell of a lot of Manties who're smart enough to realize we'd never have been able to build the units for Oyster Bay without it. So it's going to be painfully evident to anyone inclined to believe the Manties' claims that the Mesan Alignment *they're* talking about would have to have a bolt-hole hidden away somewhere." He shook his head. "We can't afford to leave any evidence that might corroborate the notion that we simply dived down a convenient rabbit hole. If we have to inflict some 'collateral damage' to avoid that, then I'm afraid we're just going to have to inflict the damage."

Benjamin looked at him for several seconds, then nodded unhappily.

"All right," Albrecht said again. "Obviously, we're both responding off the cuff at the moment. Frankly, it's going to take a while for me, at least, to get past the simple shock quotient and be sure my mind's really working, and the last thing we need is to commit ourselves to anything we haven't thought through as carefully as possible. We need to assume time's limited, but I'm not about to start making panicked decisions that only make the situation worse. So we're not making *any* decisions until we've had a chance to actually look at this. You say Collin's on his way?"

"Yes, Sir."

"Then as soon as he gets here, the three of us need to go through everything we've got at this stage on a point-by-point basis. Should I assume that, with your usual efficiency, you've brought the actual dispatches about all of this with you?"

"I figured you'd want to see them yourself," Benjamin said with a nod, and reached into his tunic to extract a chip folio.

"One of the joys of having competent subordinates," Albrecht said in something closer to a normal tone. "In that case," he went on, holding out one hand for the folio while his other hand activated his terminal, "let's get started reviewing the damage now."

Chapter Eighteen

"WELCOME ABOARD, CHIEN-LU. It's good to see you again."

"And you, Honor," Chien-lu Anderman, Herzog von Rabenstrange, said warmly as he shook the offered hand.

The Andermani admiral, who just happened to also be Emperor Gustav's first cousin, was a smallish man, not much larger than Honor's Uncle Jacques. And like Jacques Benton-Ramirez y Chou and Honor herself, he had dark, almond-shaped eyes. At the moment, as they stood in the admiral's day cabin aboard HMS *Imperator*, those eyes were as warm with genuine pleasure as his tone, and he smiled broadly. Not that he and Honor had always been on such excellent terms.

"I'm glad—and surprised, actually—they managed to get you back here so quickly," she went on, and he shrugged. It was six days by courier vessel from the Manticore Binary System to the Andermani capital in the New Potsdam System by way of the Junction's Gregor Terminus. To get here this quickly—less than one full day after Benjamin Mayhew's arrival—Rabenstrange must have departed within no more than twenty-four standard hours after the arrival of Elizabeth's courier to Emperor Gustav.

"I won't pretend travel aboard something as crowded and plebeian as a dispatch boat is truly suited to one of my towering aristocratic birth, but it does have the advantage of getting you where you're going in a hurry. Although"—Rabenstrange's smile faded slightly—"perhaps not as much of a hurry as certain other people can achieve, if this business about the 'streak drive' has any validity."

His voice rose very slightly with the final sentence, almost (but not quite) turning it into a question, and it was Honor's turn to shrug.

"All I can tell you about that is that as far as Nimitz and the other treecats are concerned, Simões is telling the truth to the best of his own knowledge. And as far as Admiral Hemphill and the rest of her tech people are concerned, what he's told them so far seems to be holding together. The general feeling among our intelligence types is that all the technical information he's provided so far appears to be both genuine and theoretically valid."

Rabenstrange gazed into her eyes very steadily, then nodded, and Honor tasted his satisfaction. She couldn't be positive, of course, but it seemed to her that he was satisfied on several levels. At least with her.

"That's what I expected to hear," he said after a moment.

"You expected to hear that I thought he was telling the truth, or you expected me to *tell* you he was telling the truth anyway, like a good, loyal Queen's officer?" she asked with a smile that was a bit more crooked than usual.

"That you'd tell me what you personally believe to be the truth ... and that you'd distinguish between what can be realistically evaluated and what can't be," he said.

Honor's eyebrows rose a millimeter or so at the unusual candor—or un-diplomat-like directness, at least—of his response, and he snorted in amusement.

"Honor, you're never going to make a good liar," he told her, "and only a fool—which Empress Elizabeth obviously isn't—would expect you to be any good at it. I'm quite sure that's why she wants me to talk to *you* before *she* talks to me."

"Why is everyone always telling me I'm an incompetent liar?" Honor demanded a bit plaintively. "I admit, I don't get as much practice as, say, a professional diplomat or a used air-car saleswoman, but still—!"

"It's nothing personal," Rabenstrange told her with a reassuring smile, "but no one can be accomplished at everything. It's just that you've been too busy learning how to blow up starships and things like that to master the difficult arts of duplicity and chicanery as well." He reached out to pat her on the arm. "Don't take it too hard."

"I'll try to remember that," she promised with an answering smile.

"Good."

"But I'd still be interested to hear your interpretation of why Elizabeth sent you to me first."

"It's simple really. She wants me to satisfy myself that she and Pritchart have been telling the Emperor the truth *before* she and I sit down to discuss the details. She wants that settled in my mind so that I can listen to what she's proposing without worrying about whether or not she's telling me the truth about her reasons for proposing it."

"I see."

Honor cocked her head thoughtfully. Elizabeth hadn't told her exactly why she wanted her to speak to Rabenstrange first. Oh, the Empress had touched on several reasons, including the professional and personal rapport Honor and Rabenstrange had established over the years. Yet Honor had sensed that wasn't everything Elizabeth had in mind. Now, as she thought back over the way the Empress' mind-glow had tasted at the time, she decided Rabenstrange had a point.

"Well, if you're right about that," she said, "I suppose we should go ahead and discuss the rest of what Simões—and McBryde—had to say. But first, have a seat."

She gestured at the comfortable armchairs, and Rabenstrange nodded. The two of them crossed the day cabin, followed by Major Shiang Schenk and Captain Spencer Hawke. Schenk, whose uniform bore the skeleton shoulder flash of the *Totenkopf* Hussars, the elite regiment of the Andermani Empire, was technically Rabenstrange's senior military aide, but that was simply a polite fiction. In fact, the *Totenkopfs* were responsible for the personal safety of members of the Anderman Dynasty, and Schenk and Hawke had developed a comfortable relationship based on mutual respect and professionalism. Neither of them was entirely happy about the sidearm riding at his counterpart's hip, but they'd been forced to learn to deal with it, since both of them were responsible for protecting people who were required by law to be accompanied by armed bodyguards at all times.

That restriction could make things awkward enough under most circumstances, but the situation was worse than usual in Rabenstrange's case, despite his and Honor's personal friendship. In fact, it would have been the next best thing to impossible if Emperor Gustav hadn't granted a very specific dispensation in Honor's case to his across-the-board rule that no one aside from assigned *Andermani* security personnel was allowed into proximity with any member of the Anderman Dynasty when armed. Partly that was because Andermani security knew about the pulser built into Honor's artificial hand, which she would have found just a bit difficult to leave behind on social occasions. But it was also a special declaration of trust in her, and she often wondered how hard it had been for Rabenstrange to talk the compulsively suspicious Emperor around.

Which had a certain bearing on the present conversation, she supposed.

Rabenstrange seated himself, and she sank into another armchair, facing him. Nimitz, who'd been watching the Andermani's arrival from his perch, hopped down and sauntered across to the visitor. He looked up for a moment, cocking his head thoughtfully, then launched himself into Rabenstrange's lap, and the herzog chuckled as the 'cat stood on his four rearmost limbs and extended his right true-hand.

"It's good to see you, too, Nimitz," he said, shaking the offered true-hand. He and the treecat were old acquaintances, and Nimitz settled down on his lap comfortably.

"You do realize that *I* realize the two of you are setting out to double-team me, don't you?" Rabenstrange inquired, looking up to smile at Honor.

"If there's any double-teaming going on here, it's his idea, not mine," she protested. "On the other hand, you're probably right. He's about as shameless at manipulating the two-legs around him as any 'cat I've ever seen. Darn good at it, too."

"Yes, he is," Rabenstrange agreed, then nodded as James MacGuiness entered the day cabin. "Ah! The inimitable—and inestimable—Mr. MacGuiness!"

"Your Grace," MacGuiness responded, bowing slightly. "I was wondering if I could get you and Her Grace some refreshment?"

"Actually, if you have any of that truly excellent coffee of yours, I would kill for a cup." Rabenstrange shook his head. "We do many things well in New Potsdam. Unfortunately, brewing potable coffee isn't one of them."

"Of course, Your Grace," MacGuiness acknowledged, with only the smallest flicker of a smile, then turned to Honor. "And for you, Your Grace?" he inquired innocently.

"If Herzog von Rabenstrange is prepared to drink your coffee, then I'm happy for you, Mac," she assured him gravely. "In my own case, however, I believe I'd prefer an Old Tillman."

"Of course," he murmured once more, and departed for his pantry.

"You've really gotten to know me and my menagerie entirely too well for my peace of mind, Chien-lu," Honor said, and he chuckled.

"Perhaps I have," he acknowledged, but then his

smile faded. "Perhaps I have," he repeated in a softer voice, "but I haven't had the chance yet to tell you how distressed I was to hear about Colonel LaFollet. I know how much he meant to you."

"Thank you." Honor paused to swallow, then cleared her throat. "Thank you," she repeated, "but I'm scarcely alone in having lost people I cared about."

"No, you aren't. Which rather brings me to the most burning issue, from my cousin's perspective, I'm afraid."

"Of course it does." Honor nodded. "And on that particular point, I'm afraid I can't give you the sort of positive assurance I can provide where Simões' veracity is concerned."

"That was our impression in New Potsdam." Rabenstrange shook his head. "Of course, His Majesty and I had very little time to examine the documentation Empress Elizabeth sent to him before I got bundled aboard that miserable little dispatch boat. I had rather more time to consider it at length on the trip here, however, and it seemed evident that 'positive assurance' would be ... elusive, under the circumstances. Which puts us in what I believe novelists call 'a delicate position.'"

"I've been instructed by Empress Elizabeth and President Pritchart to inform you that if you wish to personally interview Dr. Simões, you'll certainly be free to do so. For that matter, if you wish, you can bring along an intelligence expert of your choice. And we're also willing to provide a treecat to tell you whether or not Simões is telling you the truth in response to specific questions." She shrugged. "I realize *we'd* be providing the treecat, but it's the closest we can come to providing a lie detector without risking triggering any suicide protocols that might be hidden away down inside him."

"A concern which also explains why he hasn't been interrogated with the assistance of . . . pharmaceutical enhancement, let's say," Rabenstrange observed.

"Exactly." Honor sighed. "The problem is he's the only intelligence asset we've got where this Alignment is concerned, Chien-lu. We're treating him with velvet gloves because we literally can't afford to lose him."

"Understood."

MacGuiness returned with a cup of coffee, a chilled stein of beer, and a platter of cheeses, fruit, and celery. Rabenstrange nodded his thanks as he accepted the coffee, and waited until the steward had left the day cabin before he turned back to Honor.

"I understand the limitations you're facing," he said, "and because I do, I don't think I'll be taking the Empress and the President up on their generous offer to personally interview Dr. Simões. I would like my intelligence staff to review the recordings of his debriefing sessions, but let's not do anything we can avoid which might add even more stress to his situation."

"I'm sure they'll appreciate that," Honor said sincerely, but she also cocked her head inquiringly, and he shrugged.

"Speaking to him directly isn't likely to tell me anything I won't already see from the debriefing recordings. I understand the reason for the offer—to demonstrate that your intelligence people are being as forthcoming as possible—but all a direct interrogation could do would be to give him the opportunity to reconfirm what he's already told you."

Honor nodded slowly, and Rabenstrange sipped coffee thoughtfully, eyes unfocused as he gazed at something only he could see for several moments. Then he gave himself a small shake and looked back at Honor.

"So, having said that, and bearing in mind the reservation you've already noted, do you believe this McBryde's allegations?"

"Do *I* believe them?"

"Please, Honor!" Rabenstrange shook a chiding finger at her. "You've had considerably longer to think about it than I have, you've had better access not just to Simões but to Captain Zilwicki and Officer Cachat, and there's that little matter of what almost happened to you aboard this very ship." The chiding finger stiffened and pointed at the decksole, and the herzog's expression turned much more serious. "I know you were close to Lieutenant Mears, so I know how losing him, especially in that fashion, must have hurt. Believe me, losing Colonel Hofschulte and his younger son hurt Prince Huang. For Huang—and for me—that gives you what I think we might both agree to call a special perspective."

Honor's mouth had tightened, but she nodded in understanding. She paused and took a swallow of Old Tillman, then looked back at him.

"All I can say is that both Captain Zilwicki and Officer Cachat believe that at least the majority of McBryde's information, and the business about the nanotech assassinations in particular, was the truth to the best of McBryde's knowledge. That's also Dr. Simões' belief, although he himself had no knowledge of the Alignment's clandestine operations. Having said that, Simões is clearly prejudiced in McBryde's favor. As nearly as I can tell, and Nimitz agrees with me in this, McBryde was probably Simões' only friend in the world by the time the two of them decided to defect. I don't personally believe McBryde was manipulating him as some sort of elaborate disinformation sting, but in all honesty, I can't completely rule out that possibility."

She paused, regarding Rabenstrange steadily, and tasted his slow mental nod, his satisfaction that she was doing her absolute best to be completely honest with him.

"Obviously, we all wish McBryde had gotten out along with Simões. In some ways, it's almost more frustrating to have the bits and pieces we have—or *appear* to have, anyway—without confirmation than it would have been to remain completely ignorant. Nonetheless, everything we've been able to check tests out, Simões believed he was telling the truth, and the gross description he gave of how the nanotech is supposed to work is fully consistent with what I personally saw in Lieutenant Mears' case."

"How so?" Rabenstrange asked gently.

"McBryde was a security agent, not a scientist." Honor's tone became almost clinical. "He couldn't explain the actual mechanisms, and, to be honest, we're all confident he was holding back details he could have given us as bargaining chips further down the road. And as added incentives for Zilwicki and Cachat to get him and Simões out in the first place, of course." She shrugged ever so slightly. "I don't see how any reasonable person could blame him for that, under the circumstances.

"At any rate, according to his explanation, the Alignment's developed an extremely sophisticated, virus-based, organic nanotech. Personally, I think that's evidence of just how crazy they all are, but that might be the Beowulfer in me, and they, at least, are apparently confident of their ability to control it and keep it from mutating. All I can say is that I hope they're right about that."

Rabenstrange nodded soberly, and she continued.

"McBryde said—I've seen the recording he provided to Captain Zilwicki, and I'll see to it you get a copy, as well—that the nanotech has to be specifically engineered for its target. They have to get their hands on a sample of the target's genetic material, then build the nannies around that material. If McBryde's right about that, that's almost certainly the primary reason no forensic examination has turned up any evidence of it. It breaks down almost instantly after completing its function, and it's all tagged as a legitimate component of the target's own body.

"McBryde either didn't know or didn't say exactly how sophisticated the nanotech's 'programming' can be, but our best estimate based on what he did say is that it has to work something like transferred muscle memory."

"I beg your pardon?"

"Transferred muscle memory," Honor repeated. "ONI consulted my father as one of the Star Empire's leading neurosurgeons as soon as they started trying to evaluate McBryde's claims"—she didn't add that he'd also been called in because of his personal connection with her and the monumentally high security clearances which went with it, but she really didn't have to—"and I've discussed it personally with him. He doesn't like the implications one bit, but he says it's at least theoretically possible. In fact, he thinks there are probably some similarities between the way the nanotech works and the way *this* works."

She held up her artificial left hand and flexed its fingers.

"When I was learning to handle this, I had to relearn all the muscle memory using the new neural connections—connections which were significantly different from the organic ones I'd always had. Apparently, if my dad's right, what they do is to use a human . . . call her a 'host,' for want of a better word, to 'train' the nanotech pretty much the same way I trained my prosthesis and my own brain. Again, assuming he's right, they can only train it to carry out limited and probably very specific physical actions. That doesn't mean the physical actions can't be *complex*, according to my dad, but that they can probably only put them together in specific combinations, and there's a data-storage limitation—probably a pretty severe one—on what they can actually pack into the nanotech. For example, I've viewed the bridge imagery of the day Tim was killed."

Her voice roughened suddenly, her mouth tightened, her eyes darkened, and she paused again before she could continue.

"I've viewed the bridge imagery"—her soprano was almost as clinical, as detached, as before when she went on once more—"and aside from drawing Simon's pulser and opening fire, he never moved from the instant whatever was controlling him took over. He simply stood in one place, held the trigger down, and swept his fire across the bridge. Looking at the security imagery of the Havenite ambassador's chauffeur shooting Admiral Webster, you see very much the same thing. He draws his weapon, he opens fire—hitting three other people, not just the Admiral—and simply stands there until he's shot in turn. No attempt to escape, no effort to take cover or evade return fire, nothing. We haven't had the opportunity to look at any imagery your security people may have of Colonel Hofschulte, so I can't say how consistent that is in his case, but that's the pattern we're apparently seeing.

"Now, according once again to my dad, there has to be another component, some sort of organic AI, you might say. His best guess is that it probably sets up residence in some corner of the target's brain, but it wouldn't necessarily have to be located there as long as it has access to the central nervous system. Presumably the AI is issued with a set of triggering criteria that it looks for before activating whatever 'muscle memory' may have been installed in the nanotech. Obviously, the criteria can't be too complex."

Rabenstrange nodded again. The ancient cybernetic hope of achieving true sentience in an "artificial intelligence" had never been realized. Enormous strides had been made in crafting "brilliant programs" which could mimic intelligence—hence the continued use of the term "AI," even though it was technically incorrect—but those programs could react only to parameters the programmer could anticipate. The ability to discriminate triggering criteria in something as complex as normal human interactions was notoriously complicated, unless the programmer had a very specific grasp of the interactions likely to arise or could build in a mechanism the program could use to gain additional information and extrapolate from it. An AI designed to deal with customer-service inquiries, for example, or to operate an air taxi, and which had the opportunity to clarify situations and desires by asking questions, could give an incredibly convincing imitation of genuine sentience within its area of competence. Outside that area of competence, however, and without that ability to expand its information base, the situation was completely different. And if Dr. Harrington was right, the AI in this case certainly wouldn't have the opportunity to ask any "clarifying" questions before it acted!

"At any rate, if my dad's right about this, the AI only triggers under very specific circumstances. In fact, they probably err on the side of *not* triggering when they set up the original programming, even when that means missing possible opportunities, in order to avoid the sorts of accidents which might have started someone wondering what the heck was going on. And the specific actions which can be triggered are only those which have been 'muscle transferred' to the target. So, assuming he's right, this stuff couldn't force someone to, say, enter a computer code that's in *his* memory, not the nanotech's. And it can't access his knowledge or make his *conscious* brain do what it wants—force him to make up a lie in order to penetrate security, for example, or come up with his own plan for some assassination or act of sabotage. Daddy says it would probably be theoretically possible to . . . pre-record, let's say, a lie, although he doesn't know whether it would sound like the target's voice or the voice of whoever provided the muscle memory to the nanotech. But it's not like . . . oh, like hypnosis or adjustment. It couldn't trick its victim into supplying the proper code-word response to a challenge—or even force him to respond in the first place—unless whoever programmed it had the proper challenge ahead of time."

"But if the programmer *had* the challenge, knew the computer code, he could cause the 'target' to enter it?" Rabenstrange asked, eyes narrow.

"Probably. Well, *possibly*, anyway." Honor shrugged. "We're shooting in the dark, Chien-lu. As you say, we've had more time to think about this and more complete information, but without the kind of specifics McBryde either never had or at least never gave us, all of this is theoretical."

"Understood." Rabenstrange leaned back in his armchair once more, right hand stroking Nimitz's spine, and grimaced. "Understood, but it poses almost as many questions as it 'theoretically' answers, doesn't it?"

"You might say that." Honor smiled without a trace of amusement. "On the other hand, I personally think Dad's onto something. If they could actually reach into someone's mind and memories with this stuff, they wouldn't need assassins. They could simply program people in key positions—like a prime minister or a president—to start doing whatever it was they wanted them to do. Or they could simply have targeted someone else on *Imperator*, someone besides Tim, who had access to a fusion reactor or a hyper generator or any of a dozen other critical systems I can think of right offhand. Someone who could have destroyed the entire ship, not just killed me. But getting anyone into a position to do any of that, to initiate the proper procedures, would have required access to information the programmer didn't have and couldn't build into the muscle-memory transfer."

"I don't know how much confidence I'm prepared to invest in that, but it sounds reasonable," Rabenstrange said thoughtfully.

"Well, one thing we do know is that treecats can sense the moment in which whatever it is kicks in," Honor said. "And the 'cats have volunteered to help protect 'their two-legs.' I don't know how well we'd do at convincing one of them to relocate all the way to New Potsdam, though. To be honest, I think separating any 'cat not bonded to a human living in New Potsdam from the rest of his or her clan would cause the 'cat severe mental distress, so I'm not at all sure we could or should ask it of them. On the basis of what they've already volunteered, though, I'm confident we could provide a treecat early warning system for any Andermani flag officer or ambassador"—she smiled lopsidedly at him—"here in the Star Empire or serving with our fleet anywhere."

"I see." Rabenstrange looked down at Nimitz, still stroking the treecat's fluffy pelt, and nodded. "Some of my fellow Andermani may have a little trouble with that, I'm afraid. They don't know any treecats the way I've come to know Nimitz, and they're likely not to understand why Elizabeth can't send all the 'pets' she wants to the Empire. His Majesty, on the other hand, probably *will* understand."

"You think so?"

"I'm almost certain. I've discussed Nimitz with him often enough for him to grasp that treecats are just as much sentient beings as humans are, at any rate. And all well-deserved traditions of Andermani imperial arrogance notwithstanding, we do understand that we can't always compel the free citizens of someone else's star nation to do what we want."

"I'm relieved to hear that. One of the things I've been worrying about, to be honest, was whether or not our 'refusal' to send 'cats to the Empire would be seen as some sort of deliberate slight or maneuver. Or as if we're 'holding out' to try to compel the Empire to do what we want."

"Oh, believe me, it *will* be seen as exactly that by all too many members of our aristocracy!" Rabenstrange snorted. "It just won't be seen that way by *Gustav*—or Huang or me, for that matter—and to be honest, that's all that really matters at this point."

The two of them sat in silence for a handful of minutes, and then Rabenstrange cocked his head at Honor.

"May I ask exactly what it is Elizabeth is planning to propose to me in"—he checked his chrono—"two hours and twenty-seven minutes?"

"I don't think I—" Honor began.

"Oh, don't be silly, Honor! Surely you don't think for a minute that I think Elizabeth is going to make a recommendation to me without having run it by you first, do you?" He shook his head. "She's not clumsy enough to do something *that* dumb!"

"Well, I suppose not," she admitted.

"Then you might as well go ahead and tell me. I'm going to decide to recommend to Gustav whatever I'm going to decide, and I don't see where letting me get started thinking about it before I sit down with Elizabeth could do any harm."

Honor could think of several scenarios in which it

certainly wouldn't help *Manticore's* position, but she regarded him thoughtfully for a moment, then shrugged.

"Basically, I think she's going to suggest the Andermani Empire should declare its effective neutrality in our confrontation with the League. With the Republic backing us, we shouldn't need your battle squadrons to deal with Filareta when he gets here. For that matter, we shouldn't *need* them even if the situation gets significantly worse and we find ourselves in a general conflict with the Sollies. Not until they manage to come up with pod-layers and MDMs of their own, at any rate."

"I can see where that would probably be true, but there are going to be people in New Potsdam who wonder what sort of Machiavellian maneuver those nefarious Manties are up to this time. Adding the Empire to the pot in an effort to make the Sollies realize their current policy is . . . ill-advised, let's say, would seem to make a lot of sense. From your perspective, at least."

"If the Sollies were going to make any kind of a realistic appraisal of the actual balance of military capabilities, they'd never have sent Filareta out here in the first place. There's not much point in making logical arguments to someone who's already decided to ignore inconvenient truths, so they'd probably never even notice the Empire if we did add it to the mix." Honor shrugged. "That being the case, Elizabeth and President Pritchart have decided it makes more sense to get you out of the line of fire, as far as the League is concerned. That doesn't mean they can't foresee some future circumstance under which it might make sense for you to go ahead and sign on to the anti-Solly alliance, assuming Gustav's willing and Kolokoltsov and the other Mandarins are ready to push things that far. I think what they're really after at this point is leaving you some freedom of maneuver. For that matter, they could even see some situations in which having you available as a third party—a go-between—might make a lot of sense."

"And it would *also* leave us free to go after the Mesan Alignment, wouldn't it?" Rabenstrange observed shrewdly.

"Oh, I think you could take it as a given that that's one possibility which has crossed their minds," Honor agreed with a faint twinkle of genuine amusement. "Mind you, Elizabeth isn't the sort to let anyone else 'go after' Mesa if she can possibly do it herself, especially after the Yawata strike. But if it should happen that we find our hands full with the League, I suppose it *could* be convenient if there just happened to be another modern navy, with its own pod-layers and a bone of its own to pick with Mesa, who could stand in for her."

She leaned forward and selected a cheese wedge from the platter MacGuiness had put between them, then looked back up innocently.

"You wouldn't happen to know where she might be able to find one, would you, Chien-lu?"

✦ Chapter Nineteen

IT WAS UNDOUBTEDLY, Honor thought, surveying the outsized conference room, the most unlikely meeting she'd ever attended. In fact, it was the sort of meeting no Manticoran could have imagined outside a drug dream as recently as last month.

Empress Elizabeth, President Pritchart, Benjamin Mayhew, Michael Mayhew, Prime Minister Grantville, Foreign Minister Langtry, and Secretary of Commerce Nesbitt sat ranged around the head of the enormous conference table. (Nesbitt was substituting—not without some obvious reservations—for Leslie Montreau, who'd been sent home with the daunting task of presenting Elizabeth's and Pritchart's draft treaties to the Havenite Senate.) Stretched along one of the table's long sides were Honor herself, Hamish, High Admiral Judah Yanakov, Sir Thomas Caparelli, Admiral Pat Givens, and Admiral Sonja Hemphill. Stretched along the other were Thomas Theisman, Admiral Lester Tourville, Kevin Usher, Vice Admiral Linda Trenis, and Rear Admiral Victor Lewis. And at the end of the table, facing Elizabeth,

Benjamin, and Pritchart, were First Director at Large Fedosei Demianovich Mikulin and Third Director at Large Jacques Benton-Ramirez y Chou.

The one star nation conspicuous by its absence was the Andermani Empire, but that was by design. Chienlu Anderman had decided to recommend that Gustav take Elizabeth and Pritchart's advice and stand aside from the Star Empire's confrontation with the League. Accordingly, the Andermani battle squadrons attached to Eighth Fleet had been withdrawn to Trevor's Star, and no Andermani officers were present.

If they were missing, however, there were more than enough *treecats* present to make up for their absence.

Nimitz, Samantha, and Ariel would have been there anyway, but now treecats sat on the backs of Benjamin's, Pritchart's, Theisman's, Tourville's, her Uncle Jacques', Caparelli's, and Grantville's chairs as well, and it was virtually certain that everyone else sitting at that table would be receiving his or her own personal furry bodyguard very shortly.

Most of the Havenites still seemed a little awkward, a little unsure about the notion of allowing an entire crew of telepaths inside all of the security systems protecting whatever was said and discussed in this conference room. It wasn't that they thought any of the 'cats were going to turn out to be Solarian or Mesan spies. They just weren't used to them yet, despite Nimitz's constant presence at Honor's own diplomatic meetings with most of the same people in Nouveau Paris.

But that'll change, she told herself, and tried not to smile as she looked at Lester Tourville.

Alone of the Havenites, Tourville had acquired at least a little fluency in reading sign during his period as a POW here in the Manticore Binary System. He couldn't sign himself—very few humans could do that, even in the Star Empire—and his ability to understand what his newly assigned guardian's fingers were saying remained limited, to say the very least. Despite that, however, he was considerably ahead of the others. And it didn't hurt any that the basic personality of his new treecat companion—Lurks in Branches—complemented his own so well. Both of them had a "cowboy" streak about two meters wide, but under those ebullient surfaces, they were also intensely focused and sharp as a vibro blade.

In fact, *all* of the new guardians—from Pritchart's Sharp Claw to Theisman's Springs from Above—had personalities which were remarkably compatible with their human charges.

I think the memory singers may have sampled more than just Nimitz's and Samantha's impressions of Simões before they handed out assignments, she thought dryly. *Interesting that everyone who's been "catted" at this point is someone both of them have met, anyway. I wonder how they actually handled it, though? Did the memory singers mix and match, or did they just "sing" the mind-glows so the volunteers could pick the ones they wanted?*

Either way, she could taste the way the 'cats were already settling into comfortable acceptance of their two-legs. It wasn't remotely like the intensity of her own bond with Nimitz, but it felt . . . nice. Like the beginning of a long, close friendship, she supposed, although she could also tell the 'cats were more than a little frustrated by the Havenites' lack of signing fluency. For one thing, the inability to hold two-sided conversations of their own was the biggest reason most of those Havenites, despite their very best, most sincere efforts, still had trouble deep down inside thinking of the small, fluffy creatures as full-fledged guardians and protectors and not cute little pets.

Once they do learn to read sign, they're going to figure out on an emotional level, not just an intellectual one, that treecats are people, too, she thought. *And when that happens, they're not going to be worried about having them sit in on meetings like this one, either. They'll realize the 'cats are* partners ... *and they can't do that a moment too soon to suit me!*

Nimitz made a very soft sound of agreement and confidence from the back of her chair, and she sent him an affectionate mental caress before she looked back up the table at the two heads of state.

"So I'm afraid Ambassador Carmichael's correct," Langtry was saying in somber tones. "If Kolokoltsov were going to call Filareta off, he'd have already done it. In fact, unless there's already someone en route—which I very much doubt is the case!—he doesn't even have the option anymore. There's not time for him to change his mind and get somebody out here to call it off, even if he wanted to."

Heads nodded. If Filareta had managed to keep to his original operational schedule, he'd be arriving in Manticoran space within the next twenty-four hours.

"I agree with Foreign Minister Langtry." Nesbitt sounded even more sober than Langtry. "They're not going to order him to stand down."

"They really are idiots, aren't they?" Grantville observed caustically.

"I think it's safe to say they don't represent sterling

examples of competence and wisdom, yes, Mr. Prime Minister," Benton-Ramirez y Chou said dryly. "On the other hand, we really don't know what Filareta's orders are." He raised one hand. "Oh, we know the basic plan for 'Operation Raging Justice,' but we don't know what kind of secret clauses may have been inserted into his instructions."

"Like a pre-existing order to abandon the operation if it turns out we really can blow his ass off, you mean, Mr. Director?" Kevin Usher inquired with a grin.

"Something like that, yes," the Beowulfer replied with a smile of his own. Although this was the first time they'd met, Benton-Ramirez y Chou and the massively thewed Usher had already discovered they were kindred souls. And of all those present, they seemed least oppressed by thoughts of the cataclysm towards which all the entire explored galaxy seemed to be sliding.

"I think we're all in agreement that a clause like that would represent an act of simple sanity," Elizabeth observed. "Unfortunately, we haven't seen any other evidence of sanity out of them!"

"Actually," White Haven said, "I'm not at all sure *letting* Filareta stand down at this point would be in our interest."

There was a moment of absolute silence, with every set of eyes turning to him. Except for Honor's, that was. Unlike any of the others, she (and Emily) had already discussed this with their husband, and while she wasn't certain she shared his and Emily's logic completely, she *was* certain she agreed with what he was about to propose.

"Perhaps you'd care to explain that, My Lord?"

Eloise Pritchart invited after a moment, topaz eyes narrowed intently.

"Of course, Madam President." White Haven looked around the conference table. "It's possible Filareta really does have a secret clause directing him to back off if it turns out he's likely to get reamed. It's also possible that even without any such clause, he'd be smart enough to do it anyway. But if he does, and he just turns around and sails back off homeward without a shot being fired, where does that leave us?"

"Well, to begin with," Mikulin observed, "it leaves a lot of people alive who'd be dead otherwise. And it pretty conclusively demonstrates that their navy can't stand up to Manticoran weapons technology."

"Does it?" White Haven asked. "Demonstrate they can't stand up to our weapons, I mean?"

"Excuse me?" Mikulin looked perplexed, not incredulous, and White Haven shrugged again.

"What happened to Crandall's *already* demonstrated that to anyone with a working IQ," he pointed out. "Despite which, they've sent this entire fleet all the way out here. The damned 'Mandarins' are still that willing to risk getting millions of people killed—and that *un*willing to even consider admitting they might conceivably be in the wrong. The name they've assigned this abortion is proof enough of that! '*Operation Raging Justice*'?" The scorn in his voice was withering. "Pretty much shows how they plan on selling this to the League, doesn't it? They're still trying to game the system, and they don't give a single solitary *damn* about the fire they're playing with as long as it's someone *else* who gets burned!"

He paused and looked around the table, his eyes like fiery blue ice.

"So what happens, what do they do, if the fleet they've sent after us turns around and goes home without anyone firing a shot?" he went on. "Do they suddenly decide to *admit* their entire so-called strategy was a recipe for disaster that they walked straight into with their eyes wide open? For that matter, do they admit they pulled back because they've figured out they can't take us out? Do they even admit we *let* them back off instead of blowing their entire fleet into dust bunnies? No. What they'll do is try their damnedest to pass it off as another example of *their* 'restraint' in the face of *our* belligerence. They didn't turn around because they knew they'd get their ass kicked if they kept coming; they turned around because they realized our leadership was so hopelessly stupid and bloodthirsty it was really going to fight, *despite the fact that we couldn't possibly win*, and they weren't prepared to slaughter all our personnel. After all, none of our spacers are responsible for our government's hopelessly corrupt and imperialistic policy. Isn't that the way they've already been selling all this? Of course it is! So rather than press matters, once they realized Her Majesty here was perfectly prepared to throw away all of those lives, they've decided to exercise restraint."

"That's—" Grantville paused for a moment, looking at his brother, then shook his head. "I'm sorry, Ham, but that'd be too much for even the Solly public to swallow!"

"Maybe," Vice Admiral Trenis said, her expression thoughtful. "In fact, probably. That doesn't mean they wouldn't *try* it, though, Mr. Prime Minister. As Earl White Haven says, it's certainly compatible with the propaganda the Mandarins already have out there, anyway. And let's face it, they've managed to sell their public a lot of things that were almost equally preposterous."

"Tester knows *that*'s true enough," Benjamin agreed. "I'd really prefer for Hamish to be wrong, too, Willie, but I'm very much afraid he isn't."

"And even if they couldn't hope to sell it in the long run," Mikulin said with a scowl, "they might figure they could make it stand up in the *short* run as long as all of them lied loudly enough with straight enough faces. Long enough for them to get a formal declaration of war through the Assembly, say."

"All right, I'll accept that they may be thinking that way, even if I don't think they'd be likely to get away with it," Grantville said, although his tone was still doubtful. "Having said that, though, what do you propose we do about it, Ham?"

"We don't give them the choice," White Haven said flatly.

"Hamish," Elizabeth said, "given my reputation, I can't quite believe I'm the one who's about to say this, but I'd really prefer not to kill anyone we don't *have* to kill."

"I'm not proposing we slaughter them out of hand, Your Majesty." White Haven smiled thinly. "Mind you, the notion does have a certain appeal, especially given how cynically they're taking advantage of the Yawata strike. Reminds you of a carrion hawk circling a sand buck with a broken leg, doesn't it? Or maybe more of a dune slug getting ready to strip the carcass before it's quite dead. But what I'm saying is that we need to create a situation in which whatever happens here represents an unambiguous, undeniable, *decisive* defeat for the SLN. Something no Solly spinmeister's going to be able to convince even some credulous three-year-old was a 'voluntary act of restraint' on the League's part. We don't have to blow them all out of space to do that, either."

"You're thinking of forcing them to *surrender*, aren't you, Milord?" Thomas Theisman said slowly, his eyes narrowed.

"That's exactly what I'm thinking," White Haven agreed. "After what happened at Spindle, they'd find the surrender of another four hundred or so ships-of-the-wall *damned* hard to explain. Well, to explain as anything except an admission of total military impotence, anyway."

"There's something to that, Your Majesty, Madam President," Langtry said. "On the heels of Lacoön and Spindle, the fact that we've simply captured the biggest single fleet the Solarian League's ever assembled—hopefully without firing a shot or harming a single hair on anyone's head—would have to just about finish off any remaining public confidence in Battle Fleet. Not to mention taking another four hundred-plus ships-of-the-wall out of Rajampet's order of battle. I don't care how many obsolete wallers he's got in the Reserve; even *he's* got to eventually figure out he's running out of ships. Or out of trained crews to put *aboard* them, anyway!"

"And if Filareta doesn't have any 'secret orders,' or if he's just plain too stupid to surrender without getting a lot of his ships blown out of space first?" From Theisman's tone, he wasn't disputing Langtry's or White Haven's analyses. He was simply a military man who wanted to be sure the civilians around that table fully understood what was being discussed.

"If we arrange things properly, Tom," Honor said, entering the discussion for the first time, "we can create a tactical situation in which he'll *have* to recognize the hopelessness of his position. In fact, you and I have already done that, haven't we?" It was her turn to smile coldly. "The only change we'd have to make would be to wait a bit longer, let him actually cross the limit before we pull the trigger. If he's not willing to surrender under those conditions, then he's another Crandall, and he wouldn't be willing to surrender under *any* conditions. And if that's the case, he'd probably try to bull straight in until we stopped him the hard way, no matter what. Which means—"

"Which means we'd have to open fire on him, anyway." Pritchart finished Honor's thought for her.

"Exactly, Madam President." Honor sighed. "Like Her Majesty, I don't want to kill anyone we don't have to kill. But if Filareta's determined to fight anyway, then I want the deck as heavily stacked in our favor as possible. And I want him hammered so hard even *Sollie*s have to get the message that going after us is a really, really bad idea. That this isn't just another of their business-as-usual manipulations or some kind of sporting event, with rules they can game any way they like or walk away from any time they choose. That it's a *war*—*their* war—and that wars have consequences. We didn't start it; they did, when Byng massacred Chatterjee's destroyers. And we didn't send a fleet to attack the Sol System; they've sent one to attack *us*. For that matter, the fact that so many of their people got killed at Spindle was Crandall's fault, not ours, and she obviously meant to kill any of *our* people who got in her way."

Honor's eyes were hard, and even as she spoke, she wondered how much of the grim, cold determination she felt inside was aimed at the Solarian League and how much of it was aimed at any convenient target. Was her anger, her vengefulness, the product of New Tuscany and Spindle? Or were they the product of the Yawata strike, directed at the Solarian League because she couldn't get at the ones who'd actually murdered so many people she'd loved?

And did it matter which it was?

"They're bringing this war to us, when they don't have to," she went on coldly. "Bringing it to us when we've *warned* them they're being played by Mesa. When we've specifically warned them they're sending their superdreadnoughts into an effective death trap! There's a limit to what *we* owe *them*, how far over backward we're required to bend to keep from killing people who're here for the express purpose of invading and conquering our star system and our homes. I support Hamish on this one. Don't let them off. Don't let them 'magnanimously' step back. Smack them down in a way that *forces* them to admit the stupidity of sending Filareta out here in the first place, and then see how well Kolokoltsov and his Mandarins deal with the fallout!"

✧ Chapter Twenty

MASSIMO FILARETA STOOD in one of his favorite "thinking" poses, feet spread, hands shoved deep into his tunic pockets, and brow knitted while he gazed down at the detailed star-system schematic. At the moment, that schematic showed both components of the binary system which was his objective, but he wasn't really interested in the secondary component. Not yet.

Although John did have a point, he reflected. *They're bound to be expecting anyone who comes calling to hit Sphinx or Manticore, especially after what happened to them in February. That's where they're going to have their fleet strength concentrated. And the bulk of any system-defense missiles they have left has to be deployed to cover Manticore-A, too. They can't really afford to lose any of their home-system planets, but they could afford to lose Gryphon a lot more than they could either of the other two. And they have to know that if they spread themselves too thin...*

He grimaced. The notion of hitting Gryphon first, of starting by attacking their weakest point, had an undeniable appeal. Part of that was the "dipping a toe in" aspect of not getting any deeper than he had to before he'd tested the waters. That was scarcely the stuff of military derring do; then again, professional naval officers were supposed to avoid derring do whenever possible. "Derring-do" was usually what happened only after someone had screwed up by the numbers and had to figure out how to save his ass from his own mistakes. And given that he'd been forced to accept that he really was facing the wrong end of a tech imbalance, seizing an objective the Manties would be forced to retake, compelling them to come to him on his terms, had a lot to recommend itself in terms of cold military logic. Especially if they really were depending on pod-launched system-defense missiles—which were effectively fixed defenses—to make up the combat differential against the League's superior numbers.

Unfortunately, his orders were to go directly for the Star Empire's capital world, and that meant attacking Manticore-A.

Yeah, those are the orders. But the people who gave them aren't here, and you are. Don't pretend you wouldn't . . . modify them in a heartbeat if you really thought it would make a difference.

He snorted mentally, wondering yet again if one reason he'd been chosen for this mission—chosen by his *official* superiors, not Manpower, that was—was precisely because those superiors realized he'd treat their orders as no more than suggestions if it came down to it. He hoped it was, at any rate, because he'd already decided that was precisely what he was going to do.

I'm sure Manpower does have its reasons for sending me out here, but I'll be damned *if I do a Crandall for them! If this brainstorm of Rajani's looks like it'll really work, all well and good. If it doesn't . . . Well, sorry about that, Manpower, but we are* out *of here!*

He didn't much care to contemplate the repercussions of disappointing his "sponsors," but he liked contemplating the deaths of a couple of million Solarians—including that of one Massimo Filareta—even less.

"All right," he said finally, turning from the display tank, "does anybody have any last-minute thoughts, inspirations, or concerns we need to discuss before we all grab some sleep?" He smiled thinly and took one hand from a tunic pocket to wave in the direction of the time display which was counting steadily downward towards Eleventh Fleet's scheduled alpha translation back into normal-space. "We've still got a whole ten hours to think about them!"

That evoked the smiles and smothered laughs he'd hoped for. There was an edge of nervousness in some of that laughter, but that was inevitable. More importantly, there was an even stronger edge of . . . not *confidence*, perhaps, but something close to it. Or a lot closer to that than to *dread*, at least. The simulations they'd carried out with their new missiles during the lengthy voyage had a lot to do with that. He still had more unhappy questions than answers about where those missiles had come from—and why—but he had to acknowledge their impact on Eleventh Fleet's capabilities. He'd been as conservative as he could in evaluating their potential, but by his calculations the pods alone had tripled his wall of battle's striking power at the very least. And if he was willing to accept a long enough ballistic phase between drive activations, the new missiles had enough endurance, even in the tube-launched version, to give him a powered engagement envelope far in excess of anything his fire control could hope to handle. That *had* to have gone a long way towards offsetting the range imbalance.

"Seriously," he continued, allowing his own smile to lapse, "the initiative's ours. If anybody *has* had a last-minute thought, we can still put a hold on the operation while we consider it."

He looked around the faces of his seated staffers and their assistants. Their expressions were sober now, but they met his eyes steadily. Then he surveyed the faces of his task force and senior squadron commanders, looking back at him from the solid wall of com displays. One or two of them looked a bit more nervous, but they, too, returned his measuring gaze levelly, and he nodded.

"Good! In that case, John"—he turned to Admiral Burrows—"let's just hit the high points one more time."

"Of course, Sir."

The portly chief of staff stood and walked around to the lectern at the head of the flag briefing room's table. Normally he would have remained seated in his usual place, but today was scarcely "normal," and every man and woman in that compartment or looking in from the display wall knew it.

"The key to our plan is the system's astrography," he began formally, entering the command that zoomed in the holo display on Manticore-A and its planets. "In particular, the location of the planet Sphinx." He entered another command, and a twenty-two-light-minute sphere around the G0-class star suddenly turned amber. "As you can see, Sphinx's position means that—"

✧   ✧   ✧

"Well, better late than never, I suppose." Mercedes Brigham made a face. "Not that I'm not grateful for the extra prep time, but you'd think even Sollies could hit within, say, a couple of days of their ops schedule."

"Now, now," Honor said mildly, studying CIC's preliminary analysis. "We've missed a few operational schedules ourselves, Mercedes."

"True, Your Grace," Rafael Cardones agreed. Her flag captain had been standing beside her, studying the flag-bridge plot, but now he turned away from it to look at the chief of staff. "And far be it from me to point this out, Commodore, but this is amateurs' night. This is Battle Fleet, you know. Frontier Fleet might at least have been able to find its backside if it got to use both hands, but these people?" He shook his head. "They sit on their asses while Frontier Fleet does all the work, and you've seen the kind of 'gimme' sims Lady Gold Peak pulled out of their computers! For somebody with exactly zero real operational experience and such miserable training doctrine, coming *this* close to meeting their schedule is downright miraculous, when you get down to it." He smiled sourly. "As a matter of fact, I'm still trying to cope with the surprise that Solly SDs were really able to make it all the way out here in the first place. I didn't think the engine-room hamsters had it in them!"

Honor's lips twitched unwillingly, but she gave him a moderately stern glower.

"It may be 'amateurs' night,' Rafe, but these people may also be a lot closer to ready for the major leagues than we think. They've certainly been given plenty of incentive to . . . reconsider their training standards, at least. On the other hand, Mercedes"—she looked at the older woman—"Rafe's got a point. For someone with zero real experience, they've done well to hit this close to their deadline."

Brigham looked back at her for a moment, then nodded.

"You're probably right, Your Grace—both of you. And either way, they're here now."

"And pretty much where we anticipated they'd arrive, Ma'am," another voice said.

There was more than a hint of satisfaction in Captain Jaruwalski's observation, and Honor nodded. Not that it had taken a tactical genius to recognize the Sollies' most probable approach vector.

She wasn't accustomed to knowing her adversary's actual instructions before battle was ever joined, but she wasn't about to complain when it finally happened. Nor was she about to rely blindly on that sort of advantage, which was why she'd copied Michelle Henke's Spindle tactics and deployed system-defense pods and most of her heavy cruisers and battlecruisers to cover Gryphon, just in case Filareta had chosen to strike that way instead. Still, despite any insurance policies against unlikely contingencies, she'd been confident in her own mind that he would head straight for Manticore-A, as both his orders and the Solarian Navy's fundamental strategic doctrine required.

Even so, that had left the question of which of Manticore-A's inhabited planets he'd choose to attack. In the eleven T-months since Lester Tourville executed Operation Beatrice, Sphinx had moved out of the resonance zone, the conical volume of space between the Junction and Manticore-A in which it was virtually impossible to translate between hyper-space and normal-space. That meant the planet was no longer shielded from a direct approach, which left Honor's home world—barely 15.3 million kilometers inside the hyper limit—very little defensive depth.

Personally, Honor would have found that very exposure a temptation to attack Manticore rather than Sphinx, on the theory that her opponent would have been forced to deploy her forces to protect the more exposed target. Given the two planets' current positions, a good astrogator could actually have dropped a fleet back into normal-space closer to Manticore than any mobile units deployed around Sphinx. It would have been riskier in some ways, since attacking the capital planet would require a deeper penetration of the hyper limit. That would make it more difficult to withdraw into hyper if the attacker ran into an unanticipated ambush, yet the potential payoff in catching the defense out of position might well prove decisive.

But if Filareta was as much smarter than Crandall as she believed, he wasn't about to get any deeper than he had to. He'd want to stay shallow enough to break back across the limit and escape into hyper quickly if it turned out the reports about Manticoran missile ranges were accurate, after all. No, he'd go for Sphinx, not Manticore, specifically so he could cut and run if it all went south on him.

Which she had no intention of allowing him to do.

Her eyes hardened at the thought, and she felt Nimitz stiffen on her shoulder as he shared the bleak bolt of savage determination that went through her.

Her expression never even flickered, but she made herself draw a deep mental breath and step back from the brink of that fury.

Down, girl, she told herself firmly. *The object is to make these people* surrender, *not just massacre them. Whatever else they may be guilty of, they* aren't *the ones who carried out the Yawata strike, and you know it.*

"What's their projected vector look like, Theo?"

Her soprano was calm, almost tranquil, unshadowed by hatred or anticipation, and Lieutenant Commander Theophile Kgari, her staff astrogator, double-checked his readouts before he replied.

"They came in about twelve light-seconds shy of the limit, Your Grace," he said. "Call it eighteen-point-niner million kilometers to Sphinx. Current velocity relative to the planet is thirteen hundred kilometers per second, and it looks like they're taking their acceleration easy. At the moment, they're building Delta V at just over three-point-three KPS-squared. With those numbers, they could make a zero-zero intercept of the planet in seventy-three-point-six minutes. Turnover at thirty-three-point-six minutes, range to planet niner-point-five-seven million klicks. Velocity at turnover would be just over seven-point-niner thousand kilometers per second."

"Thank you."

Honor never looked away from the plot as she considered the numbers, which confirmed her own initial rough estimate. As she thought about them, however, she was acutely conscious of the brown-haired officer who stood gazing into the plot beside her with another skinsuited treecat on his shoulder. Some people might have worried that an officer of Thomas Theisman's towering seniority would be tempted to do a little backseat driving, or at least kibitz, no matter whose flagship he was on. Yet what Honor tasted from him most clearly was something very like serenity, and she wondered if she'd ever be able to stand on someone else's flag bridge at a moment like this without simply *itching* to start giving orders.

That question was only a secondary thought, however, while the majority of her attention was on the coming engagement's geometry.

The maximum powered range from rest of the SLN's standard shipkillers was just under 7,576,000 kilometers. From a launch speed of 7,900 KPS, that powered range would be as close to 9 million kilometers as made no difference, however. So within the next thirty-five minutes or so, Filareta would have brought anything in orbit around Sphinx into his powered missile envelope . . . assuming, of course, that nothing changed.

And assuming "standard shipkillers" are what he has in his tubes, she reminded herself. *We still don't know exactly what Mesa used on Roszak at Congo, Honor. Of course, we also don't know that this "Alignment" is prepared to hand the same weapons to the Sollies, either.*

Under their initial defensive planning, they would have concentrated on stopping Filareta short of the limit (and convincing him to withdraw), long before he ever got that close to the planet. She still intended to *stop* him before he got that close to her home world, but as for the rest of it . . .

"I don't see any reason to change our minds at this stage," she said, her soprano as cold as it was calm. "We'll go with Cannae." She looked up from the plot at Lieutenant Commander Brantley. "Pass the preparatory signal to High Admiral Yanakov and *Timberlake*, Harper."

❖   ❖   ❖

"Signal from Flag, Ma'am."

"And that signal would be exactly what, Vitorino?" Lieutenant Commander Jacqueline Summergate, HMS *Timberlake*'s commanding officer, inquired, looking up from the small tactical repeater deployed at the base of her chair.

"Sorry, Ma'am." Ensign Vitorino Magalhães was on the young side for the senior communications officer in any starship's company, even that of a somewhat elderly destroyer like *Timberlake*, and he colored slightly. But if he was flustered, there was no sign of it in his tone, at least. "'Execute Cannae Alpha,' Ma'am."

"Very well." Summergate nodded; she'd been anticipating exactly that since the first Solarian superdreadnought made its alpha translation.

Now, now, Jackie, she reminded herself. *You mean the first* unidentified *superdreadnought. After all, there's no* proof *these are Sollies invading your home star system without benefit of any formal declaration of war. Why, they could be from Andromeda, instead!*

She smiled very slightly at the thought, then glanced at Lieutenant Selena Kupperman, *Timberlake*'s tactical officer.

"Is your tac data updated yet, Guns?"

"Just about, Ma'am," Kupperman replied. "The last of it's coming in now."

"Very good." Summergate nodded. "Astro, take us out of here. We have some mail to deliver."

❖   ❖   ❖

So far, so good. Filareta felt his lips twitch, but he restrained the smile as he sat motionless in his command chair, watching the plot. *I wonder what's going through their minds?*

"Nice job, Yvonne," he said out loud.

"Thank you, Sir," Admiral Yvonne Uruguay replied.

Eleventh Fleet's alpha translation had been as neat as any Filareta had ever seen, with minimal scatter of its units and on almost the exact heading he'd wanted. Oh, Uruguay had been off slightly—he'd wanted to shave the margin on the hyper limit even tighter—but that was inevitable after such a long hyper trip. The hyper log gave an astrogator a reasonably accurate running position, but "reasonably accurate" over interstellar distances could leave just a bit to be desired, and allowing for the difference in intrinsic velocities between departure point and the arrival star system could be tricky, too. Getting an entire fleet to the right place at the right time, in the right formation, and keeping it that way through an alpha translation while simultaneously carrying the desired relative velocity across the hyper wall was an art, as well as science, in a lot of ways.

On the other hand, skilled at her job or not, Uruguay would have been much too senior for a staff astrogator in most navies, even on the staff of a fleet the size of Filareta's current command. He knew that, and ever since this business with the Manties had blown up, he'd been thinking about the rank inflation that was such an integral, ancient, and time-honored part of the Solarian League Navy.

Assuming we don't *end up finishing this whole business this afternoon*, he reflected, *we're going to have to do something about that. Our entire rank structure's so frigging bloated it's no wonder we've all got hardening of the professional arteries! But I have to say, Yvonne did do a damned good job.*

"How long do you think it's going to take them to get around to challenging us, Sir?" Admiral Burrows asked.

"Well, they have to have noticed we're here," Filareta replied dryly. "We didn't exactly go for subtle, after all."

He pursed his lips thoughtfully, considering Burrows' question. His orders had left how he presented the League's demands to the Manties to his own discretion, and he and Burrows had considered the matter at some length. One thing Filareta had been determined to avoid was any repeat of Sandra Crandall's asinine antics at Spindle. He wasn't going to hold any two-way conversations with minutes-long delays built into the middle of them. And he wasn't going to hang around for a couple of days before getting down to business, either.

On the other hand, there was something to be said for letting the other side sweat. The ancient term "swinging in the wind" came forcibly to mind as well, and he'd decided to let the Manties worry about opening communication. Four hundred-plus superdreadnoughts ought to be enough to get their attention . . . especially when the superdreadnoughts in question were headed straight for their capital star system's hyper limit. The psychological advantage in forcing the other side to initiate contact might seem like a small thing, but at this point Massimo Filareta was prepared to go for any edge he could beg, borrow, or steal.

"We're over a light-minute from Sphinx," he continued, "and whether or not this FTL communicator they're supposed to have actually exists, *we* sure as hell don't have it. Give them four or five minutes to kick the original sighting report upstairs and their superior officers to stop crapping their drawers, then another couple of minutes for them to kick it over to the civilians. Three or four minutes for the civilians to get back to the uniforms, and then a minute of light-speed lag to get the challenge to us." He shrugged. "To be honest, I'll be surprised if we actually hear anything from them in less than ten minutes or so."

Burrows nodded slowly, his own expression thoughtful, and Filareta climbed out of his chair and strolled across to Admiral Daniels' station. The operations officer was monitoring CIC's data and seemed unaware of Filareta's approach for a moment. Then he looked up quickly with an apologetic smile.

"Sorry, Sir. Didn't notice you."

"If it's a choice between noticing me and keeping your eye on the Manties, I'd just as soon you kept your eye on the Manties," Filareta replied dryly, and Daniels' smile broadened for a moment. "I know it's early, Bill," the fleet admiral went on, "but is there anything you can tell us yet?"

"Not really, Sir." Daniels shrugged. "The recon platforms are headed in-system, but we haven't been here long enough to pick up anything from our light-speed systems. We've got quite a few impeller signatures on the gravitics, but they're scattered around the inner system—or moving back and forth between the inner system and the Junction, it looks like, which takes them well clear of our approach vector—and all of them appear to be civilian traffic. We are picking up a scattering of gravitic pulses, though."

He met Filareta's eyes, and the fleet admiral nodded,

thinking about his earlier comments to Burrows about FTL coms. The Manties' apparent ability to transmit data at faster-than-light speeds had given all of them more concern than they really wanted to admit. The advantages of real-time or near real-time communication of tactical data were enough to make anyone who didn't have them nervous about facing anyone who did. And all the fragmentary information available to Eleventh Fleet when it pulled out of Tasmania had insisted the Manties were doing it using grav pulses, possibly to somehow manufacture modulated ripples along the alpha wall's boundary with normal-space. Theoretical gravitics were scarcely Filareta's area of expertise, and he had no idea how the Manties might be pulling it off. For that matter, it didn't sound to him like any of the gravitic theorists—even among the handful who would admit it might be possible—had a clue about how to actually do it. Given the penalties the SLN had already paid for its institutional arrogance, however, he and his staff had decided to accept the probability that the *Manties* could do it.

Funny how the apparent confirmation that we were right doesn't make me feel a whole lot better, he thought.

"Any pattern to the sources?"

"Not really, Sir. Or not one we can identify yet, at any rate. It looks like they're directional as hell, so the only ones we're actually getting a good look at are coming from directly out-system of us. They might be scattered all around the system periphery without my being able to pick them up yet." He grimaced apologetically. "We're still spreading the platforms, Sir. And, to be honest, I'm not sure how good they'll be picking up this sort of datum in the first place.

Our gravitic arrays just aren't set up or calibrated to detect or differentiate signals like this."

"The best you can do is all you can do," Filareta said, much more philosophically than he actually felt.

Daniels nodded and returned his attention to his displays.

Filareta walked back across to the master plot and unobtrusively checked the waterfall display on one of the secondary plots which showed the status of Eleventh Fleet's hyper generators. A hyper generator built to the scale of a superdreadnought like *Philip Oppenheimer* was a substantial piece of equipment, and it took time to cycle. In fact, it would have taken *Oppenheimer* thirty-two minutes—over half an hour—to go from powered-down status to translation into hyper. Recovering from a translation took time as well, although nowhere near that long. In fact, *Oppenheimer*'s generator could return to standby readiness in only twelve minutes, but it would take another four to cycle all the way up to an actual translation, for a total of sixteen minutes. Unfortunately, they'd been only about *nineteen* minutes' flight time from Manticore-A's hyper limit when they made their alpha translation. That was why his operations plan had specified bringing those generators back to full readiness as quickly as possible, and he gave a mental nod of satisfaction as he observed their progress and then glanced at the time display.

Five minutes since they'd crossed the alpha wall, he noticed.

    ♦   ♦   ♦

"Looks like this is it, Sir," Ensign Brynach Lacharn said quietly (and redundantly, in Lieutenant Hamilton Trudeau's opinion).

The Junction traffic-control net had just gone berserk as the bulk carriers and passenger vessels queued up for transit got their first intimation that something untoward was occurring a few light-hours away in the direction of Manticore-A. Given what had happened to the star system a few months ago—and the possibility that the people who'd done that might choose to hit the Junction after all, if they went for a repeat visit—Trudeau could hardly fault the merchies' evident consternation. Not that he was particularly pleased by how quickly that consternation had manifested itself. It only confirmed what he and the rest of the ship's company of SLNS *DB 17025* had already decided had to be the case: the Manties really did have FTL communications.

"Anything from Junction Astro Control?" he asked.

"Not yet," Lacharn replied, then shrugged. "Well, aside from the initial announcement that 'unidentified starships' are approaching the Manticore-A limit, at any rate. That's what set off this entire clusterfuck!" He waved in the direction of the obviously overworked petty officer monitoring the communications net. "Now that everyone's yammering away, I don't have any idea how soon ACS is going to manage to restore some kind of order."

"Great."

Trudeau shook his head in disgust. When he and the rest of *DB 17025*'s crew had been designated for this operation, he'd thought it was a particularly . . . ill-advised notion. He'd even said so—tactfully, of course—although no one had paid him any attention. Which just went to show that brainpower wasn't necessarily a requirement for high rank. They were a miserable *dispatch* boat, for God's sake! Even assuming Junction ACS would be willing to let *anyone* make transit through the Junction at a time like this, a dipshit little courier boat wasn't going to be very high in the queue. Which completely overlooked the fact that *DB 17025* was a Solarian vessel. Of course, the geniuses who'd come up with this had probably done it before they realized the Manties were closing every wormhole terminus they could reach against Solarian traffic, but still . . .

On the other hand, we're not just any *Solarian dispatch boat*, he reflected.

"Stay on it, Brynach," he said. "Sooner or later, they're going to start taking calls from *somebody*, so lean on them. Remind them about our INS credentials."

"Yes, Sir."

Lacharn nodded, although he had even more reservations about their orders' basic assumptions than Trudeau. One of his sisters worked for the Ministry of Education and Information, which meant he knew exactly how the "independent reportage" of the Solarian media worked, and in his opinion, Solarian newsies were the very last people the Manties ought to be allowing to use the Junction. For that matter, the Interstellar News Service Corporation had never been high on the Manties' list of favorite people—something to do with INS' "accommodations" with the People's Republic of Haven's Office of Public Information. Still, it *might* work, he supposed, since—unlike the League—the Manties actually gave at least a little more than pure lip service to the concept of a free and independent press.

And if it *didn't* work, it was no skin off Ensign Brynach Lacharn's nose.

❖   ❖   ❖

"Fleet Admiral, we've got impeller signatures!" William Daniels reported sharply, and Filareta nodded as he saw the crimson codes of starship impeller wedges appearing in the plot. They weren't moving, just sitting there.

"CIC's identified two separate groups," Daniels continued. "The larger group—designate Tango One—is about midway between Sphinx and Manticore, range approximately two-seven-zero-point-niner million kilometers. Call it fifteen light-minutes. The smaller group—designate Tango Two—is a lot closer. Range one-five-point-one million kilometers, about two million klicks this side of Sphinx. All we've got right now are the signatures themselves—they just lit off—but preliminary count makes Tango One approximately sixty sources. Tango Two's only about forty and—"

The operations officer paused for a moment, listening to the earbug linked to *Oppenheimer*'s Combat Information Center, then nodded.

"Tango One's begun to accelerate towards us, Fleet Admiral," he said. "Acceleration's just under four hundred and seventy gravities—call it four-point-six KPS-squared. Assuming constant acceleration, they could make a zero-zero with our current position in just under four-point-two hours. A least-time approach would get them here in right on three hours, but they'd have a final velocity of almost fifty thousand KPS."

"Understood," Filareta acknowledged, eyes narrow as he considered the new signatures and projected vectors in the master plot.

Eleventh Fleet had been accelerating towards Sphinx for almost twelve minutes now, and his task forces had traveled roughly 1.8 million kilometers, halfway to the hyper limit. They were up to a closing velocity of 3,683 KPS, 17.1 million kilometers from the planet. But Daniels' recon platforms, with their far higher acceleration, were only about 5.3 million kilometers from the nearer Manty formation, closing on it at 36,603 KPS. That meant they were 9.8 million kilometers ahead of Eleventh Fleet's battle squadrons, however, which imposed a transmission delay of almost thirty-three seconds on their telemetry, so it was going to be a while before they got light-speed confirmation of the FTL-detectable impeller signatures.

"It may be smaller, but Tango Two's also directly between us and the planet, Sir," Burrows observed quietly in Filareta's ear.

"Like I said, we didn't exactly go for 'subtle,'" Filareta replied equally quietly. "And how much of a mastermind would it take to figure this was any attack force's most probable approach vector?" He shrugged. "It looks like they're screwed anyway, though, given how far away Tango One is." He jutted his chin in the direction of the larger cluster of crimson icons beginning to scramble towards the approaching sledgehammer of his fleet. "I don't care if they *do* have a powered missile envelope of forty or fifty frigging million kilometers, there's no way anybody this side of God could hit a missile target at the next best damned thing to *three hundred* million!" He shook his head. "No, they've let us catch them outside mutual support range. Tango Two's on its own, and whoever's in command over there, he's got to be pissing himself about now."

"You don't think it's Harrington?" Burrows asked

with a slight smile, picking up on the pronoun in Filareta's last sentence.

"If Harrington's in space at all and not stuck dirt-side somewhere, she's with Tango One," Filareta said flatly. "She'd want the more powerful of her two task forces under her own personal control."

"Makes sense, Sir," Burrows agreed, then smiled thinly. "On the other hand, it looks like they may have been hit even harder than Intelligence estimated."

"Maybe."

Filareta kept his tone noncommittal, but Burrows might have a point. ONI's best estimate of the Manty's wall of battle before the last attack on the star system had given the RMN around two hundred SDs, twice the number they'd detected. Of course, ONI could have been wrong about that, and he wasn't going to pretend he wasn't going to be *delighted* if the Manties were a lot weaker than their pre-battle analyses had suggested. But the division of their forces... That puzzled him, and he didn't like things that puzzled him at a moment like this.

I said it wouldn't take a mastermind to predict our approach, but if that is Harrington in command over there—and given how everybody out here worships the deck she walks on, that's who it's got to be—I wouldn't have expected her to split her forces this way. Still, I suppose anybody can screw up. For that matter, she might have wanted to maintain concentration and been overruled by the civilians. This is their capital star system, and I shudder to think how Kolokoltsov and the rest of the 'Mandarins' would be standing over the shoulder of any poor SOB responsible for defending the Sol System!

Not for the first time, he found himself fervently wishing he had better intel on the other side's senior officers. Burrows and Commodore Ulysses Sobolowski, his staff intelligence officer, had done their best, but what Filareta was most aware of was his frustrating ignorance.

There'd been no time to send back to Old Terra for updated data dumps, given the operation's time constraints. Of course, any *competent* planner should have considered the desirability of sending updated appreciations of the most probable enemy fleet commander along with orders for the operation, but he supposed that would have been asking too much. Or *expecting* too much, at any rate.

Without any updates, Sobolowski (whose relatively junior rank for the staff of a Solarian force Eleventh Fleet's size was, unfortunately, an all-too-accurate reflection of the secondary—or even tertiary—importance the SLN in general attached to the intelligence function) had gone through his own files with a microscope. He'd pulled out every scrap of data Eleventh Fleet had on Harrington . . . and come up with very little. Worse, most of what they did have on her were simply clippings from the standard news services, almost all of which had clearly been written by newsies who knew exactly zero about naval operations. They were basically fluff pieces about 'the Salamander' (who always had made good copy on a slow news day), with almost no hard data on her tactics or operational concepts but plenty of hyperbole. Hell, based on *those* sources, the woman had to be at least five meters tall, and she probably picked her teeth with a light cruiser!

He snorted quietly at the thought, then gave himself

a shake. Yes, there undoubtedly were a lot of exaggerations (and very few facts) in the news accounts, but one thing was clear—she truly did have a formidable record. Once upon a time, Filareta had been as inclined as the rest of his colleagues to write that off. After all, how good did some neobarb have to be if all she was going to do was beat up on other neobarbs? That had been before the Battle of Spindle, however. *Since* the Battle of Spindle, he'd revised his estimate of *all* Manticoran officers significantly upward.

Presumably, the Republic of Haven's technological capabilities had to at least generally match the Manties', since the war would have been over a long time ago if they hadn't. That had been an unpleasant conclusion as well, especially since Filareta remembered a time when the technologically backward *People's* Navy had been desperate for any scrap of Solarian tech it could get. But the critical point at the moment was that if Harrington—clearly the cream of the Manty crop—had racked up an unbroken string of victories against an opponent who could come remotely close to matching Gold Peak's performance at Spindle, she was obviously no one to take lightly, so—

"Update!" Daniels snapped suddenly.

Filareta wheeled back around just in time to see what looked like several hundred additional impeller signatures appear in the plot. They were much smaller and weaker than the earlier ones: far too small and weak to belong to starships. But they were also at least two million kilometers closer to Eleventh Fleet and—

"LACs, Sir," Daniels said a moment later, his tone bitter. "They must have pretty damned good stealth, too. We never got a sniff of them until they brought their wedges up, and the bastards just killed every one of my advanced platforms."

"I see."

Filareta understood Daniels' anger, but as he studied the sidebars on the weaker impeller signatures, he was more concerned about the timing. Daniels was right. They had to be light attack craft, but their signatures were more powerful than any LAC impeller wedge Filareta had ever seen. And they'd killed the advancing front of Daniels' reconnaissance shell five million kilometers short of Tango Two. They'd done it with energy weapons, too, which suggested they had an awful lot of reach for such light units. Still, recon drones were fragile. They relied far more on stealth than evasive maneuvering for survival, too, and, as Daniels said, they hadn't had a clue the Manties were out there. Assuming the other side had picked them up early enough, there'd been plenty of time to track them and establish hard locks while they came bumbling in all fat, dumb, and happy. And if the LACs had been able to generate firing angles that avoided the platforms' impeller wedges...

He frowned unhappily at the thought of what that said about Manty sensors and their ability to track elusive targets, but LACs were still LACs. No matter how accurate they were, they couldn't pack in the firepower to seriously threaten a waller! And the Manties had let the platforms get close enough to do a hard count on the SDs in Tango Two before they killed them, too. Which meant he knew there weren't any more wallers hiding out there. No admiral this side of Sandra Crandall or Josef Byng would leave his ships sitting with cold impellers if there was even a *chance* missiles might be flying around shortly. And no matter how good Manty stealth might be, an SD's impellers would have burned through it at *that* piddling a little range.

They're close enough I can get to them and too far from Tango One for anyone to support them.

Anticipation glowed within him, even hotter because he'd never dared to hope Harrington would present him with an opportunity like this one, and he made himself stand back and think.

Alpha or Bravo, Massimo? he asked himself. *Take it slow, or run right in?*

He glanced at the chrono. His original ops plan had called for him to make the decision about his final approach to the hyper limit at about this point anyway, but the Manties' faulty dispositions lent added urgency to the choice. Under Approach Alpha, Eleventh Fleet would begin decelerating, reducing its velocity to a relative crawl by the time it hit the limit in order to minimize how long it would take to get back *across* the limit, if that became necessary. Under Approach Bravo, the fleet would maintain acceleration all the way in, which would get it into effective range of the planet (and any defenders) as quickly as possible but also meant he'd have to go far deeper into the system before he could kill his approach velocity and get back to the hyper limit.

The truth was that he'd seen Bravo as a desperation move, the rush of a boxer trying to get close, inside a larger opponent's longer, heavier reach, where he might be able to get in a few punches of his own. And, he admitted, given the Manties' reported higher acceleration rates, he hadn't really expected it to work.

But he'd caught Tango Two just *sitting* there. The acceleration numbers Tango One was putting up now that it had its impellers on line were fairly shocking, of course, despite earlier reports. In fact, they indicated the Manties had an advantage of almost forty percent over his own current acceleration. But Tango One was a minimum of three hours away, even so, whereas Eleventh Fleet could reach *Tango Two*'s current position in thirty-five minutes—and Sphinx orbit in thirty-eight. And it would take Tango Two *forty-seven* minutes just to match velocity with him, even assuming it began accelerating directly away from him this instant. He'd close the range to less than 10 million kilometers before that happened, though . . . and he'd be 6.9 million kilometers *inside* Sphinx's orbit when it happened.

Tango Two wasn't going to let that happen. Not when he'd be able to take control of Sphinx's orbitals and legitimately demand the planet's surrender. The Manties might move away from him, fall back *closer* to the planet, to hold the range open as much as possible. That would be the smart move on their part, anyway, although he doubted they'd let him get any closer to it than they had to before engaging him. But maintaining his own accel would tighten the time window on them, keep them from opening the range as *far* before they stood and fought, and that was no minor consideration, given how poor missile accuracy had to be at such extended ranges. Indications were that Manty accuracy was going to be significantly better—at least—at long range than his own, too, so keeping Tango Two from staying any farther away from him than he could (and punching his lights out with its longer-ranged missiles) struck him as a very good idea. And so did the notion of finishing Tango Two off as quickly as possible, while he was still able to engage it completely isolated from Tango One's support!

And I can still change my mind and translate out before we hit the limit if something new enters the picture.

"Well, at least we know they know we're here now," he said. "Get some additional recon platforms in there, Bill. In the meantime"—his nostrils flared slightly as he committed himself—"we'll go with Approach Bravo." He smiled thinly. "And I expect we'll be hearing something from them shortly."

Chapter Twenty-One

"STILL NO TRANSMISSIONS from our visitors, Harper?"

"No, Your Grace. Not yet, anyway," Brantley replied.

"Correct me if I'm wrong, Your Grace," Cardones, back on his own bridge, said from the dedicated display linked to *Imperator*'s command deck, "but aren't these people here to demand our surrender?"

"That's my understanding of their mission orders, yes, Captain Cardones," she replied, almond eyes still gazing thoughtfully at the master plot.

"Then don't you think they ought to be, well, *demanding* it?"

"I'm sure they'll get around to it when they think the time is right, Rafe," she said soothingly. "Don't forget, as far as we're aware, none of them has a clue we even knew they were coming." She shrugged slightly. "They may figure on letting panic soften us up before they announce their surrender terms."

"Maybe, but we just killed a bunch of recon platforms, Your Grace," Cardones pointed out. "And not even a Solly could've missed seeing our wedges come up. I'd think that would be a pretty good indication we're not feeling especially hospitable, and they're only six minutes from the limit. If I were them and I intended to do any talking at all, I'd be thinking about opening the conversation sometime real soon now."

"That's because you're a naturally talkative soul," Honor replied with a chuckle she didn't really feel. "Some people are the strong, silent type."

Cardones snorted, and she smiled, but the smile faded as she contemplated the steadily developing situation. So far, everything was proceeding according to plan, yet that didn't make her feel a lot better. As Cardones said, time was getting short, and she was always nervous when things appeared to be going this well. In her experience, Murphy always put in an appearance somewhere, and she'd anticipated from the outset that if he planned on showing up *this* time, he was most likely to do it in the next handful of minutes.

She'd thought a lot about the timing for this entire operation, especially this part of it, and her thinking had been forced to allow for both Filareta's probable acceleration and what he was most likely to do with his recon platforms.

Unlike the RMN, the SLN still adhered to the "maximum power" limit of eighty percent of power on its inertial compensators, and those compensators were a lot less efficient than her own. After considering what little she knew about Filareta, she'd decided he might well shave his impeller margin a bit closer than that and decided to assume he'd go with an eighty-*five* percent setting. That would have given him an accel of 3.5 KPS^2, but he'd come in at only 3.311, the old eighty-percent setting, and that bothered her.

Not because it was going to make a lot of difference, but because he was apparently being more cautious than she'd allowed for. Under the original planning for his visit, that would have been a good thing from her perspective; given the revised objectives of Operation Cannae, she would vastly have preferred someone more reckless.

Well, up to the last little bit, at least, she reminded herself wryly.

The really tricky part of the timing, however, had focused on the recon drones, and she'd had better numbers to work with there. Without Ghost Rider's onboard fusion plants, Solarian reconnaissance platforms had both lower acceleration rates and—compared to their Manticoran counterparts—pitiful endurance. Five thousand gravities was about the best they could turn out, and they couldn't maintain even that power level for very long. On the other hand, Operation Raging Justice obviously contemplated a very...direct approach to its objectives. Filareta wasn't going to need a lot of dwell time out of his reconnaissance shell, and he probably had more than enough platforms to replenish it if he really needed to, anyway.

On that basis, she'd assumed they'd come straight in at their maximum acceleration, and she timed her wedges' activation accordingly. The trick had been to make sure Filareta got a really good look at what she wanted him to see before her outer LAC screen put out his advanced eyes, and she was pretty sure she'd accomplished that. Now he knew she really did have only forty superdreadnoughts under her immediate command, without any more of them hiding anywhere near at hand. Hopefully, he'd also seen the "superdreadnoughts" between Sphinx and Manticore, as well. There was no way he'd had time to get any of his platforms close enough to realize that *they* were only Navy supply ships with military-grade impellers and compensators, however, and she meant to keep it that way.

Her own heavily stealthed platforms were deployed to cover a sphere over ten light-minutes across, centered on HMS *Imperator*, and Ghost Rider's sensors were far better than anything they'd seen examining Sandra Crandall's surrendered hardware. She had detailed information on Filareta's superdreadnoughts, and Ghost Rider was managing to keep pretty fair tabs on the Sollies' platforms, as well. As a result, she knew Filareta had reacted to the destruction of his advanced drones much as she'd hoped he would. He was vectoring his more distant, surviving platforms in on Honor's ships, trying to get them close enough to replace the ones he'd lost. In his place, she'd almost certainly have done exactly the same thing.

And, hopefully, it's going to bite him on the butt just as hard as it would have bitten me when I did, she thought with grim amusement. *Now if I can only convince him to keep on accelerating. . . .*

"Excuse me, Your Grace," Andrea Jaruwalski said. "The forward recon platforms confirm their superdreadnoughts are deploying pods."

"Deploying them? Or were they towing them all along and we just now noticed them?"

"Deploying, Your Grace," Jaruwalski said firmly. "They must have had them tractored inside their wedges."

"You were wondering if that accounted for their

accel rate, Your Grace?" Brigham asked, and Honor nodded.

"It would have been one explanation. Any sign their acceleration's dropping further now that they've deployed, Andrea?"

"Not so far, at least, Your Grace," Jaruwalski responded, "and given the numbers they seem to have deployed, maintaining their current accel has to be pushing up their compensator loads by a good eight to ten percent. So I'd say the fact that they're not reducing power is a sign they're feeling pretty serious."

"Point," Brigham conceded. "The thing I'm wondering most about is what's in the pods, though. Last time I looked, the Sollies didn't *have* any missile pods."

"You're thinking about those Technodyne pods Terekhov ran into at Monica, Ma'am?" Jaruwalski said thoughtfully.

"Something like that. Or whatever the hell Mesa used against Roszak at Congo." Brigham shrugged. "Either way, I don't think they'd bother with them unless they were stuffed with something they figure is superior to their standard tube-launched birds. I don't like the thought that they might have a point about that, but if they *are* thinking that way, it's going to have at least some impact on how willing—and eager—they are to bring it to us."

"I think you're exactly right," Honor said. "And bearing that in mind, I also think it's time we welcomed our visitors." She looked at Brantley. "Ready, Harper?"

"Yes, Your Grace."

"And are *you* ready?" Honor asked, turning to Theisman with a crooked smile.

"Oh, I believe you could say that, Your Grace," he replied. "And I'm sure Lester is, too."

"Then just make sure you're out of the pickup's field of view until the appropriate moment."

She made shooing motions, and Nimitz bleeked in laughter as the Havenite Secretary of Defense obeyed the gesture. The 'cat's skinsuit kept him from flirting his tail the way he would have under other circumstances, but his amusement was obvious, and Springs from Above (who'd been fitted with his own skinsuit) laughed back from Theisman's shoulder.

Honor waited another moment to make sure everyone was where he or she was supposed to be, then nodded to Jaruwalski.

"Send *Cantata* through to Admiral Tourville, Andrea."

❖   ❖   ❖

"We've got clearance, Skipper!" Brynach Lacharn said suddenly. "Number seven in the queue!"

Hamilton Trudeau looked up in surprise at the announcement. He hadn't really expected the Manties to let DB 17025 make transit at all, and certainly not this early in the queue. Maybe the people who'd picked the INS cover weren't as dim as he'd thought they were.

"All right, Tommy," he said briskly, turning to Ensign Thomasina Tsiang, the dispatch boat's astrogator and third in command, "get us in line! The last thing we need is to miss our slot now that they've given us one."

"Aye, Skipper."

The dispatch boat was small enough for Tsiang, who enjoyed being hands-on whenever possible, to take the helm herself instead of simply passing orders to someone else, and *DB 17025* accelerated smoothly, sliding out of the mass of waiting freighters and passenger liners. Trudeau suspected there were some alarmingly high blood pressures on the bridges of the ships they were leaving behind, but that was fine with him. He only wished he had some better intelligence—like *any* intelligence—on how the rest of Operation Raging Justice was making out.

Somehow, he felt sure, Admiral Tsang would probably wish the same thing.

❖   ❖   ❖

"Are we sure this is a good idea, Ma'am?"

Christopher Dombroski's tone sounded more than a bit doubtful as he watched the dispatch boat's icon moving towards the terminus to Beowulf.

"Define 'good idea,'" Admiral Stephania Grimm replied with a wry smile.

"Well, it just seems to me it would have been simpler all around to sit on them," Captain Dombroski said. "I mean, they wouldn't be going anywhere without our permission. We could've just kept them cooling their heels right here until it was all over one way or the other, without ever bringing the Beowulf end into it at all. Seems to me that keeping Beowulf up our sleeve as a holdout card in case we need to play it even worse later on might have a lot to recommend itself."

"In some ways, I'm inclined to agree with you," Grimm acknowledged. Given their positions and the role they had to play, she and Dombroski knew quite a lot about the thinking behind this part of the plan. And in Grimm's opinion, the captain had a very valid point. But . . .

"It'd be a hard call for me, either way," she said finally. "I'm sure it was for everyone else involved, too.

In fact, even though no one's told me this in so many words, I think it was ultimately the Beowulfers who made the decision, not anyone at our end. And I think the deciding factor was probably that they're really and truly *royally* pissed off at this Mesan Alignment. There's no way in this universe they're going to sit on the sidelines when we go after them, and they're about as disgusted as anyone could possibly get with the way Kolokoltsov and the Mandarins have botched the entire situation. For that matter, they're disgusted as hell with all the rest of the League for letting itself get turned into such a bitched-up *mess* instead of a star nation in the first place. So this is their way of punctuating all the reasons they're doing what they're doing—jumping ship to sign up with us, I mean. And I think they want to draw Admiral Tsang in, get her to openly commit to her part of 'Operation Raging Justice,' so they'll have that additional evidence of just how fast and loose with the League Constitution Kolokoltsov's apparatchiks are really willing to play."

She paused, lips pursed in thought, then shrugged.

"Anyway, senior and better-paid heads made the decision, not us, so that's the way it's going to be. And"— she smiled slightly—"I have to admit I'm going to be interested as *hell* to see how it all works out in the end."

✧   ✧   ✧

"All right, Harper," Honor said as she watched HMS *Cantata*'s icon disappear from her plot. "Why don't you go ahead and put me through to Admiral Filareta now?"

✧   ✧   ✧

"Fleet Admiral, we have an incoming communications request."

Filareta glanced at Admiral Burrows and arched one eyebrow at the announcement. At 14,875,000 kilometers, the grossly outnumbered Manty wall of battle remained motionless, holding position relative to the planet, fifty light-seconds from his own far larger formation. He was astonished that they hadn't even begun accelerating away from him, but he wasn't going to complain about it.

"I wondered how much longer it would take them," he said.

"Frankly, I'm surprised they managed to wait this long, Sir!" Burrows replied with a harsh chuckle.

"Who's the message from, Reuben?" Filareta continued, turning his back on the main plot to face Captain Reuben Sedgewick, his staff communications officer.

"It's from Admiral Harrington, Sir," Sedgewick replied, but there was something odd about his tone, and Filareta frowned. Any light-speed com request had to be coming from Tango Two if it had reached them this soon, and he was a little surprised Harrington was there, instead of with Tango One. But that wasn't enough to account for the odd note in Sedgewick's response.

"Is there a problem, Reuben?"

His own tone was a bit colder than it had been.

"It's just . . ." Sedgewick paused, then shrugged very slightly. "It's just that she asked for you, specifically, by name, Fleet Admiral. And she, ah, asked for you as the commanding officer of Eleventh Fleet."

Filareta felt his expression stiffen. He gazed at the com officer a moment longer, then looked back at Burrows. The chief of staff's amusement had vanished, and he met his superior's eyes with a frown.

"So much for operational security," Filareta observed.

"Yes, Sir." Burrows shook his head in disgust. "Somebody must have blabbed back on Old Terra."

"One of the many joyful disadvantages of having to come the long way round while the other side can get intelligence reports directly through the damn Junction."

Filareta's light tone was almost whimsical; his expression was not.

"I wonder how long they've known?" Burrows continued, thinking out loud.

"That *is* an interesting thought, isn't it?"

Filareta showed his teeth. Burrows had an excellent point. If the Manties had learned of his orders far enough in advance, there was no telling what sort of welcome they might have decided to set up.

Stop it, he told himself firmly. *Yes, they must have known you were coming, but knowing a two hundred-kilo sumo wrestler is about to rip your head off doesn't help a lot if you weigh fifty kilos dripping wet. It only means you can watch it coming longer, not that you can get out of the way. And it sure as hell doesn't mean you can* beat *the bastard once he gets his hands on you!*

"Time to the hyper limit, Yvonne?" he asked calmly.

"Just under six minutes, Fleet Admiral. Call it one-point-five-seven million klicks."

"Thank you."

Filareta looked at Burrows again. Their current velocity, relative to Sphinx, was up to 3,882 KPS; by the time they crossed the hyper limit, it would be up to over five thousand, exactly as Approach Bravo specified. At that velocity, it would take twenty-six minutes just to decelerate to zero, and they'd be the next best thing to 3.9 million kilometers *inside* the limit when they did. From that position, they'd need *another* twenty-six minutes to get back across the limit, where they could reenter hyper-space.

All of which meant they theoretically had six minutes in which they could break off with relative impunity... after which they would be stuck inside the Manticore-A limit for the next best thing to an hour.

Interesting timing, a corner of his mind thought. *Did they wait this long to contact us—and let us know they already knew we were coming—in an attempt to panic me into breaking off before we cross the limit?*

"Bill."

"Yes, Fleet Admiral?" Admiral Daniels looked up from his console.

"I want the entire fleet scheduled for an alpha translation twenty seconds short of the limit."

"Excuse me, Sir?" Daniels looked as if he couldn't quite believe what he'd just heard. Which wasn't too surprising, perhaps, given his superior's decision to go with Approach Bravo.

"Is that a problem for you, Admiral?" Filareta asked, looking at his operations officer coldly.

"Uh, no, Sir. Of course not! I just... wasn't expecting it."

Filareta continued to eye him coolly for a second, then relented.

"I didn't say we were actually going to translate," he pointed out. "We can abort any time up to the last fifty seconds of the cycle, correct?"

"Yes, Sir." Daniels nodded, his eyes narrowed as understanding dawned. "You just want to have the extra three minutes in hand if you need them, is that it, Sir?"

"Exactly." This time, Filareta smiled. "It'll give me at least another couple of minutes to think, anyway."

Daniels nodded again, more energetically, and began passing instructions while Filareta looked back to the communications officer.

"All right, Reuben," he said. "Put it on the main display."

"Yes, Sir."

Filareta turned towards the indicated display as the holo image of a very tall woman appeared above it. She wore a white beret, rather than the black beret that was standard for Manty flag officers, but he recognized her immediately from the file imagery. Even if he hadn't, her skinsuit carried the four broad cuff bands and four golden stars of a fleet admiral, and the six-limbed creature on her shoulder would have been sufficient clue if it hadn't. She also had remarkably cold brown eyes as she gazed out of the display at him.

Alexander-Harrington's recorded image stood motionless for a moment, until Sedgewick entered the "play" command.

"Fleet Admiral Filareta," she said then, her soprano voice as cold as her eyes. "In case you haven't already figured it out, my name is Alexander-Harrington. I have the honor to command the forces assigned to the defense of this star system, and the fact that I know both your name and that you're the commanding officer of Eleventh Fleet should be an indication that I know precisely why you're here. In case you require further evidence of just how thoroughly your plans have been blown, however, I'll add for the record that I also know you're here to execute 'Operation Raging Justice,' which I find a rather . . . ironic way to describe the forcible conquest of the Star Empire of Manticore by the Solarian League Navy without the bothersome details of niggling little things like a formal declaration of war or any consultation with the League's own Assembly. I suppose that's just the way the League's grown accustomed to doing things, and it's worked fairly well for it so far.

"But trust me, Admiral. *This* time it isn't going to happen."

Her smile was a razor, and the treecat on her shoulder bared needle-sharp-looking fangs.

"I suppose you may actually believe your intelligence services' conclusion that the Yawata strike has crippled our defenses. I assure you, that isn't the case. I suppose it's also possible you believe that the fact that I have only forty superdreadnoughts in my wall indicates you have the force advantage. If you should be thinking anything of the sort, I suggest you remember what happened to Admiral Crandall, when Admiral Gold Peak had *no* superdreadnoughts in her order of battle."

She paused, as if to allow that to sink in, then continued in that same icy voice.

"I hereby inform you, Admiral, that you are in violation of Manticoran territorial space. I further inform you that the Star Empire of Manticore considers your presence here, given the many previous instances of blatant and unprovoked Solarian aggression against the Star Empire, an act of war. Should you not immediately depart Manticoran territorial space, Her Majesty's Navy and its allies will respond to that act of war with deadly force. Should you cross our hyper limit after this warning, I am instructed to inform you that Empress Elizabeth and her government will take it as incontrovertible proof that, despite its pious diplomatic protestations and posturing, the Solarian League in fact actively desires a state of war between it and Manticore. Should that be the case, we will certainly give you one."

She paused once more, briefly, her brown-flint eyes hard with confidence.

"Whatever the people who sent you here may have thought, Admiral, you have no chance whatever of completing your mission. If you attempt to do so, especially after this warning, the consequences—including the thousands of your own personnel who will die and the general war between the Star Empire and the Solarian League which most assuredly *will* result—will rest upon your head and those of the corrupt bureaucrats who sent you here without a single shred of legal authority or moral justification.

"Alexander-Harrington, clear."

She stopped speaking, and in the silence which enveloped SLNS *Philip Oppenheimer*'s flag bridge, it required all of Filareta's willpower to keep his own face expressionless.

She sure as hell doesn't sound like she's bluffing. And she obviously does know—or seems to, anyway—all about our orders. But, damn it, she's got less than fifty wallers! And nobody could fight as many battles as this woman is supposed to've fought without learning to bluff convincingly!

"Record for transmission," he heard himself say.

"Yes, Sir," Sedgewick replied. "Live mike."

"Admiral Alexander-Harrington"—he made himself match the chill of her own smile—"obviously you *do* know why I'm here. That being the case, I see no reason not to cut right to the heart of matters.

There's obviously a wide difference between your star nation's interpretation of recent events and the Solarian League's, and I have no intention of debating those interpretations. While I might not choose to use 'conquest' to describe my mission orders, I *am* here under orders to demand, in the name of the Solarian League, the stand down and surrender of all Manticoran military forces, the reopening of the wormholes you have illegally closed to all Solarian traffic as an act of economic warfare against the League in direct contravention of every principle of freedom of trade and passage, and the surrender of your civilian government. You may genuinely believe you have the capacity to defeat my forces. For that matter, you may actually have that capacity, although I beg to differ. Even if you do, however, you won't accomplish it without taking significant losses of your own, and you might want to consider the fact that in addition to the other fifteen hundred superdreadnoughts actively in commission, the Navy has over eight thousand more in the Reserve. My presence here should indicate to you just how seriously the League takes this situation, and I assure you that, however many of those other ten thousand ships-of-the-wall it may require, the Solarian League *will* win in the end."

He paused to let her consider his words, then straightened his shoulders and looked straight into the pickup.

"I intend to complete my mission, Admiral Alexander-Harrington, and I will. To use your own words, if you persist in resisting, the consequences—including the thousands of your personnel who will die—will rest upon your head and the Star Empire of Manticore's. I demand that you stand down your fleet immediately. If you refuse, I *will* engage you.

"Filareta, clear."

✧　　✧　　✧

"Well, that wasn't exactly unexpected," Honor observed fifty-odd seconds later. "Except for the bit about reopening the termini. I guess there was time for Old Chicago to tell him about that before he sailed, after all."

"It's certainly *arrogant* enough for me to believe it came from a Solly," Mercedes Brigham half muttered, her expression baleful.

Honor shook her head, smiling faintly, but she also checked the digital timer counting down in one corner of the main plot. She could have used the Hermes buoys planted along with the stealthed recon platforms to conduct her conversation with Filareta in what amounted to real-time. In this instance, though, the lag of light-speed communications worked in her favor, and she glanced at Lieutenant Commander Brantley.

"Time for round two, Harper."

"Yes, Your Grace." The communications officer nodded. "Live mike."

"I see rationality still isn't a hallmark of the Solarian officer corps, Admiral Filareta," she said, looking straight into the pickup. "I can't say that comes as a dreadful surprise, given the uniformly disastrous decisions Solarian flag officers—and especially *Battle Fleet* flag officers, now that I think of it—seem to have been making for some time now. Hasn't anyone in Solarian uniform noted that you haven't come out on top in a single one of the engagements you've provoked? Except, of course, when your courageous personnel choose to open fire without warning on ships which don't even have their wedges up. Which, I point out to you, is *not* the case in this instance."

Her lip curled, brown eyes glittering with scorn, and the contempt in her expression and her voice was genuine.

"Obviously, I can't prevent you from sailing your entire fleet into an even worse disaster than Sandra Crandall's. I do warn you, however, that this entire exchange has been recorded and will be provided—at no charge—to the prosecution at the court-martial I'm sure you'll be facing, should you happen to be one of the survivors of the fresh debacle the Solarian Navy is about to experience. I repeat my original warning. If the forces under your command cross the hyper limit of this star system, you will be engaged and destroyed and a state of war will exist between the Solarian League and the Star Empire of Manticore and its allies.

"Alexander-Harrington, clear."

❖   ❖   ❖

"Alexander-Harrington, clear."

Massimo Filareta's nostrils flared at the cold, biting disdain in that soprano voice, yet he made himself stop and think.

So far, the exchange had used up two and a half minutes, leaving him just over three minutes from the hyper limit. He'd bought himself a little extra cushion with his instructions to Daniels, but even so, he had to make the call within the next two minutes.

The woman had to be insane. She was outnumbered ten to one, with a base velocity of zero relative to the planet, while Eleventh Fleet came at her at over five thousand kilometers per second. She'd have to have one hell of a lot more of a compensator advantage than even the wildest tales suggested if she hoped to pull away from him under those circumstances!

Unless she seriously believes she can pound us to pieces with those damned missiles of theirs before we get into our range of her, despite our velocity advantage, he thought. *That might be it. But she's* already *in our powered range, whether she knows it or not. Accuracy may suck, but we can* reach *her, and I've got* ten times *as many ships as she does! And I'm not going to get another chance like this one. Not another tactical situation where the frigging Manties* can't *stay away from us, pick us apart from outside our effective range. This is a chance to take out what looks like it's at least a third of their remaining wall of battle, and they can't survive that kind of loss rate even if they take out my entire command in return.*

But, damn it, she's got *to know that, too! So why is she* goading *me this way?*

He glanced at the time display again, then drew a deep breath and made his choice. He waved one hand sharply at Sedgewick.

"Live mike, Sir," the com officer told him, and he glared into the pickup.

"You obviously have a very high opinion of your capabilities, Admiral," he said coldly. "Well, I have a high opinion of my *fleet's* capabilities as well. I think we'll just have to see which one of us is correct. You have ten minutes to decide what you're going to do. If you have not struck your wedges in preparation to surrender your vessels at that time, you will not be given another opportunity to do so.

"Filareta, clear."

Chapter Twenty-Two

"*Cantata*'s MADE TRANSLATION, SIR."

"Thank you, Frazier."

One thing Commander Frazier Adamson hadn't done during their prolonged visit to Manticore, Lester Tourville reflected, was to grow an imagination. When it came to *anything* beyond the purview of his operational responsibilities, he was still the same unflappable, my-brain's-busy-elsewhere-so-don't-bother-me sort he'd always been, and that could still be irritating as hell. It did have its advantages upon occasion, however. In fact, there were times Tourville wondered if having a little less imagination wouldn't have been a good thing for him, too.

Probably not, though. He'd needed a certain... mental flexibility to handle the rapid-fire sequence of events which had snatched him abruptly out of captivity and made him once again the commander of Second Fleet (although it wasn't the Second Fleet *he'd* brought to the Manticore System) and assigned that fleet as the Havenite component of what had become known as Grand Fleet.

The designation had been suggested by Eloise Pritchart, and Tourville supposed it made sense. It had been one way to avoid submerging any of its constituent fleets into subunits of someone else's fleet. He didn't think that would have bothered him particularly, but he knew it would have bothered quite a few Havenite officers. And it for *damned* sure would have pissed off any number of politicians back in Nouveau Paris. Especially the ones who figured they could make some sort of political capital out of being pissed off over it. Hell, enough of *them* were going to be offended that Duchess Harrington had been named to command it without even worrying about what the damned thing was called!

Hitting the ground running with that sort of an assignment had been no picnic, but at least he'd been permitted to keep his staff together during their stay in Manty custody, and its members had been kept busy dealing with his many responsibilities as the senior officer of the original Second Fleet's surrendered personnel. (For that matter, he'd been the most senior Republican POW taken during the entire war, which he considered a somewhat dubious distinction.) As a result, it had remained a functional, well-integrated team when he needed it, although getting all of its members used to the notion of fighting *with* the Manties, rather than *against* the Manties, hadn't been the easiest thing he'd ever done. Which was fair enough. Getting *himself* used to the notion after so many years had taken some doing. In many ways though, Tourville suspected, Adamson's lack of imagination had actually made it easier in the operations officer's case.

"Signal from Commander Pruitt, Sir." Lieutenant Commander Anita Eisenberg remained far and away the most youthful staff officer Tourville had ever had, but her promotion from lieutenant during her stay as a POW had been amply merited. He hadn't had all that much need for a communications officer per se, yet she'd made herself invaluable in dozens of other ways. "*Cantata's* initiating download now."

"Thank you, Ace." Tourville gave her a brief smile, then looked back at Adamson. "Any changes, Frazier?"

"Don't see any, Sir." Adamson's tone was a bit absent as he watched his side plot updating from HMS *Cantata's* download. "Looks like Filareta's maintaining acceleration. If he does, he's going to cross the limit in about another four minutes. At which point"—the ops officer's tone shifted from absent to intensely satisfied; he did have a lively imagination when it came to *tactics*, and he'd been looking forward to this ever since the ops plan had been explained to them—"he is going to be well and truly screwed."

Tourville nodded. His expression was thoughtful, but his fingers were busy unwrapping one of his trademark cigars, and it was a bit hard to hide the smile which might have undermined his flag officer's gravitas as he realized every officer and rating on RHNS *Terror's* flag bridge was watching him. Those cigars were part of his image, and he felt ripples of anticipation radiating outward, as if those men and women—most of whom had known him only by reputation until he arrived to take command—had been waiting for the evidence that they truly were going to do this.

The treecat perched on the back of his command chair, on the other hand, made a soft sound of mingled resignation, amusement, and scolding. Lurks in Branches didn't like the smell of burning tobacco. Or he *claimed* he didn't, anyway; Tourville had caught him sniffing at it with what looked suspiciously like appreciation once or twice. Either way, he seemed willing to put up with it as part of the price of looking after his assigned two-leg, although he definitely wasn't above making his public attitude clear. Tourville's ability to read sign was still rudimentary, but he didn't need to be able to read it fluently to understand Lurks in Branches' message when the 'cat's long-fingered true-hands sealed his skinsuit helmet as soon as the human started unwrapping the cigar.

"Then I suppose we should get ready to dance," he said dryly, and smiled at the hermetically protected treecat as he stuck the cigar into his mouth. He made sure he had it at the proper, jaunty angle before he looked at the com displays which tied him to the flag bridges of the brand-new Second Fleet's three constituent task forces.

He'd worked hard to fit into his new command assignment ever since he'd found out he was going to have it, and it helped that he knew all three of his task force commanders reasonably well. It still hadn't been easy. After the next best thing to a solid T-year away from a command deck, he'd felt undeniably rusty, and he'd wondered how the three of them were going to feel about taking the orders of an admiral who'd rather decisively lost the last battle he'd fought in this very star system. For that matter, he still wondered how Admiral Pascaline L'anglais, the commanding officer of Capital Fleet, had felt when almost seventy percent of her wall of battle was suddenly stripped away and sent off to fight under someone else's command. In her place, Lester Tourville would have been royally pissed, and he wouldn't have cared who knew it.

Of course, at that point the plan had been for *Thomas Theisman* to command the reconstituted Second Fleet, and not even someone with L'anglais' well-known temper would have cared to argue that point. That had changed along with the initial plan for dealing with Filareta, however. The suggestion that Theisman might actually contribute even more effectively from someone else's flagship had come from Duchess Harrington, but somewhat to Tourville's surprise, Theisman had embraced the idea enthusiastically, which had left Second Fleet with no flag officers who'd ever actually commanded a full-scale fleet in action.

Except for Lester Tourville, that was.

"All right, people," he told his task force COs. "Commander Adamson is sending all of you the execute signal now. The timer's ticking. Any last immortal words anyone wants to say?"

He raised his eyebrows, then produced an old-fashioned silver lighter, activated its tiny plasma bubble, and puffed the fragrant tobacco carefully alight.

"I don't know about 'immortal words,' Admiral," Vice Admiral Oliver Diamato said with an off-center smile, "but I guess we're about as ready as we're going to get." He shook his head. "I have to say, though, I'm still wondering when we're going to wake up and find out this was all a really weird dream."

"It may be a dream, Oliver," Vice Admiral Jennifer Bellefeuille said from her quadrant of the display, "but, frankly, the thought of fighting Sollies instead of Manties makes it more pleasant than quite a few I've had!"

Vice Admiral Sampson Hermier, Tourville's third task force commander, only shook his head with a rather bemused smile of his own. He was almost as young as Diamato, which was an accomplishment for an officer of his seniority, and he was one of the few survivors of what had once been a moderately prominent Legislaturalist family. Tourville knew him less well than he did Diamato or Bellefeuille, but his combat record was excellent. If it hadn't been, Thomas Theisman would never have tapped him for task force command.

Especially not command of one of *these* task forces.

"Well," Tourville said thoughtfully, squinting through a haze of smoke before the ventilators wisped it away, "with the exception of Sampson, here, we've all had our butts kicked at one time or another by the Manties. So I'll grant you it feels a bit bizarre. But to be honest, Jennifer, I think you've got a point. And speaking only for myself, I have to admit part of me really wants to see these goddamned arrogant Sollies taken down a peg. Besides"—his smile disappeared— "we know who the *real* enemy is now."

His eyes had hardened along with his tone, and his subordinates looked back at him in grim agreement. He held their gazes for a moment, then continued more briskly.

"Hopefully, this is going to work out without anyone else's getting hurt. It may not, though, depending on how stupid Filareta's feeling. And if it doesn't, then we are going to *hammer* these people. Clear?"

All three vice admirals nodded, their expressions hard.

"Good."

He glanced at the digital display counting steadily downward in one corner of the plot, then at Molly DeLaney, his chief of staff.

Captain DeLaney looked back at him, and something dark and hungry flickered in her eyes. She had more reservations than the staff's younger members about the Republic's allying itself with the Star Empire, if only because she'd lost so many more friends than they to the wars with Manticore. She'd kept those reservations to herself well enough that anyone who didn't know her well could be excused for not realizing she felt them, but she'd also been with Tourville longer than any other member of his staff. He *did* know her well, yet as he looked into her eyes, he felt no doubt about her commitment to whatever was about to happen. Not, in her case, because she hated Sollies, although she was no fonder of them than any other naval officer who'd ever had to deal with their arrogance, but because she was impatient.

Filareta was only a distraction, as far as she was concerned. The entire *Solarian League* was only a distraction, when it came down to it, and one she wanted disposed of as promptly as possible. Molly DeLaney might not like Manticorans, and she might have a few qualms about finding herself allied to them, but those were secondary considerations whenever she remembered the nightmare slaughter of the Battle of Manticore. She didn't really blame the Manties for the carnage. She might not like them, but she did respect them, and they'd only been doing exactly what *she* would have done if someone had attacked her home star system. Besides, she knew now that the Star Empire had been manipulated just as skillfully as the Republic by someone who intended to see both of them destroyed. And because she knew that, she *wanted* the people who'd sabotaged the Torch summit talks and sent Second Fleet into that holocaust. She wanted them with a pure and blazing passion, and she was willing to fight beside anyone who might help her get to them.

"On the clock, Frazier," Tourville said, looking away from DeLaney. "On the clock."

❖   ❖   ❖

Eleventh Fleet crossed the hyper limit, charging towards Sphinx with a closing velocity of just over five thousand kilometers per second. There was no actual physical sensation involved, yet in the instant the flagship's icon crossed the perimeter of the amber sphere indicating Manticore-A's hyper limit, something like a deep, silent sigh went through SLNS *Philip Oppenheimer*'s flag bridge.

Fleet Admiral Filareta stood silently, expression controlled but with grim eyes locked to the plot. Tango Two was still just *sitting* there, not even trying to evade him, and anticipation pulsed somewhere deep inside him, hot and eager. He felt the same emotion coming back at him from the staff assembled about him, yet he felt something else as well. A sense that there was no turning back. Win or lose, they were committed, and despite all of their simulations with the new missiles, despite their huge margin of superiority over Tango Two, the reports of what had happened to Sandra Crandall echoed and reechoed in the depths of their minds.

Hell, they'd be more than human if they weren't worried! he thought coldly. *But whatever happens to us, Tango Two is screwed. There's no way in this universe that forty superdreadnoughts can match the defensive firepower of four hundred and thirty of them!*

A minute passed. Two minutes. Three.

Eleventh Fleet's velocity rose to 5,647 KPS. The hyper limit lay 963,000 kilometers behind *Oppenheimer*, and the range to Tango Two had fallen to 12.3 million kilometers. The Manties were 3.2 million kilometers inside Cataphract's powered envelope, even with no ballistic phase built into the attack run, although projected accuracy at forty-one light-seconds would be abysmal. On the other hand, he only had to worry about forty targets, and each of his superdreadnoughts had twelve missile pods towing astern. That gave him over five thousand pods, each containing ten missiles, which didn't even count his tubes. Each of his superdreadnoughts had given up a pair of tubes in each broadside to squeeze in Aegis, but that left them thirty per side. If he flushed all of his pods and fired a full broadside from each of his superdreadnoughts, he could put over 64,000 missiles into space simultaneously.

Their simulations had demonstrated that they couldn't hope to usefully control more than 17,000 or so at a time, of course. But if he used only 4,200 pod-launched missiles to back his broadsides each time he launched, he could fire twelve salvos that size before he exhausted them. That would be better than four hundred missiles per launch for each and every one of Tango Two's wallers, and his fire plan concentrated his entire first salvo on only half his potential targets. No superdreadnought ever built could fend off eight hundred and fifty capital ship missiles arriving in a single, cataclysmic salvo! So it was only a matter of them—

"Status change!" William Daniels snapped suddenly. "New impeller signatures. *Many* new impeller signatures!"

Massimo Filareta's eyes flew wide as the plot abruptly changed.

Tango Two suddenly sprouted additional impeller signatures—*hundreds* of signatures! None of them were powerful enough to be starships. They had to be still more LACs, but there were so *many* of them! They glared like a solid, curved hemisphere between Eleventh Fleet and Tango Two's superdreadnoughts, and still more of them appeared even as he watched.

That would have been surprise enough all by itself, but it wasn't by itself. A brand new cluster of signatures, signatures so powerful they clearly *were* ships-of-the-wall, had burned to sudden life a million and a half kilometers *beyond* Tango Two.

That's why they killed the recon platforms, a preposterously calm corner of Filareta's brain said. *They killed them before they could overfly Tango Two and possibly pick up the people hiding in stealth* behind *them. And what did* I *do?* I *let Harrington sucker me in like a goddamned stage magician, that's what I did. I vectored all my surviving platforms in on Tango Two instead of spreading them farther out to try and figure out what they might have been trying to hide!*

"Designate new force Tango Three." Daniels' staccato voice was crisp, harshly professional, yet Filareta heard his operations officer's own shock, his awareness of how thoroughly they'd been duped, echoing in its depths. "Estimate Tango Three at one hundred and fifty—repeat, one-five-zero—superdreadnoughts and a minimum of eight hundred additional LACs."

Filareta's jaw muscles clenched as he abruptly found himself confronting five times the number of wallers he'd thought he was about to encounter.

But we've still got them by better than two to one, and Tango Two's still over a million kilometers this side of Tango Three, he told himself. *That's going to limit how much Tango Three can bolster Two's missile defenses. I can still gut the closer one, and then—*

"Status change!" Daniels barked yet again, and Filareta could literally feel the color draining from his face as yet another huge cluster of impeller signatures appeared in the plot. These weren't in front of him; they were *behind* him, ten million kilometers outside the limit, arriving in the biggest, most powerful hyper footprint he'd ever seen.

"Designate this Tango Four," Daniels' voice was flat now, that of a man face-to-face with total disaster, holding off despair by pure, dogged concentration on his duty. "Estimate Tango Four at minimum two hundred fifty additional superdreadnoughts. Minimal escorts, but—"

The ops officer paused, then he cleared his throat.

"Sir, we're getting additional LAC signatures with Tango Four. They're just *appearing* on the plot. They must have used some kind of carrier ships—some of those 'superdreadnoughts,' maybe—to carry them across the wall."

The silence on *Oppenheimer*'s flag bridge was absolute.

They mousetrapped me. Filareta felt something like admiration even through his shock. *They keyed the entire thing to my own approach. They showed me Tango Two's impellers to suck in the recon platforms and keep me coming, then they timed Tango Three's wedges to come on line only after I crossed the limit. And they had Tango* Four *waiting in hyper the entire time. They must've sent a courier across the alpha wall to alert their backdoor force... and* they *timed their hyper translation to catch me on the wrong side of the limit, too.*

It was all timing, he realized. Every bit of it tied to his own maneuvers. He wondered if Tango Four would ever have dropped out of hyper at all if he *hadn't* crossed the limit?

Probably, he thought. *It wouldn't have given anything away, either way, since the only way I could have avoided crossing the limit would have been to hyper out short of it, before they ever turned up. All of my sensors would have been on the other side of the alpha wall, where they couldn't see a thing, when they dropped into normal-space. And did I think of detaching a couple of picket destroyers to watch and see what happened in a case like that? Of course not.*

Humiliation glowed at the core of him as he realized how totally he'd been manipulated. No, not manipulated: *anticipated.* Anticipated the way a veteran—or an adult—might anticipate some inexperienced novice full of his own omnipotence. They hadn't had to manipulate him, because it had been so easy for them to *predict* him, and that made it almost worse.

"Sir," Reuben Sedgewick said in a very careful voice, "I have a com request from Admiral Harrington."

❖   ❖   ❖

"So, has it occurred to you that things may not be quite as simple as you thought they were, Admiral Filareta?"

Harrington sounded whimsical, almost amused, Filareta thought resentfully. He glowered into the com pickup, his face as expressionless as he could keep it, and "the Salamander" smiled thinly.

"I did point out to you," she continued, "that your intelligence agencies' estimate of how badly our defenses had been eroded by the Yawata strike were in error."

"Yes, you did," he acknowledged, showing his own teeth briefly and settled back for the eighty-second two-way transmission lag. But—

"You should have listened, then," Harrington said after little more than a *single* second. Despite his best efforts, Filareta's eyes widened in surprise, and she smiled again. "It's called a Hermes buoy, Admiral. We have quite a few of them seeded around the system to serve as FTL relays. Convenient, don't you think?"

Flinty brown eyes bored into his, and icy fingernails scraped down his spine at the proof that Manticore truly did have faster-than-light communications capability.

"I'm aware," she continued, "that up until a minute or so ago you believed you had the force advantage. You don't. Nor, for that matter, do you face only the Royal Manticoran Navy. At the moment, a significant percentage of our own forces are...elsewhere, let's say, on another mission. So we asked some friends to fill in for them. The ships you've been tracking between Sphinx and Manticore are, unfortunately, only freighters with military-grade impellers and inertial compensators. We wanted you looking at them so you wouldn't notice the force I'm sure you've now detected just in-system from my own...which represents two task forces of the Grayson Space Navy, as well as the Protector's

Own. If it should happen your intelligence has failed to pick up on it, Grayson's war-fighting technology is identical with our own. As for the ships which have just completed their alpha translation astern of you, they represent three task forces of the Republic of Haven Navy. And I think it should be apparent to you that the Republican Navy wouldn't have survived this long if its war-fighting technology couldn't match our own as well."

She paused, as if inviting a response, and the treecat on her shoulder cocked its head to one side, green eyes bright and whiskers twitching gently.

Filareta felt as if he'd just been punched in the belly. The *Havenite* Navy? ONI and BuPlan had always recognized that Grayson might be stupid enough to stand up beside its Manticoran allies. They were religious fanatics, after all, even more backward than most of their fellow neobarb monarchies. So there'd always been a possibility he'd encounter at least some of their units, as well . . . although no one had ever suggested that a single star system so recently removed from hopeless primitivism could have put *that* many superdreadnoughts into a wall of battle! But Haven? They'd been at the Manties' throats for decades! What could possibly have induced *Haven* to range itself alongside its mortal enemy in defiance of the Solarian League's juggernaut? It was preposterous! Of course, one answer might be . . .

"I trust you'll forgive a certain skepticism, Admiral Harrington"—he managed to keep his tone almost normal—"but I find it just a bit difficult to believe Haven would come rushing to your rescue in a situation like this." He twitched a smile. "Given the size of your star nation's merchant marine, I find myself wondering if that force behind me isn't just another batch of freighters."

"It would have been an interesting ploy," Harrington replied. "And it occurred to me that you might wonder that. So I've brought along someone who can vouch for my veracity."

She nodded, and a stocky, brown-haired man—a man in a Havenite admiral's skinsuit—stepped into the display image with her.

"Allow me to introduce Admiral Thomas Theisman," she said coldly. "You may have heard of him? If so, you know he's the Republic of Haven's Secretary of War *and* its Chief of Naval Operations. As such, I believe you can assume he's in a position to speak officially for the Republic."

"Yes, I am in that position, Admiral Filareta." The brown-haired man's voice was just as chill as Harrington's. "And I'm addressing you from Duchess Harrington's flagship so there can be no question of just where my star nation stands. If you should happen to doubt that I'm who I say I am, I invite your ONI representative, should you actually have one on board, to consult his records. He may not have the data available, but I've dealt personally and directly with the Solarian League Navy in the past. Admittedly, I wasn't a flag officer at the time, but your intelligence people—such as they are and what there are of them—may have kept the recordings. For that matter, they may actually have been smart enough to provide them to you before sending you out into this region of space."

His tone made it clear he very much doubted anyone had been smart enough to do anything of the sort,

Filareta thought grimly. Which, given the monumental intelligence failure his current situation demonstrated, was hardly an unreasonable assumption.

"While they're checking that," Theisman continued, "simply allow me to say that every word Duchess Harrington's just said is fully supported by both myself personally and my government. The Solarian League's current lunacy is only the most recent and spectacular manifestation of its arrogant, corrupt foreign policy. The League's blatant disregard for any interstellar law, treaty, or independent star nation which happens to get in the way of its own desires and the expansion of its OFS 'protectorates' has been tolerated by the rest of the galaxy for far too long. The fact that no one in the League seems bright enough to figure out how your star nation's allowed itself to be played like a violin by an even more corrupt regime which isn't even a League *member* only makes you even more dangerous to any other star nation. To *all* other star nations, in point of fact. As such, the Republic of Haven is fully prepared to stand with the Star Empire of Manticore and its allies against the Solarian League's most recent unprovoked aggression."

Theisman stopped speaking, and Filareta looked over his shoulder. Commodore Sobolowski was working frantically at his console. Then the intelligence officer's eyes widened, and he looked up at Filareta and nodded once.

The fleet admiral's stomach muscles clenched at the confirmation that it really was Theisman. Or a damned convincing facsimile of him, anyway, although he couldn't imagine what in the name of sanity the

Havenite secretary of war was doing on a *Manticoran* flag bridge. And what the hell was *Theisman* doing with a treecat on his shoulder?

Filareta shook the questions aside. However perplexing—or vital—they might be in the greater scheme of things, they had exactly zero relevance for his present position. He turned back around to the pickup and opened his mouth, but Harrington spoke before he could.

"Before we go any further, Admiral Filareta, let me summarize the tactical situation," she said coldly. "Your fleet is between two hostile forces, which combined have effective parity with your superdreadnought strength. Our recon platforms report that you have approximately fifty-one hundred pods on tow behind your ships. Each of those pods has ten missile cells, for a total of fifty-one thousand missiles. In addition, each of your superdreadnoughts has a broadside of thirty tubes, allowing for the two you've taken out and replaced with Aegis fire-control stations. We're assuming the missiles in question are at least equal in capability to the ones Mesa supplied to the mercenary fleet dispatched to carry out a genocidal attack on the planet of Torch not so very long ago. Under those circumstances, I estimate that my own forces are currently inside your powered envelope."

She paused, as if inviting comments, and Filareta fought to keep his face from sagging at the accuracy with which she'd summarized his capabilities. It just got worse and worse, he thought. She must have had her platforms practically *inside* his wall to get that kind of information, and his sensors had never even *seen* the damned things!

"My own forces have rather more pods deployed," she said, and Daniels sucked in sharply behind Filareta.

"Sir—!"

"*What?*" Filareta snapped, venting some of his own tension as he wheeled to face the operations officer.

"Sir, the plot..."

Filareta looked back at the master plot and felt his blood turn to ice. She hadn't paused to invite comments, he realized distantly; she'd paused until the light-speed transmissions from the beacons which had suddenly turned the plot into an almost solid mass of point sources could reach *Philip Oppenheimer*.

"Those are *my* missile pods, Admiral," a soprano icicle told him. "Or *some* of them, to be more precise. I imagine you're having a little difficulty getting a detailed count, so I'll save you the effort. There are just over a quarter million of them...which represents less than ten percent of the total available to me. Moreover, every missile in those pods has a powered engagement range of better than forty million kilometers. And unlike you, *we* have the advantage of faster-than-light data transmission for fire control and electronic warfare management."

"Which won't do you personally a great deal of good if my admittedly inferior missiles blow you and every damned superdreadnought in company with you into plasma," Filareta heard his own voice say harshly.

"No, it wouldn't. But that's not going to happen, Admiral. First of all, we've had the advantage of examining Sandra Crandall's units in some detail. On the basis of that examination, we know your fire control is capable of managing salvos of no more than seventeen to eighteen thousand missiles. Each of *my* superdreadnoughts, on the other hand, can manage more than two hundred missiles apiece ... in real-time, without transmission lags. I'll let you do the math."

She looked at him coolly.

"Bearing in mind that capability, do you really think we haven't developed a defensive doctrine to deal with far heavier volumes of fire than your fleet can possibly lay down or control? I'm sure you've observed all of the LACs screening my forces, for example. I'm also sure you dismissed them as 'only' LACs. Before you do that, however, you might want to remember just how badly you've underestimated the *rest* of our hardware."

She showed her teeth in another of those icy smiles as she let that sink in, then continued with the same cold dispassion that was more terrifying than any rant could ever have been.

"Each of those LACs has more missile defense capability than one of your *Rampart*-class or *War Harvest*–class destroyers," she told him. "In fact, they probably have more antimissile capability than one of your cruisers. And at this moment there are two thousand of them deployed with each of my forces. Which doesn't even consider what our onboard defenses and EW will do to your birds." She shook her head. "Your fire isn't getting through my defenses, Admiral. Not enough of it to do you one bit of good."

Filareta's jaw tightened. He wanted, more than he'd ever wanted anything in his entire life, to believe she was lying. That it was all still an elaborate bluff. But he knew better. There was too much certitude, too much confidence in those frozen brown eyes. And her body language—for that matter, the body language of every officer and rating in her pickup's field of view—was just as confident as her eyes.

Silence lingered for several seconds. Then he drew a deep breath and squared his shoulders.

"And your point in explaining all of this to me is...?"

"For the last eight T-months, the Solarian League government—or, rather, the corrupt bureaucratic clique which dictates the Solarian League's policies—has ignored every effort on the Star Empire's part to divert it from a catastrophic collision," Harrington said in that same battle-steel soprano. "We've repeatedly sought a diplomatic resolution of the crisis provoked and sustained by the League. The unelected bureaucrats ruling the League with complete disregard for the League's own constitution, however, have made it clear they prefer the path of military confrontation, regardless of how many human beings—including men and women in the uniform of the Solarian League Navy—might be killed along the way. We've recently discovered, and have shared with the League through our ambassador in Old Chicago, evidence that strongly supports our contention that the crisis between our star nations was deliberately engineered by certain parties in the Mesa System. We also invited Permanent Senior Undersecretary Kolokoltsov and his... associates to send someone through the Junction to Manticore with the authority to order you to stand down before anyone was killed. That invitation was declined, from which we can only conclude Kolokoltsov continues to prefer war to a peaceful resolution."

She paused once again. Her eyes narrowed, and Filareta wondered if she'd seen something in his own eyes when she mentioned Mesa.

"Since war is clearly what he prefers, and since no one in the League seems to be prepared or in a position to dispute his policies, then war it will be." Harrington's voice was colder than the space beyond *Oppenheimer*'s hull. "Which leaves you with a decision, Admiral Filareta. The Star Empire and its allies are prepared to accept your surrender and the surrender of the vessels under your command. Should you so surrender, we will guarantee your personnel proper treatment under the Deneb Accords. We will further guarantee your personnel's repatriation to the Solarian League as soon as a reasonable and mutually satisfactory resolution of all disputes between us and the League has been concluded. Should you choose not to surrender, we *will* engage you, and the consequences for your fleet will be disastrous. You have five minutes to consider our terms. At the end of that time, if you have not announced your surrender, struck your wedges, and scuttled your missile pods, we will open fire.

"The choice is yours. Alexander-Harrington, clear."

The tall, implacable image disappeared from Filareta's com, and he turned to face his staff.

Every one of them looked as stunned as *he* felt.

"Well, John?" He gave Burrows a smile he suspected looked as ghastly as it felt. "Do you think she's bluffing?"

From his expression, Burrows wanted desperately to say exactly that. Instead, he shook his head.

"No, Sir," he said flatly. "She set all of this up too well. She knows too much about our ops plan, and she's showing us too much tactical detail. Worse, she's showing us *way* too much about their capabilities—things like their platforms' stealth and sensor reach, the number of pods she's got deployed, those LAC carriers or whatever the hell they are the Havenites must have." He shook his head again. "She wants us to know what she has, *wants* us to know exactly what she can do to us, and she wouldn't be giving us that good a look if she wasn't just as confident as she sounds. She may be exaggerating her antimissile capabilities, but I don't think so. And even if she is, it won't make any difference to *us* once the wreckage cools."

"And I went charging straight over the limit, so we can't even try to run, instead." Filareta heard the bitterness in his own voice.

"It's what our orders specified, Sir," Burrows replied with a shrug. "Whoever thought this operation up was obviously operating on the basis of a few...flawed assumptions. Now we've been handed the shit-end of the stick."

Filareta nodded slowly, yet unlike Burrows, he very much doubted that "whoever" had truly come up with this operation had been operating on "flawed assumptions." No. Harrington had it right; Mesa was ultimately behind it all. He couldn't imagine why, or what Mesa hoped to accomplish, but it didn't matter, either. There were over four hundred superdreadnoughts on his plot, and if they were even half as capable as Harrington had described, they were more than enough to cut through every active unit of Battle Fleet like a laser through ice cubes. Which didn't even consider what would happen to him personally, or to the almost three million men and women aboard Eleventh Fleet's starships, because they wouldn't even work up a light sweat dealing with *his* command.

"Bill?" He looked at Daniels.

"Sir,"—the operations officer's expression was desperately unhappy—"I think she's telling the truth—about her capabilities, anyway. And if she is, we're ... Well, John's right, Sir. If she pulls the trigger, we're toast. We may be able to hurt them more than she's suggesting, but there's no *way* we survive."

❖   ❖   ❖

"What do you think he's going to decide, Tom?" Honor asked quietly.

"Given the options, he's going to strike his wedges and blow those pods, unless he's a complete and total idiot," Theisman replied succinctly. "Of course, he may *be* a complete and total idiot, but I think you made our position eloquently clear. For that matter," he smiled slightly, "I doubt my own modest contribution hurt."

"No, I don't think it did," she agreed, right cheek dimpling with a sudden, much broader smile of her own.

"You do realize you weren't exactly truthful with the poor shmuck, Your Grace," Rafe Cardones pointed out from his com screen, and she cocked an eyebrow at him. "You didn't fall all over yourself giving him accurate info on our capabilities," her flag captain expanded, and she shrugged.

"I disagree with your assessment, Rafe. I didn't tell him we could do a single thing we *can't* do, I just ... understated the numbers a bit. Sooner or later, at least some of these people will be going home again—at least I darned well *hope* they will!—and I don't see any reason to give away all our little secrets before they do. Hopefully, we're finally going to put the brakes on this thing today. If we don't, though, I want to keep the Sollies guessing about the actual ceiling on our abilities for as long as I can."

"I agree completely." Theisman nodded firmly. "Keeping at least some of your capabilities in reserve as long as possible is always a good idea. Besides"—he snorted dryly—"they might not have believed you if you'd told them how good your tech—*our* tech—really is! He might've decided you were lying and running a bluff after all."

"I'm with Admiral Theisman, Your Grace," Mercedes Brigham offered. "Besides, you didn't *need* to tell the bastards everything. What you did tell them was plenty bad enough from their perspective, and while I'll agree you were both pretty eloquent, I think the tactical situation's even more persuasive." She shook her head. "I've never seen a fleet in a worse hole than this one, even in a simulation, and"—she glanced at Theisman for a moment—"that's saying something, after some of the scrapes we've been in." She shook her head again. "Surrender's the only option you've left him."

"That was the general idea, Mercedes," Honor said softly, her eyes on the crimson icons of Eleventh Fleet.

❖   ❖   ❖

Massimo Filareta took one last look at the horrific array of firepower which had closed its battle-steel jaws on his command. He remembered the shock with which the SLN had responded to the surrender of Josef Byng's task force. The even greater shock—and disbelief—of what had happened to Sandra Crandall. The impact of this was going to dwarf all of those other shocks, all of that other disbelief.

And there wasn't one damned thing he could do about it.

Well, actually, there is, he told himself. *I can at*

least put one right in those Mesan bastards' eye and refuse to be an even more disastrous Crandall for them.

"Very well." His voice sounded flat, defeated and broken, even to him. "Strike our wedges and send the pod self-destruct command, Bill."

"Yes, Sir," Daniels said.

"I suppose you should go ahead and get Harrington back, Reuben," Filareta continued, turning to the communications officer. "She'll want—"

Admiral William Daniels reached for his console to transmit the orders Admiral Filareta had given him. He was still in a state of shock, of disbelief, yet what he felt most strongly was relief. Relief that Filareta had been willing to recognize reality. Relief that Eleventh Fleet wasn't going to be destroyed after all.

Relief that abruptly vanished as he saw his own hand flip up a plastic shield and hit the button under it.

Filareta stiffened in horrified disbelief as fifty-one hundred pods launched fifty-one *thousand* missiles in a single enormous salvo.

"What the *fuck* d'you think you're do—?!"

The fleet admiral never completed the question. Before he could, William Daniels' hand, still under someone—or some*thing*—else's command, kept right on moving. The operations officer fought desperately to stop it, but it moved smoothly, efficiently, punching in a numerical command code he'd never learned or even seen before.

The command that detonated the bomb a petty officer named Harder had installed in his console and killed every man and woman on SLNS *Philip Oppenheimer*'s flag bridge.

❖   ❖   ❖

"Missile launch!" Andrea Jaruwalski barked. "Multiple missile launches! Fifty thousand-plus, incoming!"

Honor Alexander-Harrington's breath stopped. For just an instant, she couldn't believe what she was seeing. Couldn't believe anyone, even a Solly, could be that insane. That *arrogant*. That willing to see his men and women slaughtered.

But someone obviously could.

She looked at that incoming tide of destruction for perhaps another two seconds. Then she drew a deep breath.

"Engage the enemy," her soprano voice said evenly. "Fire Plan Thermopylae."

Chapter Twenty-Three

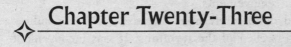

FLEET ADMIRAL IMOGENE TSANG sat up as the attention signal on her bedside communicator chimed. She raked hair out of her eyes, glanced at the time display, and grimaced. She'd been down for less than three hours, her eyes felt dry and scratchy, and the throbbing ache behind her forehead suggested that last pair of tequila sunrises might have been just a bit too much.

The com chimed again, and she stabbed the voice-only key with a vicious forefinger.

"*What?*" she snapped.

"Sorry to disturb you, Ma'am," Admiral Pierre Takeuchi said quickly, "but the dispatch boat just came through the terminus."

"It did?" Tsang turned sideways, sitting on the edge of her bed and planting her feet on the decksole. "How long ago?"

"Just over three minutes, Ma'am." She sensed Takeuchi's unseen shrug. "It took Lieutenant Trudeau, the dispatch boat's skipper, a couple of minutes to spot *Ranger* and for *Ranger* to relay to us."

"Understood." Tsang felt a spike of irritation she knew was completely irrational (and probably owed at least a little of its strength to her headache). There was no way this Trudeau could have known where TF 11.6 was located relative to the Beowulf Terminus before he actually arrived. And it wasn't as if the slight extra delay was going to make any difference to Tsang's movements.

She'd deliberately held the task force ten million kilometers clear of the terminus. It was inconvenient as hell, and it was going to take the better part of an hour to reach the terminus with a zero-zero velocity and make transit, but it had the benefit of keeping her far enough out to avoid offending Beowulfan sensibilities any worse than she had to. She'd considered deploying recon platforms and communications relays closer to the terminus, where she could cut down on any confusion on the part of the incoming courier boat. That would have been pretty blatant, though. It would undoubtedly have undone her efforts to placate Beowulf's ire, and it wasn't as if the Beowulfers were going to sneak up on her and attack!

Even from here, though, her gravitic sensor sections had monitored the impeller signatures of at least sixty or seventy Beowulfan freighters shuttling back and forth through the terminus. Obviously, while that terminus might be closed to *other* Solarian shipping, the Beowulfers were doing quite a bit of trade with the Star Empire. She'd gone so far as to ask the system government for an explanation, and been informed that what she was seeing were "humanitarian relief" efforts, not anything so crass as "trade."

Sure, and I can believe just as much of that as I

want to, she thought sardonically. *Oh, I don't doubt those cargoes are being used as part of the Manties' rebuilding effort, but I'll bet Beowulf's making a pretty centicred off their "humanitarian" concern!*

Beowulfan profiteering hadn't been very high on her list of concerns, however; steering clear of any avoidable incident *had* been, and so she'd contented herself with observing their activities from afar. And she'd also concentrated on staying far enough out from the terminus that none of those freighters were likely to see very much of her actual strength. There was no telling which of the merchant skippers sailing back and forth through the terminus might be tempted to tell friends in Manticore about the enormous SLN task force hovering on the far side. Fortunately, commercial-grade sensors weren't going to pick up diddley at just over half a light-minute.

She'd gone ahead and posted a single destroyer, SLNS *Ranger*, closer in, however, with her transponder online. The courier boat ought to have spotted that without too much difficulty, even allowing for the limitations of dispatch boat's sensor suites, but there was no point pissing or moaning over a couple of minutes either way.

"Have you already waked Franz?" she asked, massaging her temples with both hands.

"I told Sherwood to get him up while I got *you* up, Ma'am," Takeuchi said wryly, and Tsang snorted. Admiral Franz Quill, her operations officer, tended to wake up grumpy, and he didn't like Captain Sherwood Marceau, her com officer, very much anyway.

"As soon as you and I are done here," Takeuchi continued, "I'm getting Captain Robillard up, too. I already put out the general order to bring up the task force's impellers, and I figure she'll forgive me for waking you up first."

"Probably."

Actually, Tsang wasn't all that sure about Sanelma Robillard's forgiveness. Robillard was good, or Tsang wouldn't have picked her as her flag captain, but she was also a prima donna, even by the often prickly standards of the Solarian Navy. She was likely to make herself a pain in the ass if she decided Takeuchi had trespassed against her prerogatives by passing an order which would have *her* engineering department up and stirring before she was informed, even if he *was* the task force's operations officer.

"All right," the fleet admiral said. "It sounds like you've done everything right so far, Pierre. I'll meet you and the rest of the staff on Flag Bridge in twenty minutes. Clear."

❖   ❖   ❖

It was actually twenty-five minutes later, not twenty, when Tsang, headache banished by a quick squirt from her preferred morning-after inhaler, stepped onto SLNS *Adrienne Warshawski*'s flag deck. Not that the extra five minutes really mattered. A quick glance at the readiness display showed that *Warshawski*'s impeller nodes were still fifteen minutes from full readiness.

"Where are we, Pierre?" she asked brusquely.

"We should be able to get moving in another fifteen or twenty minutes, Ma'am," he replied, twitching his head in the direction of the display Tsang had already consulted. "Franz transmitted the preparatory order for Arbela twenty minutes ago, and all tactical crews have acknowledged. And Sherwood's copied Lieutenant

Trudeau's transmission to your console if you want to view it personally."

"I'll take a look at it in a minute," she said. "Unless there's something in it you think would affect Arbela?"

"No, Ma'am." Takeuchi grimaced. "All he knows is that the system was reported under attack. Well, that and he did confirm that assuming the Manty traffic-control people were giving accurate time chops, they really do have FTL com capability."

"Marvelous," Tsang said sourly. It wasn't that much of a surprise by now, but the confirmation emphasized the Manties' tech capabilities unpleasantly. Especially now, when Operation Arbela had moved from a future probability to a present certainty.

"All right," she went on a moment later. "I'll take a look at Truman's message. Meanwhile I think you and Franz should probably get on the net and touch base with our squadron commanders. Be sure we're not looking at any unanticipated delays."

❖   ❖   ❖

"Captain Robillard would like to speak to you, Fleet Admiral," Sherwood Marceau said, and Tsang looked up from her CIC repeater.

"Put the Captain through," she said.

"Yes, Ma'am."

The image of *Adrienne Warshawski*'s commanding officer appeared on Tsang's com a moment later.

"Sanelma," Tsang said. "What can I do for you?"

"I just wanted to report we're ready to proceed, Ma'am," Robillard replied, and Tsang suppressed an ignoble temptation to smile. Her flag captain's tone could not have been more respectful, yet there was a certain tartness to it. She was obviously still irritated by Takeuchi's decision to wake Tsang—and to order the entire task force (including *her* ship) to bring up its impellers—before he woke Robillard. She must have been sitting there, watching the engineering displays with her thumb on the call key to make *sure* she got Tsang notified before Takeuchi could. For that matter, she might even have instructed her engineer not to simultaneously report readiness to her and the task force operations officer, as SOP required.

"Thank you, Sanelma," the fleet admiral said as gravely as she could.

"You're welcome, Ma'am," Robillard responded with barely a trace of satisfaction, and Tsang chuckled as the display blanked.

"So I guess I *did* piss her off," Admiral Takeuchi observed with a wry smile.

"She'll recover," Tsang said dryly, and glanced at Admiral Quill.

"Let's get the task force moving, Franz," she said.

"At once, Fleet Admiral!"

Of all of Tsang's staffers, Quill came closest to being genuinely enthusiastic about Operation Arbela. In fact, he was the one who'd come up with the operation's name. Personally, Tsang was less confident than he was that it was going to work out as well for TF 11.6 as the original battle had for Alexander of Macedon, but she'd been willing to go along with his chosen name. And at least it wasn't as if Quill were one of those hidebound, blinkered, Solarian bigots who refused to acknowledge the possibility that the Manties might actually be able to give the SLN a genuine fight. A skeptic where the more extravagant claims about Manticoran technology were concerned, yes, but not a *blind* skeptic...unlike certain other officers Tsang could have named.

She stood watching the master plot for two or three minutes as her task force began accelerating towards the terminus. Then she turned back to Marceau.

"Sherwood."

"Yes, Ma'am?"

"I suppose you'd better go ahead and notify Terminus Traffic Control that we're going to be making transit shortly."

"Yes, Ma'am."

"Well, I bet *that's* going to make the Beowulfers happy," Takeuchi murmured, his voice low enough for only Tsang to hear.

"They're just going to have to live with it," Tsang replied flatly. "And it's not as if they haven't had enough time to adjust—"

"Excuse me, Fleet Admiral."

Tsang broke off in midsentence and turned back towards Marceau, eyebrows rising as the com officer's peculiar tone registered.

"Yes, Sherwood?"

"You've got an incoming priority com request, Ma'am."

"From Traffic Control?" Tsang was surprised. She didn't doubt the traffic-control authorities were going to be unhappy with her announcement that she was coming through their terminus anyway, whatever the Beowulfan system government might have decreed. But the terminus was thirty-three light-seconds from *Warshawski*; there was no way Marceau's transmission could have reached it yet, and any response would be at least a half-minute behind that.

"No, Ma'am," Marceau said, still with that peculiar

edge to his voice. "It's originating from near the terminus, but it's from Vice Admiral Holmon-Sanders, not Traffic Control."

Tsang glanced quickly at Takeuchi. Marianne Holmon-Sanders was the Beowulf System Defense Force's senior in-space officer, ranking just behind Admiral Corey McAvoy, the chief of naval operations. She was also the commanding officer of the BSDF's First Fleet—its *only* fleet, really—which made the fact that the incoming message was from her even more interesting.

"I see," the fleet admiral said after a moment, and walked across the flag bridge to her command chair. She took her time, settling herself comfortably, then nodded to Marceau.

"Put her through, Sherwood."

"Yes, Ma'am."

The woman who appeared on Tsang's display a moment later had brown hair, brown eyes, a wide, firm-lipped mouth, and a determined chin which went just a little oddly with her pert, undeniably snub nose. But what Tsang noticed most strongly, what caused her eyes to widen, was the fact that Holmon-Sanders wore not the maroon tunic and charcoal gray trousers of the Beowulf System Defense Force's usual uniform, but a skinsuit.

And so did every other officer and rating visible behind her. The officers and ratings manning their consoles and displays on what was obviously a capital ship's flight deck at general quarters.

"Vice Admiral?" Tsang said after a moment, slightly but firmly emphasizing Holmon-Sanders' lower rank. "What can I do for you today?"

She sat back to wait the minute necessary for her transmission to reach the terminus and Holmon-Sanders' reply to reach her, but then, barely one second later—

"You can stand down your impellers and assure me you have no intention of making transit through this terminus against the expressed will of my star system, Fleet Admiral," Holmon-Sanders said flatly.

Tsang's head whipped around towards Sherwood Marceau's station. She heard Takeuchi mutter something short, pungent, and surprised sounding, then cursed herself almost instantly for revealing her own astonishment so clearly. But—

Marceau was staring at his own console and looked, if possible, even more surprised than she felt. He looked down for another moment, then raised his eyes to hers.

"Another transmitter just came online, Ma'am," he said. "It must be some kind of relay. It's less than ten thousand klicks out from *Warshawski!*"

"No doubt your com section has detected my communications relay, Admiral Tsang," Holmon-Sanders' voice continued, and Tsang looked back at her display. "It's a receiver, as well as a transmitter, you know. I thought it would probably be a good idea not to have any . . . avoidable delays in our conversation. Particularly given the strength and clarity with which my government has set forth the Beowulf System's position on your proposed operation. Again, I formally request clarification of your intentions."

Tsang had her expression back under control, and her mind raced. Holmon-Sanders hadn't just idly decided to speak to her in real-time. She'd done it to make a point; that much Tsang was certain of. But *what* point? So far as Tsang knew, the only people who were even rumored to possess FTL communications ability were the Manties and—possibly—the Havenites. Which meant the only place Holmon-Sanders could have gotten her FTL relay was from Manticore. But *why* had she gotten it? And why was she telling Tsang she had it? Surely not even the *Beowulfers* had been crazy enough to—!

"Use their damned relay, Sherwood," she said.

"Yes, Ma'am. Give me just a second." He entered the commands to redirect his communications laser to the far closer relay, then nodded to Tsang.

"My intentions, Vice Admiral Holmon-Sanders," the fleet admiral said then, her voice hard, "are to carry out my orders, as previously explained to your system government."

"In other words," Holmon-Sanders said, still with that impossible quickness, "you *do* intend to transit this terminus?"

"I do," Tsang said flatly.

"Then I hereby inform you that you will not be permitted to do so," Holmon-Sanders said, just as flatly. "The federal government has no authority to overrule the Beowulf System government in this regard in the absence of a formal declaration of war. Do you happen to be in possession of such a formal declaration, Fleet Admiral?"

"I've already had this discussion with Director Caddell-Markham," Tsang replied. "I told him then, as I tell you now, that my understanding of the Constitution is that the federal authority supersedes that of any single star system in this situation. And, as I also informed him at the time, I intend to carry out my orders regardless of your own system government's interpretation of their legality."

"I don't think you want to do this, Fleet Admiral," Holmon-Sanders said, and smiled thinly. "I *really* don't think you want to do this."

That smile sent a bolt of anger through Imogene Tsang's surprise and confusion. There was no amusement in the expression, only challenge. And, even more infuriating, more than a hint of disdain. Possibly even contempt. Somehow, that smile made Tsang abruptly aware that she'd felt more anger over the Manties' defiance of the might, majesty, and power of the Solarian League than she'd previously realized.

"In that case, Admiral, you think *wrong*." Her tone was an icicle. "I have every intention of carrying out my orders."

All *my orders*, she thought, remembering the secret clause covering her response to this very situation. *My God, I wondered what whoever wrote that part must've been smoking. Now it turns out they nailed it!*

"And *I*, Fleet Admiral Tsang, have every intention of preventing you from endangering the lives of Beowulfan citizens of the Solarian League," Holmon-Sanders replied equally coldly.

"Ma'am," Franz Quill said quietly, "I'm picking up sensor platforms."

Tsang glanced at the display, and her mouth tightened. Cascades of icons appeared as at least two or three hundred reconnaissance platforms went active, lashing her starships with radar and lidar. Some of them were even closer than the FTL relay, and threat receivers warbled in warning. She had no idea how they'd gotten that close without being detected in the first place, but there was no mistaking Holmon-Sanders' message. She was telling Tsang that, unlike Tsang, she had detailed tactical information on the SLN task force.

"Status change!" Quill announced an instant later, and Tsang's right hand clenched on her chair arm as thirty-six impeller signatures appeared on her plot, roughly nine million kilometers from *Adrianne Warshawski* . . . and directly between her and the Beowulf Terminus.

"Thirty-six superdreadnoughts at eight-point-eight-seven million kilometers," Quill confirmed. "Impellers active. I can't tell yet if their side walls are up."

"Are you actually proposing to fire on units of the *Solarian Navy*?!" Tsang demanded, eyes blazing at Holmon-Sanders.

"I'm proposing to exercise the sovereign right of my star system to defend its citizens against the orders of an unelected clique of corrupt bureaucrats with no trace of constitutional authority to give the orders you propose to execute," Holmon-Sanders replied. "And you, Fleet Admiral, know as well as I do that they have no authority. That if you proceed with this operation you will be doing so in direct violation of the Constitution you swore an oath to protect and defend. That may not mean much to you, but it means quite a lot to us here in Beowulf."

Anger darkened Tsang's face. How *dare* this jumped-up pretense of a flag officer in her comic-opera little system-defense force talk to her that way? Of course she'd sworn to protect and defend the Constitution! Every Solarian officer did that. But the Constitution was what accepted practice made it, not some dead-letter document which hadn't functioned properly in over six hundred T-years! Holmon-Sanders knew as well as she did that the League would have fallen apart centuries ago if the people truly responsible for governing hadn't made accommodations with the more absurd provisions of Holmon-Sanders' precious Constitution!

"I disagree with your . . . unique interpretation of current constitutional law," she said flatly. "And I repeat that I intend to pass my command through that terminus."

"Not without the assistance and cooperation of Terminus Traffic Control, you aren't," Holmon-Sanders replied. "I'm sure your staff astrogator will be aware, even if you aren't, of just how disastrous any effort to make a simultaneous transit through this terminus without Traffic Control's guidance is going to prove. Do you intend to place armed parties on the control platforms and compel our personnel to coordinate your transit at pulser point?"

"I intend to do whatever it requires, Vice Admiral! And if that means my Marines are forced to take control of your control platforms and 'compel' your personnel to do their duty as Solarian citizens, then that's precisely what I'll do!"

"And the instant you attempt to do so, the Beowulf System Defense Force will open fire upon you in defense of our citizens."

Tsang inhaled sharply as the words were finally spoken.

"In that case, Admiral Holmon-Sanders, you will commit an act of treason."

"In that case, Admiral Tsang, *one* of us will have committed an act of treason," Holmon-Sanders replied, and her contemptuously challenging smile was no longer thin.

"And you and the vast majority of the personnel aboard your superdreadnoughts will also be *dead*," Tsang said flatly. "You'll be in my powered missile envelope in approximately nineteen minutes. If at that time you have not stood down and withdrawn your units, I *will* engage you, and the deaths of your spacers will be on your own head and that of your system government."

"I take it that's your final word on the matter?" Holmon-Sanders inquired almost calmly.

"Damned right it is." Tsang glared at her. "Get out of my way now, *Admiral*, or I will by God blow every one of your fucking ships out of space!"

"I think not," another voice said suddenly, and the image on Tsang's display split as another woman appeared on it, speaking from another command deck.

The blue-eyed newcomer had golden hair...and her skinsuit was definitely *not* Beowulf-issue.

"Vice Admiral Alice Truman, Royal Manticoran Navy," she identified herself coldly. "You might want to reconsider your belligerence, Fleet Admiral Tsang."

"Status change!" Admiral Quill's sharp voice wrenched Tsang's eyes from Truman's image back to the master plot as at least fifty new icons appeared on it. "Confirm sixty—repeat, *sixty*—additional superdreadnoughts!" Quill continued, and the bottom seemed to fall out of Tsang's stomach as her numerical superiority over Holmon-Sanders abruptly disappeared.

Impossible. *Impossible!* There was no way sixty

Manty superdreadnoughts could possibly be here in Beowulf space! Even if they'd dared to divert any of them, how could they have gotten them here? It was ridiculous, unless—

"I think you should have taken a closer look at the freighters moving back and forth between Beowulf and Manticore, Admiral Tsang," Truman said in that same cold voice, smiling faintly. "Surely not even the SLN was stupid enough to think we couldn't foresee the possibility of something like this once we figured out Filareta was coming! Or perhaps you really thought we couldn't. Especially if you judged us by your own service's demonstrated levels of competence."

The contempt in Truman's tone bit like a lash, and Tsang felt her jaw muscles bunching.

"I knew your system government was being run by lunatics," she grated, glaring at Holmon-Sanders, "but I hadn't realized they were goddammed *traitors*!"

"An interesting characterization coming from someone who proposes to kill Solarian citizens for having the audacity to resist the unconstitutional, illegal policies of a bevy of unelected bureaucrats," Holmon-Sanders replied.

"Don't hand me that bullshit!" Tsang snapped. "You've actively connived with a hostile star nation in time of war to offer armed resistance to the League's own military!"

"In time of war?" Holmon-Sanders cocked her head. "Not unless there's been that formal declaration of war you don't seem to be able to provide me with, Fleet Admiral Tsang." Her tone could have frozen a volcano.

"Don't you *dare* parse semantics with me! I represent the Solarian League!"

"You, Admiral Tsang," Truman said dispassionately, "represent Innokentiy Kolokoltsov, Nathan MacArtney, and the rest of their bureaucratic clique. And, as the Star Empire has repeatedly warned the League, they—or their policies, at least—are being manipulated by a non-Solarian power."

"*Bullshit!* Don't any of you ever get tired of that same old tired song-and-dance routine?!"

"In this case, no," Truman replied. "Since, unlike the nonsense you've just been spouting, it bears at least a nodding acquaintance with the truth."

"You wouldn't know the *truth* if it bit you on the ass!" Tsang snarled back. "And even if there were some tiny particle of truth to it, that doesn't change the fact that the Beowulf system government has actively colluded with another star nation which has killed God only knows how many Solarian naval personnel!"

"In resisting God only knows how many illegal, unilateral acts of aggression, you mean?" Truman inquired.

"Stop twisting my words!" Tsang's face was dark with anger. "And no matter how you try to twist things around to make it *our* fault, how do you think the League is going to react to this shit? You think the rest of the League's member systems are going to side with *Beowulf*? After Beowulf's actively connived to help you *ambush* a Solarian task force in *Solarian* space?!"

"Your ability to interpret a tactical situation would appear to be every bit as good as Josef Byng's and Sandra Crandall's, Admiral," Truman observed with icy disdain. "If we'd wanted to 'ambush' you, you'd be as dead as they are by now. Your reconnaissance provisions were so pathetic that the first thing you would have known about our presence would've been the impeller signatures of incoming missiles! Fortunately for you, nobody's particularly eager to murder spacers whose only crime is serving under criminally stupid superiors. If *that* was what we'd wanted to do, we would have *let* you make transit straight into the fire of our Junction forts and killed every one of your ships before you even scratched our paint. Instead, we've chosen to save your lives—or your crews' lives, at least—from the towering incompetence and unbridled arrogance of the Solarian League Navy's senior officer corps."

For the first time in her life, pure, distilled fury reduced Imogene Tsang literally to speechlessness. She could only glare at the Manticoran officer as Truman continued in that same precise, scalpel-edged voice.

"Had you shown a modicum of reasonableness, even a trace of respect for your own constitution and the constitutional rights of the Beowulf System and its citizens, you would have chosen to abide by the Beowulf System government's decision to deny you transit through this terminus. And had you done that, my forces would simply have stood by in stealth as observers, without interfering in any way. Unlike the League, we have no desire to kill anyone we can *avoid* killing. But you couldn't do that, so we found it necessary to present . . . an additional argument in favor of sanity, shall we say."

"And, as for how the rest of the League's systems are going to feel about this," Holmon-Sanders put it in, "every word of our conversation has been and is being recorded, and it will be released to the news media, without cuts or censorship, as soon as possible. You'd made your intention to violate our sovereignty—and the Constitution—abundantly clear long before the first Manticoran naval unit arrived in Beowulf space, Fleet Admiral. Indeed, the only reason Admiral Truman's ships remained stealthed as long as they did was to give us time to let you explain yourself for the newsies' benefit. I don't think there's going to be very much question in the mind of anyone who bothers to think about it that if Admiral Truman hadn't been here, you would indeed have opened fire on the units under my command in pursuit of what you know, whether you admit it or not, is an unlawful order. Of course, the odds have changed somewhat from the ones you thought obtained when you were so courageously prepared to slaughter your fellow Solarian citizens in pursuit of that order, haven't they?"

The Beowulfer showed her teeth, and her brown eyes were just as hard, just as cold, as Truman's blue ones.

"As Admiral Truman says, we don't want to kill anyone who doesn't have to die. But if you're still prepared to fight your way through this terminus, Fleet Admiral Tsang, then you just bring it on."

Chapter Twenty-Four

"WHAT THE HELL was he *thinking*?!" Elizabeth Winton snarled.

The Empress of Manticore stood glaring at the monstrous casualty list, brown eyes smoking like twin furnaces as the names of dead and damaged Solarian starships crawled endlessly up the conference room's display wall.

"You had him dead to rights. He *knew* he you did! How could even a *Solly* be so *stupid*?!"

"I don't know," Honor said drearily. She stood beside her monarch, and her own eyes were dark and haunted, not fiery. Anger hovered in their depths as well, but it was a cold, bitter anger overlaid by equally bitter regret... and guilt.

Nimitz made a soft sound from his perch on a chair beside the conference table, then straightened up and raised both true-hands as she looked at him.

<Not your fault,> he signed sharply. <You tried. You did everything you could. It was his fault, not yours.>

"Nimitz is right." Elizabeth's voice was softer, gentler,

and Honor returned her gaze to the Empress. "You *did* do everything you could, Honor."

"Everything except not back him into a corner," Honor replied.

"Don't you dare second-guess yourself over this!" Eloise Pritchart said sharply. "Yes, you and Earl White Haven pushed for an ops plan which would force them to surrender. I supported you in that, though, and so did Tom and Elizabeth and Protector Benjamin. And the reason we did, is that the two of you were right. And, as you yourself said, anyone crazy enough to open fire in the tactical situation you'd created was going to open fire no matter *what* happened!"

Honor looked at the Havenite president for a second or two, then nodded. Pritchart was probably right about that, but that didn't make Honor feel any better over two hundred and ninety-six destroyed Solarian superdreadnoughts . . . and 1.2 million dead Solarians.

Why? she asked herself yet again. *Why did he do it? Because I* humiliated *him in the way I demanded his surrender? Was he really so stupid, so* . . . vain, *that he was willing to get himself and all of those other men and women* killed *rather than swallow his pride and back down in front of a bunch of "neobarbs"?*

She didn't know, and she never would, for there had been no survivors from SLNS *Philip Oppenheimer*. And of the four hundred and twenty-seven superdreadnoughts Massimo Filareta had led into the Manticore Binary System, only sixty had managed to surrender undamaged. Two hundred and ninety-six—including *Oppenheimer*—had been destroyed (most of them outright, although some had merely been turned into hopelessly shattered and broken hulks), and another seventy-one might have been repairable, assuming anyone was interested in returning such obsolete, outmoded death traps to service.

Well, you wanted them to understand there was a price to war, Honor, she thought bitterly. *Maybe when they add this to what happened to Crandall, they'll finally start to get the message. It would be nice if* something *good came out of it, anyway.*

Her pain was almost worse because Grand Fleet's casualties had been so light. She'd learned long ago that every death took its own tiny bite out of her soul, yet she'd also learned the lesson she'd wanted the *Sollies* to learn. Wars cost. They cost starships, and they cost billions of dollars, and they cost *lives.* No matter how well you planned, how hard you trained, they cost lives, and she'd been incredibly fortunate to escape with "just" two thousand dead, most in her screening LACs, and minor, readily repairable damage to eleven of her own superdreadnoughts.

That was still two thousand dead men and women too many, though. And what hurt worst of all was that she'd been so certain Filareta was going to recognize the hopelessness of his situation. His expression, his body language, his obviously bitter appreciation of the tactical situation . . . all of them had convinced her he would accept surrender on honorable terms rather than see so many of his spacers killed.

"It must have been a panic reaction," Thomas Theisman said slowly, reaching up to the treecat on his shoulder as Springs from Above's muzzle pressed against the side of his neck. "I didn't see it coming, either, Honor, but that has to have been what it was."

"I think Admiral Theisman's right," High Admiral

Judah Yanakov said. He stood beside Admiral Alfredo Yu, technically Honor's second-in-command of the Protector's Own but for all practical purposes its actual CO. "It wasn't even coordinated fire!"

"*Was* it a panic reaction, though?" Admiral Yu asked softly.

Everyone turned to look at him, and he smiled faintly at Theisman. Once upon a time, Alfredo Yu had been Thomas Theisman's commanding officer, mentor, and friend. In fact, he'd transmitted his interest in the history the Legislaturalists and the Committee of Public Safety had both, each for its own reasons, done their very best to erase or rewrite, to a very junior Lieutenant Theisman. And it was his own study of that history which had helped lead a much more senior Citizen Admiral Theisman into his ultimate opposition to Rob S. Pierre and Oscar Saint-Just. Of course, that had been twenty T-years ago. A lot had changed in the intervening decades, but the Havenite-turned-Grayson still recognized the look in his old student's eyes.

"No, it's not a trick question, Tom," he said with a crooked smile. "I mean it. *Was* it a panic reaction?"

"It had to be, Alfredo," Yanakov said. "That was a classic gone-to-hell desperation launch. They couldn't possibly have targeted that much fire."

"Oh, I agree," Yu replied. "They just flushed the pods at us, threw everything they had right at Lady Harrington's command in hopes the missiles' onboard seekers would find something to kill, even without any direction, and that the sheer mass of fire would saturate her defenses. I've planned last-ditch, desperation attacks like that of my own."

"Exactly," Honor said slowly, her eyes intent as she tasted the emotions behind Yu's handsome, bony face. Some thought was working its way out in his brain. She could feel it, even though she had no idea what it was. She wasn't even certain *he* knew what it was yet. But she knew Alfredo Yu well, and she respected his instincts.

"We've all put together that kind of fire plan," she continued, waving her right hand in a gesture which took in the assembled flag officers. "Even when you don't expect to *need* it, you put it together, just in case. But, Alfredo, you don't *use* it when someone's offering to let you surrender your ships and your people *alive*. You just don't."

"No, you don't," Hamish Alexander-Harrington said softly. "But I think that's Alfredo's point, Honor."

White Haven was gazing very thoughtfully at Yu, and Samantha cocked her head to one side, considering Yu even more intently than her person.

"It is," Yu said after a moment. "My point, I mean. Look, when you set something like that up, you know it's only going to be used when the tactical situation's gone totally straight to hell, right?"

Honor nodded, almond eyes intent, and he shrugged.

"So you set it up so you can get the shot off with zero lost time," he continued. "I don't know for sure about the *Solly* Navy, but I do know that when we set up something like that in the GSN or the Protector's Own, we usually tie it to a single macro, or at the most a very short, easily remembered keycode on the ops officer's panel. That's the way the People's Navy did it, too."

"And the Republican Navy still does it the same way," Theisman said.

"Of course it does." Yu nodded. "You don't want something that's going to go off by accident—not unless you're criminally insane, anyway!—but you *do* want something that can get that shot off *no matter what else is happening* with the shortest possible delay between the order to fire and the actual launch. And what does that suggest?"

"Are you saying," Benton-Ramirez y Chou asked in a very careful tone, "that you think we're looking at another example of McBryde's damned nanotech, Admiral?"

"That's ridiculous," Pritchart said, yet her voice was far more thoughtful than denying, and Yu looked at her.

"Why, Madam President? If you assume they could get to Filareta's ops officer at all, why not set up something like this? Especially if there was some way for the people who programmed him to know or to guess how *he'd* go about setting up a gone-to-hell fire plan? Maybe they had access to recordings of simulations where he'd set up plans like that. For that matter, maybe they had someone else inside Filareta's staff passing them that kind of information, probably with no idea at all what the Alignment meant to do with it. I can think of at least three ways, right offhand, a Peep flag officer back in the bad old days could've gotten that information about any operations or tactical officer in the People's Navy anytime he'd wanted to, and the SLN's at least as badly riddled by patronage and 'favor buying' as the Legislaturalists ever were. And if Filareta's tac officer *did* have a pattern, did have a standard way of setting up for that kind of plan..."

His voice trailed off, and silence enveloped the

conference room as the people in it looked at one another.

"Tester, you may be right," Yanakov said softly into that silence at last. "It *could* be, anyway."

"I think he *is* right," White Haven said grimly. "Think about it. If they'd gone with a standard fire plan, they had the fire-control channels to've fired at least three *targeted* salvos out of those missile pods. There'd have been time to feed actual target coordinates to their birds, and those salvos would have been in final acquisition by the time anything *we* fired could've reached their ships. Sure, we'd have stopped a lot of them—most of them—before they inflicted any damage, but their chances of actually getting through with at least some hits would have been a lot higher than they could do simply trying to saturate our defenses without even assigning targets!"

"And look at the delay between that first launch and the first follow-on salvo from their broadside tubes," Lester Tourville said, eyes distant. "It was a good—what? Ten seconds? Something like that?"

"Thirteen," Theisman said. "You're right, Les."

"Pat hasn't had time for any prisoner interviews yet," Sir Thomas Caparelli said thoughtfully, lips pursed. "I wonder if anyone's going to be able to explain that delay to us? It does almost sound like there was a hole of some kind in the order queue, doesn't it?"

"Possibly," White Haven agreed. "But that doesn't change the fact that Filareta could have used the time Honor gave him to set up a sequenced, targeted, *controlled* launch, and he didn't. Why not?"

"Because that would have required a *series* of actions?" Yu murmured, then nodded slowly. "They'd have to select the pods to be enabled. Then they'd have to choose the targets, feed the coordinates, enable at least the first salvo's telemetry links, update their electronic warfare plan. It would have taken more than one man, and it would have taken a *complex* series of commands and keystrokes. Whereas—"

"Whereas this way, if you're right, all they needed was for some poor damned soul to punch one button and they could count on *me* to kill over a million people for them," Honor grated harshly.

More than one of the humans present winced. Her husband reached out to lay one hand on her forearm, and she looked at him with bitter eyes.

"You didn't have any choice," he told her. "Not with fifty thousand missiles coming at your command."

"I could have just taken the fire," Honor replied flatly. "Look at how few people we lost anyway! I could've waited to be sure—"

"Oh, stop it!" Thomas Theisman snapped, and Honor's head snapped around in surprise at the genuine anger in his voice.

"No, you could *not* have 'just taken the fire'!" the Republic's secretary of war told her sharply. "And if you *had* done something that stupid, you'd deserve to be broken for it!"

"But—"

"Don't you 'but' *me!* You didn't know—you *couldn't* know—if they'd come up with some kind of fire-control fix we'd never heard of before. You had no right, not one *shred* of a moral justification, to risk the lives of personnel under your command just because somebody on the other side had done something suicidal! Your responsibility is to *your* people, not theirs! It's your job to neutralize an enemy before he kills *them*, and you'd *damned* well better do it if you're going to be worthy of the uniform you wear!"

His brown eyes blazed, and she tasted the white-hot fury, the total sincerity, behind them.

"*That's* your responsibility, Admiral Harrington, and you lived up to it! You reacted to the threat you knew about, the one you saw, and I was right there on that flag bridge with you. It took those missiles three minutes to reach us, and you had a Hermes buoy sitting right off his flagship's bow. There was *plenty* of time for him to get on the com and tell you the launch was a mistake, if he hadn't meant to launch it! Correct me if I'm wrong, but I don't believe he did that, now, did he? Not only that, but thirteen-second lag or not, the *rest* of his damned fleet was firing full broadsides at you on its heels! I understand that real-izing you gave the order to kill that many people has to make you sick to your stomach. It makes *me* want to puke, and I didn't have to give it. But the only ones responsible for what happened to Filareta and the people under his command are whoever arranged to get him sent here and—assuming there's any basis to all this speculation in the first place—whoever got to his tac officer. Not you; not me—*them*!"

She looked around the conference room and saw the agreement in every other face. More than that, she *tasted* the agreement, and her brain knew they were right. Maybe someday she'd be able to accept that as easily as they did. But even if that day came, she would never be free of the soul-deep regret she felt.

Silence lingered for several moments, then Pritchart cleared her throat.

"How do you think the League is going to react to all this?" she asked the group at large.

"Poorly?" Tourville suggested with a sour smile.

"Oh, I think you can take that for granted," White Haven agreed. "And I don't think it's going to be a very good idea for us to suggest Mesa somehow manipulated Filareta into firing." He rolled his eyes. "Even if anyone in Old Chicago were willing to entertain any evidence which might support our 'ridiculous conspiracy-theory paranoia' in the first place, we don't *have* any evidence. We'd play straight into Abruzzi's hands if we handed him that kind of propaganda hook."

"And there are plenty of Sollies ready to go along with him," Elizabeth agreed sourly, then gave herself a shake and drew a deep breath. "Not that I suppose I can blame them, really, given the official party line, Solly newsies' well-known impartial reporting, and how ridiculous the whole notion still seems to *me* sometimes!"

"The fact that we can't blame them for it doesn't keep their refusal to entertain the truth from being inconvenient as hell," Pritchart observed even more sourly. "And the fact that Tsang is going to get to Old Terra with what happened in Beowulf well before anybody in Old Chicago finds out what happened out here isn't going to help one bit. The Mandarins are going to have at least a few days to start drumming up anti-Beowulf sentiment before word of what happened to Filareta lands on them like a nuke, and just imagine what the 'faxes are going to be like *then*."

"Not exactly something we didn't anticipate," Benton-Ramirez y Chou sighed. "Mind you, we'd all have been happier if Tsang had been bright enough to back down without Admiral Truman having to take a hand."

"At least she was smart enough not to pull a Crandall or a Filareta," Honor observed grimly.

"Or else Mesa didn't have time to get to anyone on *her* staff," Tourville muttered.

"They can't get to *everybody*, Les," Theisman pointed out a bit tartly.

"And they can't predict every situation," Yanakov added, nodding his agreement with Theisman's observation. "Tester knows they seem to do a better job of anticipating and manipulating than I'd like, but there have to be limits somewhere. And, frankly, the last thing we can afford is to actually succumb to—what was it you called it, Hamish?—'ridiculous conspiracy-theory paranoia' and start seeing Alignment machinations behind *everything* that happens."

"Either way, Honor has a point," Benton-Ramirez y Chou observed. "Nobody got killed in Beowulf, and as the President says, they won't have a clue what happened to Filareta until the first newsies get to the Sol System from Manticore. So they're going to come out like attack dogs, without any idea of the next bit of news in the pipeline. I'm not sure how that's going to play with League public opinion, but I'm pretty damned sure that when word of Filareta's disaster reaches Old Chicago, things are going to go to hell in a handbasket. I wouldn't be too surprised if some of the real lunatics don't press for direct military action against Beowulf."

"Some of them are going to see your actions as real treason, Mr. Director," Yu pointed out. "They're not going to worry about constitutional niceties, and they *are* going to be looking for someone to blame, especially when they find out what happened to Filareta. If there's any justice in the galaxy, they'll blame Kolokoltsov and Rajampet, but it's been my observation that justice is conspicuous by its absence when it comes to politics and entrenched, self-serving regimes."

"We have had just a little experience of our own with that, haven't we?" Pritchart said wryly, but she was looking at Theisman, not Yu. "On the other hand, Tom, I remember something you said about Kolokoltsov and Frontier Security."

"Something *I* said?" Theisman's eyebrows arched.

"Yes. It was while we were discussing the implications of the Battle of Spindle and how the Sollies might react. I said something about how little impact Solarian public opinion ever has on the League's decisions. Do you remember what you said to me?"

"Not exactly, no."

"I think this is pretty nearly a direct quote, actually," she told him. "As I recall, you said, 'The citizens of the People's Republic didn't have any real political oversight over its bureaucracies, either. A situation which changed rather abruptly when the Manties' Eighth Fleet came calling and Saint-Just got distracted dealing with that minor threat.'"

There was silence for a moment, then Benton-Ramirez y Chou nodded.

"That's becoming a steadily more likely scenario," he said grimly. "And that's hard." He shook his head, his expression sad. "I've known the League was rotten at the core for almost my entire life, but it was still the *Solarian League*. It was still the heir of all Mankind's greatness, and for all its warts, it was still *my* star nation. And now this." He shook his head again. "Now it looks like I'm going to be directly party to the actions which bring the whole tottering edifice crashing down. And I can't be sure we're not doing exactly what those Mesan bastards *want* us to be doing."

"The last thing we can afford to do is allow ourselves to be paralyzed for fear we might be doing what they want, Uncle Jacques," Honor said quietly, almost gently. "Judah's right about that. And I know you. For that matter, I know *Beowulfers*. If it comes down to doing what you think is right or sacrificing your most basic principles to preserve a system as corrupt as the League's proving it is, I know what you're going to decide."

"Always so black-and-white for you Manties," her uncle teased her gently, and Elizabeth chuckled.

"And you decadent Beowulfers always trying to convince us that you see *only* shades of gray," she riposted.

"Well, usually, that's what it is." Benton-Ramirez y Chou's tone was suddenly much more serious. "But sometimes it isn't, and my long, tall niece here has a point." He smiled a little sadly at Honor. "Comfortable or not, when those 'sometimes' come along, the only coinage history seems willing to accept is our lives, our fortunes, and our sacred honor."

✦ Chapter Twenty-Five

"TELL ME AGAIN how maneuvering Beowulf into a false position was supposed to *help* us, Innokentiy. I seem to be having a little trouble following the logic."

Omosupe Quartermain's voice was uncharacteristically harsh, and her blue eyes were hard as she glowered at Innokentiy Kolokoltsov across the table. The two of them sat in a high-security conference room in an unusual private, face-to-face meeting with neither their colleagues nor a single aide present, and the permanent senior undersecretary of commerce was not a happy woman.

"I think it still is going to help us in the long run," Kolokoltsov replied patiently. "I don't say it worked as well as I hoped it would, because it sure as hell didn't. And I don't know if it's going to help us *enough*, either, but please remember that I never said it was a *good* option in the first place. I only said it was the best one available to us."

"But look what those two bitches had to say!" Quartermain snapped. "You've seen what Beowulf's dumped to the media, Innokentiy, and Holmon-Sanders is bad enough all by herself! The newsies are going to eat up that business about violating the Constitution, and 'unelected bureaucrats', and federal overreach, and you know it. God help us once *O'Hanrahan* gets hold of it! But that Manty admiral, that *Truman...*" She shook her head. "The *contempt* that bitch showed! She was *daring* Tsang to cross the line, and she didn't show a trace of doubt that she could hammer our ships into wreckage any time she wanted. Worse, she didn't pull any punches about dumping full responsibility on *us*—on us, personally—any more than Holmon-Sanders did, Innokentiy! That's going to resonate with the woman in the street in a way no 'principled response' of ours is ever going to match, and you know *that*, too."

"Admittedly, it never occurred to me Beowulf might be so far gone as to actually invite Manty wallers through into Beowulf space to threaten the League Navy," Kolokoltsov conceded. "On the other hand, I never expected Admiral Tsang to be so frigging stupid as to actually try to fight her way through when Beowulf told her no, either!" It was his turn to shake his head, his expression disgusted. "She was *supposed* to back off 'in deference to Beowulf's expressed wishes'—to *let* the Beowulfers stand on their 'constitutional rights' so we got the credit for showing restraint in the face of their irrationality!"

"Well, she didn't get *that* part of it right, did she?"

"No, she didn't. And I find it interesting that Rajani's still so busy debriefing her."

"What do you mean?" Quartermain's eyes narrowed, and Kolokoltsov shrugged.

"I mean I want to talk to the good admiral personally," he said in a flat, hard voice. "I want to find out exactly what her instructions from Rajani actually were. God knows, after Crandall's performance I'm willing to accept that every serving flag officer in the Navy is a frigging idiot, but were her actions all her own idea? Or did somebody over at the Admiralty cut her a set of orders we didn't know anything about?"

"Why the hell would Rajani have done something like that?" Quartermain frowned, her expression intent. "He knew what we were after as well as we did!"

"I certainly explained it to him using nice, short, simple words," Kolokoltsov said bitingly. "But he's been pushing this confrontational stance against the Manties from day one, and he never has explained why Crandall picked the Madras Sector, of all damned places, for her training exercise. Or exactly why he failed to mention her presence in the vicinity to us after what happened at New Tuscany. Or even how Filareta just 'came to be' so conveniently placed at Tasmania when he came up with Raging Justice in the first place. I know he's an arrogant prick who despises every neobarb ever born, and I know he takes the Manties' attitude as a personal affront to *his* Navy, but I'm starting to wonder if there might not be more to it even than that."

"*Please* don't tell me you're buying into this grand conspiracy nonsense the Manties are spouting!"

"I'm not," Kolokoltsov said, yet his tone lacked a little something, Quartermain thought.

"Centuries-long conspiracies?" She threw up both hands. "Fleets of invisible starships? Plans to replace us all with genetically engineered super-Scrags of some sort? Some kind of mind-controlling nanotech? And the entire institution of genetic slavery's only a front for all of this 'Alignment's' evil plans? We're supposed to believe the nasty Mesans managed to keep all of this completely secret for six hundred *years* when all the 'proof' the Manties can provide is the unsupported testimony of a single lunatic scientist? One who actually threatened to *kill* one of Mesa's leading geneticists—not one of Manpower's hacks, but the Chairwoman of Maternal and Fetal Genetics at one of the finest hospitals on Mesa!—over his daughter's death?"

"I agree it sounds insane," Kolokoltsov replied. "But parts of it are going to make people wonder, if they really stop and think about it. Like the fact that the Republic of Haven, of all people, believes it, too. That Haven actually brought the entire story to Manticore in the first place!"

"That's what the Manties are *telling* us happened," Quartermain shot back. "And if I were them, I'd have damned well been telling us anything I could think of that might have convinced us to go ahead and send somebody to Manticore to order Filareta to stand down the way Carmichael kept demanding!"

"You think they're lying?"

"Actually, I think it's possible as hell," Quartermain said flatly. "If Carmichael could've sold us on their version and gotten us to whistle Filareta off, wouldn't it have been worth it? I mean, even if we later found out they'd lied to us, we'd already have recalled him. We're going to send him all the way back out there just because we're pissed off that they *lied* to us? We'd look like complete clueless bunglers—first for letting them bluff us to begin with, and then for sending him back to kick their ass, like a playground bully in a temper tantrum, just because they outsmarted us the first time!"

"What about Pritchart?" Kolokoltsov challenged.

"What about her? *I've* never met the woman, have you? How hard would it be to find an actress to stand in for her? Especially with a little judicial computer enhancement? What—you think the Manties are going to worry about pissing off the head of state of a star nation they've been fighting for the last twenty years when she finds out they used her in a psychological-warfare operation against us? What's she going to do? Declare war on them?!"

Omosupe had a point, Kolokoltsov reflected. One he hadn't actually considered, in fact. He wasn't convinced she was right—not by a long chalk!—but it was a plausible alternative, and he made a mental note to suggest it to Malachai Abruzzi. It might just come in handy in the not too distant future.

"Well, be that as it may," he said, pulling the conversation back to its original topic, "and in answer to your earlier question, even with the way Tsang screwed up, we've still got Beowulf dead to rights refusing our own ships passage. And however big a mouth that Manty admiral might've had, the fact that Beowulf invited her in ahead of time—obviously connived to cover and conceal the movement of her ships through the Beowulf Terminus for the express purpose of killing Solarian spacers if it *had* turned into a shooting exchange—is perfect from our perspective. I've already talked to Malachai about it, and he's priming the pump with 'unnamed source' briefings for some of our more reliable newsies. And

I've got three of our more prominent friends in the Assembly—including Tyrone Reid—ready to move for a formal inquiry into Beowulf's actions."

Quartermain looked at him for a moment, eyes thoughtful, and then nodded slowly. Tyrone Reid was a senior assemblyman from the Sol System itself. A member of the Judiciary Committee, he'd carefully crafted the public image of a senior and thoughtful jurist, and the camera liked him. His photogenic patrician face and the polished perfection of his Old Terran accent made him one of the newsies' favorite talking heads, and that in turn made him one of the most widely known political figures in the entire League. He'd be perfect for the part, whether he adopted the persona of an infuriated firebrand or the "more in sorrow than in anger" attitude of a regretful constitutional scholar debunking Beowulf's flawed position.

"And if it turns out Filareta's screwed up as badly as Tsang did?" she inquired after a moment, and Kolokoltsov grimaced.

Assuming Operation Raging Justice had proceeded as planned—and the dispatch boat which had transited to Beowulf seemed to prove Filareta had reached Manticore at least a week ago, just about on schedule—they should already have heard from him. The fact that they hadn't didn't necessarily prove things *hadn't* gone as planned, however. Battles between fleets the size of Eleventh Fleet and whatever the Manties had scraped up might last days or even weeks as the opponents maneuvered against one another. For that matter, even if Filareta had captured all three of the Manticore Binary System's inhabited planets, he still would have had to get past the forts at the Manticore end of the Junction—and past the combined BSDF and RMN detachments in Beowulf space at the other end—before he could have gotten a message back to Old Chicago.

None of which kept Kolokoltsov's nerves from tying themselves tighter and tighter while the silence stretched out.

"That's one reason Malachai isn't giving the newsies any 'official' position statements," he admitted. "And the reason I've *primed* Reid and the others without turning them loose yet. We're not going to jump either way until we know what Filareta did, but Malachai and I have discussed our options. Obviously, if he's pushed ahead and the Manties have collapsed, figuring out how to spin it is no problem. If he's backed off, on the other hand, we point out that both he and Tsang have demonstrated yet again the Solarian League Navy's abhorrence for the kind of blood fests the Manties seem perfectly willing to embrace."

"And if he's gotten his ass blown off like Crandall?" Quartermain asked grimly.

"My feeling is that he's smarter than Crandall. I think he'll have backed off if it looked to him like he was going to get hammered. And I think the Manties will have let him, to be honest."

"Why?" Quartermain could have sounded incredulous, but her tone was genuinely curious.

"I think they're crazy, but I don't really believe they're the bloodthirsty maniacs we've been describing to the newsies, Omosupe, and neither should you. Think about it. They had Tsang dead to rights, and they didn't even try to engage her. They let her turn around and hyper out. With her tail metaphorically between her legs, perhaps, but they let her *go*. If they were really contemplating pushing a war against the League, would they have let that many of our superdreadnoughts get away from them? 'Live to fight again another day' is the phrase, I believe."

"I don't know how much faith I'd care to invest in that particular theory, but it's not as completely insane as I thought it was going to be before you explained," Quartermain said. "On the other hand"—her eyes narrowed once more—"that still doesn't explain why you specifically wanted to see me and none of the others."

"It wasn't because I wanted to see you and *none* of the others," Kolokoltsov corrected. "I wanted to see you without seeing *all* of the others. In particular, without seeing Nathan and Rajani. I figure there's actually a pretty good chance the two of us can stay below their radar horizon, but if I'd started adding others..."

He let his voice trail off, and she nodded. She'd thought that might be it. For that matter, she'd made a mental bet with herself about the topic he wanted to discuss.

"All right," she said. "We're here; they aren't. What is it you want to talk about?"

"This damned Manty blockade," he said frankly. "One reason I didn't want Nathan or Rajani here was because the last thing we need right now is more posturing. But having said that, I have to admit the Manties have moved faster and a lot harder than I thought they were going to. Closing their own termini is bad enough; if these reports that they're closing down other people's termini are true, they've escalated it further than I really expected they were going to."

Quartermain started to say something sharp and pungent, but she didn't. At least he was admitting he'd made a mistake. Besides, it wasn't as if kicking him the way he deserved was going to do any good at this point.

"And?" she said instead.

"And I need to know where we stand as of what we know right now. And where you think it's going to go in the next few months. Even in a best-case scenario, our economy's going to get hammered—assuming Filareta hasn't already solved all our problems, of course. I know that. But I need to know what you and Agatá are planning to do to mitigate the damage. I'm not expecting any kind of miracles," he added hastily as her blue eyes began to harden once more, "and that's not why I'm asking. I'm asking because I need to know how to go about positioning us to implement the best patch-up job the two of you can do. I know you and Agatá are working closely together, so I figure talking to you is pretty much the same as talking to both of you, without the problem of talking to Nathan and Rajani at the same time."

"You're going to have to talk to them sooner or later," she cautioned in a slightly mollified tone. "The economic implications for any kind of sustained war effort are going to be painful—*incredibly* painful, to be honest—in the long run. We're going to find ourselves needing the protectorate service fees worse than ever, even in the best case I can imagine, and that's going to be Nathan and Frontier Fleet's bailiwick."

"I've already figured that out, and when I have to bring them in, I will. But before I do that, I want the best briefing I can get. I want to speak to them from a position of strength, and that means knowing what the hell I'm talking about and knowing you, Agatá, and I are all on the same page. Fair?"

"Fair enough," she conceded and settled back in her chair.

"First," she began, "as Agatá and I have already pointed out, the effect on our interstellar commerce is going to—"

Chapter Twenty-Six

"ARE YOU SURE ABOUT THIS, Commodore?"

The man on Commodore Sean Magellan's display wore the gray and black uniform of Agueda Astro Control and a profoundly worried expression. Magellan didn't blame him; he was more than a little unhappy about his assignment himself.

But unhappy wasn't the same thing as hesitant, and he felt the eagerness simmering in his blood as the moment approached.

"Yes, Captain Forstchen," the commodore replied far more calmly than he felt. "I'm quite sure."

Captain Lewis Forstchen's gray-blue eyes looked even more worried at Magellan's response. He clearly didn't like where this was going, but there wasn't a lot he could do about it.

"My government's not going to like this," he pointed out.

"I'm afraid there's a lot of that going around these days, Captain," Magellan said. "And the good news is that we don't really need your help for this transit. So you can just sit back and watch, and your own sensor records will prove that's all you did."

Forstchen started to say something else, but he stopped himself in time. As Magellan had just pointed out, electronic records of his and the Agueda System in general's innocence might come in very handy in the not-too-distant future. Personally, Magellan expected that "not-too-distant" day to be considerably *more* distant than Forstchen apparently did.

On the other hand, it could turn out Forstchen had a point.

"For the record, Captain," he said, "your objection and your government's protests are formally noted. And on behalf of *my* government, I extend the sincere regrets of the Star Empire of Manticore for the potentially invidious position in which the Agueda System's been placed. Unfortunately, the current... unpleasantness between the Star Empire and the Solarian League leaves us little choice. I regret that, but I'm afraid I'll have to be moving on now." He inclined his head courteously at the com. "Magellan, clear."

The display blanked, and he turned to the compact, squarely built captain on the far smaller display linking him to HMS *Otter*'s command deck.

"Are we ready, Art?" he asked.

"Just about, Sir," Captain Arthur Talmadge replied. "Mind you, I'd really have preferred not to dispense with Astro Control's services quite so cavalierly." He smiled. "I know our charts were updated just before we left, but I find myself longing for a local guide."

"And if we could've found a local guide for this terminus anywhere in the home system, he'd be right there on the bridge with you," Magellan pointed out with a half smile of his own. "Since we couldn't, he isn't. So let's not spend our time dwelling on things we wish we had and don't."

"Point taken, Sir," Talmadge agreed and then glanced at his own executive officer. "Ready, Colleen?"

"Yes, Sir." Commander Colleen Salvatore nodded.

"David?" Magellan asked, looking at Commander David Wilson, his own chief of staff.

"Yes, Sir. Jordan just receipted *Malcolm Taylor*'s and *Selkie*'s readiness signals."

"Thank you." Magellan looked back at Talmadge. "The squadron's ready to proceed when you are, Captain Talmadge," he said in a much more formal tone.

"Very good, Sir," Talmadge responded with matching formality.

"In that case, let's move them out."

"Aye, aye, Sir." Talmadge turned his command chair to face Senior Chief Cindy Powell. "Helm, take us in."

"Aye, aye, Sir."

Otter ghosted forward at a bare twenty gravities, moving into the invisible flaw of the Agueda Terminus. Under normal circumstances, she would have been aligned for transit and cleared by Agueda Astro Control, which would have monitored her approach vector, double- and triple-checking her entry into the terminus. Under the circumstances which currently obtained, she and the rest of the Thirty-First Cruiser Squadron were on their own, dependent on their own charts of the terminus and its tidal stresses. The good news was that they'd been provided with the very latest charts for the terminus before they ever set out; the bad news was that none of the squadron's ships had ever transited this particular terminus before.

And the potentially *really* bad news was that they had absolutely no idea what they'd be sailing into on the far side.

Oh, stop that! Magellan told himself irritably. *You do know what's on the far side... more or less, anyway. And it's not like you're about to poke your nose into the Junction Forts, now, is it?*

No, it wasn't. On the other hand, if Lacoön Two was going according to plan and no one else had managed to jump the gun, he was about to become the first naval commander in history to seize a Solarian wormhole terminus by force.

And isn't that going to make the Sollies happy? he thought dryly.

Magellan's slightly understrength squadron of *Saganami-C*-class cruisers was a long way from home: four hundred and forty-five light-years from the Manticore Binary System through hyper-space, and three hundred and twenty-seven from Beowulf. Of course, he hadn't had to make the trip the long way. Instead, he'd transited from the Manticoran Junction to Beowulf, then crossed sixty-three light-years from Beowulf to the Roulette System, then transited the Roulette-Limbo Hyper Bridge and crossed another forty-nine light-years of hyper-space from Limbo to Agueda.

Spreading sunshine and light the entire way, he reflected. *Amazing how unpopular we are*.

Amazing, perhaps, but scarcely surprising. Roulette, Limbo, and Agueda were all independent (or at least nominally so) star systems. Actually, Limbo was an OFS client state, with a particularly unpleasant fellow sitting in the system's executive mansion. President for

Life Ronald Stroheim had been *most* unhappy to see a Royal Manticoran Navy task group suddenly appear through the wormhole terminus which he regarded as his personal cash cow. As a good, loyal OFS henchman, he got to keep somewhere around three percent of the terminus' total revenues for himself, which made him an incredibly wealthy man. Apparently he hadn't heard that the Star Empire had decided to start collecting termini, however, and CruRon 31's unannounced arrival had come as a distinct shock. He seemed to feel very ill used that his neighbors in Roulette hadn't warned him his guests were en route.

In fairness, the Roulette System's government hadn't been enthralled by the Manticorans' arrival in *its* system, either. Although Roulette normally enjoyed cordial relations with both Beowulf and the Star Empire, it had been deliberately distancing itself from Manticore ever since news of the New Tuscany Incident hit the Solarian 'faxes. Given that Roulette was little more than a hundred light-years from the Sol System itself, it was difficult to blame President Matsuo or the rest of his government for not wanting to irritate the League. Unfortunately for them, however, the Roulette Terminus was on Lacoön Two's list, and Magellan had swooped in across the alpha wall and secured control of the terminus before anyone could make transit through it to alert Limbo of what was coming.

He'd detached one of his escorting destroyer squadrons and the CLAC *Ozymandias* to sit on the Roulette Terminus, then headed through to Limbo, where his ships' emergence from the terminus associated with that star system had taken the locals completely by surprise. Unlike the Manticoran Junction, the Limbo Terminus was unfortified, and the "Limbo Space Navy" consisted of two elderly destroyers—only one of which seemed to be actively in commission at the moment—and eight LACs which had to be at least fifty T-years old. Despite their no doubt undying loyalty to President for Life Stroheim, the commanding officers of those antiquated death traps had declined to match broadsides with seven *Saganami-C*-class heavy cruisers.

Magellan couldn't imagine why.

He'd detached his second destroyer squadron and the CLAC *Midas* to cover the Limbo Terminus, and then moved briskly on to Agueda.

Agueda had been just as surprised as Limbo, and not much happier to see him, although he suspected that quite a bit of President Loretta Twain's fiery denunciation of Manticore's "high-handed and flagrant disregard for the rights and sovereignty of independent star nations" had been more for the official record than from the heart. Unlike Roulette, Agueda was almost three hundred and fifty light-years from Sol, and the citizens of Agueda didn't much care for the repressive government of Limbo and its ... affiliation with the Office of Frontier Security. Still, there were appearances to be observed, and Magellan had rigorously respected the Agueda System's twelve-light-minute territorial limit and restricted his activities to the terminus itself. He'd been scrupulously polite as well, and assured Captain Forstchen and President Twain that he had no intention of forcibly seizing control of Agueda Astro Control's platforms.

Of course, he also had absolutely no intention of allowing a single Solarian-registry ship to pass *through* the Agueda Terminus, either, but that was quite another matter.

One nice thing about moving along the hyper bridges, he thought. *Unless you call ahead, no one knows you're coming until you arrive.* He smiled thinly. *Pity about that.*

"Stand by to reconfigure to Warshawski sail on my command, Rung-wan," Talmadge said.

"Aye, Sir," Lieutenant Commander Hwo Rung-wan, *Otter*'s engineering officer, replied. "Standing by to reconfigure."

Talmadge nodded, watching the maneuvering plot as Senior Chief Powell gently, gently aligned *Otter* for transit. The ship's icon flashed green as Powell put her flawlessly into position.

"Rig foresail for transit," he said.

"Aye, aye, Sir. Rigging foresail—now."

Otter's wedge fell abruptly to half-strength as her foreword alpha nodes reconfigured to produce the circular disk of a Warshawski sail instead of contributing to her n-space drive. The sail was over six hundred kilometers in diameter, and completely useless in normal-space, but the forward end of HMS *Otter* was edging steadily *out* of n-space.

"Stand by to rig aftersail," Talmadge said as his ship continued to creep forward under the power of her after impellers alone. A readout flickered to life in the corner of the maneuvering plot, and he watched its numerals climb steadily upward as the foresail moved deeper and deeper into the terminus. Compared to the Manticoran Wormhole Junction, the Agueda Terminus was little more than a ripple in space, but that was still orders of magnitude more powerful than anything a ship's impeller nodes could have produced. If their charts were as accurate as everyone thought they were, he had almost twenty seconds either way as a safety margin, but if they *weren't*, and if *Otter* strayed out of the safe window before she got her aftersail rigged, they'd never even realize they were dead.

The soaring numbers crossed the threshold. The foresail was now drawing sufficient power from the tortured grav waves twisting through the terminus to provide movement, and Talmadge nodded sharply.

"Rig aftersail now," he said crisply.

"Rigging aftersail, aye, Sir," Lieutenant Commander Hwo replied, and *Otter* twitched as her impeller wedge disappeared entirely and a second Warshawski sail sprang to life at the far end of her hull.

The transition from the impeller to sail was one of the trickier moments any coxswain had to deal with, even with the full support of a terminus' traffic-control staff. If Senior Chief Powell felt any particular anxiety, however, there was no sign of it in her rock-steady hands. They moved with complete confidence, taking *Otter* through the conversion with scarcely a quiver, holding her dead center as she gathered way forward.

The maneuvering plot blinked again, and—for an instant no one had ever succeeded in measuring—*Otter* ceased to exist in Agueda and then, equally suddenly, *began* to exist somewhere else. She reappeared in a dazzling burst of azure brilliance as transit energy radiated from her sails, and Powell nodded in satisfaction.

"Transit complete," she announced.

"Thank you, Helm. Well done!" Talmadge said, but most of his attention was back on the sail interface readout, watching the numbers twinkle downward even more rapidly than they'd risen. "Engineering, reconfigure to impeller."

"Aye, aye, Sir. Reconfiguring to impeller now."

Otter folded her sails back into her impeller wedge and moved forward more rapidly, accelerating steadily out of the Stine Terminus, five and a half light-hours from the G5 primary of the Stine System.

"Five hundred gravities, Senior Chief," Talmadge said.

"Five hundred gravities, aye, aye, Sir," Powell acknowledged crisply, and Talmadge's lips twitched as he waited for Stine Astro Control to react to his ship's abrupt appearance.

❖   ❖   ❖

"Sir, they've noticed us," Lieutenant Jordan Rivera announced, and Commodore Magellan raised an eyebrow at his staff communications officer.

"Put it on the main display, Jordan."

"Yes, Sir."

An officer in the uniform of Stine Astro Control with a captain's insignia appeared on the main com display. He had a dark complexion, a shaved head, a thick mustache, and an irate expression.

"Unknown ship!" he snarled. "Reduce acceleration immediately!"

"My, he does seem a bit unhappy," Magellan murmured.

"Well, Sir," Commander Wilson observed, "we *are* exceeding the terminus acceleration limit by about four hundred and eighty gravities. I imagine that could account for a *bit* of unhappiness."

"I suppose you're right," the commodore conceded.

"God damn it, reduce your accel right *now!*" the

shaven-headed captain shouted. "What the *fuck* d'you think you're doing?!"

"I think he's going to get even more unhappy just about...now," Lieutenant Commander Sarah Tanner, Magellan's ops officer, remarked dryly as *Malcolm Taylor*, his squadron's second ship, burst out of the terminus behind *Otter*.

Malcolm Taylor peeled off on a sharply divergent vector, accelerating just as hard as *Otter*, and Magellan nodded in satisfaction. Although even a relatively small terminus was an enormous volume of space, trying something like this into or out of the Manticoran Junction would have been extraordinarily dangerous. Despite the separation between inbound and outbound lanes, there was so much traffic through the Junction that the probability of a wedge-on-wedge collision would have been only too real. In Stine's case, however, there was only a single inbound and a single outbound lane, and traffic was sparse, to say the least. He saw a single freighter's icon on the tactical display, swinging wildly away from the terminus, even though *Otter* was a good forty thousand kilometers clear of her. But that was fine with him.

"Deploy the Ghost Rider platforms, Sarah," he said. "Let's get some eyes out there."

"Yes, Sir. Deploying now."

The icons of half a dozen Ghost Rider recon platforms arced away from *Otter*'s larger, stronger light code on the tactical plot, and he saw HMS *Tiger Cub*, the squadron's third cruiser, emerging from the terminus behind *Malcolm Taylor*.

"Who the hell *are* you people?!" the astro-control captain on the com demanded furiously.

"Better go ahead and put me through to him, Jordan," Magellan said.

"Yes, Sir. Live mike in three...two...one. Now."

Magellan saw the dark-faced captain's expression change abruptly as his own image appeared on the other man's display. For a moment, the Solarian looked blank, but then his eyes first widened and then, almost as quickly, narrowed again as he recognized Magellan's black-and-gold uniform.

"Commodore Sean Magellan, Royal Manticoran Navy," Magellan said calmly.

"What the *hell* do you think you're doing?!" the captain challenged. "This is Solarian space!"

"Really?" Magellan replied. "Imagine that."

The astro-control officer's complexion turned darker than ever and his jaw muscles quivered as he glared incredulously at the commodore. He opened his mouth, but nothing came out of it, as if the sheer power of his fury had paralyzed his vocal cords, and Magellan gave him a thin, cold smile.

"Actually, Captain, I'm quite aware of where I am. And I'm quite aware that the Solarian League claims sovereignty over this terminus. Unfortunately, things like that are subject to change."

"What the hell do you mean by that?!" the captain managed to get out after another three or four seconds of rage-inspired muteness.

"I mean that jurisdiction over this terminus has just changed hands from the Solarian League to the Star Empire of Manticore," Magellan told him flatly.

"You're out of your fucking mind!"

"No," Magellan responded as the fourth and fifth ships of his squadron emerged from the terminus and shifted their vectors outward to englobe it. "I'm afraid not, Captain."

"You are if you think you can get away with *this* kind of crap!"

"Excuse me for asking this, Captain, but why do *you* think I *can't* 'get away with this kind of crap'?"

"Because—" the captain began furiously, then stopped abruptly.

"That's what I thought," Magellan said much more gently. And glanced back at the tactical display as HMS *Wolf*, the last of his cruisers, emerged from the terminus . . . closely followed by HMS *Selkie*, his remaining CLAC. He didn't know what the Solarian captain thought *Selkie* was, but she sure *looked* like a ship-of-the-wall.

"Allow me to explain this to you, Captain—?"

Magellan paused, raising both eyebrows, and waited patiently until the Solarian shook himself.

"Pálffi, Captain Cyrus Pálffi," he grated.

"Thank you, Captain Pálffi." Magellan nodded courteously. "I'm sure you're well aware of the tension between the Star Empire and the League. My Empress and her Foreign Ministry have tried from the very beginning to get someone—*anyone*—in the League's government to show even a modicum of willingness to find a nonmilitary way to resolve that tension. You may have noticed that we haven't had a great deal of success in that respect." He smiled, showing his teeth. "So Her Majesty's Government has decided that since we can't seem to get the League's attention through normal diplomatic channels, it's time to try another approach. This one."

"What do you mean?" Pálffi asked in a tone which was at least marginally closer to normal.

"I mean that this terminus is now closed to all Solarian-registry shipping, except for courier vessels and those registered to recognized interstellar news services. It will remain closed to all Solarian traffic until further notice."

"This is never going to stand," Pálffi said almost conversationally. "You and your pissant cruisers are going to need a hell of a lot more than one waller to stand up to what's going to be headed your way as soon as Sol finds out about this."

"By the strangest coincidence, Captain Pálffi, there's quite a lot more *headed* this way," Magellan informed him. "Although, to be honest, I don't think we're going to need as much more as you may believe."

While he was speaking, the ammunition ship HMS *Bandolier* emerged from the terminus, stuffed to the deckheads with missile pods and additional Mark 16 missiles for his cruisers, and he smiled.

"My pinnaces will be headed your way within the next twenty minutes, Captain Pálffi," he continued. "My Marines will come aboard your control platforms shortly thereafter. I have no desire for anyone to get hurt, and I trust you'll feel the same. I warn you, however, that my Marines will be in battle armor, and they *will* be authorized to use lethal force if they're attacked or forcibly resisted. Is that understood?"

Pálffi glared at him, and Magellan cocked his head.

"I asked if that was understood, Captain," he said in a considerably cooler voice, and his eyes hardened.

"Understood," Pálffi got out finally, and Magellan allowed his own expression to ease slightly.

"Good. As I say, I would genuinely prefer for no one to be hurt on either side. I'm not going to pretend

I'm not as pissed off as any other Manticoran, but I'm also aware that no one here in the Stine System bears any responsibility for what's happened in the Talbott Quadrant. I'd just as soon not contribute any more to the bad blood between the Star Empire and the League than I have to under the letter of my orders."

"Really?" Pálffi looked at him skeptically, then shrugged. "Maybe you *do* mean that, but it doesn't matter what you'd 'just as soon' happen, Commodore. Not anymore. You've stepped across the line this time, and you're a hell of a long way away from home."

"Manticorans are accustomed to being a long way away from home, Captain. And we're accustomed to taking care of ourselves when we are. No doubt a sufficiently strong SLN detachment could push me off this terminus, but I guarantee you that before it does, it'll lose many times the tonnage of my squadron."

"Sure it will." Pálffi snorted contemptuously. "I'm sure Battle Fleet's wallers will just be scared to death of your *cruisers*, Commodore!"

"They will be if they've bothered to read the reports about what happened at Spindle," Magellan replied calmly. "These are exactly the same class of cruisers which captured or destroyed Fleet Admiral Crandall's entire fleet, Captain Pálffi."

The Solarian's face went suddenly blank and stiff. For a moment, he only stared at Magellan. Then he inhaled sharply and shook himself.

"Pardon me if I don't exactly shake in my boots," he said in a voice which seemed to have lost just a bit of its previous certainty. "But there's not a whole hell of a lot *I* can do to stop you. Just exactly what do your Marines plan to do after they board my platforms?"

"Mostly just keep an eye on you until I can contact President Zell and get some transport dispatched out here to take your people off."

"You're kicking us off our own platforms?"

"I suppose that's one way to look at it," Magellan conceded. "I prefer to think of it as getting your people safely out of the line of fire, however. If the Solarian Navy is rash enough to attempt to retake control of this terminus by force, I don't want any stray missiles taking out control platforms full of innocent bystanders."

Pálffi's eyes examined his expression closely for several seconds. Then the Solarian nodded slowly.

"Appreciate it," he said grudgingly, with obvious reluctance.

"As I say, Captain Pálffi, I'd really prefer for no one to get hurt. So we'll just get you and your people out of the way. Because"—Magellan's expression hardened once again, his eyes bleak—"if the League does try to retake this terminus, a *lot* of people are going to get hurt."

Chapter Twenty-Seven

"WHERE'S RAJANI?" NATHAN MACARTNEY DEMANDED. His expression was not a happy one, which struck Innokentiy Kolokoltsov as a bit ironic, under the circumstances.

"He's off-planet," the senior permanent undersecretary for foreign affairs said dryly. "I understand he's out at *Hyperion One* for a staff conference on the best way to go about mobilizing and modernizing the Reserve . . . just on the off chance the Manties actually decide to fight after all, you understand."

MacArtney flushed angrily at the none too subtle jab. He started to say something sharp, then visibly restrained himself. Which was wise of him, Kolokoltsov thought acidly. He and Rajampet had burned a lot of credit with their fellow Mandarins.

"I wonder how long he can stay out there?" Malachai Abruzzi asked sourly.

"Until the energy death of the universe, as far as I'm concerned." Omosupe Quartermain's tone was even more sour than Abruzzi's, and Kolokoltsov snorted.

"I'm sure he's actually getting some work done while he's out there—if only to cover his ass when the newsies start hounding him. But it is convenient for him, isn't it? For now, at least."

Hyperion One was the SLN's primary Sol System space station. It was not only the Navy's largest single construction and service platform but the HQ location for its Logistics Command. LogCom was responsible for the vast number of superdreadnoughts mothballed not only there but at Battle Fleet installations in half a dozen other star systems. *Hyperion One* also orbited the planet Mars, not Old Terra, which left it roughly four light-minutes inside Sol's hyper limit yet much closer to the asteroid smelters which still produced the bulk of the Sol System's industrial resources—a compromise between security and convenience which was looking a little less secure, in Kolokoltsov's opinion, given the preposterous missile ranges the Manties were supposed to be attaining. At the moment, however, it offered Rajampet a different sort of security. The current distance from Old Chicago to *Hyperion One* was just over four light-minutes, which made any sort of real-time conversation impractical, to say the least. Coupled with the admiral's concern over the security of their communications, it put him safely beyond reach of the pointed interrogation he obviously knew awaited him.

"Convenient or not, he's for the long drop," Abruzzi said flatly. MacArtney looked as if he wanted to argue, but the permanent senior undersceretary of education and information went straight on. "No matter how we try to spin this one, someone's got to take it in the neck. You don't have *this* kind of disaster without determining who's responsible for it and giving him the ax, Nathan, and you know it. He's the senior uniformed officer of the Navy. That makes him the logical choice. For that matter, he's the one who really *is* responsible for it!"

"That's going to touch off a firestorm in the Fleet," MacArtney said after a moment. "I'm not saying you're wrong, I'm just saying the Navy's going to see it as a bunch of civilians stabbing the uniforms in the back to cover their own backsides."

"Of course they are!" Agatá Wodoslawski snorted. "If they don't see it that way, they'll have to admit their precious Navy couldn't organize an orgy in a whorehouse!"

More than one other person attending the high-security electronic conference winced. That sort of language was rare out of Wodoslawski, but it did capture the gist of their collective opinion rather neatly.

"What I want to know is what the *hell* Filareta thought he was doing," Kolokoltsov said flatly.

He'd replayed the recordings the Manties had sent along with Eleventh Fleet's preliminary casualty reports again and again, seen the exchange between that cold-blooded bitch Harrington and Filareta. Kolokoltsov was no trained naval officer, but it had been obvious even to him that unless Harrington was lying—and she hadn't been; that much should certainly have been clear to Filareta—Eleventh Fleet had stood the proverbial chance of a snowball in hell. She'd *had* him—had him dead to rights—and she'd given him the option of surrendering, but the maniac had chosen to fire instead!

"I don't know what he was thinking," MacArtney admitted bitterly. "And nobody ever will, now."

"And Rajani still hasn't managed to get Imogene Tsang to Old Chicago where we could ask her exactly what her orders in *Beowulf* were, either, has he?" Quartermain observed. She glanced at Kolokoltsov from the corner of one eye. "She was a hell of a lot more confrontational than she was supposed to be. I can't help wondering if maybe her instructions—and Filareta's—might not have included a couple of clauses we didn't know about."

"I can see where you'd wonder that," MacArtney acknowledged, "but I don't think that's what happened. Not in Filareta's case, anyway. I don't know what the hell *did* happen, but I have—had, I suppose—met him, and he wasn't the kind to commit suicide on someone else's orders, no matter who the someone who gave them might be."

"Even if that is exactly what he did." Abruzzi shook his head when MacArtney stabbed another sharp look in his direction. "I'm not arguing with your analysis of his character, Nathan. I'm just saying *something* caused him to commit suicide."

"Oh, for God's sake, Malachai!" Quartermain said disgustedly. "*Please* don't climb on the Manties' mind-control nanotech bandwagon!"

"I have no intention of doing anything of the sort, Omosupe," Abruzzi replied coldly. "First, because the entire notion is ridiculous. But, second, because even suggesting there might be something to the Manties' claims in that regard would be the first step in legitimizing all their other claims about this 'Mesan Alignment' and the way we've been allowing it to manipulate us."

"Well, we're going to have to issue *some* kind of statement," Wodoslawski pointed out. "The Manties' recordings of Harrington's conversation with Filareta are already hitting the news channels, and they make it pretty damn clear she gave him every opportunity to surrender, and he chose to fire on her instead. I hate to say it, but that's pretty damning evidence of who's to blame for this massacre."

"And it's only a matter of time before Felicia Hadley starts screaming about it in the Assembly," Kolokoltsov agreed. "She's been justifying Beowulf's opposition to Tsang's passage on the argument that Beowulf's refusal actually saved the lives of Tsang's crews. What happened to Filareta's only going to strengthen her position in that regard."

"The hell with Hadley!" MacArtney said harshly. "The newsies are going to be all over this. Even some of our 'special friends' in the media are going to find it hard not to join the pack on this one, because, frankly, they'll lose a hell of a lot of credibility if they don't. And that doesn't even consider someone like that incredible pain in the ass O'Hanrahan. *She'll* be all over this like stink on ... Well, you get the idea."

"One of my people over at Education and Information *may* have come up with a way we can spin it, at least in the short term," Malachai Abruzzi said. The others looked at him in disbelief, and he shrugged. "Nobody's going to be able to spin this one in the *long* term," he conceded. "The best we can do is try to get out in front and at least slow it down, plant some seeds of doubt to undermine the credibility of the early reports. The problem is that whatever we gain in the short term is likely to turn around and bite us in the long term when the Manties' version of events is independently verified."

"Then what's the point?" MacArtney demanded.

"The point is that if Malachai's people have come up with a way to buy us some time, even if it's only a few months, we may be able to pull together some coherent strategy for getting through this more or less intact, after all," Kolokoltsov replied. "At this point, frankly, I don't have a clue what that strategy might be, but the critical point is that we're looking right down the barrel of a constitutional crisis."

The sudden silence was absolute, and his colleagues looked at him as he finally said the words.

"That's been the anaconda under the table none of us have wanted to talk about from the very beginning," he continued unflinchingly. "Unfortunately, Holmon-Sanders brought that front and center when she faced down Tsang, and this is only going to make it worse. For the first time in T-centuries, people may actually be willing to look at the emperor and admit he's bare-assed naked." He looked around their holographic faces. "The Constitution was effectively dead on arrival; we've always known it never could have worked as the basis for an effective system of government the way it was written. So we found ways around it. Ways that, frankly, are completely *illegal* under the letter of the Constitution. Now people like Hadley and Holmon-Sanders are saying so openly, and a lot of other people who would've been willing to say 'so what?' and let us go on with the business of making the League work anyway are going to look at what happened to Filareta as proof we don't know *how* to make the League work. And if they decide that, and they listen to Hadley and the rest of those crazy Beowulfers, the entire League could go straight down the crapper. *That's* what this is really about now."

"That . . . has to be a little alarmist," MacArtney said tentatively. He looked around at the others. "Doesn't it?"

It was obvious to Kolokoltsov that MacArtney had been totally focused on the crisis' personal implications. That he'd never looked beyond the problem of cuffing the Manties aside so the League in general—and Nathan MacArtney in particular—could get on with business as usual the way they always had. Now, though . . .

"I don't think it is, Nathan." Abruzzi didn't like MacArtney and never had, but his tone was almost gentle as he shook his head. "I admit it sounds preposterous, but this really could take down the entire League, and when it does, God only knows what's going to happen out in the Protectorates. Hell, some of the *Core* systems don't like each other all that much! If they see an opportunity to go their own ways, maybe even get some of their own back against someone who pissed them off centuries ago, they're likely to take it."

MacArtney sat silent, his face ashen, and Kolokoltsov returned his attention to Abruzzi.

"Tell us about this time-buying idea, Malachai."

"It's actually pretty simple." Abruzzi shrugged. "In some ways, this is Spindle all over again—all we have really is the Manties' word for what happened, plus the stories filed by civilian newsies in the system. In other words, the only first-hand information is coming from official Manty sources. So we do what we did then." He shrugged again. "We lie."

"How?"

"The sequence is clear from what the Manties have released. Filareta sailed into an ambush; Harrington sprang the trap and gave him the option of surrendering or being destroyed; he opened fire; she handed him his head. Right?"

Heads nodded, and he shrugged again.

"Well, we can't possibly win if we try to defend his actions. So instead, we change the storyline. Harrington deliberately drew him into the trap; she offered him the option of surrendering as a ploy to get him to scuttle his missile pods; he *did* scuttle his missile pods . . . and the instant he'd given up the one weapon she was afraid of, she opened fire and cold-bloodedly destroyed his fleet. It was never about giving him a chance to surrender; it was always about her intention to destroy him whatever he did."

"How the hell do you expect to make that stand up?" Wodoslawski demanded. "Especially with the recordings the Manties have already made public!"

"We point out that they're the recordings the *Manties* have made public," Abruzzi replied. "They've told us they're clean copies of the actual conversation, but we have no proof of that. We point out that Filareta's orders gave him the option of standing down or even surrendering if it turned out Admiral Rajampet's estimate of the tech imbalance turned out to be in error. I don't know if they did—in fact, I doubt like *hell* they did—but by the time an official transcript of them gets released, they damned well will have! On the basis of those instructions and what appears to have been the tactical situation when Harrington demanded his surrender, we believe that's what he actually did. At which point Harrington opened fire, and everything after that point in the 'official record' they've sent us is almost certainly a skillfully edited montage of the actual battle."

"It'll never fly," Wodoslawski said flatly.

"It might," Kolokoltsov said more slowly, eyes narrowed as he considered the scenario. "It has the advantage of being consistent with what we've been saying about Spindle and the other confrontations. Sure, some people are going to see it as the same old line, but for a lot of others that continuity's going to give it a certain legitimacy. It'll fit with what those people have already accepted as the truth, and the Manties can't *disprove* it. They can provide all the sensor recordings and recorded messages they want, but all of them will be coming from official government organs, and any good, cynical Solarian citizen knows government organs routinely lie their asses off when it suits their purposes."

"Oh, yeah?" Wodoslawski leaned back in her chair. "And what about Haven throwing in with them? Validating the same story?"

"Basically, the Havenites cut a deal with the Manties," Abruzzi responded. Her gray eyes widened in disbelief, and he chuckled harshly. "I'm sure Innokentiy's Foreign Ministry sources and analysts can come up with all sorts of straws in the wind to justify it, but what obviously happened was that Manticore offered Haven a bargain. Clearly, Haven's war-fighting technology has to be roughly on a par with Manticore's for it to have survived this long. That means they've got a major tactical advantage—only a fleeting one, until our own Navy acquires matching weapons, of course—over the League, too. So Manticore's offer was simple: let's stop shooting at each other long enough for us both to rip off big, juicy mouthfuls of territory from the League and anyone else who gets in our way while we've still got the military edge to get away with it. Think of it as a variation on the old cliché about my enemy's enemy being my friend. In this case, it's a case of my enemy's helpless victim being *my* helpless victim, too. Or that's how Manticore sold it to Haven, anyway."

"You're saying that in this version of reality Haven saw the opportunity to throw in with Manticore for a piece of *our* pie and figured that was a better deal than trying to finish off the Manties and getting nothing out of it except a bunch more losses of their own and—maybe—control of the Junction at the end of it?" Wodoslawski said in a much more thoughtful tone.

"We've been explaining that the Manties are cold-blooded, cynical imperialists from the beginning," Abruzzi pointed out. "This would be just more of the same on their part, wouldn't it? And the fact that Haven, who's always hated Manpower as much as Manticore in the first place, is the one who 'confirmed' this nonsense about the so-called Mesan Alignment fits in rather nicely."

"You know, that's what bothers me the most," Wodoslawski admitted. "It was Pritchart who brought this to the Manties, not the other way around. I agree it's nonsense, but if Haven really believes it—"

"I'd just point out to you that according to the fairy tale they've been spinning, it was Zilwicki and Victor Cachat who brought this Simões home from Mesa," Abruzzi said, and rolled his eyes. "I'm sure all of us remember what a loose warhead Zilwicki was right here in Old Chicago when he claimed Manpower had kidnapped his daughter. I don't think anyone's going to call him a disinterested witness where anything to do with Mesa is involved! For that matter, if there's one scrap of truth to Mesa's version of Green Pines, Zilwicki would have every conceivable reason to come up with some far-fetched story about centuries-long conspiracies as a way to cover up his own guilt! And then there's Cachat, who's been spending the last couple of T-years getting further and further into bed with the Audubon Ballroom through his cronies in Verdant Vista, and who appears to have been *with* Zilwicki in Green Pines. Another sterling, utterly trustworthy character witness against Mesa! And, as the cherry on top, it's the Manties' treecats' supposed ability to know when someone is lying that 'proves' Simões *isn't*.

"The most charitable scenario I've been able to come up with is that Zilwicki and Cachat managed to sell this fabrication to Pritchart and her administration, at least tentatively. I think the most plausible explanation of why it took them so damned long to get back home was that they spent the intervening months holed up somewhere with Manty intelligence putting the aforesaid fabrication together and priming Simões as their ventriloquist's dummy. Then they sailed off home to Nouveau Paris, made their 'shocking revelation' to Pritchart, and convinced her to share their information with Manticore. At which point—surprise, surprise!—the mind-reading treecats of Sphinx 'confirmed' Simões' truthfulness.

"Frankly, the really interesting question is whether or not Pritchart really bought it in the first place.

We've all been around for a while, Agatá. We know how the game's played. It's possible Pritchart actually believes this nonsense, and that her statements to that effect in the messages the Manties've sent us are absolutely genuine. But I'd say it's considerably more likely she realizes full well that Zilwicki and Cachat have 'sold' her a crock of bullshit which justified her making *Elizabeth* the offer we're going to claim Elizabeth made to *her*. In other words, she saw the opportunity to get out from under the war with Manticore in a way that would put her on Manticore's side of the table at the peace conference that divvies up the Solarian League."

"You know," MacArtney said after several moments of silence, "that could actually be what happened. Or something close to it, anyway. I'm not saying Filareta didn't fire first, whatever we're going to tell everyone, but that really could be how Haven wound up in the Manties' corner."

"Maybe," Abruzzi agreed. "But we don't want to muddy the water. It's going to be a simpler, more easily presented message to stick with the Manties as the undisputed heavies of the piece. We let Haven be the 'unwitting dupe'—maybe with a *little* imperialist ambition thrown in—and we take the position consistently in our own public statements that it's a tragedy Haven has allowed itself to be deceived and manipulated in this fashion. More of an in-sorrow-than-in-anger approach. Who knows? If things take a turn for the worse for the Manties, Haven might see our attitude as providing an opportunity to jump ship to the other side."

"I don't think I'd bet very much money on that

possibility if I were you," MacArtney said dryly, "but I agree there's at least a chance we could sell this in the short term. In fact, I'll make it my business to suggest to Rajani that it would be a good thing if his in-house experts could analyze the Manties' recordings and find evidence of *possible* editing. I think a good, judicious report—one that obviously tries to be as fair-minded and restrained as possible—which concludes the records *may* have been doctored but that it's impossible to demonstrate the truth conclusively one way or the other would be more useful than an outright condemnation."

"I agree."

Abruzzi nodded with unusual approval, and Kolokoltsov looked around at the faces of his fellows.

"All right. I think we're in agreement that we'll proceed the way Malachai's recommending. And I also think it would be a good idea for you and Omosupe, Agatá, to put together a report solemnly warning about the huge economic disruptions the Manties are about to inflict upon the League as part of their imperial ambitions. Let's get that out in front of the newsies, too, and use it to aim some extra public disapproval in Manticore's direction." He smiled thinly. "I don't see how it could make any of our citizens any *less* willing to decide the Manties are the real villains."

Chapter Twenty-Eight

THE HAVENITE DISPATCH BOAT made rendezvous with *Haven One* as the official interstellar transport of the Republic's president swept peacefully about the planet Manticore in its assigned orbit. The fact that the tiny vessel was allowed to make its approach without having to take aboard a *Manticoran* helmsman to enforce the "two-man" rule which had become the norm for near-planet traffic in the Star Empire said volumes about how the relationship between Haven and Manticore had changed in a single T-month.

The high-security dispatches from Nouveau Paris were hand-transferred to *Haven One*, where they then sat for just over three hours while President Pritchart completed her current meeting with Empress Elizabeth, Protector Benjamin, and Planetary Director Benton-Ramirez y Chou in Mount Royal Palace. Partly, that was because the meeting was too important to interrupt, but there was more to it as well. Eloise Pritchart was not a cowardly woman, yet in her circumstances, only a superwoman wouldn't have felt at least a tingle or two of trepidation at the thought of mail from home.

Nonetheless, when she arrived back aboard her ship, she went immediately to her private quarters, accessed the security locks on the files, braced herself, and began to read.

❖   ❖   ❖

"No, actually I think I agree with Aretha on this one, Roger," Empress Elizabeth said. "I realize it's your wedding—well, yours and Rivka's!" she went on, smiling warmly at Rivka Rebecca Rosenfeld. "And if you insist, we can do it your way. But under the circumstances, I think involving the Navy is probably a good idea."

"I'm not disagreeing with that part of it, Mother, but it's a *wedding*, not a political statement." Crown Prince Roger Gregory Alexander Timothy Winton tried (mostly successfully) to keep exasperation out of his voice. "And unlike Uncle Mike or Michelle, I never actually served in the Navy. I'd feel... uncomfortable calling them in for my wedding, especially after what's just happened. It's not my place to use my status as Heir to order a bunch of uniforms to turn up for the wedding when they've got a lot better things to be doing. And I especially don't want to look like I'm trying to steal any of the... well, the *glory*, darn it, the Fleet's earned to make me and Rivka look more important!"

It was obvious only filial respect had kept him from using a somewhat more vigorous expletive, and Elizabeth was forced to smother a smile stillborn.

"That's not what Aretha has in mind," she began once she was sure she had the smile under control. "She's—"

"Forgive me, Your Majesty," Rivka said, "but whether it's what Dame Aretha actually intends or not, I think what she's proposing could look that way."

The young woman who was about to become Crown Princess of the Star Empire of Manticore was attractive, in a dark, understated sort of way. She was also quiet, almost bookish, but there was a brain behind those big brown eyes. And some intestinal fortitude, too, Elizabeth reflected. It couldn't be easy for a young woman who wouldn't be twenty-two T-years old for another eleven days to argue with not just her future mother-in-law but her monarch. That was one of the many reasons Elizabeth approved so heartily of Roger's choice.

"I think what bothers Roger," Rivka went on, "is the notion of turning out all those naval personnel in uniform to line the approaches to King Michael's Cathedral. I mean"—she smiled slightly—"I don't think we're going to be able to convince everyone they were all invited to the wedding and just couldn't fit into the cathedral. It's going to look like they were *ordered* to attend."

"It's going to look like that because that's what they're going to be," Elizabeth pointed out. "It's standard procedure for the military to be represented at royal weddings, baptisms, and funerals, Rivka."

"I realize that, Your Majesty. I'm just saying that I think that's why Roger feels the way he feels."

"Mother, I don't object to the Navy being *represented*," Roger said. "I just don't want to turn it into a situation where for all intents and purposes *only* the Navy is represented. Don't get me wrong—I think the Navy has every right to be represented. God knows it does if anyone does! I just don't want to look like we're ... trading on how popular the Navy is right now. Maybe it's silly, and maybe it's only because I was never commissioned, but that's the way I feel."

"I see." Elizabeth gazed at him for a moment, then cocked an eyebrow at his fiancée. "Do you feel that way, too, Rivka?"

"Maybe not as strongly as Roger does, Your Majesty. On the other hand, it's *his* wedding, too." Rivka shrugged. "All of this is still new to me, but it does seem to me that 'our wedding' is going to be a huge public event. I realize that goes with marrying Roger, and I'm not complaining, really. But if there's any way we can cut down a little bit on the intrusion of politics and do something that will make Roger feel a little more comfortable at the same time, I'm in favor of it."

Elizabeth nodded slowly, impressed once again with her future daughter-in-law's levelheadedness. She'd always thought the Manticoran Constitution's requirement that the heir to the throne marry a commoner had been one of the Founders' best ideas. Over the years, it had created its share of heartache and unhappy marriages, which was probably inevitable. And she knew from her own experience that every handsome (or beautiful) fortune hunter in the Star Kingdom was willing to take a shot at the Heir. She could have picked any of two or three dozen stunningly handsome boy-toys, but she hadn't. She'd picked Justin, and she was eternally thankful the constitutional requirement had brought them together. One or two of the young women who'd done their best to hover around Roger had worried her, but she was delighted with his final choice. Indeed, she strongly suspected that Rivka was going to prove as strong a support for Roger as Justin had proven for her.

"All right," she said. "How about a compromise? You're right that the Navy deserves to be represented, Roger, so suppose what we do is alternate personnel from the various branches of the service? What about Navy, Queen's Own, Marines, Palace Security, Navy, and repeat? If we run out of the Queen's Own, we could fill in with regular Army. Otherwise, the Queen's Own will represent the Army contingent. Could you live with that?"

"I think so," Roger agreed, then looked at Rivka as she laughed suddenly. "What's so funny?" he asked.

"I was just thinking that the Navy's going to be pretty well represented, anyway," she explained. "Your uncle's going to be present in uniform, and so is Admiral Truman, Earl White Haven, Admiral Caparelli, Admiral Givens, and Admiral Hemphill. Then there's Admiral Theisman, Admiral Tourville, Admiral Yu, and High Admiral Yanakov for the foreign contingent."

"I suppose that's true," Elizabeth agreed with a smile, not mentioning the one flag officer Rivka hadn't named and who was *not* going to be in uniform. Honor Alexander-Harrington had agreed to serve as one of Rivka Rosenfeld's matrons of honor, but she would be present in her persona as Steadholder Harrington, not Admiral Harrington.

Well, technically she'll also be present as Duchess *Harrington, I suppose*, Elizabeth thought. *On the other hand—*

"Excuse me, Your Majesty, but President Pritchart is on the com."

Elizabeth turned to the footman who'd spoken, and he bowed with a slightly apologetic air. None of the Mount Royal staff liked to interrupt the royal family when they actually had time to spend as a *family*.

"She's on the secure terminal in your study, Your Majesty," he murmured.

"Thank you, Isaac," she acknowledged with a smile, then turned back to Roger and Rivka. "All right, you two win this one on points. But I warn you, I'm going to be more adamant about the cake topper!"

She glowered at them ferociously, and Rivka laughed as Roger cowered in mock terror. Elizabeth chuckled, shook her head, scooped up Ariel, and headed for her study.

She sat down at her workstation and pressed the acceptance key.

"Sorry to keep you waiting, Eloise. I've discovered that arranging my son's wedding is just a little more complicated than arranging interstellar treaties with lifelong enemies."

"Funny you should mention treaties with lifelong enemies," Pritchart replied with a somewhat peculiar smile. "It just happens I've received dispatches from Nouveau Paris. The reception of our treaty proposals wasn't quite what I anticipated."

"Oh?" After forty T-years on the throne, Elizabeth Winton's face said exactly what she told it to say. It was a bit harder than usual to keep it that way at the moment. "In what way?"

"Remember how I told you I'd expected all along that Leslie was going to have trouble pounding them through the Senate, especially without me to back her up?"

Elizabeth nodded. There'd been strong arguments in favor of Pritchart's taking the proposed treaty home and personally presenting it to the Havenite Congress, but there'd been countervailing arguments as well. The necessity for her, as Haven's head of state, to personally oversee the delicate and difficult business of effectively coordinating the Republican Navy with the Royal Manticoran Navy after so many years of hostility had loomed large among them. But another, although Pritchart and Elizabeth had never *explicitly* discussed it, was that by remaining in Manticore, Pritchart could force a de facto acceptance of the treaty, in the short term at least, whatever the Senate ultimately decided.

"Well, it turns out I was wrong about the treaty's prospects," Pritchart went on now. "According to Leslie's dispatch, she never got a chance to pound it anywhere. The Senate jumped all over it. It was approved with a fifty-six-vote margin over and above the two-thirds majority requirement. There were only *eleven* dissenting votes!"

The president's face blossomed in a huge smile, and Elizabeth felt herself smiling back.

"That's wonderful news, Eloise!"

"I think the Senate's as tired of locking horns with you people as Thomas Theisman is," Pritchart said, shaking her head. "And according to Leslie, the fact that we not only get out of this without paying reparations, despite Giancola's games with the diplomatic notes, but that it looks like we're going to become the Star Empire's biggest trading partner in the not so distant future didn't hurt one bit. The probability that Giancola was working for Mesa the entire time and that we're on the same hit list you people are didn't hurt any, either, Leslie says. And neither did the fact that *nobody* in the Republic is especially fond of the League, for that matter."

"Completely off the record—and I'll deny it if you ever quote me—but I'd just as soon go pick on someone who isn't as tough as you guys for a change, myself," Elizabeth told her, marveling even now at how close she'd become to the president of the star nation she'd hated with every fiber of her being for four standard decades.

"There are still some questions at the Nouveau Paris end, of course," Pritchart went on in a more sober tone. "As they say, the devil is always in the details. With your permission, now that the original treaty's been approved at both ends, I'd like to go ahead and get Admiral Hemphill's mission off to Bolthole as soon as possible. I think that would help put a lot of those questions to bed with a shovel."

"Tom and Hamish are still having to knock a few heads together over at the Admiralty," Elizabeth said with an off-center smile. "I don't think there'll be any major snafus, though."

I hope *to hell there won't be, anyway*, she added mentally. She truly didn't expect any, but she'd been surprised upon occasion before. And she supposed it was inevitable that the more conservative members of the Royal Navy would be...uncomfortable about sending the entire surviving R&D staff of HMSS *Weyland* off deep into Havenite territory to share all of the RMN's technical secrets with its traditional enemies. In fact, there were times *Elizabeth* expected to wake up with a terminal drug hangover any moment now.

But crazy as it sounds, it actually makes sense—a lot of sense, she thought. *We're pretty sure that if we couldn't figure out where Bolthole was, the Sollies— and probably the Alignment—don't know, either. God knows we had a lot more incentive to find it than either of them did! So tucking our R&D projects away where no one with any invisible starships is likely to drop by to clean up what she missed the first time around strikes me as a very good idea. And from what Theisman and Eloise have shown us, Bolthole's going to be a damned good place to start putting all that new hardware into production on a really large scale quickly, once we've made a few upgrades.*

There'd been arguments in favor of using Beowulf instead. For one thing, Beowulf's basic technology was considerably in advance of the Republic's as a whole—or even of Bolthole's, for that matter. In theory, Beowulf would be better placed to hit the ground running and improve upon the existing research more rapidly than Haven could. But there was a difference between basic technology and war-fighting technology, and an even bigger difference between the mindsets required to successfully push military and civilian R&D. There was no doubt in Elizabeth's mind—or that of any serving Manticoran officer, for that matter—that Shannon Foraker fully deserved her reputation. The staff she'd put together had done miracles to close the gap between Manticore and the Republic. With the destruction of the *Weyland* and its Grayson equivalent at Blackbird, there was no one in the galaxy better qualified to push the bleeding edge of hardware development.

Besides, Beowulf was already busy doing other things.

Horrific as the casualties of the Yawata strike had been, it had actually killed only a relatively small percentage of the total Manticoran workforce. But it had killed a *critical* percentage—the technicians, the logisticians, the supervisors, and the managers responsible for building the Star Empire's starships, military and civilian. The smelters and the resource-extraction platforms were still there. Much of the system's consumer manufacturing still existed, although a frightening percentage of it had been wiped away with the space stations as well. The service personnel who'd manned the service and repair platforms associated with the Junction were still intact, still available. But the Yawata strike had destroyed the workforce whose skill set had made it the most efficient shipbuilding powerhouse in the explored galaxy. It had destroyed the heavy fabrication units, the skilled personnel who oversaw final component manufacture and assembly, the shipfitters and the ordnance specialists, the nano-farms that produced the critical manufacturing nanotech, the armorers and life-support technicians, the planners who kept it all moving smoothly. They were all gone, and their disappearance had eliminated the very skilled workforce needed to rebuild the hardware, the infrastructure, they'd once manned as well. It was a case of the chicken and the egg; to build the one, you needed the other.

As Baroness Morncreek and Countess Maiden Hill had pointed out at that first dreadful cabinet meeting after the strike, they could rebuild and retrain. They still had at least some of the people they needed, once they could be recalled or transferred from other critical sectors of the economy. And the repatriated workforce from Grendelsbane had been a godsend. For the matter, there were plenty of Manticorans who could acquire the necessary skill sets. The problem was how to do all of that quickly enough... and how even the Star Empire of Manticore could afford the price tag.

It looked like the answer was going to be Beowulf and the Republic of Haven. The loss of revenues Operation Lacoön had inflicted on the Old Star Kingdom would have been close enough to catastrophic under normal circumstances. Under the post-Yawata strike circumstances, it came one hell of a lot closer. But when Lacoön was first formulated, no one had anticipated having the Republic of Haven available to step in as a full trading partner. Nor had it counted on Beowulf's becoming for all intents and purposes a full ally against the Solarian League.

Haven offered enormous business opportunities for the Star Empire. It wasn't going to come remotely close to replacing everything Lacoön had shut down, but that didn't mean it wasn't going to help a lot. And with Beowulf's open alignment with Manticore, its economy had become part of the Grand Alliance's dynamo as well. Beowulfers had always been heavily invested in the Old Star Kingdom; now they were actually lining up to buy Manticoran war bonds.

Nor was that all Beowulf was doing. Dozens of Beowulfan repair and service ships had already streamed through the Junction, and the nuclei of new space stations were already taking shape—two each, this time, around Manticore and Sphinx. They were going to be different this time, too; built to a carefully thought-out plan that allowed for systematic expansion rather than simply growing as need required. And with powerful self-defense capability as well. There really was truth to the old saw about the burned hand teaching best, Elizabeth reflected grimly.

The tectonic shift represented by the Grand Alliance's unexpected formation had hugely reduced even the most optimistic Manticoran estimates of how long it was going to take to rebuild the Old Star Kingdom's industrial muscle. Which wasn't to say it was going to happen overnight, even now. The process was still going to take T-years, and everyone knew it.

That was why Beowulf was already establishing its first MDM production lines. It had no pod-laying superdreadnoughts of its own, but its basic technological capabilities required far less tweaking than Haven's would to begin producing the mini-fusion plants and the miniaturized gravitic components required to build something like the Mark 23-E. So for the foreseeable future, Beowulf would be the primary missile supplier for the Grand Alliance. For that matter, if things worked out the way the planners were anticipating, in the next several T-months Beowulf would begin building Keyhole-Two platforms to be installed in purpose-built Havenite SD(P)s constructed in Bolthole and sailed to Manticore for final installation of the Beowulf-built components.

Just thinking about it could make Elizabeth's head swim, but Honor and Hamish promised her it would work. As long as Beowulf remained intact, at least, and the two hundred pod-laying superdreadnoughts stationed there to protect the system suggested it would.

"Well, anyway," Pritchard said, "it looks like this is actually going to work. I have to admit, there've been times when I wasn't as confident of that as I hope I looked."

"Eloise, you and I have to be the two stubbornest, most bloody-minded females in the galaxy," Elizabeth pointed out. "If the two of *us* can agree on anything, it's *going* to happen."

"*I'm* not going to argue with you," Pritchard said with a smile. "But on that note, I'll let you get back to your family and that wedding. It's probably more fun than this anyway."

"It is, in a lot of ways," Elizabeth admitted. "And the notion of having the President of the Republic of Haven present as an invited guest isn't something I'd've given a lot of thought to until the last month or so."

"I guess not." Pritchart chuckled and started to press the button to terminate the connection, then paused. "Oh! While I'm thinking about it. One other point Leslie raised in her message was to ask where we were on the possibility of getting treecats assigned to critical personnel in Nouveau Paris. She knows that's really up to the 'cats, and she's not trying to push anybody into leaning on them, but it seems the security services back home are taking the possibility of nanotech assassinations very seriously."

"I'll discuss it with Dr. Arif and Sorrow Singer tomorrow morning, early," Elizabeth assured her. "From my last conversation with them, I'd say we'll probably be able to send at least a couple of dozen home with you after the wedding. Maybe more, for that matter."

"Thank you," Pritchard said with a warm smile. "And on that note, go back to your family, Elizabeth. I'll talk to you later. Clear."

JULY 1922 POST DIASPORA

"You are *so* going to get all of us killed."

—Lieutenant Colonel Natsuko Okiku,
Solarian Gendarmerie

Chapter Twenty-Nine

SIR LYMAN CARMICHAEL, who'd never expected to replace the assassinated James Webster as Manticore's ambassador to the Solarian League, stood at a fifth-story window and looked down at a scene out of a bad historical holo drama. His perch in one of the Beowulf Assembly delegation's offices gave him a remarkably good view of it, too.

Frigging idiots, he thought disgustedly. *Only Sollies. Nobody else in the entire galaxy would've swallowed that line of crap Abruzzi's passing out! But* Sollies? *Hook, line, and sinker.*

He shook his head. In a reasonable universe, one might have thought continual exposure to lies would instill at least a partial immunity. Looking down at the sea of angry, shouting humanity clogging the plaza outside the Beowulf residence seemed to demonstrate it didn't. In fact, he was beginning to think continual exposure actually weakened the ability to recognize the truth on those rare occasions when it finally came along.

You're being cynical again. And unfair, he admitted unwillingly. *But not too unfair. It's not like these morons hadn't heard both sides of the story—or been exposed to them, anyway—before they decided to go out and demonstrate their stupidity.*

For the moment, Carmichael was relatively safe in a personal sense, here with the Beowulf delegation. That shouldn't have been a significant consideration, but it was in this case. Under interstellar law as accepted by most star nations, his person was legally sacrosanct, no matter what happened to the relations between his star nation and another. Even in time of war, he was supposed to be returned safely to his government's jurisdiction, just as any ambassadors to the Star Empire were to be repatriated under similar circumstances.

The Solarian League, however, had never gotten around to ratifying that particular interstellar convention. That hadn't mattered in the past, since no one had been crazy enough to challenge the League, which meant Old Chicago had never been forced to deal with the problem. It left Carmichael in something of a gray area under the current circumstances, however, and he wasn't at all sure how Kolokoltsov and his cronies might choose to interpret the law in his own case. That was why he'd moved into the Beowulf residence, which enjoyed extraterritorial status under the Constitution. Assuming anyone was paying *attention* to the Constitution. On the other hand, if things kept building the way they were, Beowulf wasn't going to be enjoying any sort of legal status within the Solarian League very much longer.

He couldn't hear the individual chants or shouts through the background surf of crowd noise, not from the fifth floor through a hermetically sealed window. But he knew what they were screaming. And even if he hadn't known, he could read the placards and holo banners.

MANTICORAN MURDERERS!

BUTCHERS!

HARRINGTON + TREACHERY = MURDER!

REMEMBER FLEET ADMIRAL FILARETA!

ASSASSINS, NOT ADMIRALS!

THIEVES, LIARS, AND MURDERERS!

And there was equal time for Beowulf, of course.

TRAITORS!

MANTICORAN PIMPS!

WHOSE KNIFE IS IN ADMIRAL FILARETA'S BACK?

WHERE'S YOUR THIRTY PIECES OF SILVER?

BEOWULF HELPED MURDER ELEVENTH FLEET!

WHERE WAS ADMIRAL TSANG WHEN ELEVENTH FLEET NEEDED HER?

Carmichael sighed and turned away from the window, only to discover someone had been standing behind him.

"Madam Delegate," he said with a slight bow.

"Mr. Ambassador." Felicia Hadley, Beowulf's senior delegate to the Solarian League Assembly, returned his bow. She was a slender woman with black hair, brown eyes, and a golden complexion. She was at least several T-years older than Carmichael, but the freckles dusted across the bridge of her nose made her look much younger, somehow.

"I was just watching the show," he said.

"I know. I was watching you watch it." She smiled slightly. "Impressive, isn't it?"

"Not as impressive as the fact that Old Chicago's highly efficient police force seems somehow totally unable to break up this completely unauthorized and spontaneous demonstration." Carmichael's tone was poison-dry, and this time Hadley actually chuckled.

"The same thought had occurred to me," she admitted. "Actually, I've been wondering whether or not I should add that to my daily indictment on the Assembly floor. It wouldn't *change* anything, of course, but it might make me feel a little better."

Her expression was almost whimsical, and Carmichael shook his head.

"Forgive me, Madam Delegate, but I don't see how you've stood it so long. At best, the Assembly's turned into some sort of zoo where tourists come to see the exotic animals. Or maybe the term I really want is the endangered species!"

"Not the most tactful of descriptions, perhaps, but to the point," she said judiciously. Then she shrugged, and her expression turned more serious. "Actually, it's not a bad description at all, but, you know, I honestly believed—once, at least—that I might be achieving *something* worthwhile. Even if it was only to be the voice of the past, a reminder of what the League was once supposed to be. Now"—she stepped past Carmichael to look out his window—"all of that seems as foolish as it was pointless."

Carmichael looked at her back, conscious of a stab of regret for his own words. Not because they hadn't been accurate, but because...

"You fought the good fight, Madam Delegate," he said quietly. "There's something to be said for that. At least you didn't simply throw up your hands and acquiesce. It may be cold comfort at the moment, looking out that window, but one day history's going to get it right. And one of the nice things about prolong is that we may actually live long enough to see you—and Beowulf—justified."

"And without prolong, there's no way either of us would make it that long!" she replied tartly, looking over her shoulder at him. "I think your Duchess Harrington is right. This is going to be the end of the League, at least as anyone's ever known it. But something this big, with this much inertia behind it, doesn't go down clean and it doesn't go down easily. It's going to be a long time before anyone's in a position to be taking any dispassionate historical looks back, Ambassador Carmichael."

"I'm afraid you're right about that."

He stepped up beside her, looking back out the window himself at the screaming mob. They were beginning to throw things at the residence's ground-floor walls and windows. The security fields were stopping the tide of rocks, eggs, overripe vegetables, and occasional old-fashioned Molotov cocktails, but the symbolic acts of vandalism seemed to please the crowd. Not as much as the little knots of people who were burning the Manticoran and Beowulf planetary flags and dismembering—or igniting—effigies dressed in what they fondly believed were Manticoran and Beowulfan naval uniforms, though. As Carmichael watched, one flashily dressed, wildly tattooed flag-burner—he looked like one of the millions of long-term unemployed who collected their stipends from the planetary government every month—held on to a burning Manticoran flag just a moment too long. It was impossible to hear his howls, but the way he started leaping about and waving his hand frantically said volumes, the ambassador thought with a certain satisfaction.

"Frankly," Hadley said, "what astonishes me, even though I ought to know better after all this time, is that anyone would take Education and Information's word for anything." She grimaced. "Like I say, I ought to know better. In fact, I *do* know better. But it still seems so incredibly brainless. It's like they *want* to be lied to because it's so familiar, or because it keeps them in their comfort zone by absolving them of the need to actually *think* about things. Apparently nobody on Old Terra ever heard that cliché about 'Fool me once, shame on you; fool me twice, shame on *me*.'"

"Well, I don't know if E&I's reflected on just how badly this is going to bite them on the butt out in the Verge and the Shell," Carmichael replied. "Sure, it's tailor-made for the Core Worlds. These people are so sheltered and divorced from what's going on out on the frontiers that it's no surprise, really, that they're liable to actually believe this nonsense. And I realize Kolokoltsov and Abruzzi's immediate concern is how the Core Worlds are going to react. But they're making a huge mistake if they think the Core Worlds are all that matters, and I think they really do. I think they genuinely believe that as long as they can jolly the oldest, most 'respectable' worlds into going along with them, they'll be able—eventually, at least—to restore the 'old order' outside the Core. That 'the little people' outside the Core are going to accept their more sophisticated intellectual superiors' guidance once more, they way they ought to, once all this unpleasantness blows over." His lips twisted and his eyes were bitter. "Even that OFS and its corporate cronies will be able to go back to administering their little empires out in the Verge. And they're wrong about that."

"That's my reading, too," Hadley said, her expression troubled. "Especially with Mesa stirring the pot the way it is. Absent some probably impossible change at the center, the League's going to start shedding Verge systems pretty damned quickly, and it won't be long until the Shell follows suit."

Carmichael nodded, wondering if Hadley had been as fully briefed as he had on events in the vicinity of the Congo System and the Maya Sector.

He looked back out at the mob.

Aside from the mental myopia of mistaking Old Terra's public opinion for the entire League's public opinion, Abruzzi and his minions had actually done a workmanlike job, he reflected. The suggestion that the Grand Alliance had deliberately sucked Filareta into a death trap with false offers of honorable surrender terms just so it could be certain of wiping him out had actually struck a chord in at least a sizable portion of Old Terra's population. The Mandarins' pet newsies had come out swinging in support of the official line, and the Solarian Navy's refusal to uncategorically back that same official line had actually lent it additional credibility. It gave the story an aura of deliberation, of a refusal to rush to judgment which befitted sober-minded, thoughtful leaders doing their best to pick their way through a minefield of confusion and other people's misrepresentation.

As far as Carmichael could tell, at least some of the people who were embracing Abruzzi's version so enthusiastically had done so because it explained how the invincible Solarian League could have been defeated so completely by a patchwork coalition of neobarbs. What made it even more convincing to them, he suspected, was that it suggested the Grand Alliance was really afraid of the League. That it had resorted to such chicanery and treachery because whatever it might *claim*, it was actually terrified of facing the SLN in fair, open battle. After all, *Spindle* had been primarily an ambush engagement, hadn't it? And now there was Filareta's massacre in a similar situation. Surely that demonstrated that the League's defeats were primarily due to neobarb treachery and deceit, not the fundamental rot at Battle Fleet's core! There was no doubt in his mind that such an analysis was comforting to those frightened of admitting the League was in a position of hopeless inferiority. Not to mention those who simply resented the hell out of the way the Solarian Navy had been slapped aside like a bothersome mosquito.

And then there was the derision Abruzzi and his stable of newsies had heaped upon Manticore and Haven's assertions of Mesan complicity in the creation of the entire crisis. He'd known that was coming. In fact, *everyone* back home had known it was coming. Yet they'd had no choice but to make their information public, and at least some of the Solarian newsies—like Audrey O'Hanrahan, for example—weren't as quick to dismiss it as a combination of Beowulfan paranoia and Manticoran lies. Exactly who was going to be believed in the end was still being fought out, but it didn't look good for the Grand Alliance. Too many Solarians had bought into the Mesan claims of the Star Empire's complicity in the Green Pines atrocity. They'd invested too much emotion in that belief, which predisposed them to see the absurd allegations about hidden conspiracies as simply one more cynical Manticoran ploy to turn public opinion against Mesa and provide an excuse for the Star Empire's own support of terrorists and imperialist expansion.

I purely hate this entire frigging planet, he thought sourly. *I know it's the home world, the mother world. The place we all came from. But I'm not from here. I'm from the planet Manticore, and this place, this planet, is the epicenter of the corruption trying to hand the entire human race over to whatever those murderous bastards in Mesa are trying to accomplish. Hadley's right. The League's grown so rotten, so accepting of corruption and graft, of shakedowns and empire building, of brutal régimes propped up by Frontier Security and Gendarmerie intervention battalions, that it doesn't deserve to survive. That the sooner we're all shut of it, the better.*

And that was the fatal flaw in Malachai Abruzzi's strategy. No matter what he convinced Old Terra of, no matter what line he sold to the oldest, most comfortable of the Core Worlds, the rest of the galaxy knew better. It was far enough from the center to see much more clearly than those too close to the rot, and it was going to refuse to go along with the Office of Frontier Security and its transstellar cronies any longer.

They're not getting that *genie back into the bottle*, he thought coldly. *No matter what they do.*

❖   ❖   ❖

Fleet Admiral Rajampet Kaushal Rajani sat in his private penthouse apartment gazing out his three-hundredth-floor window at the glittering jewel box of Old Chicago. Other towers rose as high as or even higher than his own, caparisoned in glowing windows and flashing aircraft-warning lights, and gemlike bubbles drifted across the heavens as air cars moved sedately in and around them. More of the stupendous structures rose from pylons sunk deep into the bedrock underneath Lake Michigan, and their mirrored reflections gleamed up at them from night-black water swarming with the Christmas tree glow of pleasure boats. The pedestrian slide-walks so far below his window were a steady stream of late-night moving humanity amid a forest of HD billboards, subliminal advertising messages, chatter, and the frothing ferment of Old Terra's largest city. If he looked up, he could see the gleaming pearls of orbital freight stations and solar-power collection satellites, but the overpowering impression was of the incredible size, power, and wealth of the city that stretched as far as the eye could see and lit high, thin wisps of cloud with its own sleepless glow.

Rajampet loved that view. He loved looking out over it, knowing he was one of the movers and shakers who controlled the destiny of all those antlike people swarming about so far below him. He loved the taste of power—he admitted it—and for almost a hundred T-years, he'd wielded it well. But the panorama from his window was less reassuring tonight, because tomorrow he was going to have to face Kolokoltsov and the others. He didn't expect to enjoy that session. For that matter, he wasn't at all sure his position was going to survive it, and without his position, what did he truly have?

Well, he thought dryly, *you might think about that 3.6 billion credits in your private account, Rajani. Not a bad paycheck, all things considered. And you can't pretend you didn't know you were supping with the devil, although maybe you might have wanted to use a spoon that was a bit longer, now that the fucking Manties've finally tumbled onto the truth. Or part of the truth, anyway. God knows where the wilder parts of their hallucinations are coming from! Something in the water or the air out there? Talk about paranoia!*

He shook his head.

Of course, the fact that you're paranoid doesn't necessarily mean you don't really have enemies . . . even if they aren't the three-meter monsters you think they are. Like that nanotech crap. Ha! Why believe in fairy tales like that instead of simpler explanations? Crandall was so deep in Mesa's pocket she'd've picked any spot they wanted for her frigging exercise, and they could count on her stupidity to make the rest of it work out the way they wanted. Same thing with Byng, except that they probably didn't have to promise him *a thing except an opportunity to put one in the Manties' eye. And Filareta—! If that taste of his for sick games with little girls and boys had ever made it to the public eye, he—or his career, at least—would've been dead, even in the League. So getting him on board wasn't all that hard, either. And it didn't take any "mind-control nanotech" to convince you to help hit the bastards where it hurt, now, did it? Even if things are turning out a bit...dicier than you expected.*

He snorted in harsh amusement, yet the truth was that he hadn't counted on the completeness of the defeat waiting for Sandra Crandall and Massimo Filareta. He wasn't going to shed any tears for either of the admirals involved, and he wasn't going to pretend about that even with himself. But he hadn't contemplated the sheer number of other people who were going to get killed. For that matter, he'd genuinely believed the new missiles would go a long way towards leveling the playing field when Filareta reached Manticore. And he'd never thought for a moment Filareta would have been stupid enough to open fire after that bitch Harrington had mousetrapped him so completely.

Never thought Haven would be willing to side with the Manties, either, did you? he asked himself derisively. *God, who could've seen that one coming?!*

He'd asked himself, since the reports of the Second Battle of Manticore had reached Old Terra, why he'd really done it. Oh, the money was the easy answer. And so was his resentment of the way he'd been denied his proper place at the table with Kolokoltsov and the rest of those parasitic civilian leeches. Their very survival had depended on Rajampet's Navy to do the dirty jobs it took to keep them where they were, yet he couldn't even count how many times one of those arrogant "Mandarins" had shown his—or her, he thought, thinking of Omosupe Quartermain—condescension for the uniformed men and women who carried the League's mandate out to the fucking neobarbs on the backside of nowhere.

But most of all, he'd come to realize, it had been his hatred for the Star Empire of Manticore. His resentment of its merchant marine's reach and power and wealth. Of Manticore's refusal to bend to the League's demands, to show the Solarian League Navy the respect and deference it was due. For the sheer arrogance of a ten-for-a-centicredit neobarb so-called star nation—one which had laid claim to only a *single* star system as little as twenty T-years ago!—which had dared to use the unfair advantage of its damned Junction to actually tell the *Solarian League* what it could and couldn't do. In that respect, much as he hated to acknowledge the comparison, he and Josef Byng had actually had at least one thing in common.

He didn't give a single good goddamn whether the Manties actually had any imperial ambitions. He admitted that in the privacy of his own mind, because it didn't matter. He remembered one of his long-dead father's favorite sayings: "When you fuck with the bull, you get the horns." Well, it was time the Manties got the goring they deserved, and if he could do well for himself out of the process, so much the better.

Yeah, all well and good, but it's not going to make tomorrow any more fun, despite the fact that you knew something like this was coming sooner or later, he reflected. *But at least you* did *see it coming, unlike those other cretins. That's the reason you buried your tracks as well as you did. And*—he smiled thinly—*if the wheels come off anyway, you've got enough little tidbits tucked away to convince your esteemed civilian colleagues they'd better cover your back. Doesn't matter how good Abruzzi is. If your insurance files ever hit the news channels, they're all dead meat.*

There was actually a part of him that hoped they'd push him into making that very point to them. It would be so . . . *satisfying* to see the looks on their faces when they realized he had them all by the short hairs. It would be the equivalent of a nuclear exchange, of course; no way there'd be any bridges back from that kind of confrontation. But he was pretty sure they planned on stuffing him out the airlock as the sacrificial goat anyway, so he might as well get his full credit's worth out of it first.

Besides—

A ripple of musical notes, the first few bars of the overture from *Adonis of Canis Major*, his favorite opera, announced a com call on his private, priority combination. He scowled out at the city panorama, then sighed and pushed himself to his feet. He'd never felt any inclination to surround himself with the bevies of personal attendants altogether too many of the Solarian elite seemed to require. They were less efficient than properly programmed electronic servants, they chattered and pestered, they always had their noses in their employers' affairs, and every one of them was a potential security breach waiting to happen. Besides, he didn't like being fussed over in the privacy of his own home. There was enough of that in the Service!

He walked across to the living room communications

terminal and frowned as he looked at the display. He didn't recognize the caller's combination, and there weren't that many people who had *his* combination— not on this line, anyway.

He shrugged and pressed the audio-only acceptance key.

"Rajampet," he announced gruffly.

"Sid?" a voice he'd never heard before said. "Is that you, Sid?"

"No, it isn't!" Rajampet replied sharply. "Who *is* this?"

"What?" The other voice sounded confused. "I'm sorry, I was trying to reach Sid Castleman. Isn't this his combination?"

"No, it isn't," Rajampet repeated. "In fact, it's a secure government combination!"

"Oh, Lord! I'm so sorry!" the other voice said quickly. "I must've punched in the wrong combination."

"I guess you did," Rajampet agreed a bit nastily.

"Well, sorry," the other voice repeated. "Clear."

The connection went dead, and Rajampet snorted as he hit the termination key at his end. But then his eyes opened wide as the hand which had just hit the key went right on moving. It opened the drawer in the com console, the one where he'd kept a loaded pulser for the last fifteen or twenty T-years. It reached into the drawer, and Rajampet's face erupted in sweat as he watched his own fingers wrap around the pulser's butt. He fought frantically to stop his hand...without any success at all. He tried to raise his voice, shout the code to activate the penthouse's security systems...but his jaw refused to move, and his vocal cords were still.

His mind raced as the pulser rose, his thoughts gibbering like rats in a trap, and then, to his horror, his jaw *did* move. It dropped so that his own hand could shove the weapon's muzzle between his teeth.

God, God! he thought, calling out frantically to the deity he'd never really believed in. *Help me! Help me!*

There was no answer, and alloy and plastic were cold and hard as his teeth closed on the pulser's barrel.

They were right. The frigging Manties were right all along, a tiny corner of his brain realized, like a last pocket of rationality in a hurricane of terror. *The bastards* do *have some kind of nan—*

His finger squeezed the trigger.

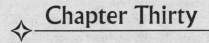

Chapter Thirty

IT WAS VERY QUIET in the file room.

People seldom came here, which was hardly surprising. The huge, cool chamber buried deep under the Solarian League Navy's primary headquarters building was only one of several dozen given over to storage of backup records of critical files. Theoretically critical, at any rate. Although this particular storage chamber—Records Room 7-191-002-A—was carried on the Navy's Facilities List as an active records repository, it was actually an archive. The "youngest" record in it was over eighty T-years old, which made it of purely historical interest even for something with the SLN's elephantine bureaucracy and ponderous, nitpicking mentality.

Despite the age of the data stored in its files, the fact that it was listed as an active records repository meant not just anybody could come wandering in. Admittance required a certain level of clearance, which the four people who'd gathered there all happened to possess. Not that any of their superiors would have approved of their visit if they'd known about it.

Hopefully, none of them ever would.

"Damn," one of the intruders said mildly, looking around at row after row of computer-chip storage drawers. There were even what looked like filing cabinets for paper copies towards the rear of the room, and he shook his head. "This looks like a thoroughly useless pile of Navy crap, Daud. And a big one, too. Don't you people ever throw *anything* out?"

The speaker was a tallish fellow in the uniform of the Solarian Marine Corps. He had wheat-colored hair, green eyes, and the collar insignia of a major. His right shoulder carried the flash of Marine Intelligence, technically a component command of the Office of Naval Intelligence, since the Navy was the Solarian League's senior service. In fact, Marine Intelligence had gone its own way long ago, operating in its own specialized world—one the Navy had never understood . . . and one where reasonably accurate intelligence was critical.

"Very funny, Bryce," Captain Daud al-Fanudahi said dryly. He was several centimeters shorter than the Marine and as dark as the major was fair. "And, yes, we do occasionally throw things out. Usually when keeping them might cause embarrassment for a senior officer. Wouldn't want to have any unfortunate evidence lying around for the court-martial, after all."

Captain Irene Teague, twenty T-years younger than al-Fanudahi and Frontier Fleet to his Battle Fleet, winced visibly. She also shook her head, brown eyes more than a little worried.

"Do you think it might be possible for you to indulge in witticisms that *didn't* make me even more nervous, Daud?" she asked testily.

"Sorry about that," al-Fanudahi said with a trace

of genuine apology. "*I* thought it was funny, but I can see where not everyone might share my sense of humor in this case."

"If there's a word of truth to your suspicions, I don't think anyone's going to think it's funny at all," the fourth member of their group said. She was easily the smallest of the foursome and only a very little older than Teague. She wore the uniform of the Solarian Gendarmerie with lieutenant colonel's insignia, and she had a sandalwood complexion, almond-shaped eyes, and close-cropped hair dark as midnight.

"Frankly, what I'm hoping is that you're going to turn out to be a totally off-the-wall, lunatic nutcase, despite Major Tarkovsky's having vouched for you," she went on, waving one hand at the Marine major, and her voice was hard. "Unfortunately, I don't think you are. Not *totally* off-the-wall, at any rate."

"I'd like to be wrong myself, Colonel Okiku," al-Fanudahi said somberly. "I'm not, though. Mind you, I'm nowhere close to having all the answers—or even *most* of the answers—but I think I've least figured out the questions we need to be asking ourselves."

"*All* of the questions?" Major Tarkovsky asked, opening his eyes wide. "Gosh, Daud! I thought we were just getting started!"

"Oh my God," Teague muttered just loud enough for the others to hear. "He's worse than Daud!"

"Oh, no, no!" Tarkovsky shook his head vigorously. "Nobody's *worse* than Daud, Captain Teague, but I do try to be at least as bad." He smiled very briefly. "It's the only thing that's kept me sane for the last few years."

His voice was much harsher on the final sentence, and all four of them looked at one another.

"All right," Lieutenant Colonel Okiku said after a moment. "I'm here at Bryce's invitation, Captain al-Fanudahi, but I understand this is basically your show. Would you like to start the ball rolling?"

"I can do that," al-Fanudahi replied, leaning back against one of the tall chip-storage cases. "But first, how much do you know about the way ONI is organized?"

"Not a lot," Okiku admitted.

"Then I'd better give you at least the high points before I get into all this.

"ONI's divided into four sections. Section One is Operational Analysis, where Irene and Bryce and I all work, one way or another, under Admiral Cheng. In theory, we're responsible for analyzing operational data—our own and reports on other navies—in order to identify trends and potential operational problems or shortcomings. We're also supposed to generate intelligence in response to specific requests or needs—for an operation against a specific opponent or star system, for example—which means we *should* have been the lead analysts for 'Raging Justice.'

"Section Two is the Office of Technical Analysis, Vice Admiral Hoover's bailiwick, which is supposed to provide OpAn with current information on tech developments—our own and those of the various system defense forces and other navies—to support our analyses. Section Three is the Office of Economic Analysis, under Captain Gweon, though he's practically brand new, which is responsible for tracking economic trends and information of specific interest to the Navy. And Section Four is the Office of Counter Intelligence, Rear Admiral Yau's shop."

He paused to give her time to digest that, then shrugged.

"Basically, I've been pretty much considered the Office of Operational Analysis' pet paranoiac for the last several T-years. I've had this peculiar notion that the Manties might actually be developing something new in the way of war-fighting technology. Ridiculous, of course. Everyone knows the invincible Solarian League Navy's technology is superior to that of everyone else in the explored galaxy!"

His tone could have eaten holes in an engine room's deck plates, Okiku noted, and his eyes were more bitter even than his voice.

"I'll confess that not even I had a clue just how far ahead of us the Manties had actually gotten," he continued. "And it wasn't really that I had any brilliant insights about Manticore to prompt my suspicions, either—not when I started. What I did know, was that OpAn, Technical Analysis, and ONI in general didn't have any damned idea what was really going on *any*where. That wasn't our job anymore. Our *job* was to come up with the feel-good reports that would tell our superiors they were still masters of the universe.

"Unfortunately, I had this odd idea that since we were the Office of *Operational* Analysis, we might actually try doing some analysis of real operational data. So I started poking my nose into things people probably wished I'd have left well enough alone, and I *really* irritated Vice Admiral Hoover. For some reason, she seemed to feel my interest in such matters suggested Technical Analysis hadn't been doing its job very well. Go figure."

He smiled crookedly.

"In the course of my journey into unpopularity, I began to realize reports of new Manticoran and Havenite weapons developments and new tactical and strategic doctrines had been systematically suppressed. They didn't suit the party line, and our own prejudices—our certainty that we *had* to have the best tech anywhere—created a natural set of blinders. That can happen to anyone, I suppose, but no one was even trying to allow for the problem or get past it to look at what was really happening, and at least some of it was deliberate, coming from people protecting their own little patches of turf. People like Admiral Polydoru over at Systems Development, for example, where any suggestion we might be dropping behind was anathema. Or, for that matter, Vice Admiral Hoover's people, who seemed more concerned with establishing that they hadn't *missed* any significant new developments than with figuring out whether or there'd *been* any new developments. And no one was even worried about the implications. It couldn't really matter what a bunch of neobarbs was up to, after all. Couldn't have any significance for the *Solarian League*, now, could it?"

He shook his head, his expression disgusted.

"I'll admit it took me years to get to the point of realizing how bad things were myself, and I was at least trying to do my job, so I suppose I shouldn't have been too surprised at what happened when I started suggesting we might want to look a little more closely at those ridiculous rumors. What *did* happen, of course, was that my career prospects took a sudden turn for the worse. I was already on the Admiralty's shit list because I'd been making waves at OpAn; the suggestion that there could be anything at all to the stories about new Manticoran missiles or inertial compensators only made it worse. Fortunately, I'd at least been smart enough not to hand over the actual reports I'd collected. As long as I was only suggesting there were vague rumors that should be looked into, I was a nuisance and a crackpot but not an active threat to anyone's career. They were satisfied to tuck me away in my dead-end little assignment and ignore me.

"That, alas, was when Irene fell into my clutches." He smiled suddenly at Teague.

"It took me a while to corrupt her properly, but after I'd exposed her to those toxic reports I'd collected, she caught the same leprosy I had. I managed to convince her to keep her mouth shut, though. Having one of us on the lunatic list was bad enough, and I figured if and when the centicredit finally dropped, ONI was going to need *someone* who had a clue. Since I also figured one of the first things they'd do would be to give me the ax for having dared to be right when the Powers That Be had been *wrong*, I hoped keeping her out of the line of fire would let her be that someone with a clue. Then this whole situation with the Manties blew up, seemingly out of nowhere, and all of a sudden people like Admiral Thimár were actually asking me for briefings.

"Not that it did Eleventh Fleet any damned good." His smile vanished abruptly.

"I did my best to convince Jennings, Bernard, and Kingsford the whole idea was insane, but they weren't interested in listening. Bernard, in particular, seemed especially eager to push Raging Justice as a viable strategic option, and she didn't want to hear anything that might have thrown cold water on her proposal."

He paused, one eyebrow arched, and Okiku nodded. She was Gendarmerie, not military, but she recognized the names. Fleet Admiral Evangeline Bernard was the CO over at the Office of Strategy and Planning. Fleet Admiral Winston Kingsford was the commander of Battle Fleet, which made him second only to Chief of Naval Operations Rajampet in the SLN's hierarchy, and Admiral Willis Jennings was Kingsford's chief of staff.

"Kingsford seemed a little more doubtful," al-Fanudahi continued, "but he wasn't arguing, and he wasn't pushing for more information. That led me to conclude that the mastermind really behind it all was Admiral Rajampet himself. I think Bernard really believed her own arguments about the Manties' morale being on the edge of collapse after that attack on their home system, but she wouldn't have pushed it that hard if it hadn't been sponsored from on high. And if *Kingsford* was less than wildly enthusiastic, that really left only one person who could be doing the pushing."

"If it was Rajampet's idea, why not push it himself?" Okiku asked.

"Doesn't work that way, Natsuko," Tarkovsky said. "It's called deniability. I hope Daud and Irene won't get too pissed with me for pointing this out, but the Navy's a hell of a lot more of a bureaucracy than a fighting machine these days, and creating the right paper trail's more important than formulating the best strategy. If Rajampet could get Bernard to push the Raging Justice concept from below, he could 'endorse' it without owning responsibility for it. He was simply listening to his subordinates—the subordinates who were *supposed* to be making strategy recommendations, giving him a menu of options, for that matter—like a good officer. And in a way, Bernard was protected, too. She'd recommended the strategy, but she had no authority to implement it. The decision to *adopt* her recommendation lay with the operational commanders—who always had the option of *not* adopting it—so once Rajampet signed off on it, *she* didn't own it, either. That meant responsibility could be dropped somewhere between her desk and his, without splashing on the career of either of them, if it went sour."

Okiku looked at him for a moment, as if she suspected he was pulling her leg. Then she shrugged and turned back to al-Fanudahi.

"I'll accept it works the way Bryce has just explained, Captain. But I don't think you arranged this thoroughly clandestine and conspiratorial meeting just to complain about having your advice ignored."

"No, I didn't," al-Fanudahi agreed grimly.

"The thing is, Colonel, that it's part of a pattern. Oh, I keep reminding myself never to ascribe to malice—or enemy action—what can be explained by good old-fashioned incompetence and bureaucratic inertia. And when you crank in Navy nepotism, cronyism, corruption, graft, and careerism, you can explain pretty much anything without requiring some kind of malign outside influence. But there's more to it this time."

He paused, clearly hesitating, and Okiku smiled thinly.

"Let me guess, Captain al-Fanudahi. You're about to suggest to me that the Manties' allegations of 'malign outside influence' in the form of this Mesan Alignment of theirs was responsible for it?"

"To some extent, yes," he said, and paused again, watching her expression closely.

"I hope you realize how thoroughly insane that sounds," she said after a moment. "And despite the strictly limited faith I normally put in Education and Information's version of galactic events, the notion that Manticore's fabricated all of this to cover its own actions and ambitions actually seems more likely than that anyone could have carried off some kind of interstellar conspiracy for so many T-centuries without *anyone* catching them at it. Permanent Senior Undersecretary Abruzzi's argument that the Manties' claims would only be expected out of someone who actually was responsible for at least enabling the Ballroom to carry out the Green Pines bombing hangs together pretty well, too."

"I see," al-Fanudahi said flatly.

"My problem here, Captain," Okiku continued, "is that I have a naturally suspicious mind. It's the reason I went into the Criminal Investigation Division. Well, that and the fact that I was never particularly interested in breaking heads out in the Protectorates for the greater glory of the Office of Frontier Security." She grimaced impatiently. "I have the sort of brain that gets suspicious when things hang together *too* well. It's a useful sort of mindset when you start picking apart suspects' alibis. And I've discovered that if it hangs together too perfectly to be true, it probably isn't. True, I mean. Real life tends to be sloppy, not neat and tidy."

"I see," al-Fanudahi repeated in a rather different tone, and she gave him a quick, fleeting smile.

"Don't get me wrong," she cautioned. "I'm not about

to buy any magic beans from you, Captain. If you want to bring me on board, you're going to have to do better than offering me some unsubstantiated suspicions. On the other hand, Bryce here"—she twitched her head in Tarkovsky's direction—"vouches for you, and I consider him a pretty good character witness. So that's going to buy you at least some credibility."

"I'll try not to abuse Bryce's confidence," al-Fanudahi promised.

"Good. And now, you were saying . . . ?"

"I have no idea at this point how much of what the Manties are selling is accurate," al-Fanudahi said. "I do know I haven't been able to come up with any reason the Star Kingdom—or the Star Empire, I suppose, now—should deliberately pick a fight with the League, though. I also know Josef Byng was an anti-Manty bigot who couldn't have poured piss out of a boot if it had the instructions printed on the heel, and when it came to finding her ass with both hands, Sandra Crandall was even worse, assuming that was humanly possible. I can't conceive of a more disastrous choice of commanders for an area where tensions were running high, yet somehow they both ended up out in the Talbott Quadrant. And I've gone back and looked at Crandall's deployment plan. She was scheduled for her 'training exercise' *before* the Battle of Monica. I haven't been able to verify whether or not Byng had already been selected for his command at that point, as well. I suspect he had been, although I'm trying to keep an open mind on that point, but it was definitely true for her. So supposing there was any truth to my suspicions that someone besides Manticore was stirring the pot out in Talbott, it was obvious it had to be someone with a lot of juice.

"Then there was Filareta's fortuitous deployment to Tasmania. You probably don't realize how unusual concentrations of ships-of-the-wall that big really are, Colonel. I, on the other hand, went back and checked the records. There have been exactly five deployments of seventy or more wallers—including Crandall's and Filareta's—in the last two hundred and forty-three T-years, and we have *both* of them taking place simultaneously."

"Suggestive, yes," Okiku said thoughtfully, "but still only speculative."

"Agreed." Al-Fanudahi nodded. "But that's where Bryce comes in."

"Bryce?" Okiku sounded a bit surprised, and cocked her head at the Marine.

"I know you're aware Marine Intelligence is under the ONI umbrella, Natsuko," he said, "What you may not be aware of, since we don't exactly advertise it, is that we're a pretty independent outfit. There are a lot of reasons for that, but, frankly, the main one is that we got dropped in the crapper once too often by faulty Navy intelligence. We got tired of taking it in the neck because a bunch of Navy pukes—no offense, Daud and Irene—didn't know their asses from their elbows where ground operations were concerned. Things work a lot better with us handling our own intel functions, and Frontier Fleet got behind us and supported us because they're the ones who usually have to carry the can from the Navy side when something goes wrong in a joint operation."

It was his turn to pause, one eyebrow crooked, and she nodded a bit impatiently to show she understood.

"Well, there's another side to it, too," he said, his

tone considerably flatter. "I know you're aware of the kind of shit the Gendarmerie gets involved in out in the Protectorates. Trust me, what the Corps gets handed can be even worse, and sometimes the poor SOB theoretically in command of the ground op doesn't have any idea what kind of snake pit he's about to drop his Marines into. What with transstellars in bed with OFS, local collaborators eager to sell out for the best price they can get, and poor damned bastards too dumb to realize they can't fight, it can turn into a clusterfuck in nothing flat. Because of that, one of the things we try to do is keep track of as many players as possible. In fact, for the last fifteen or twenty T-years, Brigadier Osterhaut's been keeping track of as many *Navy* players as possible. An awful lot of senior flag officers have crawled into bed with the rest of the bottom feeders, and she likes to be able to give our Marine expeditionary force COs at least an unofficial 'we-never-had-this-conversation' heads-up if one of the senior Navy officers involved in his operation has irons of his own in the fire."

He paused again, waiting until she nodded once more. It was a slower nod, this time—a thoughtful, considering one.

"I've been the Brigadier's point man on the garbage detail for several T-years," Tarkovsky told her. "As a matter of fact, that's how I first met Daud. And we've got some interesting dossiers in our burn-before-reading files. For example, we had dossiers on both Sandra Crandall and Admiral Filareta." His expression twisted in distaste. "Neither of them was any great prize, and some of the things we found out about Filareta are enough to make your stomach crawl. But the other thing we found out about them is that both of them had close connections—primarily financial in Crandall's case; a bit more . . . complicated in Filareta's—with Manpower of Mesa."

Okiku's eyes widened, and he nodded.

"Both of them, Natsuko. And both of them just happened to find themselves in command of major fleet deployments within striking distance of Manty territory when Mesa started getting nervous about Manty expansion in its direction. We're not sure about Byng. We know he had connections with some of the transstellars, but we haven't been able to find a direct link between him and Mesa. On the other hand, given his attitude towards Manties, it wouldn't have taken very much to convince him to go out and make trouble for them."

"And speaking as someone who's spent a few T-weeks pulling the records and analyzing Byng's career—and his performance in exercises—" al-Fanudahi put in, "he would have been the perfect choice to do exactly what Mesa wanted even without having knowingly signed on for it. He hated the Manties with a passion, and he had even more contempt for them than most Battle Fleet officers. Get him into the vicinity of any of their naval forces, and he could be absolutely relied upon to provoke an incident—almost certainly a *disastrous* incident, from our perspective, given his towering incompetence—right on schedule. Especially if someone was manipulating the situation the way the Manties claim Mesa was."

"With Crandall parked close enough at hand to sweep up the pieces after he got himself reamed," Okiku said slowly, her eyes intently narrowed.

"Or to get *herself* reamed as a way to pump extra

hydrogen into the fire," Irene Teague suggested softly. Okiku looked at her sharply, and the Frontier Fleet captain shrugged. "I thought Daud was out of his mind when he first suggested that possibility, Colonel. But the more I thought about it, the more likely it seemed. And then this brilliant idea of sending Eleventh Fleet out to repeat Crandall's experience on a grander scale came along."

"You're suggesting someone deliberately got all those spacers killed by maneuvering the Navy into battles it couldn't win? Is *that* what you're saying?"

"That's what I've started to think, at any rate," al-Fanudahi admitted somberly. "It didn't make any sense to me at first, though. Why would Manpower, which has always hated the Manties—and vice versa—arrange an anti-Manty strategy *that wasn't going to work?* Anybody willing to make a fortune off something as disgusting as the genetic slave trade probably isn't going to lose any sleep over getting a few million Solarian spacers killed, but what was the *point?* Manticore basically only had to reload between engagements. We were *that* outclassed, and I couldn't convince myself that anybody able to arrange something like this could have had such piss-poor intelligence they wouldn't realize what was going to happen."

"From what you're saying, *we* didn't realize it," Okiku pointed out.

"No, but if my suspicions were correct, *we* didn't arrange it, either," he retorted. "And then, after Spindle, there was that 'mystery attack' on the Manties' home system. Trust me, Colonel, that wasn't us. We don't have a clue how whoever it was pulled it off, and there's no way in hell we could've done the same thing. One thing that's just become pretty damned painfully obvious, however, is that Admiral Thimár's theory that whoever did it had to have crippled the Manties' defenses on his way in was out to lunch. But the salient point that occurred to me was that if it wasn't us, it was almost certainly Manpower, unless I wanted to assume there was yet another third-party out there who had it in for Manticore. Only if Manpower had that sort of resources, then it hadn't needed us in the first place."

"You're making my head hurt, Captain," Okiku complained, and he snorted.

"I had my own share of headaches trying to work my way through all of this in the first place, Colonel Okiku," he assured her.

"So where is all of it going?" she asked.

"Until the Manties and the Havenites dropped their little bombshell about this 'Mesan Alignment,' I really only had what I suppose you'd have to call a gut feeling," he said. "The only thing I could come up with was that for some reason whoever was really orchestrating all of this wanted the League involved. And the truth is we've become so frigging corrupt it wouldn't have been all that hard to arrange, especially when no one had any reason to see this coming. Just three or four senior flag officers could have put the whole thing together, if they were the right senior officers. A half-dozen would've been more than enough.

"But if whoever the plotters were realized how thoroughly we were outclassed by the Manties, then they couldn't have expected us to take them out. Not quickly or cleanly, anyway. Not without a hell of a lot of losses of our own. So why throw us into the mix at all?

"I'd already begun to suspect—that 'gut feeling' I mentioned—that the Manties weren't the real target. Or, at least, not the *only* target. And like I told Irene at the time, the only other target on the range was us. It seemed ridiculous, but it was the only conclusion I could come up with.

"And then Pritchart announced there was this vast interstellar conspiracy which had targeted both the Star Empire and the Republic of Haven. One which—assuming there was any real basis for her claims—was obviously manipulating the League's policies. And one which obviously had its own idea of how the galaxy's power structure should be arranged . . . which probably didn't include the conspirators' playing second fiddle to the League indefinitely."

"Are you seriously suggesting that this conspiracy the Manties and the Havenites are talking about not only exists but is also aimed at destroying the *Solarian League* as well as the Manties?"

"I'm not sure it wants to *destroy* the League," al-Fanudahi responded. "I do think it wants to cripple us, maybe break us up, though." He waved both hands in frustration. "Look at what's happening! The Navy's taking it in the ear; the Manties' closure of the wormhole networks means the League's economy is about to be hammered like it's never been hammered before; and we're heading into a full-blown constitutional crisis. For the first time in T-centuries, people are actually talking about the *Constitution* . . . and the fact that we haven't paid any damned attention to it in the last six or seven hundred years. And don't think for a minute that the beating we've taken from the Manties isn't going to send tidal waves through the Verge and the

Protectorates, Colonel Okiku. It is—believe me, it is! And when all hell breaks loose out there, and when the Core Worlds start looking at the worst recession they've ever seen and blaming it all on the policy of a bunch of unelected bureaucrats, I think it's entirely possible we're going to start shedding member systems. For that matter, I think it's possible we're going to see the entire federal government melt down completely. I know that seems preposterous—we're talking about the *Solarian League*—but it really could happen."

He stopped talking, and silence hovered in the records storage room for long, fragile seconds. Then Okiku shook her head.

"My God," she said softly. "No wonder people think you're a fucking lunatic! But you really could be right." She shook her head again, her expression an odd mix of wonder and fear. "You could."

"Believe me, there's nothing I'd like better than to be *wrong*," he told her equally softly.

"So, why bring *me* in on it?" she asked after a moment. "Trust me, I'm not going to be thanking you for it. If there's anything at all to this theory of yours, whoever the conspirators are—'Mesan Alignment' or someone else entirely—they sure as hell aren't shy about killing people. I'd just as soon not give them a reason to add me to their list."

"You and me both," al-Fanudahi said feelingly. Then he shrugged. "The problem is, they have to be tied in at the highest levels, and I don't have a clue how to find them. I'm an intelligence analyst, not a criminal investigator. I truly think—I'm truly *afraid*—I'm onto something here, but I don't have a clue how to go about *investigating* it, and the Office of Counter

Intelligence has been basically a place to park people with more family connections than competence for decades. Rear Admiral Yau's abilities are...less than stellar, let's say, and the rest of his section takes its cue from him. For that matter, if I were out to engineer the covert penetration of another navy, the very first place I'd set up shop would be inside that other navy's counter-intelligence service in order to make sure my operatives didn't get caught. I don't dare hand this to OCI without at least some idea of who's in whose pocket, and I can't just go to Justice or hand it over to the JAG for investigation without going to OCI first. The procedures simply aren't there, and it would just get kicked back to Yau, probably with a pretty pointed observation that I should have gone through channels in the first place. So I need your expertise, and I need it without anyone else's knowing we've talked."

"You are *so* going to get all of us killed," Okiku said grimly.

"It may actually be even worse than you know," he said, and shrugged as her eyes narrowed once more. "It hasn't hit the 'faxes yet, but they're not going to be able to hold it for long."

"Hold *what* for long?" she demanded.

"I think I've figured out who the top level of the Alignment's Navy contacts was," he told her. "And it looks to me like there may actually be something to the Manties'—and the Havenites'—wild stories about some kind of nanotech that can control minds and make people do things."

"Oh, give me a break!" Okiku's tone was testier than it might have been, probably in reaction to her own inner tension, he thought. "I may grant you vast interstellar conspiracies, but *mind control?* Please!"

"I felt the same way," al-Fanudahi said. "But that was before I found out Admiral Rajampet put a pulser in his mouth and pulled the trigger last night."

Chapter Thirty-One

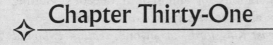

FLEET ADMIRAL WINSTON SETH KINGSFORD was barely half the age Rajampet Kaushal Rajani had attained, Innokentiy Kolokoltsov thought as Kingsford stepped into his office. He was also at least twice Rajampet's size.

And unlike Rajani, he's still alive, Kolokoltsov reflected. *Which may or may not be a good thing.*

"Mr. Permanent Senior Undersecretary," the fleet admiral said respectfully, and Kolokoltsov nodded back to him.

"Fleet Admiral Kingsford. Thank you for coming so promptly. I didn't really expect you to be able to get here for another couple of hours."

"I won't pretend things aren't still in an uproar at the Admiralty," Kingsford said. "There's not much I can contribute there at the moment, though, and it seemed important to get over here and touch base with you as quickly as possible." His mouth twisted briefly. "Admiral Rajampet's suicide leaves a lot of things up in the air at the worst possible moment."

Kingsford, Kolokoltsov thought, had a genuine gift for summing up the obvious. Then the permanent senior undersecretary kicked himself mentally. Nobody else was doing any better coping with Rajampet's death. Irritating as the man had been, he'd also been a serving officer of the Solarian League Navy for the better part of a hundred and ten T-years and chief of naval operations for almost four decades. Getting used to his absence was going to take time.

But at least Kingsford—or anyone, really—is bound to be an improvement!

"Please, sit down, Fleet Admiral," he said, and watched Kingsford seat himself. Once the naval officer had settled, Kolokoltsov sat back down himself and cocked his head. "I understand you're Admiral Rajampet's proper successor?"

"I was next in seniority, and that makes me the *acting* CNO, Sir," Kingsford replied. "Filling the post on a permanent basis is a bit more complicated. Ministry of Defense Taketomo needs to formally nominate someone for the position. Then, under the Constitution, the Assembly has to confirm the nomination."

He actually said that with a straight face, Kolokoltsov observed. Ministry of Defense Taketomo Kunimichi was a complete nonentity in terms of real power. He'd nominate whoever Kolokoltsov and his colleagues suggested, and "Assembly confirmation" would follow with automatic precision.

"I see." The permanent senior undersecretary of state smiled. "Given the fact that it's been—what? Thirty-seven T-years?—since we last had to replace a chief of naval operations, everyone's going to be a little rusty on the procedure, I suppose. I think we can assume your acting status will be confirmed and made permanent as soon as possible."

"I appreciate that, Sir," Kingsford said, then allowed himself a wry smile of his own. "Under the circumstances, I'm not sure it's going to be a very *enjoyable* job, you understand."

"Oh, believe me, I understand. I understand completely."

There was silence for a moment. Then Kolokoltsov leaned back in his chair and steepled his fingers across his chest.

"I realize you've been acting CNO for less than twelve hours, Fleet Admiral, and I don't want to pressure you unduly. At the same time, you were Battle Fleet's commanding officer, and I have to assume you've worked closely with Fleet Admiral Rajampet for some time. Frankly, that continuity is one of the reasons I believe Minister Taketomo will definitely nominate you as Fleet Admiral Rajampet's replacement. I hope it also means you're in a position to give us your evaluation of the current military situation and of how you think we should best proceed."

"That's a pretty steep order, Mr. Permanent Senior Undersecretary," Kingsford responded after a moment. "And a bit of an awkward one, too, given that Fleet Admiral Rajampet and I weren't in complete agreement on either of those points."

"No?" Kolokoltsov leaned a bit farther back. "How so?"

"I had some reservations about Operation Raging Justice," Kingsford said. "I didn't *oppose* it. In retrospect, I wish I had, but at the time it was first discussed, I only suggested that rushing it as much as we did might not be the best approach. Rajani—Fleet Admiral Rajampet, I mean—scented a possible opening and wanted to get his blow in as quickly as possible, before the Manties had time to recover from the attack on their home system. I understood the logic, but I felt the inevitable delay in projecting an attack over that great an interstellar distance was likely to give the enemy too much time to recover his strategic balance.

"In fairness, I have to admit my reservations were nowhere near as pronounced as what I've just said might indicate. For one thing, I had no more idea than anyone else that the Havenites might actually ally themselves to the Manties. I don't think *anybody* saw that one coming. I was simply concerned about getting in too deeply too quickly." He shrugged. "In my worst nightmares, I never envisioned anything as disastrous as what happened to Fleet Admiral Filareta, however. It would be grossly unfair to Rajani—and, for that matter, to Filareta—to pretend I had any better idea of what was going to happen than they did."

"Then why raise the point at all?" Kolokoltsov inquired.

"Because the reason I had my reservations about Operation Raging Justice is that I believed there was rather more truth—or *could* be, at any rate—than Rajani did to the stories about Manticoran missile ranges. I hadn't realized how thoroughly they appear to have transitioned to pod-launched missiles, or that they'd incorporated an FTL component into their fire control, but I did think evidence suggested they truly had significantly increased their missiles' effective range. Under the circumstances, I would have preferred to test the waters a little before we committed a wall of battle to action. Better to have lost a few battlecruisers here or there than to have three or four hundred SDs blown out of space."

"I see." Kolokoltsov wondered how much of that was true and how much spin. On the other hand, Kingsford had been around long enough to know how the game was played. He wouldn't have said what he'd just said if there hadn't been a paper trail of memos somewhere which could at least be interpreted to support the analysis he'd just delivered.

"Should I assume, then, Fleet Admiral, that you'd be opposed to any additional fleet actions at this time?"

"Mr. Permanent Senior Undersecretary," Kingsford said flatly, "any 'additional fleet actions' could only be one-sided massacres. Even assuming what Harrington said to Filareta in the recordings they've sent us represents a full statement of their capabilities, without holding any nasty tactical surprises in reserve, we simply can't match them at this time. There probably hasn't been this great an imbalance in combat power since the introduction of the machine-gun put an end to massed infantry assaults."

Kolokoltsov's eyes widened, despite himself, at the frankness of that response. It was refreshingly—and utterly—different from anything Rajampet had ever said.

"It's really that bad?" he asked, curious to see how far are Kingsford would go.

"It's probably worse than that, frankly, especially with Haven added to the equation," the acting CNO said unflinchingly. "For all intents and purposes, the Reserve has just become several billion tons of scrap material. The superdreadnoughts we have mothballed are the wrong ships for this war, and I don't see any way the existing hulls could be refitted to turn them into effective combatants."

Well, that's a kick in the head, Kolokoltsov thought dourly. *On the other hand, if Omosupe and Agatá are right, we won't have the cash to reactivate the Reserve, anyway. Of course, that leaves the little problem of where we're going to find the cash to build* new *wallers if we can't even de-mothball the ones we've already got!*

"Are you saying we should just go ahead and surrender?" he asked, deliberately putting an edge into his voice, and Kingsford shook his head.

"For better or worse, Sir, I don't think we can. Whether we want to fight or not, we don't have a choice after the defeats we've suffered. And that's what they were, Mr. Senior Permanent Undersecretary— make no mistake about that, because nobody in the Verge will. It's not just the Manties and Havenites we have to worry about. We're going to have other people, other star systems, pushing to see how they can exploit the situation. We can contain a lot of that, since none of those other systems will have the kind of missiles the Manties and Haven do, but if we don't ultimately defeat the people who've hurt us this badly, their example's going to remain and we'll be fighting smaller-scale wars for decades."

"I see. But if we can't send our wall of battle out to fight *their* wall of battle, what do we do?"

"Actually, Sir, if I may, I'd like to bring in one of our analysts to present a little additional background before I respond to that question."

"What sort of analyst, Fleet Admiral?"

"Captain Gweon, Sir—Captain Caswell Gweon. He's the CO of the Office of Economic Analysis over at ONI."

"Really? Only a captain?" Kolokoltsov said with a small smile, and Kingsford smiled back.

"He's already been selected for rear admiral, Sir. His name's on the next list to be submitted to the Assembly for approval."

"I see," Kolokoltsov repeated. "Very well, Fleet Admiral. How soon can Captain Gweon get here?"

"If you have the time for it now, Sir, he's waiting with your assistant."

"Ah." Kolokoltsov touched a key on his chair arm. "Astrid?"

"Yes, Sir?" a female voice said out of thin air.

"If you have a Captain Gweon squirreled away in your office, would you be kind enough to send him in now?"

"Of course, Sir."

The office door opened to admit a somewhat taller than average, immaculately uniformed SLN captain with brown hair and brown eyes. He struck Kolokoltsov as looking even younger than his rank would have suggested, and the permanent senior undersecretary frowned slightly as Astrid Wang uploaded a brief bio on to the holo display which could be seen only from behind Kolokoltsov's desk.

It was a *very* brief bio in this case, consisting of about the barest-bone vital statistics he'd ever seen. Normally, he would have expected much more, but Gweon wasn't one of the political figures Astrid would already have had prepackaged bios for.

Not as young as he'd thought, Kolokoltsov observed. Prolong could fool anyone, but it must've worked uncommonly well in Gweon's case. He scarcely looked sixty-five T-years old, at any rate! Without a more detailed bio, Kolokoltsov couldn't be certain, but it looked as if Gweon was well connected within the Navy's hierarchy, which raised the interesting question of why he'd gone into intelligence. That wasn't—or hadn't been, anyway—the fast track to senior rank. For that matter, Gweon had only inherited his present position less than five T-months earlier, when Vice Admiral Yountz managed to slip and break his neck on the wet surround of his swimming pool.

"Mr. Permanent Senior Undersecretary, Fleet Admiral Kingsford," Gweon murmured, bowing respectfully to both men.

"I understand you're one of the Navy's economic experts, Captain," Kolokoltsov replied. "And Fleet Admiral Kingsford wanted you in here to talk to me about something. What would that happen to be?"

If the bluntness of the question flustered Gweon in any way, it wasn't apparent. He only nodded, as if he'd expected it.

"I believe that would be in regard to my analysis of the economic consequences of a war with the Star Empire of Manticore, Sir."

"I think we've already come to the conclusion that the consequences are going to be unhappy, Captain," Kolokoltsov said dryly. "Should I assume you have some additional illumination to cast upon them?"

"I can't really promise to cast any *new* illumination without having had access to the reports you've already seen, Mr. Permanent Senior Undersecretary," Gweon replied calmly. "I do have the Navy's perspective on them, however."

"Then share that with me, if you would."

"Of course, Sir."

Kolokoltsov hadn't invited the captain to be seated, but that didn't seem to faze Gweon, either. The intelligence officer simply clasped his hands behind him, standing with the easy poise of someone accustomed to presenting briefings, and began.

"I'm going to assume, Sir, that you don't want the detailed statistical basis for my analysis at this time. I have that material with me, on chip, and I can provide it if you'd prefer. I've also already left a copy of it with Ms. Wang for you to review at a later time, if you wish. For now, I'll simply concentrate on the conclusions of our analysis, if that's acceptable?"

Kolokoltsov nodded a bit brusquely.

"In that case, Mr. Permanent Senior Undersecretary, the critical point is simply that any extended war with the Manties is going to be an economic as well as an overtly military conflict. At the moment, their technological advantages are overwhelming, but our economic and industrial power is many times as great as theirs, even allowing for their new alliance with the Havenites. The essential question is whether or not our size and economic capacity are great enough to withstand a concerted attack by this new 'Grand Alliance' long enough for us to produce what we need to match its war-fighting capability. And the answer, I'm afraid, is that they may well *not* be."

"I beg your pardon?" Kolokoltsov's brows lowered in surprise at hearing someone finally say that in so many words.

"A great deal depends upon the political cohesiveness of the two sides," Gweon said. "Given the lengthy period of hostilities between Manticore and the Republic of Haven, one would anticipate internal strains within their alliance which would work against its stability. I wouldn't invest much hope in that prospect, however, for several reasons, including the fact that I think both Manticore and Haven genuinely believe this nonsense they're spouting about sinister Mesan manipulation of the League's policies. Another factor would be their shared resentment for what they regard as Solarian arrogance. And yet another, frankly, would be the fact that both of them obviously smell the opportunity to make extensive territorial gains at the League's expense.

"In the case of the Republic of Haven, we're talking about a star nation with a long tradition of conquest. Even if we assume the Pritchart Administration might not wish to be as expansionist as the Legislaturalists and Committee of Public Safety, it's still confronted with a *military* accustomed to thinking in terms of expansion by force of arms, and a civilian population habituated to accept that sort of foreign policy.

"In the case of the Star Kingdom—excuse me, the Star *Empire*—of Manticore, there's no previous tradition of imperialism. Not in the territorial sense, at any rate. Manticoran power has traditionally been extended on an economic basis, by continually increasing the Star Empire's inroads into the League's shipping industries and penetrating market areas in the Verge and the Shell for its own goods. And, of course, there's the enormous advantage the Manticoran Wormhole Junction bestows on its financial sector. Yet while all of that's true, its recent expansion into the Silesian Confederacy and then into the Talbott Sector suggest there's been a fundamental change in the Manticorans' internal calculus. Our best guess over at Economic Analysis is that they believe it's time to expand their political control in order to bolster their economic dominance and give them greater strategic depth. This may actually be a result of their conflict with the Havenites, a response to the awareness that a single-system star nation, however wealthy, is at a serious disadvantage when fighting a much larger multi-star system star nation because a single defeat can cost it everything. Which is rather ironic, I suppose, since the star nation it was worried about fighting is currently its ally against us.

"Regardless of the motivations in Haven and Manticore, however, we probably have to accept that the ambition for expansion will reinforce all the other reasons they believe they have for standing together against us. In which case, their alliance is going to have a lot more stability and staying power than anyone in the League would prefer."

He paused politely to allow Kolokoltsov to digest what he'd already said, and the permanent senior undersecretary nodded slowly. He was impressed. Gweon might be young, but he was also articulate, and it sounded as if he had a much clearer and more detailed appreciation of the situation out in the Verge than any of the Navy briefers *Rajampet* had ever brought along with him.

"If I'm correct," Gweon continued after he'd given Kolokoltsov a few moments, "and we can't realistically expect the 'Grand Alliance' to self-destruct, we have to look at the balance of economic power as it exists and to consider just how stable we are ourselves.

"Economically, we have many times more industrialized, heavily populated systems. Almost all of our Core Worlds have tech bases at least as good, overall, as the Manties and probably superior to anything Haven can produce at this time. Some of them don't, and we need to be aware of that, as well. On balance, though, it would certainly appear the scales are heavily weighted in our favor.

"Appearances, I'm afraid, can be deceiving, however." Gweon's expression turned somber. "With the withdrawal of Manticoran freighters and the holes their closure of so many wormholes has blown in our shipping routes, our economy's been very severely damaged. It's not evident to most of our citizens yet, but I'm afraid they'll be figuring it out shortly. With the curtailment of available shipping, our star systems are going to be thrown back on their internal resources. Most of them will ultimately be able to absorb the blow, especially if we can expand our own merchant marine to compensate for at least some of what we've lost. It's going to take a lot of time, though, and there's going to be a lot of pain involved. Civilian morale is going to suffer, and even worse from the federal government's perspective, it's going to mean a major loss in revenues at the very time military expenses are going to be skyrocketing."

He must have been reading Wodoslawski's and Quartermain's reports, Kolokoltsov thought sourly.

"In the meantime," Gweon continued, "Manticore's dealt its own economy a very significant blow, especially coupled with the damage their home system apparently took from the recent 'mystery' attack upon it. However, they're actually in a position to begin recovering from it much more rapidly than we are, for several reasons. One is that they have access to the Silesian Confederacy and now to the entire Republic of Haven. The latter, in particular, represents an entirely new market for them—one which has been completely closed for the last twenty or thirty T-years. In addition, they have control of the wormholes they've denied to us, which means they can continue to reach markets and trading partners in the Verge and even in the Shell we literally *cannot* reach. In those areas, they'll be in a position to pick up the direct trade, not just the carrying trade, which was previously dominated by Solarian manufacturers and transstellars. When those opportunities are coupled with the fact that—unlike the citizens of the League—both Manticorans and Havenites are experienced in and thus far better inured to the strains and tensions of interstellar warfare, their alliance is probably in a position to recoup everything it's lost as a result of the Manties' closure of our trade lanes within a very few T-years. Certainly in a shorter time than *we* can recover. In fact, our projections over at Economic Analysis indicate that we'll reach a tipping point at which the combined economies of Manticore and Haven will effectively match the economic power of the League within no more than ten to fifteen T-years."

"You're joking." Surprise startled the comment out of Kolokoltsov. That was a considerably grimmer projection than Agatá Wodoslawski or Omosupe Quartermain had yet presented to him.

"No, Mr. Permanent Senior Undersecretary," Gweon said respectfully. "I'm afraid I'm not. Those projections, including the data upon which they rest and the models and methodology we employed, are included in the data chips I've left with Ms. Wang. I'd be happy to sit down with your own analysts and explain our thinking to them. For that matter, I'd welcome an outside critique of our results. At the moment, however, I believe those projections are solid. And I'm very much afraid that even they rest on some fairly optimistic assumptions."

"*Optimistic?*" Kolokoltsov's eyes widened.

"Yes, Sir," Gweon said grimly. "The two most problematic of those assumptions are that, first, we'll be able to muster the resources on the federal level to support an ongoing, lengthy conflict. And, second, that the League will maintain its political cohesiveness long enough for us to overcome the other side's technological advantages.

"As far as the first assumption is concerned, to be honest, we simply don't know what revenues will be available. We can make a good guess at the percentage of revenues we'll lose because of lost shipping duties, and it isn't pretty. What we can't begin to estimate at this point is how badly our revenue stream from the Protectorates is going to be affected. Frankly, if I were the Manties, I'd be doing everything I could to further disrupt the Protectorates. For that matter, I'd be stirring up all the unrest I could among the Office of Frontier Security's . . . client states."

The captain's tone shifted very slightly on the last two words, and Kolokoltsov grimaced mentally. Apparently Gweon wasn't one of the greater admirers of OFS' policies in the Verge.

"Whether Manticore does that deliberately or not, there's going to be a lot of unrest, anyway," Gweon continued. "Worse, anywhere we lose control, the

Manties will be able to move in and begin taking our place. So they'll very probably gain most of the revenue *we* lose, which will have a highly adverse affect on the bottom line. In fact, that's one of the main reasons we believe we'll reach that tipping point I mentioned so quickly.

"It's certainly possible we'd be able to compensate for those losses, but I'm afraid the only solution we've been able to see over at Economic Analysis would require an amendment to the Constitution." Gweon met Kolokoltsov's eyes with a levelness which told the civilian the naval officer understood the realities as well as he did. "Essentially, the federal government would have to impose direct taxation in some form in order to compensate. There's an enormous amount of wealth in the League's economy, even—or especially—in the Core Worlds, alone. If there were some way to tap that wealth, it would completely transform our current analysis of the competing economic trends."

"Perhaps so, Captain," Kolokoltsov said with a wintry smile. "Speaking as someone with a modicum of political experience, however, it might well be easier to beat the Manties militarily than to accomplish a structural change of that magnitude."

"Obviously that's outside my area of competence, Sir," Gweon acknowledged. "Nonetheless, it brings me to my second optimistic assumption: that the League will maintain its political cohesiveness long enough to defeat its adversaries. Frankly, I think that's unlikely."

Silence hovered for several seconds. Then the permanent senior undersecretary of state cleared his throat.

"That's a . . . remarkable assertion, Captain," he observed.

"I realize that, Sir, and I don't wish to appear alarmist. Nonetheless, I think we have to acknowledge that there's enough resentment of current League policies in the Protectorates, the Verge, and even in some Shell systems to make their loyalty to the League... uncertain. Quite a few systems in those regions would ask nothing more than to slip out of the League's control. They might or might not prefer some sort of arrangement with the Manties, possibly along the lines of what happened in Talbott, but they'd certainly like to throw out the transstellars and, undoubtedly, nationalize their investments and property. In terms of those systems' contributions to the League, it doesn't really matter whether they decide to remain independent or sign up with the Manties.

"That's bad enough, but I think we also have to assume some of the systems in the Shell will see an opportunity to strike out on their own. They're full-member systems of the League, which means they have the constitutional right to secede whenever they wish. I realize that option's never been exercised, but the League's never been at war with a multi-system star nation with superior war-fighting capabilities, either. It seems extraordinarily unlikely that the possibilities inherent in the situation won't occur to power-minded individuals and star systems throughout the Shell.

"And, finally, given that same constitutional right to secede, there's no guarantee some of the Core star systems won't follow suit. Especially not if they find themselves facing the sort of tax mechanism necessary to sustain a long-term war effort. And that situation would almost certainly be exacerbated in both the Shell and the Core by Manty offensive operations designed to erode our military capabilities, to encourage those who might wish to secede from the League or even align with them, and to *punish* those who do *not* choose to secede or align with them."

He paused once more, then shrugged very slightly. It was a gesture of weariness, not dismissal, and he shook his head.

"I don't like my own conclusions, Mr. Permanent Senior Undersecretary," he said levelly, "but if those conclusions are accurate, we stand a greater chance of losing this war than we do of winning it, and even if we 'win' in the end, it's likely the League will be severely damaged by the time the shooting stops."

"I see," Kolokoltsov said after perhaps thirty seconds. Then he gave himself a mental shake.

"I see," he repeated. "And I thank you for a very comprehensive piece of analysis and for honestly presenting conclusions you obviously would have preferred not to have reached. If you'll excuse us, now, though, I think Fleet Admiral Kingsford and I need a few moments."

"Of course, Sir."

Captain Gweon came briefly to attention, nodded courteously to both of his superiors, and quietly withdrew.

A fresh, lengthy silence lingered until Kolokoltsov finally broke it.

"I rather wish Fleet Admiral Rajampet had carried out that analysis before he advised us to launch Raging Justice," he said bitingly.

"I'm not in a position to say why he didn't, Sir," Kingsford said, "and I have no desire to speak ill of someone under whom I served for so long. At the same time, I have to agree with you."

"Yet you're still saying you believe we have no choice but to continue this war that Captain Gweon's just demonstrated we're probably going to lose. Is that correct, Fleet Admiral?"

"Captain Gweon is a very skilled and insightful analyst, Sir. He's not omniscient, however, and what he actually said was that we have a greater *chance* of losing than of winning, not that we *can't* win. If we don't even attempt to win, I'm very much afraid most of the catastrophic consequences he just painted are going to come to pass, anyway. If that's the case, we won't be any better off if we don't fight or any *worse* off even if we fight and lose. If, on the other hand, we fight and *win*, our position at the end will probably be recoverable. I'm sure we'd still have to make a lot of changes and adjustments, but the League would survive. So it seems to me that it comes down to whether or not that possibility is worth fighting for. If it isn't, if the decision—which is a political choice, not a military one—is that the price and risk aren't worth the possible outcome, we need to stand down our forces immediately and ask the Manties and Havenites for terms."

Kolokoltsov's face tightened as Kingsford put the options so bluntly.

"What about a third possibility?" he asked. "What if we offered the Manties and Havenites terms to get the shooting stopped, then pushed our own R&D until we could match their weapons? Bought time to redress the military balance?"

"Again, that's a political decision, not a military one, Sir. Having said that, I think the other side would have to anticipate that that was precisely what we were doing. That being the case, I don't see them accepting any terms we might find bearable. I could be wrong, but even if I'm not, it's going to take us a long time to duplicate their hardware, and they'll be using all that time to consolidate their current position. I'm sure they'll be pushing their own R&D, looking for still more improvements in their existing capabilities, which will stretch out the time we'll require to catch up with them. And I'm equally sure they'll be consolidating their spheres of economic power, not to mention continuing to expand their own navies. The upshot will be that when we finally do face off with them again, they'll be far more powerful in economic and territorial terms than they are right now. So even if we can match their technological capabilities, we'll be facing a much tougher and more powerful adversary. In which case, the consequences of a long war like the one Captain Gweon just sketched out for us would probably come into play once again."

"Well, if we're screwed if we *do* fight, and screwed if we *don't* fight, exactly what do you propose we do?" Kolokoltsov demanded. He wished he hadn't heard so much exasperation in his own tone, but he couldn't help it, and Kingsford took it without apparent offense.

"As I said earlier, Sir, I think we have no choice but to fight. At the same time, as I also said, I don't think we can afford to send our wall of battle out to fight their wall of battle. And what that leaves us, Sir, is a policy of commerce warfare. A raiding strategy."

"Explain . . . please," Kolokoltsov said.

"At the moment, the Manties' problem is that the League is very, very big, and they have only a finite number of starships and a finite supply of manpower,"

Kingsford responded. "The ability to control and consolidate territory is dependent upon the ratio of your available military power to the volume to be controlled and consolidated, and those sorts of duties actually eat up more manpower and more tonnage than pitched fleet combat does. I'm Battle Fleet, Mr. Permanent Senior Undersecretary, but the plain truth is that Frontier Fleet's always had to have more hulls—more hyper-capable platforms—than Battle Fleet precisely because establishing and maintaining that sort of control was its primary mission.

"In addition, even including its Silesian territories, the Talbott Sector, and all of the Havenite star systems combined, their alliance has a much smaller number of star systems. They can't afford the attrition we can, yet they have enough systems that if we can compel them to divert forces to protect them, we can significantly reduce the striking power of their fleets.

"Moreover, as Captain Gweon's just pointed out, their ability to sustain the war effort against us is largely dependent on their ability to absorb the economic power we're losing. So anything we can do to prevent them from doing that would be very much worthwhile. Attacking their commerce and the support facilities in areas trading with them—both of which are legitimate targets under the rules of warfare—is one way to slow that absorption down. If we can in the process inflict sufficient pain on people who've attempted to shift from our camp to their camp, we might also be able to discourage further defections. And perhaps most importantly of all, the real focus of the strategy would be to force them to divert combat power from offense to defense. If we're hitting them everywhere we possibly can with in-and-out raids, they'll be forced to tie down millions of tons of warships in system protection and convoy defense."

He paused, and Kolokoltsov nodded slowly, expression thoughtful.

"All right, that makes sense," he said. "I'm not clear on why you think we'll be able to do that, though, given what you and Captain Gweon have both just said about the Manties' current tactical advantages."

"Sir, the strategy I'm proposing would depend primarily on battlecruisers and lighter units, not ships-of-the-wall. That would mean we wouldn't face the expense of trying to mobilize a vast tonnage of capital ships that would only tie up manpower, suck up resources, and provide virtually nothing in terms of actual combat power. We already have a lot of battlecruisers in Frontier Fleet, plus those assigned to Battle Fleet, of course. And we can build more *battlecruisers* a lot faster than we could build more superdreadnoughts. Moreover, I think we have to assume the 'exaggerated reports' of Manty increases in inertial compensator efficiency may actually have been accurate. If that's the case, our battlecruisers probably come a lot closer to being able to match the acceleration curves of their *superdreadnoughts*. Our capital ships certainly wouldn't be able to.

"One of the points on which I differed with Rajani was his belief that even if the Manties had a significant missile advantage, a big enough force of superdreadnoughts would have the anti-missile defenses to blunt their attack. I felt what had happened to Admiral Crandall suggested that wasn't necessarily true; in my opinion, what's happened to Admiral Filareta *confirms* that it wasn't. Until we can develop and build capital ships that can stand up to the kind of enormous salvos Harrington employed against Eleventh Fleet—and I'm sorry to say it, Sir, but that's going to take quite some time—capital ships aren't going to be any more survivable against heavy Manty or Havenite firepower than battlecruisers. Or, to put it another way, battlecruisers are going to be *as* survivable as superdreadnoughts under those circumstances.

"Considering all of that, and considering the pod-launched missiles Technodyne made available to Eleventh Fleet, I believe our best option at this time is to go with a commerce and infrastructure-raiding strategy, carried out by battlecruisers and lighter units equipped with missile pods, while simultaneously pushing further development of the new Technodyne birds with the greatest urgency possible. We know the Manties and the Havenites have developed missiles which are at least as long-ranged and which clearly have heavier warheads and substantially better electronic warfare capabilities than Technodyne's do. Knowing that, we also know it's possible to develop such missiles, and I'm confident we'll find it's faster to duplicate what they've done than they found it to develop the capabilities from scratch.

"What I'm proposing is what I believe is our best option for driving them back onto the defensive, or at least blunting their own offensives against us, in a way which will give us time to improve on the present Technodyne platform until, hopefully, we'll be in a position to match their performance. I think it's likely our individual missiles' performance will still be inferior to theirs, but with sufficient superiority in numbers, that's acceptable."

"And you believe this is an attainable strategy?" Kolokoltsov asked.

"I believe it's the closest to an *achievable* strategy available to us, Sir," Kingsford replied unflinchingly. "Obviously, there are political and economic aspects to it which I'm not in a position to address. For example, the point Captain Gweon raised about possible direct taxation, since we'd definitely require large amounts of money. Nowhere near as much as we'd require if we were trying to modernize the Reserve or build new capital ships, but still a far bigger budget than the peacetime Navy's. I realize that's going to open an entirely different can of worms for the political leadership, but I'm not really qualified to address that aspect of the problem."

Kolokoltsov nodded once again, lying back in his chair and thinking hard.

It's a pity Rajani didn't shoot himself months *ago*, he thought sourly. *Of course, Kingsford probably would've shot from the hip, too, if he'd been in Rajani's position and known what Rajani knew at the outset. Even if that's true, though, he's clearly a wiser and more cautious man these days. The question is, is he* wise *enough?*

"All right, Fleet Admiral," he said finally. "You've given me a lot to think about. As you say, there are political aspects to this that lie outside the military's purview. My colleagues and I will have to consider those aspects before we can decide whether or not to pursue the strategy you've sketched out. I'll try to get that decision for you as quickly as possible. In the meantime, however, I'd like you—and perhaps Captain Gweon—to produce a more detailed strategic plan. One that shows us what forces you'd contemplate using, where and how you'd employ them, what the logistic requirements would be, and all of that sort of thing."

"I've had Admiral Jennings, my chief of staff at Battle Fleet, working on the concept for several weeks, Sir. I'm pretty sure we could have what you're asking for in no more than a few days."

"Good." Kolokoltsov stood and extended his hand across the desk, indicating the end of the meeting, and Kingsford rose and gripped the hand.

"I won't say I've enjoyed hearing what you and Captain Gweon had to say," Kolokoltsov continued. "I do, however, appreciate the clarity with which you both said it."

❖   ❖   ❖

"So, how did it go?"

Captain Caswell Gweon looked up from his martini with a smile as the extremely attractive red-haired woman slid into the chair on the other side of the small, private table.

"Fine, dear. And how was your day?" he asked with a smile.

"Boring, as usual," she replied. "And don't change the subject."

"It's known as small talk, dear," Gweon pointed out. "The sort of thing people who are seeing one another seriously or, oh, I don't know, *engaged* to each other, tend to do when they meet."

"Point taken," she admitted with a smile, then leaned across the table, cupped the side of his face in the palm of her right hand, and kissed him with a thoroughness which drew at least one laugh of approval from the bar's other patrons.

"*Much* better!" he told her with an even broader smile of his own. He looked around the dimly lit bar, as if seeking the person who'd laughed. Nobody confessed, but several people smiled at him, and he shook his head, then waved one of the waiters over.

"Yes, Captain?"

"Would it be possible for us to get one of the private booths?" Gweon produced a credit chip which somehow magically teleported into the waiter's hand.

"Oh, I think we can probably arrange something, Sir," the waiter assured him with a brilliant smile. "If you and the lady would follow me, please?"

Gweon stood and pulled back his companion's chair, then offered her his arm as they followed along in the waiter's wake. He showed them to a large, comfortable booth in the rear of the attached restaurant—one with first-rate privacy equipment.

"Will this do, Captain?"

"It looks perfect," Gweon said approvingly. "If you could, please let us have a few minutes before sending someone to take our order? We'll signal"—he indicated the panel on the table—"when we're ready."

"Of course, Sir."

The waiter bowed with another smile and departed.

Gweon watched him go, then ushered his companion into the booth, seated himself opposite her, and activated the privacy equipment. They were instantly enclosed in a bubble which allowed them to see the restaurant around them clearly, but prevented anyone else from seeing in. That bubble was also supposed to be impervious to any known eavesdropping equipment, but Gweon pulled a small device from his pocket, laid it on the table between them, and activated it.

"And how wise is that?" his companion asked a bit sharply, and he shrugged.

"I'm the head of one of ONI's main sections, Erzi, and I'll be a flag officer in another couple of weeks. Rank hath its privileges in the SLN, including the use of officially assigned anti-snooping equipment while necking with my fiancée. Trust me, nobody's going to find this remotely suspicious unless they're already suspicious for some reason. In which case, we're already screwed and might as well not worry about it."

"I hate it when you get logical this way," she complained with a pout, and he chuckled.

He sat back, surveying her, and reflected that he could have done far worse for a control. Erzébet Pelletier was every bit as smart as she was attractive. She was also athletic and a pleasant armful in bed. Not only that, they got along well, and he knew she genuinely liked him. In fact, it might even go a little further than that, although both of them had to remember the risks of getting overly emotionally involved in their roles.

"All right," Erzébet went on after a moment. "You told that nice young man we'd order in a few minutes, so why don't we go ahead and get the dreary details out of the way?"

"Suits me," he agreed.

He wished they could have held this conversation in their comfortable apartment, but it was a given that the apartment was bugged. Not very effectively— Rear Admiral Yau's Office of Counterintelligence was pretty inept, and its bugs were no more than pro forma, since it was extraordinarily unlikely anyone in OCI cherished any suspicions where Gweon was concerned. Unfortunately, there was no good excuse for using his anti-eavesdropping equipment at home, whereas there were plenty of reasons someone might do that in public. So it actually made more sense for the two of them to exchange critical information in a "public" venue.

"First," he told her, "there's no sign anyone thinks there's anything suspicious about Rajampet's suicide." He shrugged. "Given all that's happened and the grilling he could expect from Kolokoltsov and the others, it's easy to figure he had more than enough reasons to kill himself."

"So it went off cleanly?" she asked.

"Evidently. It was his pulser, after all." He grinned suddenly; he'd never much liked Rajampet. "It was a thoughtful of him to keep the damned thing in the same place for so many years. It was a lot cleaner and neater to have him shoot himself with a gun we knew how to find. God knows what kind of mess it would've made if we'd had to jump him out of a window that high, instead!"

"True." Erzébet's tone carried a certain delicate distaste. She hadn't been much fonder of Rajampet than Gweon, and she was pleased by how neatly his demise tied off that particular loose end, but she didn't share her companion's amusement at the circumstances of the ex-CNO's death.

Gweon sensed her reaction and grimaced an apology.

"Sorry, Erzi. Maybe I shouldn't be so flip about it, but if you'd had to put up with that arrogant little prick as long as all of us who had the joy of working for him did, you'd probably feel like hoisting a few, too."

"You may be right about that, and I guess I'm glad I *didn't* have to put up with him. Either way, we've got other things to think about, and the courier's leaving for Mesa tomorrow evening, so let's go ahead and get the rest of your report out of the way."

"Fine." He nodded. "First, I'm pretty sure I'm in the process of cementing my credentials with Kolokoltsov. I'm giving him good analysis, and he knows it. Same for Kingsford, although I've revised my opinion of his IQ upward. I always knew he was smarter than Rajampet; I'm beginning to think he may be smarter even than I'd allowed for, and I better be a lot more cautious than I have been around him. There's no such thing as cautious *enough*.

"I wasn't present when Kingsford pitched his new strategy to Kolokoltsov, but judging from the additional analysis he asked for after leaving Kolokoltsov's office, it sounds to me as if—"

✧ Chapter Thirty-Two

"SO WE'RE AGREED?" Kolokoltsov asked, and looked around the faces of his fellows.

"I'm still not sure this is the best policy," Agatá Wodoslawski said unhappily.

"I'm not wildly enamored of it myself," Malachai Abruzzi told her, "but we've damned well got to do *something*. Something that looks at least moderately aggressive, I mean. And after what happened to Filareta, I don't see a lot of other options."

"And at least Kingsford's being more realistic than Rajani was," Nathan MacArtney put in. The permanent senior undersecretary of the interior was unwontedly subdued. Rajampet's suicide had hit him particularly hard. It wasn't so much that he'd *liked* the CNO, but they'd worked together for far too many years in policing the Protectorates, and they'd had far too many shared priorities, for MacArtney to take his sudden demise—and its circumstances—in stride.

"Yes, that does seem to be the case," Kolokoltsov agreed in a tone of deliberate understatement, and

MacArtney flushed. He looked as if he might be about to say something, but then he bit his lip. Kolokoltsov gazed at him for a moment longer, then sighed.

"I'm sorry, Nathan," he said. MacArtney looked back up quickly, and Kolokoltsov shrugged. "We're in a hell of a mess, and Rajani had a lot to do with our getting here. And, yes, you and he were our point team for the Protectorates. But the two of you didn't act alone, and it's obvious Rajani wasn't keeping you fully informed any more than he was keeping the rest of us fully informed. So I suppose it's about time I got past taking out my own fear and uncertainty—and I *am* scared, don't doubt that for a moment—on you." He smiled thinly. "Trust me, there's been more than enough screwing up involved in getting us to this point to go around. And a lot of it comes to roost right here."

He tapped his own chest, his expression grim. MacArtney gazed at him for a few seconds, then nodded. No one else said anything else, and Kolokoltsov didn't blame them. Quartermain and Wodoslawski had persistently cautioned all of them about the potential economic consequences of a conflict with the Star Empire of Manticore, yet all of them—including Quartermain and Wodoslawski—had disastrously underestimated the Manties' *military* capabilities. That was Rajampet's fault, in many ways, yet that didn't absolve them from their own disastrous mistake in accepting his assurances that Battle Fleet's numbers were more than enough to compensate for any "minor" Manticoran advantages.

Especially not when we should've known—when I should've known—how much our own attitudes were being influenced by wishful thinking and arrogance. We walked into this one step—one avoidable step—at a time, and now we're stuck with it.

"The only thing I wonder about," Quartermain said now, her tone more hesitant than usual, "is whether we shouldn't still be pursuing a back-burner diplomatic resolution?" She looked at the others. "After what's happened in the Assembly, especially, I'm more worried than ever about the long-term consequences of the Manty blockade. The political consequences, I mean. If there's any way to get them to back off on that..."

Her voice trailed off and she grimaced unhappily.

"We all know what you mean, Omosupe," Kolokoltsov told her. "But if I were the Manties, I wouldn't be real interested in negotiating with us at the moment. Not when they know how badly that blockade has to be hurting us. And not when they've got the momentum and the combat advantage, either. I'm sure they'd be prepared to give us terms, but I'm also pretty sure any terms they'd be willing to accept would do us more harm than good in the Assembly. Not to mention what people who think Beowulf has a point about what would've happened to Tsang if they'd let her through their damned terminus might do if the news got out we were negotiating with one hand while 'sacrificing Navy ships and lives' with the other."

Quartermain nodded slowly, although he wasn't certain she fully agreed with him. For that matter, he wasn't certain he fully agreed with himself. But he *was* certain they dared not show any evidence of weakness.

"We do need to be prepared to sit back down at the table with them," he went on. "In fact, I think it's essential that we put together a proposal we could live with and update it constantly, keep it current, so we can send it to the Manties as soon as the opportunity offers."

"'As soon as the opportunity offers'?" she repeated, and he shrugged.

"Before we can expect them to give any ground, entertain a peace settlement we could accept without the internal political situation coming apart completely, we're going to have to score at least some victory."

"Excuse me, but that doesn't seem likely to happen anytime soon," Wodoslawski pointed out a bit sharply, and Kolokoltsov shrugged again.

"Not in any pitched battle between fleets, no," he conceded. "On the other hand, that's not the sort of campaign Kingsford is proposing, is it? If we can do an end run around their battle fleet and start hammering *their* star systems and *their* commerce, inflict some of the hurt their blockade is inflicting on *us*, they may become more amenable to reason. And if we can do that and sell it to our own public as proof we're actually accomplishing something militarily, then we could probably risk opening negotiations without sending the League's morale and confidence even further into the crapper."

Both women looked dubious, and he leaned forward, his expression intense.

"Right now, there's a lot of floundering around in the Assembly and on the news channels. If Reid's motion succeeds the way I think it will, it should refocus a lot of that blathering and posturing, though. At the very least, it will refocus it on Beowulf and off of *us* for at least a few T-months, and that should help a lot. If nothing else, it should drive Hadley back onto the defensive and lower the temperature of the debate about our policies and competence. And I think reminding people about Beowulf's 'treachery' is going to get quite a few of the other system governments started looking around fearfully at the threats *outside* the League. The ones that are most comfortable with the existing system are worried about the example Beowulf's actions represent. In fact, they're likely to see Beowulf's decision to let the Manties in as an act of *aggression*, one aimed directly at *them*, since it threatens the integrity—and defense—of the system they're so invested in. And even better, from our viewpoint, the uncertainty, the sense that the entire galaxy is coming unglued, should make even systems whose governments are unhappy about our policies nervous about rocking the boat at a time like this. We may have gotten hurt, and they may not like everything we're doing, but we're still the biggest, most powerful haven around, so there's a herd instinct at work in our favor at the moment. But we have to accomplish something, or at least be able to *sell* something as an accomplishment, if we want to keep that instinct working for us instead of against us. That's why Kingsford's approach offers us the best chance in terms of military options."

"And how good do you think that chance really is?" Quartermain asked softly.

"Frankly, I don't know. I don't think anyone does." Kolokoltsov leaned back once more, raising his hands as he admitted his uncertainty. "I only know every other option looks even less likely to succeed. And if this does manage to buy us enough time to push the development on those new Technodyne missiles, the situation's going to change radically. We're still way too damned big for them to possibly think they could *occupy* all of our star systems. We just have to hold everything together long enough to get weapons good enough to give us a chance against them into production. If we can do that, that ratio of force to volume that Kingsford was talking about comes into play on *our* side, not theirs."

He looked around the table again and inhaled deeply.

"So, I repeat the question. Are we in agreement that we should authorize Admiral Kingsford's commerce and infrastructure-raiding strategy?"

No one spoke. But then, slowly, one by one, heads nodded all around the table.

✧　　　✧　　　✧

The Chamber of Stars, the official meeting place of the Solarian League Assembly, was enormous. It had to be for something which seated the delegation of every single star system which claimed League membership. *Every* system was entitled to a minimum of one delegate; additional delegates were apportioned on the basis of population. The majority of delegations consisted of no more than two or possibly three members. Indeed, almost a third of all delegations boasted only a single member. More populous systems, obviously, had a greater representation, however, and the Beowulf Delegation consisted of nine members, headed by Felicia Hadley.

At the moment, all nine of those members were on the floor of the Chamber. Most were gathered around Hadley in their delegation's box, but three of them were out circulating. The delegation's staff reviewed every poll, clipped every editorial, and reviewed the majority of op-ed pieces every day, but Hadley was a firm believer in taking the pulse of the Assembly one-on-one and face-to-face.

Especially on days like this.

"Felicia."

Hadley turned and found herself facing Hamilton Brinton-Massengale, the delegation's third-ranking member. He was a pleasant, unassuming man with brown hair, a ready smile, and a certain amiable lack of focus which was highly deceptive. That made him one of Hadley's best pulse-takers, and she felt her nerves tighten as she absorbed his expression. The usual quick smile was nowhere in evidence.

"Yes, Ham?"

"I think the rumor was right," Brinton-Massengale said quietly. "An awful lot of people don't seem to see me when I signal for a word." He grimaced. "I don't think they've all been struck blind, either."

"Depends on what you mean by blind, doesn't it?" Hadley smiled thinly.

"I made a special effort to check in with Heimdall, Cyclops, Trombone, Strathmore, and Kenichi," Brinton-Massengale told her, and she nodded. All five of those star systems were within thirty-five light-years of Beowulf. In fact, Heimdall was barely fourteen light-years away, and all had been trading partners and (usually) political allies for many decades.

"And?" she asked when he paused.

"And Routhier, Reicher, and Tannerbaum were some of the people who seem to be having vision problems. Fang Chin-wen was at least willing to exchange a few words, but I had this sense she was looking over her shoulder the entire time. In fact, the only one who seemed ready for an actual conversation was Gook Yang Kee."

Hadley nodded again, although not happily. Kjell Routhier was one of Cyclops' delegates. Aurélie Reicher was from Heimdall, and Charlotte Tannerbaum was from Kenichi, while Fang Chin-wen was the assistant delegation leader for Trombone and Gook Yang Kee was the junior member of the Strathmore delegation.

Hadley wasn't that surprised about Tannerbaum, since Beowulf's relations with Kenichi had never been particularly close. Routhier was more of a disappointment, especially after the way Hadley and her delegation had helped grease the skids for his delegation chief to meet personally with Permanent Senior Undersecretary Kolokoltsov a few T-months back. The real disappointment, though, was Aurélie Reicher. Heimdall and Beowulf did a tremendous amount of business with one another, given their proximity, and there was more intermarriage between Beowulfers and Heimdallians than almost any other star system except Manticore itself.

I don't like the possibility that Heimdall's decided to pull the plug on us, Hadley thought. *Still, Reicher's a pain in the ass on her best day. And she resents the fact that our delegation's got two more members than hers does. Talk about petty! So it's possible she's simply decided on her own that there's no point getting splashed if we're about to get whacked.*

"What did Fang have to say?" she asked.

"Not a lot, mostly just everyday platitudes. I had the impression she was making conversation to be polite. On the other hand, that may have been for the benefit of the rest of her delegation."

"Why do you say that?" Hadley's eyes narrowed intently.

"Because she's the one who told me to go have a word with Yang Kee...and she did it very quietly, when no one else from her delegation was in easy earshot."

"Okay." Hadley nodded in understanding.

Despite the Chamber's size and the thousands of human beings who inhabited it when the Assembly was in session (and its members bothered to attend), its magnificent design included sound baffles around each delegation's formal box. The baffles couldn't completely deaden the never-ending, rustling surf of that many human voices, but it did reduce the background noise to just that—a background—within each box against which voices *inside* the box were clearly audible. So it would have made sense for Fang to babble away meaninglessly as a time killer until she could find a moment no one was close enough to overhear her.

Assuming she had something to say she didn't want the rest of her delegation to know about, at least.

"So what did Yang Kee say when you found him?" she asked.

"Not a hell of a lot," Brinton-Massengale replied frankly. "But that was because he didn't *know* a hell of a lot. He says the senior members of the delegation seem worried, and nobody seems really eager to talk to any of them, either. One thing he did find out, though."

"What?"

"He's not on the official list, but Tyrone Reid's going to move a special motion."

"Yang Kee's certain of that?" Hadley felt herself

leaning towards Brinton-Massengale, her expression tight. She knew her body language was revealing too much to anyone watching her closely, but she couldn't help it.

"As certain as he can be." Brinton-Massengale shrugged. "You know how it is, Felicia. But he says the fix is definitely in. Reid isn't on the Speaker's List, but Yung-Thomas is, and Yung-Thomas is going to yield in Reid's favor. That's what Yang Kee had from someone on Neng's staff."

"I see." Hadley thought for several seconds, then inhaled deeply. "Ham, I want you to go back to the residence."

"Can I ask why?" There was no argument in Brinton-Massengale's tone, but he looked surprised.

"I want an official member of the delegation, not just one of the staffers, to sit on Sir Lyman. Someone nobody with an official position is going to try to shove his way past."

"You think somebody's going to try to put the arm on the Ambassador?" Brinton-Massengale looked even more surprised, and Hadley shook her head.

"No, not really, but I don't want to take any chances. Make sure you've entered your proxy code in my favor before you go, so I can cast your vote if I have to. Not that it's going to do much good."

"Sure," Brinton-Massengale said again. He entered the appropriate code, then looked at her before leaving the delegation's box. "What do you think this is all about? Other than something we're not going to like, I mean?"

"It could be several things," Hadley said grimly. "With Reid fronting for them, though, they're probably going for something fairly heavy. Probably—" She broke off and shook her head. "No, I'm not going to speculate. We'll know soon enough. Now scoot!"

✧　　✧　　✧

Jasmine Neng, the Speaker of the Assembly, was a native of the Sol System (speakers tended to be chosen from mankind's home star system). Born and raised in one of the belter habitats, she was tall and very slender with a pale complexion and striking dark eyes. She also knew exactly where the real balance of power lay in the Solarian League, or she would never have been chosen for her current position.

She sat in the Speaker's luxurious chair at the Chamber of Stars' central podium. The Speaker's position was a towering pinnacle mounted on a twisting, faceted column of varicolored marble—honey and cream, obsidian black and golden, warm green and umber—eight meters tall. It loomed above the closest floor-level delegation boxes, although the upper perimeter of the Chamber rose even higher above it. The Chamber's indirect lighting was designed to provide a soft, muted ambience under the huge, hemispherical dome of its ceiling, where Old Luna rose in the east and the glittering wealth of stars stretched out endlessly overhead. In the midst of that dim lighting, the Speaker's marble column gleamed, picked out and illuminated by floor-mounted spotlights, and a beautifully detailed hologram of Old Terra's blue and green globe floated above Neng's console.

Hadley had always thought the Chamber had a beautiful, magnificent presence. And so it should, as the meeting place of the democratically elected delegates of the most powerful human nation ever to have existed. But beautiful though it was, magnificently though it had been reared, it was all a sham, and the woman sitting atop that marble spire knew it.

The delegate who'd been speaking—droning away about something one of his constituents had wanted in the ORA, the Official Record of the Assembly—came to the end of his allotted time and sat back down. Hadley had no idea if he'd finished what he meant to say, but he could always sign up for additional time and take up exactly where he'd been interrupted. It wasn't as if most of the delegates had anything more important to do with their time.

She looked around the Chamber again. It was always difficult to tell, since many of the delegations didn't illuminate their boxes or even chose to engage the privacy shields, but it looked to her as if more delegates were present than usual. It was normally a toss-up as to whether or not there'd be enough attendees to make a legal quorum, although attendance had averaged higher since the crisis with the Star Empire had blown up. If her impression was right, however, more delegates than even that could account for were either in their boxes or wandering about the Chamber's floor.

"Thank you, Mr. Terry," Neng said to the delegate who'd just seated himself. She had a strong, resonant voice which always seemed a bit strange coming from such a slender frame but was probably part of the reason she'd been chosen for her position. Her hugely magnified image in the HD projection hovering just below the Chamber's ceiling looked down at the display at her console.

"The Chair recognizes Mr. Guernicho Yung-Thomas, of Old Terra. The Honorable Delegate has requested ten minutes of the Assembly's time. Mr. Yung-Thomas."

Her image disappeared, replaced by that of a somewhat portly, dark-complexioned man with sandy blond hair and gray-green eyes. He was a familiar sight to most of the Assembly, and more than one of the delegates either groaned when they saw him or decided the next ten minutes would be an excellent time for them to visit the men's room or the women's room or something else equally important. Yung-Thomas had a veritable passion for hearing his own voice, and he could be counted upon to put his name on the Speaker's List at least every couple of T-weeks. Worse, his seniority in the Assembly meant he usually got the time he'd requested. Which he then used to give what he fondly imagined were ringing orations on the most boring topics imaginable.

Hadley had never really understood what made Yung-Thomas tick. Did he simply want go down in history as the delegate who'd single-handedly put the most words into the Official Record? Was he trying to prove it really was possible to bore a thousand human beings to death? Or did he actually believe he was the magnificent orator he caricatured whenever he rose to speak? She didn't know, but the fact that he was allowed to use up the Assembly's time—whatever his motivation—was one more proof of how utterly irrelevant that Assembly truly was.

Yet today, Yung-Thomas' expression was different. It was more intent, almost excited, and Hadley felt her nerves tightening.

"Thank you, Madam Speaker," he said, then looked out of the HD at the Chamber floor. "I thank you for the opportunity to speak to you, my fellow delegates, but a matter of some urgency has been brought to my attention. Accordingly, Madam Speaker, I yield the balance of my time to the Honorable Tyrone Reid."

Neng actually managed to look a bit surprised when her image replaced Yung-Thomas' on the HD. Perhaps acting ability had been another qualification for her position.

"Mr. Reid," she said, "Mr. Yung-Thomas has yielded to the balance of his time to you. You have the floor."

"Thank you, Madam Speaker. And thank you, Mr. Yung-Thomas."

Reid's image appeared—tall, with the bronzed complexion of a skier and yachtsman, carefully arranged black hair, and Nordic blue eyes which Hadley knew (although she wasn't supposed to) he'd had altered from their original brown coloration. He was certainly physically impressive. She'd give him that. And the newsies loved him.

"Fellow delegates," he said now, his deep voice grave, his expression somber, "I apologize for coming before you under somewhat irregular circumstances. I realize this time is officially designated for addresses to the Assembly, not for the transaction of business. Nonetheless, I feel I must claim privilege for an emergency motion."

The background murmur of conversations ebbed suddenly. It didn't quite cease—Hadley couldn't conceive of anything short of a kinetic-weapon strike that could have accomplished that!—but it certainly dropped to one of the lowest levels she'd ever heard. Not surprisingly. There were very few circumstances under which a motion took privilege over the scheduled addresses from the Speaker's List.

"May the Chair ask the basis for your privilege claim, Mr. Reid?" Neng asked.

"The basis for my privilege claim, Madam Speaker, is a threat to the security of the Solarian League," Reid replied soberly. "And a grave matter of constitutional law."

The silence intensified, and Hadley had to restrain a sharp, fierce bark of laughter. Constitutional law? Kolokoltsov and his accomplices were suddenly concerned about *constitutional law?* If the idea hadn't made her want to vomit, it would have been hilarious.

"The Honorable Delegate has requested privilege for a motion on the basis of a threat to the League's security," Neng intoned. "Does anyone second his request?"

"Seconded!" a voice called from the Seacrest delegation's box.

"A request of privilege has been made and seconded," Neng announced. "The Chair calls the vote."

Hadley thought about voting against the request, but it wouldn't have made any difference in the end. The fix, as Brinton-Massengale had said, was obviously in.

Several minutes passed while the delegates who were bothering to vote punched the buttons in their boxes. The computers tallied results, and Neng looked down at them.

"The request of privilege is granted," she said. "The Honorable Delegate may proceed."

Her image disappeared once more, giving way to Reid's. He looked out across the Chamber for several seconds, then cleared his throat.

"Fellow delegates," he said, "I'm sure there's no need for me to recapitulate the grievous events of the last few T-months. The League has found itself at odds with the so-called Star Empire of Manticore over what should have been a relatively minor dispute on the frontiers. Unfortunately, the Star Empire has chosen to adopt an increasingly aggressive and militant response to the League's efforts to insist upon the sanctity of national borders, to safeguard fair and impartial elections, and to protect neutral third parties from unilateral aggression on the part of apparently imperialistic naval powers."

He paused, and Hadley rolled her eyes. She supposed that was one way to describe what had been happening.

"As you know, Fleet Admiral Sandra Crandall's task force was attacked and virtually destroyed by Manticoran naval forces in the Spindle System in what the Star Empire has dubbed the Talbott Quadrant and seen fit to annex as the result of a highly questionable 'constitutional convention' in the Talbott *Cluster*. We are still seeking to determine precisely what happened in Spindle, but the fact of Fleet Admiral Crandall's ships' destruction and the massive casualties inflicted by the Manticorans is beyond dispute. They themselves acknowledge the shocking death toll. Indeed, their leaders, their news media, and even some of their friends here in the League have actually *boasted* of the overwhelming nature of their victory. As if the deaths of so many men and women were a matter for celebration rather than regret and grief.

"In the face of such heavy losses and the obvious intransigence of the Manticorans, of their refusal to meet the League's proposals for compromise on our competing claims, the Admiralty dispatched a fleet to the Manticore Binary System under the command of Fleet Admiral Massimo Filareta. We all know what happened to that fleet once it had been duped into surrendering and destroying the missile pods which represented its best weapon for inflicting damage upon its enemies. According to the Manticorans, Eleventh Fleet did *not* send the self-destruct command to its missile pods. Instead, for some unknown reason, Fleet Admiral Filareta, although fully aware of the ultimate hopelessness of his position, chose to fire... leaving the 'Salamander' no option but to open fire and cold-bloodedly massacre almost two million—*two million!*—Solarian spacers."

There was a sound from the Chamber, a sort of low, deep growl, and Hadley's jaw tightened.

"I realize there are some Manticoran apologists who would argue with my interpretation of events," Reid continued. "And in the tradition of presumed innocence until guilt is proven, the Admiralty has declined to officially state that the visual records so kindly provided to us by the Star Empire have been edited. Despite that, I'm sure most of us have heard the opinions of acknowledged technical experts to the effect that they were. In the fullness of time, I feel certain, the truth of that matter will be sifted and the League will respond fittingly to the slaughter of so many of our uniformed personnel. I leave that for the future, and for the impartial determination of formal inquiry into all the facts of the case.

"There is, however, another matter. One which requires no access to a hostile star nation's records for determinations. I refer, of course, to the Star System of Beowulf's refusal to allow a Solarian task force under the command of Fleet Admiral Imogene Tsang to transit the Beowulf Terminus of the Manticoran Wormhole Junction in support of Fleet Admiral Filareta. It is, of course, impossible to know now how the sudden appearance of an additional hundred superdreadnoughts would have affected the Manticorans' murderous intentions. We will *never* know, because Beowulf refused to allow her passage. Not only that, but Beowulf had knowingly permitted Manticoran warships to pass through the Beowulf Terminus without warning Fleet Admiral Tsang of their presence. And Beowulf had done so for the purpose of actively collaborating with those Manticoran warships in barring Fleet Admiral Tsang's transit."

His beautifully trained voice had grown progressively harsher as he spoke, and his somber expression had turned into one of anger.

"I am not a naval officer. I have no special expertise in these matters. Nonetheless, it strikes me as likely that the sudden and unexpected appearance of a twenty-five percent increase in Admiral Filareta's combat strength would have at least forced the Manticorans to stop and think. And, if nothing else, it would have provided us with independent witnesses—records we knew were reliable—of exactly what happened when the infamous Admiral Harrington called upon Fleet Admiral Filareta to surrender and then opened fire.

"None of that happened because a member star system of the Solarian League *collaborated* with a hostile star nation to *prevent* it from happening. Oh, no! It did so on the basis that its constitutionally mandated autonomy within its own territory superseded the federal authority. This, mind you, despite the fact that the Beowulf Terminus is not the territorial space of the Beowulf System—a point the system government itself made to the Admiralty messenger sent to acquaint them with the details of Fleet Admiral Tsang's planned movement ahead of time. At a time of such critical urgency, Beowulf not only chose to deny its own responsibility within the twelve-hour limit on the pettifogging basis of a treaty independently negotiated with Manticore, but then presented the ludicrous claim that a Solarian League *flag officer* was actually *threatening* the physical safety of Solarian citizens and used that baseless slander on Admiral Tsang's honor as an excuse to commit its own military units to assist a hostile star nation in threatening units of the Solarian Navy acting as a vital component of a major operation.."

The ugly sound from the Chamber was louder than it had been, Hadley noted.

"We cannot demonstrate that Beowulf's actions led directly to the massacre of so many of Fleet Admiral Filareta's brave men and women," Reid continued heavily. "The possibility clearly exists, however. And whether that may be true or not, there's *no* question of Beowulf's actions. And so I rise to move that this Assembly impanel a special commission to investigate and determine the basis and full extent of Beowulf's actions. To specifically examine whether or not those actions constitute—as I believe they do—treason under the Solarian Constitution. And to determine precisely what Beowulf was promised by Manticore in return for the opportunity to plant a dagger in Eleventh Fleet's back by preventing Fleet Admiral Tsang from moving to its support!"

"*Second the motion!*" someone screamed, and then bedlam broke out.

✧   ✧   ✧

It took some time for Speaker Neng to restore order, and Felicia Hadley sat very still, waiting, looking straight ahead and ignoring the shouts and loud conversations raging back and forth across the Chamber floor.

Reid's motion wasn't really a surprise, even though they'd managed to keep her from learning it was going to be presented today. And she'd expected him to present it effectively. But she hadn't counted on the degree of genuine anger she'd heard coming back from the floor. She was pretty sure there were more delegates who *hadn't* shouted than who had, yet that was remarkably cold comfort at the moment.

She'd already pressed her own attention key, requesting the floor. In fact, she'd pressed it before Reid rose to speak, since she'd gotten enough warning to realize what was coming. The rules of the Assembly required that the first request for the floor received it, and her own panel showed she'd gotten in before anyone else. Despite which, she wondered if Neng was going to obey the rules this time.

She was almost surprised when Neng's image replaced Reid's and the Speaker looked directly at the Beowulf delegation's box.

"The Chair recognizes the Honorable Delegate from Beowulf," Neng announced, and sudden quiet descended upon the Chamber. The vast room was hushed, closer to silence than Felicia Hadley had ever heard it, and her image appeared on the huge HD.

"Mr. Reid," she began flatly, with none of the customary ceremonial formulas, "has leveled serious and inflammatory accusations against my star system and its government.

"While hiding behind a pretense of impartiality and fair-mindedness, he's obviously already reached his own judgment as to precisely what happened to Admiral Filareta's command when it invaded the Manticoran Binary System without benefit of any formal declaration of war and following repeated warnings from the Star Empire of Manticore that it was aware Admiral Filareta was coming and was prepared to destroy his entire fleet if necessary to protect its own people and sovereignty. In case any of you are in any doubt about that, the Manticoran Ambassador—*before* Eleventh Fleet ever reached Manticore—made public the recordings of his entire diplomatic correspondence with Senior Permanent Undersecretary Kolokoltsov in which he repeatedly requested—almost *begged*—the League to send an officer to Manticore with orders for Filareta to stand down while a diplomatic resolution to the disputes between the Star Empire and the League was sought.

"The federal government refused to send that officer. Ambassador Carmichael's requests, his formal diplomatic notes, weren't even responded to. So far as we know, none of the official ministers of the Solarian League's government ever even *saw* them! Although no one is in a position to prove that at this time, it's the firm belief of the Planetary Board of Directors of Beowulf that the decisions regarding those notes—*and* Admiral Filareta's and Admiral Tsang's movements—were made at the permanent senior undersecretary's level by *bureaucrats*. Men and women who'd never been elected to their positions, without any sort of open debate, committed the Solarian League Navy to an act of war against a sovereign star nation without ever requesting a formal declaration of war as our own Constitution requires!"

She realized her voice had risen, sharp as a battle-steel blade as fury at Reid's cynicism and the opportunity to finally speak her own mind clearly, without any circumlocutions, fueled her anger. She made herself stop, draw a deep breath, and heard one or two lonely voices raised in angry rejection of what she'd said. Aside from those voices, the Chamber was silent, and she wished she could believe it was the silence of thoughtfulness and not the silence of sullen anger.

"Completely irrespective of any actions on Beowulf's part," she continued after a moment, "the action of those bureaucrats in committing the Solarian League—without the constitutionally required declaration of war—to war against a star nation whose war-fighting capabilities were far superior to the League's surely constitutes an act of treason against the League.

"I observe, however, that Mr. Reid has not moved to investigate *their* conduct. No, he's chosen to accuse Beowulf of treason and collaboration with the enemy. Although he's been very careful never to call Manticore 'the enemy,' hasn't he? He's referred to the Star Empire repeatedly as 'a hostile star nation,' but not as a formal enemy. And the reason he's avoided that term is because *there's been no formal declaration of war.*"

The last seven words came out slowly, precisely spaced and enunciated, and she let them fall into the Chamber's silence.

"I remind all of you that while the Constitution recognizes the paramount authority of the federal government in time of *war*, in time of *peace* the self-defense forces of the League's member star systems are not subject to the federal authority. They remain answerable to the star system which buids, mans, and maintains them. And the territorial autonomy of member star systems is absolute *except in time of war*. Precisely how is Beowulf supposed to have committed treason while acting solely and entirely within the letter of the Constitution *in time of peace?*

"Yet let that question lie for the moment. Instead, let's consider the question of system autonomy and our actions in conjunction with Admiral Truman's task force to bar Admiral Tsang's passage through the Beowulf Terminus.

"There were Beowulfan personnel on the terminus traffic-control platforms. Solarian citizens, employed by the Beowulf Terminus Astro Control Service, a joint Beowulfan and Manticoran Corporation. They were civilians, not subject to the orders of the Solarian military, and with all the civil rights of Solarian citizens. Yet Admiral Tsang had made it clear she intended to take possession of the platforms by force and to compel those citizens—against their will—to pass her vessels through the terminus. Indeed, she specifically *said* that in so many words. Not only that, when Admiral Holmon-Sanders announced her intention to defend her fellow citizens from the assault of their own military, Admiral Tsang informed her that her hundred-plus superdreadnoughts would open fire on Admiral Holmon-Sanders' *thirty-six*. Clearly the decision of a fearless naval officer fully aware of her constitutional obligations and the need to avoid loss of Solarian lives."

Hadley's tone cut like a scalpel, and her nostrils flared in contempt which was not at all feigned.

"The only thing which prevented Admiral Tsang from carrying through on her *courageous* threat against an enemy she outnumbered three-to-one was the sudden discovery of the presence of a Manticoran task force. A Manticoran task force which could, had there been any truth to this bizarre notion that Admiral Filareta was massacred for no good reason after he'd surrendered, have annihilated Admiral Tsang's entire command from stealth before she even knew those ships were present. Instead, the Manticoran commander gave warning of her presence and allowed Admiral Tsang to withdraw without the loss of a single life on either side."

She paused once more, letting her words sink in, then straightened and squared her shoulders.

"Mr. Reid has made what he obviously believes is an eloquent case for how the sudden appearance of Admiral Tsang's fleet in the Manticorans' rear might have somehow prevented the destruction of Eleventh Fleet. He's been very careful to avoid saying unequivocally that it would have, yet he's clearly implied that the sudden appearance of a twenty-five percent increase in Admiral Filareta's strength would have influenced the Star Empire and its allies. He was also careful to say that he is no naval officer. That much, at least, is obvious . . . since any trained naval officer would have known that no more than thirty to thirty-five capital ships—less than an *eight*-percent increase in Admiral Filareta's strength—could have been put through the Beowulf Terminus in a single transit. And that putting *that* many ships through would have destabilized the terminus for many hours before any additional vessels could be passed through it.

"It would have been possible to pass them through in a sequential transit, instead of a simultaneous transit, of course, had not Admiral Holmon-Sanders and Admiral Truman prevented it. Had Admiral Tsang done so, however, her ships would have emerged one by one, at intervals of several seconds, into the concentrated fire of the Manticoran fortresses protecting the Junction. Fortresses which each have many times the firepower of a regular Manticoran ship-of-the-wall. The truth is, it wouldn't have mattered whether she'd attempted a simultaneous or a sequential transit; in either case, anything which passed through that terminus, as my government has repeatedly pointed out since the event, would have been annihilated. By preventing her from making transit at all, Admiral Holmon-Sanders and Admiral Truman *saved the lives* of well over a *hundred thousand* Solarian military personnel. If you wonder what malevolent, Machiavellian motives we might have had for allowing those Manticoran warships to transit a terminus of the *Manticoran* Wormhole Junction without informing Admiral Tsang of their presence, look no further than those lives. If we had slavishly rolled over before the unconstitutional assertion of federal authority over Solarian citizens and an autonomous star-system government in time of peace, those people would be *dead* today."

She looked out across the Chamber, huge holographic eyes sweeping scornfully over the men and women seated in the boxes spread across its floor, and shook her head.

"We all know what's happening here. We all know

the script, although the exact schedule may still be in some doubt. And we all know where this little play is headed and who's directing and producing it. So I don't expect truth and rationality to be any sort of effective defense. But the record will show what actually happened in Beowulf that day. Someday, the record of exactly what happened to Admiral Filareta will also be clearly and undisputedly available to anyone looking back at Mr. Reid and his motion and its consequences. A clean conscience and a reverence for the truth may not be much in demand in this Assembly today, but both of those are very much in demand in the Beowulf System. So bring on your inquiry. Present your case, and we'll present ours. Not because we give one single solitary damn for your prepackaged, predetermined 'impartial conclusions,' but because we care about history. Because unlike you, we *do* care about truth. And because someday your successors, whoever they may be, will have a record of what you actually do here and will revile your memory with all the contempt and all the disdain your actions will so richly merit."

✧ Chapter Thirty-Three

ORGAN MUSIC SWELLED, and the massed choir's voices rose in the words of the ancient hymn which had announced every marriage in the groom's family for over four T-centuries:

> "Though I may speak with bravest fire,
> and have the gift to all inspire,
> and have not love, my words are vain,
> as sounding brass, and hopeless gain."

The groom, clad in the blue and silver of the House of Winton, stood before the altar rail and turned to face down the nave towards the narthex of King Michael's Cathedral as the music soared about him. The cathedral itself was packed as it had not been in years—not since the somewhat premature state funeral of one Honor Harrington. Which was rather ironic, since Duchess Harrington was a member of the wedding procession, and the current representatives of the star nation which was supposed to have executed her sat in the pew set aside for them as they, too, turned to watch that procession move down the cathedral's central aisle towards the waiting sanctuary.

The cathedral was like an immense jewelry box, packed with aristocrats in the formal court dress and colors of their houses and commoners whose sartorial splendor and jewelry tended to put the understated elegance of court dress in the shade. Stained-glass windows glowed with late morning light, filling the cathedral's interior with pools and patterns of gleaming, slowly moving brilliance. Centuries-old wooden paneling glowed in that light, the deliberately antique organ's bronze pipes shone with hand-polished brilliance, vestments glittered with rich embroidery, candle holders flashed back the light, and the crowds of newsies had been banished to the discreet concealment of the balconies just inside the narthex.

Against all of that visual splendor, that richness of texture and color, of light and sound, the slender, white vision with the armful of flowers and one hand on her father's arm at the bridal procession's heart stood out with heart-stopping purity as she moved gracefully through the music.

Brides, and especially royal brides, were always beautiful. That was an incontrovertible law of nature—just ask any publicist or newsy. In this case, however, it was true, Honor decided. Not because Rivka Rosenfeld was a stunning beauty, because she wasn't, although she was undeniably attractive, with a face full of wit and intelligence touched with the bloom of her youth. And not because of the hours of effort the Star Empire's best cosmeticians had put in, either. No, it was because of the glow in her eyes as they met Roger Winton's down the length of that long, long cathedral aisle.

And, Honor conceded, it was also because of Rivka's own impeccable taste.

Rivka's mother, Shamirah, had lived to see her daughter engaged, but she'd been visiting relatives in Yawata Crossing. The loss had been devastating, and Honor had found Rivka turning to *her* to fill—or *try* to fill, at any rate—Shamirah's role in the planning of her wedding. It had been a complication Honor scarcely needed on top of everything else, yet it had never occurred to her to do anything but accept the honor of Rivka's trust. Her official duties as matron of honor had been less extensive than those of Lord Chamberlain Wundt or Aretha Hart's, but *they'd* been focused on the official aspects of the day. Honor had been focused on *Rivka*, and on more than one occasion she'd found herself acting as her champion as the motherless young woman fearlessly stood up against the demands of an occasion of state.

Rivka had held out steadfastly for an elegantly simple wedding gown, without glamour or elaborate embroidery or glittering jewels, and Honor—whose own tastes ran in very much the same direction, if the truth be told—had supported her strongly. Not that simplicity implied cheapness, of course. Honor had become far more knowledgeable about fashion matters and designer gowns than she'd ever expected to, and she knew how expensive that deceptively simple, flawlessly fitted gown had actually been. Yet it was also perfect, the inevitable setting for the slim, dark-haired and dark-eyed young woman advancing to meet her fiancé.

The one concession she'd made was her bridal train, which stretched far down the aisle behind her as she advanced to meet her waiting groom. Honor and her maids of honor were careful to avoid treading on it as they followed her, and at Rivka's insistence, Faith Harrington led the entire procession, scattering flower petals across the rich-toned carpet with solemn concentration. Her brother, James, followed her, carrying the Royal blue cushion with the waiting wedding rings and the princess' coronet.

Arranging it all had been a long journey and plenty of hard work for everyone, Honor reflected, following Rivka in her own Grayson-style gown and overtunic in deep, rich "Harrington green" with the Star of Grayson glittering about her throat on its crimson ribbon as her only jewelry. Yet despite the bittersweetness of watching Rivka face her wedding without Shamirah, she'd found all that hard work a welcome burden in the aftermath of what had happened to Massimo Filareta and his fleet.

Of course, finding time for all of it had been something of a challenge. Fortunately, her subordinates had happily conspired to take as much responsibility for running Grand Fleet as they could off her shoulders, and she was grateful to all of them. She'd always liked Rivka; after the last few months, she'd come to understand exactly why Elizabeth approved of her son's choice so strongly.

She's going to do well, Honor thought. *She's exactly what Roger needs. If anyone can keep him sane when he finds himself on his mother's throne, it'll be Rivka.*

Not that Rivka didn't have some qualms of her own. Even now, Honor could taste the undercurrent of trepidation in the composed young woman's mind-glow. Becoming the future queen consort of the Star Kingdom of Manticore at the age of twenty would have been daunting enough for anyone; becoming the future empress consort of the Star *Empire* of Manticore was even worse. And the fact that the Star Empire in question faced a fight for its very life against all the ponderous might of the Solarian League was downright terrifying. But somehow Rivka had coped with all of that, and as she and Roger looked at one another, the clean, focused taste of her mind-glow, the joy and eagerness which infused it—and Roger's—despite her mother's death and all of those worries, all of those future threats, told Honor how well they both had chosen.

The procession reached the groom and his party and dispersed into its perfectly choreographed components, and Hamish Alexander-Harrington, standing with Roger, smiled at his wife as she stepped up beside Rivka and took the bridal bouquet—made up of native blossoms from each of the old Star Kingdom's habitable planets—before the bride stepped forward to join Roger under the white silk canopy of the *chuppah*. The cathedral roof had been modified with a retractable skylight above the sanctuary to let sunlight stream down from the deep blue heavens of Manticore, and Honor smiled back at Hamish across that shaft of radience, remembering how much simpler (if unexpected) her own wedding had been. Then she stepped back with the flowers as Rivka took Roger's hand and both of them turned to face Bishop Robert Telmachi and Rabbi Yaakov O'Reilly.

Planning a wedding within the traditions and canon

of the Catholic Church and Judaism had required a certain flexibility of all concerned. In fact, there would be *two* weddings this day, and the formal pronunciation that Roger and Rivka were man and wife would wait until both had been completed. One or two of the protocolists had seemed a little taken aback by the notion, but it was important—to both families, and especially in light of Shamirah Rosenfeld's absence. And at least Honor's experiences on Grayson had accustomed her to dealing with far thornier problems than this! She, Telmachi, and O'Reilly had taken the entire project in stride.

The Archbishop of Manticore and his Jewish colleague didn't simply smile—they beamed. Their eyes were alight with happiness, and Honor could physically taste the joy within them. She'd come to know Telmachi well over the past few years, and she recognized his personal joy—his gladness for two young people who were deeply important to him—and the almost equally powerful joy as he recognized this wedding's healing power for an entire star nation. She knew O'Reilly less well, and he was a calmer, less effusive man by nature, yet in some ways his joy as he'd watched the young woman he'd known since birth walk towards him was even brighter and stronger than Telmachi's.

The rabbi recognized this wedding's healing power just as clearly as Telmachi, yet there was a deeper echo of Honor's own awareness of what a huge and ultimately unfair weight those hopes and expectations were to lay upon such youthful shoulders. But as the people of the Star Kingdom always had, in times of trouble they looked to the house of Winton. They were part of that house themselves—all

of them—when it came down to it, because of the
Constitution's requirement that the heir marry outside
the aristocracy, and the Winton dynasty had done far
better than most at remembering that bond and the
responsibilities which went with it. The deep compact
between the Star Kingdom's subjects and their rulers
went far beyond the mere letter of the law, and that
compact turned Roger—and especially Rivka—into
the promise of the future.

O'Reilly looked at Roger, and the crown prince
handed him an illuminated scroll. The rabbi unrolled
it and looked out over the packed pews of the Chris-
tian church.

"For our non-Jewish friends," he said with a smile,
"this is the *ketubah*, the wedding contract between
Rivka and Roger. It forms an important part of our
tradition, and it is part of that tradition that it be
read aloud at this time."

He looked back down at the document, signed by
Roger and Rivka and witnessed by himself, by Chaim
Rosenfeld, and by Justin Zyrr-Winton, then began to
read aloud in Aramaic. Honor couldn't speak that language, but she didn't have to. She'd read the *ketubah*
in translation, and even if she hadn't she could taste
the clean, joyous communion flowing between Rivka
and her groom as the words were read.

O'Reilly finished, rerolled the scroll, and stepped
back slightly, and it was Telmachi's turn to look out
over that same church.

"Dearly beloved," he began, "we are gathered
together here in the side of God, and in the face
of this company, to join together this man and this
woman in holy matrimony; which is an honorable

estate, instituted of God, signifying unto us the mystical union that is betwixt Christ and his Church: which holy estate Christ adorned and beautified with his presence and first miracle that he wrought in Cana of Galilee . . ."

The ancient, simple words spilled out into the hushed, listening silence, and Honor Alexander-Harrington reached out as well. She touched Hamish's mind-glow as he stood close beside her, and Emily's mind-glow, where her life-support chair sat at the end of the front pew on the bride's side of the cathedral. She reached out farther, touching her mother and feeling the happiness within her. Touching her father, and tasting the pain still burning at his core . . . and the healing sifting down to it, as it sifted down to her own, borne upon those ageless, joyous words. The entire cathedral was filled to the bursting point, not simply with human bodies, but with human minds, and thoughts, and hopes, and joy. They pressed in upon her from every side, soaking into her like the sea, but this was a sea of light, of energy—of focus and purpose and promise. It flowed into her like the sun itself, and tears starred her vision as she found herself wishing desperately that everyone else in that Cathedral could have tasted and known what she tasted and knew in that moment.

It was a simple ceremony, despite its importance and despite the reconciliation of the two faiths represented in it. It was O'Reilly who officially pronounced them man and wife, but it was *Telmachi* who knelt to place the glass on the carpet before Roger Winton. The crown prince took Rivka's ringed right hand in his, raised his foot, and brought his heel down on the glass, hard. The clear, crisp shattering sound filled the hushed cathedral, and Roger looked directly into Rivka's eyes.

"If I forget thee, O Jerusalem"—he recited the even more ancient words softly but clearly, his voice carrying throughout the church—"let my right hand forget her cunning. If I do not remember thee, let my tongue cleave to the roof of my mouth; if I prefer not Jerusalem above my chief joy."

He reached out, cupping her face between his palms. Then he leaned forward, and their lips met at last.

✧　　✧　　✧

"I've been to some remarkable weddings in my time," Jacques Benton-Ramirez y Chou said, "but *this* one..."

He waved his champagne glass at the glittering crowd thronging the grounds of Mount Royal Palace. Security was tight, and treecats were much in evidence. Many of them rode on shoulders threaded throughout that crowd, and others—*dozens* of others—perched cheerfully on the branches of landscaped trees, on ornamental gazebos and roofs. They could be heard every now and then, even through the steady surf of human voices and the music of the live orchestra, bleeking to one another as they enjoyed the human mind-glows swirling about them like rich, heady wine. But there was a perpetually poised, ready watchfulness even in the midst of their delight, and armed air cars and sting ships loitered overhead while the personnel of half a dozen star nations' security watched the 'cats like miners watching canaries in some ancient coal mine.

No one at the reception could possibly tune out that omnipresent security, yet most of the guests had become accustomed to their guardians' presence. There might be new wrinkles to the threats those guardians were deployed to counter, but there would *always* be threats, and no one was prepared to let that awareness dampen this day.

Honor had finally managed to slip away to steal a few moments with her uncle and her family. She'd given her matron of honor's speech, and with the assistance of scores of personnel from Dame Arethea's office, she'd made sure the thousands of wedding gifts Rivka and Roger had received had all been properly stored and labeled. Rivka had announced her intention of sending personal thank-you notes for every single one of them, and Honor felt sure the redoubtable young woman would do exactly that...however long it took.

With that task out of the way, she'd disappeared with Rivka long enough to help her change out of her wedding gown and into the equally expensive (and equally simple yet elegant) formal court dress badged in Winton blue and silver to which she was now entitled. Of course, Honor's "help" had consisted mainly of offering moral support as Rivka looked forward to her very first day as the crown princess consort of Manticore. It would have been unfair to say Rivka had experienced a case of cold feet at the prospect, but her toes had definitely felt the chill as she prepared to shoulder the public responsibilities which would be hers for the rest of her life.

Honor had felt the way the young woman braced herself, straightening metaphysical shoulders to bear up under that burden. And as she had, she'd realized that one of the reasons Rivka had been so strongly drawn to her was that Honor, too, had been born of yeoman stock. Neither of them had ever dreamed, during their childhood, of ascending to such dizzying heights, and as she'd tasted Rivka's trepidations surging once more, she'd put an arm around the younger woman's shoulders in a brief, comforting hug.

"It's not so bad, really," she'd said, and Rivka had turned her head to give her a smile that was ever so slightly lopsided.

"Are my willies *that* obvious?"

"Well, I do hang around with treecats, you know," Honor had replied with a smile of her own. "For that matter, I didn't exactly start out in this crowd myself."

"Your mother did, though," Rivka had pointed out.

"Yep, and she ran away from it with indecent haste as soon as she got the opportunity. And I promise you, she didn't bring me up to be queen of the ball, either!" Honor had snorted with amusement at the very thought. "I'm not saying it didn't help—some—to be descended from the Benton-Ramirez y Chou family, but they were only *family*, if you know what I mean, and Mother made darned sure it stayed that way. I think that's probably one of the reasons I stayed as far away from politics as I could for as long as I could, and I never saw any of *this* coming until Benjamin dumped the steadholdership on me. And then the Queen—your mother-in-law, now that I think about it—decided to open up *her* toy box!" She'd shaken her head. "Believe me, it's survivable. And the reason you're here today, married to Roger, is because of *who* you are, Rivka, not *what* you are or what anyone expects you to be." She smiled again, more gently. "You just go on being you, and you're going to do fine. Trust me."

Now, as Honor looked across to where Roger and Rivka stood on the terrace, smiling easily, laughing as they chatted with one guest after another, she knew how right she'd been.

"It is an impressive guest list, I suppose, Jacques," Hamish said now, his tone judicious.

"*'Impressive'*?" another voice repeated. "What? Is that your studied understatement of the day?"

Honor turned with a chuckle as a life-support chair slid up beside her.

"I think it's probably as good a description as Uncle Jacques's 'remarkable,' Emily," she said. "And you have to remember the source. Neither of them is all that good with the language, you know."

"You'll pay for that later," Hamish promised her with a devilish glint, and Nimitz bleeked a laugh on Honor's shoulder.

"I await the moment with trepidation," Honor told her husband sweetly, then turned back to her uncle. "However, I have to say that in your own language-challenged ways, you're both right. I wonder if there's ever been a wedding quite like it?"

"I doubt it," Emily said. "In fact, I'm pretty darn sure there hasn't been one like it since the Diaspora got everybody off Old Earth, anyway! Let's see, we've got the Empress of Manticore, the President of the Republic of Haven, the Protector of Grayson, the chairman of the Beowulf Board of Directors, Queen Berry, and the Andermani emperor's first cousin. Not to mention your own humble self as Steadholder Harrington and the commander of the Grand Fleet, followed by a scattering of mere planetary grand dukes, dukes, earls, members of the Havenite cabinet, three other members of the Beowulf Board of Directors, the chairman of the Alliance joint chiefs of staff, the First Space Lord, the Havenite chief of naval operations, the *Beowulfan* chief of naval operations, High Admiral Yanakov, Admiral Yu, two or three dozen ambassadors, and God alone only knows who else. I'm sure there've been other weddings that had the same guest count or better, but bringing all of these people together in one place?"

She shook her head, and Honor found herself nodding in agreement.

"I wish those cretins in Old Chicago could see this," her uncle said in a much more somber tone. She raised an eyebrow at him, and he shrugged. "They still just don't get it. I think the true problem is that nobody outside their own little world is actually quite *real* to them. We're all just inconveniently obstreperous tokens they're moving around on a game board somewhere. All that really matters is that damned echo chamber they live in."

"That's how we got *into* this mess," Hamish agreed, "but I'll guarantee you there are some other sounds leaking into that 'echo chamber' of yours by now, Jacques! They don't like it, and they're trying to stuff their fingers into their ears, but they can't keep it up much longer."

"They've kept it up long enough to leave all of us one hell of a mess to clean up," Benton-Ramirez y Chou replied, and Hamish nodded.

"No argument there. The question in my mind is how long they're going to be able to stay on the back of the hexapuma. I think they've pretty much demonstrated that they're determined to go on trying to game the situation until the ship sinks under them. But when that happens, when someone else steps into their place, how's that someone else going to react? That's going to be the key to the way this whole thing shakes out in the end, Jacques."

"And to how many more people we have to kill before it's all over." Honor's mouth tightened as the chill of her own words touched the warmth and pleasure of the day, and Nimitz made a soft sound and stirred on her shoulder.

"And that," her husband agreed, putting an arm around her and hugging her tightly. "I'd like to tell you we wouldn't have to kill—or lose—anybody else, but it's not going to work out that way."

"I know." She hugged him back and sighed. "I know. And I promise I'll try not to rain all over Roger and Rivka's party."

"Oh, your credit's pretty good with the happy couple, Honor," Emily told her with a chuckle. "I don't think they'll hold a minor drizzle or two against you. No *cloudbursts*, now, though!"

"No, Ma'am," Honor promised obediently with a demure little smile, and her uncle laughed.

"You three deserve each other," he said, smiling warmly at all of them. "And I'm glad you've *got* each other. Hang on to it, because, trust me, it's something special."

"I agree," Honor said softly, reaching down to touch Emily's working hand, then looked up as the orchestra stopped playing and another round of official toasts began. It was Chyang Benton-Ramirez's turn to propose the first toast, and afternoon sunlight burned golden in the heart of his wine as he raised his glass. Their sheltered little nook was too far away for any of them to hear his actual words, but they heard the applause when he finished.

"What?" she heard, and looked at her uncle.

"What 'what'?" she asked, cocking her head slightly.

"You're thinking deep thoughts again," Jacques Benton-Ramirez y Chou accused her. "Getting ready to find something else to worry about, if I know you!"

"I am not!" she protested.

"Oh, yes, you are," he shot back. "Nimitz?"

He, Hamish, and Emily all looked at Nimitz, who gazed back thoughtfully for a moment . . . and then nodded.

"Oh, you *traitor!*" she told the 'cat.

"Come on, out with it!" Jacques commanded. "Let's get it all out in the open and get rid of it before you have to go back over and do some more of that matron of honor stuff."

Honor glared at him for a moment, then shrugged.

"You may actually have a point, although I find it hard to believe I hear myself saying that."

"I *always* have a point," her uncle replied with dignity. "It is, alas, simply my fate to be surrounded by people unable to fully appreciate the needle sharpness and rapier quickness of my intellect. Now trot it out!"

Honor made a face at him, then sighed.

"All right. I was just watching Chairman Benton-Ramirez, looking at how cheerful and unconcerned he seems, and thinking about the vote on Reid's motion."

The others looked at her. Simultaneity was a slippery concept when applied to interstellar distances, but the vote on Tyrone Reid's motion to investigate Beowulf's "treason" against the Solarian League would be occurring on far-off Old Earth in less than twenty-four hours.

"There's not much point worrying about it," her uncle said after a second or two. "We all know how the vote's going to come out, after all. And Felicia has her instructions for what to do when it does." He twitched his shoulders. "And it's not as if there's much question about how the electorate's going to respond in the end. Every single opinion poll and electronic town meeting we've held underscores that, Honor. And you've seen the editorials and the public postings!"

"I know. Remember, I *am* half-Beowulfan, Uncle Jacques. But it's just such a big step, and I'm worried about how the Mandarins are going to react."

"There's not a lot they can do about it," Jacques pointed out.

"The problem is whether or not they realize that," Honor countered, "and their track record to date doesn't exactly inspire me with confidence in their judgment. I keep reminding myself that they're not *really* stupid. Blind, arrogant, bigoted, and so far out of touch with us uppity 'neobarbs' that they *act* stupidly, but within the limits of their worldview, they truly aren't idiots. And that means they have to be able to see the writing on the wall when their nose gets rubbed in it hard enough, doesn't it?"

"Probably." Jacques nodded. "You'd think so, at any rate, wouldn't you?"

"And that's what worries me," Honor said frankly. "It's obvious to me—to *us*—where Beowulf's actions are going to lead. I think we have to assume it's going to be obvious to them, too. And if it is, based on their actions to date, I think we have to assume they'll try to do something about it before that happens."

"I don't think there's a great deal they *can* do about it, in the short term, at least," her uncle replied.

"Maybe not, but I'd feel a lot better if we had a couple of dozen *Invictus*-class wallers in Beowulf orbit."

"I'm not sure I disagree with you," Jacques said slowly, "but that was a political decision, and I can see their point. It's one thing for us to call on Manticoran assistance to prevent Tsang from forcibly seizing control of the Beowulf Terminus. And I don't think anyone on Beowulf has any problem with the notion that your navy is going to make damned sure it hangs on to the terminus and deploys however many ships it has to to do it. But if we start putting Manty ships-of-the-wall in orbit around the planet, it's going to look coercive as hell. Beowulfers who have reservations about our joining the Alliance—and there *are* some of those, after all—are likely to feel threatened, and that's not what we want in the run-up to the vote. For that matter, if we had Manty wallers orbiting Beowulf, it could only make Reid and Neng's job in the Assembly even easier. A lot easier to convict us of treason under those circumstances, don't you think?"

"But as you just pointed out, we already know how that vote's going to come out in the end, anyway," Honor shot back.

"I said I wasn't sure I disagreed with you." Benton-Ramirez y Chou shook his head. "But there's another consideration to it as well. Felicia's going to drop her little nuke in the Assembly as soon as the votes are tallied on Reid's motion, and we can't afford to let the Mandarins or their mouthpieces cast doubt on the legitimacy of her actions *or* of the vote. If there's anything but Beowulfan warships in orbit around the planet, you *know* they're going to claim that whatever the Board of Directors says or however the electorate votes, it was all coerced by the threat of Manticoran warheads."

"I hate to say it, but I think they've got a point, Honor," Hamish pointed out, and even Emily nodded in agreement.

"I didn't say they didn't have a point, Hamish," Honor said a bit tartly. "What I said is that I question whether or not it's a good *enough* point to park all of our modern wallers far enough out that some Solly idiot could decide they're too far from the inner system to intervene if something...untoward happens."

"Which is why we're we're taking the belt-and-suspenders approach and working on Mycroft," Hamish pointed out, and Honor was forced to nod in acknowledgment. Sneaky of him to use Mycroft, since she was the one who'd first suggested the concept to Sonja Hemphill.

One of the problems the Alliance was bound to face if the situation continued to deteriorate was the need to free up capital ships for mobile operations rather than tying them down in static defenses. Honor, as the unwilling beta tester for Shannon Foraker's Moriarity system, had developed a profound respect for the effectiveness of massed MDM pods in the system-defense role. Michelle Henke's success at Spindle had reconfirmed that respect even before Filareta's spectacular demise. Which was why Honor had devoted quite a bit of thought to ways in which Moriarity's system-wide network of dispersed sensor and fire-control stations could be updated to take advantage of the Mark 23 and the Mark 23-E. The answer Hemphill had come up with was Mycroft, named for a character out of the same pre-space detective fiction which had given Foraker Moriarity in the first place.

Essentially, Mycroft was simply a couple of dozen Keyhole-Two platforms parked at various points in a star system. It was a little more complicated than that, since the platforms were designed to operate on beamed power from their motherships, so it was necessary to provide each platform with its own power plant. And it was also necessary to provide the raw fire control and the rest of the supporting hardware and software which was normally parked aboard the platform's deploying ship-of-the-wall. Those were relatively straightforward problems in engineering, however, especially with an entire planet to work with, and tech crews were working at breakneck pace even as Honor stood with her uncle and her spouses to meet them.

Mycroft's advantages over Moriarity would be profound. Unlimited by Moriarity's lightspeed control links, Mycroft would be able to take full advantage of the Mark 23-E and the FTL reconnaissance platforms which were also being thickly seeded throughout the system's volume. And unlike Moriarity—which had been unarmed and defenseless when Honor used Hemphill's Baldur to take it out—Keyhole-Two platforms were simply crammed with active antimissile defenses. No doubt they could be taken out, but it would be a difficult task, and enough of them were being deployed as part of Mycroft to ensure survivability through sheer redundancy.

"I agree that once Mycroft's up and running, especially, anybody who goes after Beowulf is going to get bloodied in a hurry," she said now. "I guess my main concerns are that, like the terminus picket, Mycroft isn't a *visible* deterrent, especially since we're keeping it so completely under wraps till it's actually up and running, and, secondly, that it *isn't* up and running yet and won't be for at least another couple of months. Maybe longer." She shook her head. "It's that window that worries me," she said soberly. "In the Mandarins' place, I'd make it a point to assume that we had to be aware of Beowulf's vulnerability and be doing something about it, but I'm not at all sure they will."

"Well," Benton-Ramirez y Chou said with a shrug that was just a bit more philosophical than his mindglow tasted, "I guess there's one way to find out."

"And that's what I'm afraid of, Uncle Jacques," she said. "That's what I'm afraid of."

Chapter Thirty-Four

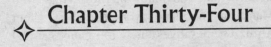

FELICIA HADLEY SAT ONCE MORE in the Beowulf delegation's box in the Chamber of Stars.

Her head was erect, her shoulders squared, and anyone looking at her could have been excused for not recognizing the mixture of anger, weariness, frustration, grief, and…emptiness behind those outwardly tranquil eyes. After all, she couldn't sort out all those feelings herself, so why should she have expected anyone else to understand the way she felt?

The two weeks of scheduled debate on Tyrone Reid's motion had been the ugliest Hadley could remember ever having seen. That was hardly a surprise, given the position Kolokoltsov and the rest of the Mandarins faced. They'd pulled out all the stops to focus the League's fear and anxiety on someone else in order to save themselves, and they knew all the tricks of the game. The attacks had been carefully orchestrated, aimed from every imaginable quarter and endlessly repeated by flocks of coopted newsies and media talking heads, to give them maximum

credibility with the public. There were a few report-
ers, like Audrey O'Hanrahan, who genuinely seemed
to be trying to cover both sides of the debate, just as
there were some Assembly delegates who'd tried to
get the truth out. But those delegates, like the newsies trying to do their jobs, were drowned in the tide
of attackers. There were simply too many members
of the Assembly—and too many in the media—who
owed the Mandarins too many favors (and about whom
Malachai Abruzzi's operatives knew too many secrets)
for there to be any other outcome.

Two things *had* surprised her, however. One was the
degree of genuine hatred some of her fellow delegates
had spewed out in their attacks on Beowulf. Reid's
allies had placed *their* darts carefully, wrapping their
fiery denunciations around a core of cold calculation,
but others had joined the assault on their own, lashing out in an almost incoherent fury that didn't care
what the law might say, wasn't concerned with why
Beowulf might have done what it had done. No, that
fury fed only on panic-stricken reports of the Manticorans' superior weaponry and fear that Beowulf's
"treason" had somehow freed that weaponry to ravage
the entire Solarian League. Of course, no one had
bothered to explain how Beowulf's permitting Imogene
Tsang's fleet to be massacred would have *averted* that
threat, now, had they?

Well, be fair, Felicia, she told herself. *It's not all
fear of what the Manties' weapons can do, now, is it?
Some of those people have started getting messengers
from transstellars based in their home systems. A
glimmer of what withdrawing all those Manticoran
merchantmen and shutting down the hyper bridges*

really means is starting to sink in, and they don't like that a bit. They want the hide of anyone associated with the people getting ready to inflict that much hurt on their corporate sponsors.

No doubt they did, yet what had surprised her even more than the fury coming at her home system from so many quarters was the fact that some of the other delegations had actually spoken in Beowulf's behalf. Not that Beowulf's actions met with complete approbation even from them, because they didn't. But at least some of the League's elected representatives truly did seem more concerned about getting at the truth, or even considering the legal and constitutional implications of Bewoulf's acts, than with simply scapegoating someone else.

Of course, there weren't very many of them.

Oh, be fair, she scolded herself again, rather more seriously. *Standing up to this kind of hysteria at all requires more guts than anyone running for the Assembly ever expected to need! You always recognized it was really only a rubber stamp for people like the Mandarins, didn't you? Sure, you wanted to change that, but you knew damned well deep inside that you weren't going to. Nobody was.*

And now nobody's ever going to have the chance to.

She gave herself a mental shake as that last thought ran through her mind. They weren't going to break the Mandarins' grip today, no. She knew that. But there was still hope for the future, wasn't there? Didn't there *have* to be? Look at what had happened in the Republic of Haven. They'd recovered their constitution, and it looked like they were making that stand up, too. Of course, the Republic was a lot smaller than the League, and its corruption had been given nowhere near as long to sink into the blood and the bone of their political processes. Yet people like Eloise Pritchart and Thomas Theisman *had* pulled it off, and that meant it truly was possible for the League as well.

And it looks like the League's going to get just as badly hammered militarily as the People's Republic ever did, she reminded herself glumly. *The question's whether or not it'll learn enough along the way to—*

The shimmering reverberation of a deep-toned musical chime echoed over the Chamber of Stars' vastness, interrupting her thoughts.

The Assembly was in session.

❖   ❖   ❖

The usual pointless opening ceremonies seemed even more meaningless than usual today. They'd never actually been more than the hollow forms of a representative body which had long since lost any meaningful political power. Lip service to a dream which even Hadley had to acknowledge had never been more than a dream, really. Yet that pretense that the Assembly's delegates actually represented the will of the Solarian electorate grated especially painfully on her nerves this morning.

She was scarcely surprised when Speaker Neng moved through those ceremonies more briskly than usual, though. After all, the Speaker had a job to do for the people she *really* represented, and after so many days of vicious debate it was time to get to it.

The last empty formality was completed, Speaker Neng pronounced the presence of a legal quorum, and then her gavel cracked.

"The Assembly will come to order," she announced

crisply. She waited a heartbeat, then continued, "The Honorable Delegate from Old Terra has the floor."

Tyrone Reid's image replaced hers on the huge display. As the originator of the motion, it was his right under the Assembly's rules to move for the vote now that all time allocated for debate had been expended. He stood there, his expression grave, his eyes artistically troubled, and then drew a deep breath.

"Madam Speaker, I call for the vote."

Neng reappeared on the display.

"Honorable Delegates, the vote has been called on motion AD-1002-07-02-22, to impanel a special commission to investigate the alleged treason of the system government of Beowulf in aiding and abetting an enemy of the Solarian League. All debate having been completed, the Chair now calls the vote."

Her image stood there, hovering in the air, while votes were cast throughout the enormous chamber. It didn't take long.

She looked down, considering the numbers, then raised her head once more.

"The vote is eight thousand seven hundred and twelve in favor, two thousand nine hundred and three opposed. The motion is carried."

A roar went up, and Hadley's jaw clenched. Not in surprise, but in anger. The only surprise was that almost a quarter of the Assembly had voted *against* the motion. That was a dangerous sign for the Mandarins, given the massive effort they'd mounted to pass the motion in the first place. It suggested all sorts of unpleasant things, yet that was for the future. For now . . .

She punched her attention key and sat back, arms folded, while she waited. The roar of approval continued for several seconds before it finally trickled off slowly into something approaching quiet. Then Neng looked back down at her panel, and her gavel cracked again.

"The Assembly will return to order!" Her tone was sharp, chiding, and the delegates who were still out of their seats, still celebrating their victory, looked up at her in surprise. Then they—slowly—obeyed the command, and she waited another few moments before she looked in Hadley's direction.

"The Chair recognizes the Honorable Delegate from Beowulf," she announced.

Hadley didn't bother to stand as her image replaced the Speaker's. She simply sat there, looking out of the display as a silence settled over the thousands of delegates. She could feel all those other eyes, almost taste the burning curiosity behind them. How would defeated Beowulf respond? What could she possibly say in the wake of this totally unprecedented public humiliation . . . and scapegoating? She let them wonder for several endless seconds, and when she spoke, her voice was cold and hard.

"I have served as Beowulf's representative to this Assembly for almost forty T-years. In that time, I've tried without success to find some trace, some fragment, of the power and the responsibility and the high standards of personal conduct envisioned for it by the drafters of our Constitution. There's no question of what the drafters intended, what they expected from this Assembly. The words are there for anyone to read and understand. The expectations are clear. Yet instead of finding those things, I've become intimately familiar with the 'business as usual' mentality of this Chamber. Like all of you, I've also become aware of where the true power in the formulation of federal law, regulations, and policy lies. Even if I hadn't, even if I continued to cherish the slightest illusion that the elected representatives of the League's citizens had one shred of authority at the federal level, this vote has just demonstrated the true owners of power in the Solarian League once again. It is nothing more nor less than a rubber-stamped approval of the unelected bureaucrats who illegally wield power far beyond anything the Constitution ever granted them. A rubber-stamp dutifully affixed to their effort to silence all internal opposition to the disastrous policy—and war—to which they've committed the League. Beowulf's reward for attempting to prevent that war—or to at least cut it short before it consumes still more millions of lives and trillions upon trillions of credits—is to be investigated for 'treason' because it asserted the autonomy guaranteed to every member star system of the League. The same autonomy the home star system of every delegate who just voted in favor of this motion takes for granted every single day."

She paused, brown eyes hard with contempt and disdain. The Chamber of Stars was deathly still, its quiet broken only by a handful of voices shouting denials of her assertions.

"We expected nothing else from a morally, ethically, and legally bankrupt institution," she continued finally, her voice colder than ever. "However, there is another right which the Constitution guarantees to every member star system, and Beowulf chooses to exercise that right today. If we cannot oppose the 'Mandarins'' criminal and disastrous policies from inside the system, we will no longer attempt to.

Instead, as the leader of Beowulf's delegation, acting on the instructions of my star system's legally *elected* government, I hereby announce that Beowulf will hold a system-wide plebiscite two T-months from today to determine whether or not the Beowulf system shall withdraw from the Solarian League."

The lonely voices shouting insults and denials vanished suddenly into a deep, singing silence, and she smiled grimly.

"That vote will be fairly, legally, and publicly taken, but speaking personally, I have no doubt whatsoever what its outcome will be. And, again speaking personally, I caution all of you to have no illusions upon that head. You've passed your motion, and you're welcome to investigate anything you choose to investigate, but Beowulf will no longer be party to the blood-soaked policies of a corrupt and venal oligarchy prepared to murder entire star nations rather than admit even the possibility of wrongdoing on its part. We reserve the right to disassociate ourselves from criminal enterprises and murder on an interstellar scale, and to take whatever actions the citizens of our star system believe are required of it in the crisis which Permanent Senior Undersecretary Kolokoltsov and his fellow 'Mandarins' have created. For those of you who have chosen to vote in favor of this motion, we wish you joy of your actions . . . but I don't think you'll find it."

She hit the key that cleared her image from the display, and the Chamber of Stars went berserk.

Chapter Thirty-Five

"SO, ARE YOU STILL so blasé about how easily Reid's motion is going to 'neutralize' Beowulf, Innokentiy?" Nathan MacArtney's voice was rather caustic, Innokentiy Kolokoltsov thought.

"I was never 'blasé' about it, Nathan," the permanent senior undersecretary for foreign affairs replied. "And I never said it would neutralize them. I said I expected it to shift the focus of the debate from us to Beowulf and put a muzzle on Hadley, and I think that's exactly what's happening. I'll admit I never expected even *Beowulfers* to go this far, and sure as hell not to go this far this *quickly*, but it does look like we're going to take Beowulf out of play in the Chamber of Stars, doesn't it? I believe it's called looking for a silver lining." He smiled thinly. "Since we can't do anything to stop it, we might as well try to find a bright side to look on once it's done."

Hadley's bombshell announcement had completely blindsided him. He admitted it. He'd envisioned quite a few possible outcomes of Reid's motion, but never that Beowulf would simply walk away from its seven centuries of membership in the League. No one had *ever* done that, and most people had assumed that, like so much more of the original Constitution, the right of secession had withered and was no longer applicable.

Beowulf's government obviously didn't see it that way, and while the system's secession had not yet become a fact, there seemed to be very little chance of the plebiscite failing. Benton-Ramirez and his fellow directors undoubtedly had better access to polling data on Beowulfan public opinion than anyone on Old Earth did, but what the Mandarins did have access to made grim reading. At least eighty-two percent of the system population supported the Board of Directors' decision to accept Manticoran assistance to prevent Imogene Tsang's transit of the Beowulf Terminus against Beowulf's wishes. An only slightly lower percentage—seventy-five to seventy-eight percent, depending on whose poll one chose—firmly believed it had prevented thousands of additional Solarian deaths. And somewhere around eighty-*five* percent favored an outright military alliance with the Star Empire against the boogie man of this "Mesan Alignment" figment of the Manties' imagination. It was only a very short step from an alliance against Mesa to one against anyone perceived as serving the "Mesan Alignment's" purposes, and while Kolokoltsov hadn't seen any specific data on the question of outright secession from the Solarian League, against that sort of public opinion background, he was sickly certain Hadley was right about the final vote on the question.

Worse, there seemed to be very little the federal

government could do to stop it from happening. Not with the Royal Manticoran Navy and its allies only a single wormhole transit away. That was bad enough, but according to his agents within the Assembly, it appeared the system delegations of Strathmore, Kenichi, and Galen were strongly inclined to recommend that their own star systems follow Beowulf's example! He didn't know if any of them had actually made their recommendations yet, but their system governments certainly seemed angry enough to take the plunge once they did, especially if Beowulf succeeded in its defiance of the entire League, and the thought was terrifying. The average population of the four star systems was over six billion, and the decision of *twenty-four billion* Solarian citizens to withdraw would be a body blow to the federal government's authority and prestige.

No, he thought, *not to the federal government, but to the federal* system. *To us, sitting right here. And, damn it, sometimes I think they'd be* right! *But what other alternative is there? We can't reform a system that's been in place for the better part of a thousand T-years on the run. Especially not in the middle of a military and constitutional crisis! The entire League would come apart! Before we can fix the League's problems—assuming anyone* can *fix them—we have to hold it together long enough to* be *fixed.*

"Well, personally, I don't think your silver lining's especially bright," MacArtney said sourly. "I've been hearing from a lot of people who aren't any too happy about the invasion highway Beowulf offers if the Manties decide to come after us right here. For that matter, I'm not too crazy about it, either!"

"The worst thing the Manties could possibly do—from their perspective, not ours—is to attack the Sol System." Kolokoltsov barked a laugh. "In fact, I wish they *would!* It's the one thing I can think of practically guaranteed to get *all* the Core Worlds lined up to back us!"

"You really think so?" Agatá Wodoslawski sounded doubtful. "I mean, if they—and the Havenites, too; let's not forget them—were to take out Old Terra, you don't think that would terrify the rest of the League into throwing in the towel?"

"Only in the shortest possible term," Kolokoltsov said positively. "Personally, I think it would convince most of the other Core Worlds that the Manties and their friends are just as expansionist and arrogant as we've been telling them they were all along. It would sure as hell knock any notion of distant, plucky little neobarbs defending themselves against Solarian aggression on the head and turn them into cynical imperialists striking at the very heart of the greatest star nation in human history! The most likely thing for the rest of the Core Worlds to do in that case would be to sue for a cease-fire just long enough to figure out how to build matching missiles of their own, then hammer this 'Grand Alliance' flat, and the Manties have to know it."

He shook his head and looked straight at MacArtney even as he spoke to Wodoslawski.

"I don't see the Manties wanting to pump that kind of hydrogen into the fire, Agatá. Not unless we drive them to it. For that matter, I don't see Beowulf wanting to piss off so many of its neighbors by *allowing* that sort of attack. Whatever happens to the League, eventually Beowulf's going to have to live with the star systems around it again. If the Beowulfers stick that kind of knife into the League's back, most of those star systems are going to be gunning for them once the smoke clears and the tech imbalance has leveled out again."

"Assuming the damned Beowulfers are smart enough to figure that out," MacArtney grumbled.

"I think they are," Kolokoltsov said with just a bit more confidence than he actually felt.

"Maybe so," Wodoslawski said, "but there are other factors to consider. Like what's going to happen if someone else decides to follow Beowulf's example on this one. It could turn out Beowulf's only the first drop of rain, and if that happens, we may find out just how badly screwed we really are."

Kolokoltsov grimaced and decided—again—not to mention his agents' reports about Beowulf's neighbors. There'd be time for that once he'd been able to confirm the accuracy of those reports. But the permanent senior undersecretary of the treasury had a point, and he nodded as he was forced to concede it.

"That's one of the things I'm hearing about from the transstellars, too," MacArtney said. "They're all worried that even if the Manties don't use Beowulf to go after the League from the inside out, Beowulf's example is going to cause other Core Worlds to decide to sit this one out. That'd be bad enough, but what happens when the *Shell* hears about this?" He shook his head. "You know that even a lot of the League member systems out there aren't all that fond of our policies. I won't say they feel as exploited as the Protectorates and the Verge, but they know we've consistently favored the Core World economies over their own. And a lot of them are a hell of a lot closer to Manticore and Haven than they are to us, even leaving the wormhole network out of the equation. If they see us starting to shed *Core* systems, what's to keep them from deciding to jump ship and look for a better deal out of the Manties, too?"

What you mean, Nathan, Kolokoltsov thought, *is that your buddies in the transstellars are worried about somebody's seceding from the League and nationalizing their investments. That's what they're really worried about. And it's what they're turning the screws on you about, too. They could care less whether or not the entire Shell stays in the League as long as it goes on being business as usual for them! Which it won't, of course, if the people they've been exploiting for so long see a chance to get out from under them.*

He nodded gravely once more, keeping his thoughts out of his expression. And the truth was that what MacArtney was describing would become an all-too-plausible scenario if things went all the way south on them. For that matter, Kolokoltsov had entertained the occasional nightmare about what would happen if the *transstellars* started trying to cut deals with the Manties. Given the way their tentacles completely permeated the League, they could do an enormous amount of damage if they decided to throw in openly—or, possibly even worse, clandestinely—with the Manties and Havenites. He had no idea how likely the Manties would be to accept an offer like that, but he never doubted that the "loyal and patriotic" men and women who ran the transstellars would make it in a heartbeat if they thought it would benefit them.

Which meant he had to keep them happy—or as happy as he could, at least—too.

Wonderful.

"I think Nathan has a point," Omosupe Quartermain said. She didn't much like MacArtney, and she didn't sound very happy about supporting him, but the permanent senior undersecretary of commerce was probably the only person hearing more from nervous transstellars than he was. "I just have this feeling the avalanche is still accelerating," she continued, looking around at the holographic faces of the electronic conference room. "It's only going to get worse and worse, at least for the immediate future, and if we don't do something to at least slow it down, we may run out of time to do anything else."

Wodoslawski looked at her colleague, and Kolokoltsov's heart sank as the permanent senior undersecretary of the treasury nodded slowly. The nature of Wodoslawski and Quartermain's responsibilities meant the two female Mandarins ended up supporting one another more often than not, and Kolokoltsov didn't like the way he thought this was headed.

"What would you like us to do to try and slow it up, Omosupe?" Malachai Abruzzi asked.

"I don't know," Quartermain admitted. She raised her right hand, waving it in an uncharacteristically helpless, worried gesture. "I just know that if we let Beowulf do this, if we just stand back and wave goodbye, we're establishing a precedent. The exact kind of precedent Nathan's worrying about where the Shell systems are concerned. Right this minute, the jury's still out on whether or not Beowulf really does have the constitutional right to leave. But if we let them go, aren't we saying for all the galaxy to see that they *do?* And if *they* do, then *every* member system does!"

"Maybe, but the simple truth of the matter is that we can't stop them," Abruzzi pointed out with unwonted gentleness. "They've got to have a hundred or so Manty SDs sitting on top of the Beowulf Terminus right this minute. After what happened to Filareta, we all know what would happĕn if we got into shooting range of them, too." He shrugged. "That constitutes a pretty conclusive rejoinder as to whether or not we have the 'right' to stop them, I'm afraid."

"But the fact that we can't stop them doesn't mean we have to *condone* their actions," MacArtney said, his expression mulish.

"Meaning what?" Kolokoltsov asked.

"Meaning we don't have to admit their actions are legal." MacArtney tapped an index finger on his desk for emphasis. "We can condemn them, announce that they're *illegal*, and that we intend to take firm action at the earliest possible moment."

"Which will only underscore the fact that we can't take any kind of 'firm action' right now," Abruzzi retorted. "It'd make us look ridiculous, Nathan!"

"Maybe, and maybe not," Quartermain said, her expression suddenly hopeful. "Oh, I agree it would underscore the fact that we can't take action against *Beowulf*, but the entire League knows Beowulf's in a very special astrographic position, thanks to its direct connection to Manticore. Most people understand how that limits our options where it's concerned. But if we make that our guiding principle, then we'll have positioned ourselves to react . . . more forcefully in the case of star systems we can actually reach."

"Basically, you're saying we reject anyone's right to secede, whatever they may think the Constitution says, and use force to prevent any additional secessions?" Wodoslawski said with the air of a woman wanting to be certain there was no confusion on the point.

"If we have to," Quartermain replied unflinchingly. "I don't like the thought, and, frankly, there are a lot of potential secessionist systems we probably *couldn't* reach militarily. But we'd be able to reach a lot of them, and if they don't have the super missiles the Manties and the Havenites do, Frontier Fleet should be more than capable of keeping them in line."

"We probably could," Abruzzi conceded. "It'd be hard to spin that as anything except us using the iron fist, though. I mean, after everything else we've already had to throw out there in the 'faxes since this thing began."

"Well, if we're going to take the position that Beowulf has no right to secede," MacArtney said, "then Hadley and the rest of their delegation have just committed treason." He smiled nastily. "That being the case, I think they should be arrested and prevented from leaving the system!"

Oh, that's a marvelous *idea*, Kolokoltsov thought bitterly.

"Nathan's probably right," Quartermain put in, and Wodoslawski was nodding again.

"And if we're talking about arresting the bastards for treason over this secession crap," MacArtney went on, "I think we should consider whether or not their decision to harbor Carmichael doesn't constitute *another* act of treason!" His smile was even uglier than before. "If we put the arm on *them*, then we're in a position to put the arm on *him* as well."

"Whoa! Just slow down, Nathan!" Abruzzi said sharply. "If we start throwing terms like 'treason' around now, and start strong-arming *Assembly delegates* before this plebiscite of theirs has even been voted on, the rest of the delegates are going to raise merry hell. Not because they're all that fond of Beowulf, either! You think they won't see that as a precedent that could come home to bite *them* too?"

"I'm not so sure it would be a bad thing if they did," MacArtney shot back. "If they figure out we're going to hammer anybody who looks like they're turning on us, then they'll probably think twice—or even three times!—about doing just that."

"This isn't the Verge, and we're not talking about OFS protectorates," Abruzzi said flatly. "We're talking about Core Worlds. We're talking about star systems that have the internal industry to build significant navies of their own if the urge strikes them. We're already looking at a confrontation against somebody whose weapons technology we can't match, and you want to go around irritating our own star systems into deciding they have to build a military capability to protect themselves from *us?*"

The permanent senior undersecretary of education and information shook his head, his expression incredulous, and MacArtney flushed angrily. He opened his mouth to snap something back, but Kolokoltsov raised one hand in a "stop" gesture.

"Calm down, Nathan. And you, Malachai." He shook his head. "You and Omosupe and Agatá have raised valid concerns, Nathan. But Malachai has a point, too. If we start resorting to the kind of tactics you're suggesting, we up the ante for everybody, and right this minute, we can't afford that."

"We can't afford *not* to," MacArtney replied stubbornly, and Quartermain nodded. Wodoslawski seemed more torn, however, Kolokoltsov noted. "If we don't get our heel firmly on this kind of thing now, we never will."

"But Malachai's right that we *can't* get our heel on it right now," Kolokoltsov said inflexibly. "We literally can't. So if we try to grab Hadley and Carmichael, we only run the risk of alienating the other Core Worlds at a time when our weakness is going to be obvious to everyone. Especially when grabbing Hadley and Carmichael is the *only* thing we can do, because we sure as hell aren't going to be able to follow through by arresting the *rest* of the Beowulf system government!"

He shook his head.

"No. We can't make this about whether or not secession is legal. Not now. That's something we're going to have to address later, but it's not anything we want to go anywhere *near* at a moment when we know other Core Worlds are at least considering it."

"We don't have any choice," McCartney began, "and if you think—"

"Wait, Nathan," Wodoslawski interrupted, gazing intently at Kolokoltsov. The permanent senior undersecretary of the interior looked affronted, but he also closed his mouth, and Wodoslawski cocked her head to one side.

"What did you mean 'we can't make this about whether or not secession is legal,' Innokentiy?" she asked.

"I mean we have to make it about whether or not Beowulf's actions threaten the security of the League in general and the Core Worlds in particular, instead,"

Kolokoltsov replied. "I think we have to take a more or less hands-off position on the entire issue of secession's legality for the moment. That's something we should probably hand over to Reid and Neng once they get the inquiry into Beowulf's collaboration with Manticore underway. I'm sure Reid will be able to come up with a whole stack of legal precedents he can convincingly claim have invalidated a supposed 'constitutional right' nobody's exercised in seven hundred years! Jurisprudence and living constitutional law have moved on, you know."

He smiled, and Abruzzi actually chuckled out loud. Even MacArtney looked a little more thoughtful.

"At that point," Kolokoltsov continued, "we argue that secession from the League *isn't* legal, but for now we formally reserve judgment on the subject. We make it clear we're not conceding that Beowulf has the right to leave, but that we're not prepared to make an ugly situation even worse until there's been time for the courts to rule on whether or not their actions are legal."

"We let the erring sister go—for now, at least—more in sorrow than in anger, you mean?" Abruzzi asked, his eyes narrowed in thought. "And when we do, we leave ourselves the option of deciding later that Beowulf was wrong and taking whatever remedial action seems appropriate *then?*"

"More or less." Kolokoltsov nodded. "What I'm trying to do here is to defang the emotional aspects of the issue. I'd love to get this resolved before anybody else starts holding referendums on secession, you understand, but I doubt we're going to be that lucky. So what I'm looking to do right this minute is to avoid handing any extra ammunition to the people who'd be likely to agitate *for* secession in the referendums we may not be able to prevent in the first place."

MacArtney and Quartermain still looked profoundly unhappy, but Wodoslawski actually looked a bit hopeful, Kolokoltsov thought.

"All well and good," MacArtney growled after a moment, "but it doesn't do diddley about Beowulf right *now*."

No, and it's not going to make any of those transstellars any happier with you, either. Not right now, at least, Kolokoltsov thought trenchantly. *Unfortunately, all we can do is all we can do!*

"I'm not saying we shouldn't take any action at all against Beowulf, Nathan," the permanent senior undersecretary for foreign affairs said coolly. "Mind you, I'm not sure what kind of action we're going to be in a *position* to take, but I'm in favor of doing anything we realistically can. I just don't want it to be over the legality or illegality of secession at this point."

"That's what you meant about not making it about whether or not secession is legal," Wodoslawski said.

"Exactly." Kolokoltsov tipped back in his chair. "I think we need to get Kingsford in here, let him take a look at any military options we may have—*workable* military options, I mean—where Beowulf is concerned. If there's one that will work, I'm entirely in favor of using it, but not because they illegally seceded from the League. At this point what we need to do is to make it over the security threat to the League Beowulf represents because of its association with the League's avowed enemies. As Omosupe said, everybody knows about Beowulf's effective proximity to Manticore. That means everybody knows Beowulf does, indeed, represent that 'invasion highway' Nathan was talking about. We'd be fully justified in taking military action against *any* star nation that was in a position to enable a Manty invasion of the very heart of the Solarian League. I don't think they'd be remotely stupid enough to do it, you understand, but we can make an ironclad case for taking action to deprive them of the *capability* to do it. But making certain that they can't would be a simple matter of self-defense, and one we'd have no choice but to pursue. We'd be derelict in our responsibilities to the rest of the League if we didn't!"

"Which lets us hammer Beowulf as hard as we want—assuming we can find a way to do it, that is—without ever even touching the question of secession!" Abruzzi said enthusiastically.

"Exactly," Kolokoltsov repeated. "And, Nathan, there's no way anyone out in the Shell who might be thinking in terms of seceding is going to miss the subtext. There won't be a single official word about secession in anything we have to say on the subject, but everyone will hear it anyway."

"And once the immediate furor dies down, Reid and Neng's committee reports back that Beowulf's actions were treasonous before it seceded," Wodoslawski said thoughtfully.

"*After* which Reid produces the precedents to establish that the right of secession's lapsed with the passage of time," Abruzzi said, nodding energetically.

There was silence for several seconds, then MacArtney shrugged irritably.

"I don't like it," he grumbled. "We're still pussyfooting around the issue, and a lot of people are going to realize it."

"I agree with you, Nathan," Quartermain said, "but I think Innokentiy and Malachai have made some valid points, too." She shrugged. "Given the practical limits on what we can actually *do* at the moment, I'm afraid I'm going to have to side with them. *But*"—she glared suddenly at the others— "whatever our justification for going after Beowulf, we need to do it just as hard and just as quickly as humanly possible. Because Nathan's got a point, too, people. The situation in the Verge is going to go straight to hell on us, no matter what we do, but the last thing we need is to have the Shell going up in flames right along with it. We need to get a handle on this, and we need to do it fast!"

❖   ❖   ❖

"You're kidding me," Irene Teague said, staring at Daud al-Fanudahi. The two of them sat on benches across a small outdoor table from one another, eating their lunch as the warm summer sun spilled down across them. Lake Michigan's waters stretched limitlessly towards the horizon below the restaurant perched on a two-hundredth-floor balcony of the Admiralty Building, and gaily colored sails and powerboats dotted that dark blue expanse as far as the eye could see.

Not that either of them was in much of a mood to appreciate the view at the moment.

"I wish I were." Al-Fanudahi sounded entirely too calm for Teague's mood, and she glared at him.

"Calmly, Irene," he said, gazing serenely past her towards the lake water so far below. "I don't think anyone's listening to us out here, but I'd just as soon not give anyone a reason to think they *should* be listening to us, if you know what I mean."

Teague looked at him for a moment longer, then nodded and reached for her own fork.

"Granted," she said. "But I stand by my original reaction. *Please* tell me you were just making a really bad joke."

"Wish I were," he repeated with a sigh. "Unfortunately, the official request for intelligence updates will be coming through this afternoon sometime. As far as I can see, they're very serious about it."

"After what happened to *Filareta?*" She scooped up a forkful of delicious tuna salad and chewed without tasting it at all. "I knew Rajampet wasn't what anyone would've called brilliant, but I thought Kingsford had a working brain!"

"As far as I can tell, he does," al-Fanudahi replied. "I don't know that this is his idea, either. But given the kinds of intelligence data they're going to be requesting, there's no question what they're looking at."

"A military operation against Beowulf?" She shook her head. "That's got to be the worst idea I've heard since Operation Raging Justice itself!"

"I don't know." Al-Fanudahi shrugged. "It depends on the mission parameters and the available resources, I guess."

"*Mission* parameters?" She rolled her eyes at him. "Just what sort of 'mission parameters' are going to make our superdreadnoughts survivable against *their* superdreadnoughts, Daud?"

"None that I can think of right offhand," al-Fanudahi conceded. "But the evidence from the merchies who've been passing through Beowulf since Raging Justice does seem to suggest that the Manty forces in Beowulf space are concentrated around the terminus, not the planet."

"So what?" Teague demanded. "Superdreadnoughts are *mobile*, you know!"

"Yes, and the Beowulf System Defense Force is a nasty handful all on its own, which doesn't even consider the system's fixed defenses," al-Fanudahi agreed. "What I suspect our lords and masters are thinking about is that the Manties *appear* to be trying to avoid stepping on any Solarian sensibilities, especially until the final tally is in on Beowulf's plebiscite. It may be politics on their part, for all I know."

"Politics?"

"If they want to encourage other star systems to follow Beowulf's example—to encourage the fragmentation of the League—they'd want to avoid any suggestion that they're using force majeure to turn Beowulf into some sort of Manty puppet régime, don't you think? One way to do that would to be to let Beowulf defend Beowulfan space while *they* defend the terminus, instead of putting a batch of their wallers into Beowulf orbit. It avoids the appearance of iron-fist pressure on Beowulf's voters at a particularly delicate moment . . . and just happens to put their superdreadnoughts a couple of light-hours away from Beowulf itself."

"You mean Kingsford and Bernard are thinking in terms of pouncing on Beowulf—coming straight in across the hyper limit and going flat out for the planet—before any Manty forces at the terminus can intervene?"

"I think that's about the only thing they *could* be thinking of," al-Fanudahi said. "I don't know if it would work, but assuming Beowulf hasn't been completely surrounded by new and nasty missile pods, a big enough force of superdreadnoughts, especially with enough of the new Technodyne missile pods, probably could fight its way in through the BSDF and the fixed defenses. And once they controlled the planetary orbitals, they'd be justified under interstellar law in demanding the system's surrender."

"And exactly where in this fascinating analysis of yours do the *Manty* superdreadnoughts come in?" Teague inquired politely. "You know, the ones over at the terminus? The ones who are going to come right back over to Beowulf and kick our sorry asses out of the star system?"

"Oh, *those* superdreadnoughts?" Al-Fanudahi smiled crookedly at her. "Well, I suppose the idea would be that once the system government surrendered to us, we'd announce special emergency elections—called at the insistence of the Beowulfan public, of course—in light of the existing Board of Directors' high-handed and probably treasonous actions. And no doubt that new, legitimate system government would denounce the *previous* system government's decision to even consider seceding from the Solarian League. Obviously, it would be incumbent upon us to recognize the new, legitimate—I did mention that it would be *legitimate*, didn't I?—system government's position. And, equally obviously, Manticore would be on very thin ice when it came to *denying* the legitimacy of that new system government, given their desire to avoid the puppet-master image. So the logic, I imagine, is that since what Manticore really needs is control of the Beowulf *Terminus*, the Manties would recognize a fait accompli when they saw it and let us have the Beowulf *System* back."

"And if the Manties don't roll over that way?"

"In that case, I would imagine, our fleet commander negotiates a withdrawal from the star system. Probably on the grounds that the orders which sent him there in the first place had misread the true sentiments of the Beowulfers. Now that he's had the opportunity to observe firsthand that the decision to secede enjoys genuine popular support, of course he's prepared to acknowledge that and retire from the lists. Of course, if Manticore is so unreasonable as to deny a negotiated, peaceful withdrawal with no further combat, our commander can't be held responsible for any collateral damage that might befall the system infrastructure—and population, unfortunately—in the course of an unprovoked Manticoran attack upon his peaceably departing forces."

Teague scooped up another forkful of salad, chewed slowly, and swallowed, all without taking her incredulous gaze from al-Fanudahi. Then she shook her head.

"That may be less totally insane than Rajampet's attack on the Manty home system, but that's not saying a hell of a lot, is it?" she observed caustically.

"No. On the other hand, they're in a hell of a crack at the moment," al-Fanudahi pointed out. "I think they figure they've got to do *something*, and I'm afraid they may decide this is the best option they've got. And there's actually at least a chance—a remote one, I'll grant you, but still a chance—they could pull this one off."

He shrugged and popped an olive into his mouth.

"Personally, I wouldn't want to make any heavy bets on our ability to get away with it, but the Manties *are* going to be cautious about inflaming Solarian public opinion any more than they have to, especially if Kingsford can get this up and running before any of the other Core Worlds choose to follow Beowulf's example. The question would be whether Manticore would decide it would look more like an outside tyrant intervening to protect a collaborationist clique or like a liberator intervening to prevent the reimposition of an illegitimate, unconstitutional tyranny of bureaucrats."

He chewed and swallowed, then inspected his salad plate for another olive before he looked back up at Teague.

"Interesting choice, don't you think?"

The following is an excerpt from:

TO SAIL A DARKLING SEA

JOHN RINGO

Available from Baen Books
February 2014
hardcover

CHAPTER 1

Robert "Rusty" Fulmer Bennett III wasn't a guy to just sit around if he could help out. But he also wasn't, still, in the best of shape.

When he'd boarded the cruise ship *Voyage Under Stars* with his buddy, Ted, he'd weighed 337 lbs, nekkid. By the time the rescue teams from Wolf Squadron found him, Ted had long before zombied and Rusty weighed 117 lbs and *was* naked, covered in bed sores and mostly unconscious on his filth covered bunk. Since he was still 6' 7", and, honestly, big boned, 117 was pretty bad. The one nurse Wolf had found so far, no doctors, said it was a miracle he'd survived.

So he still wasn't in the best shape of his life when he sat down in the "Wolf Squadron Human Resources" office. In the four weeks since he'd been found he'd put on about twenty pounds but that wasn't much. And he could barely work out at all. He wasn't sure that he could hack it as a "clearance specialist" but he was all up for killing zombies.

He filled in his name on the clipboard and took a seat. Then he opened up a packet of sushi and started to munch.

"Still putting on weight, huh?" the guy next to him asked.

"I never thought I'd like sushi," Bennett said, offering some of the rolls. "Anything is, like, *the best food in the world*, now. Except hummus. If I never eat hummus again I'll be so glad."

"Gotta try fish eyeballs," the guy said, taking one and nodding. "Mmmm... tuna is sooo much better raw than dolphin. Brad Stevens."

"Rusty Bennett," Rusty said. "Actually, it's Robert Fulmer Bennett Third. But everybody calls me Rusty. Like, you ate a *dolphin*?"

"Not the Flipper, ark, ark, kind," Stevens said. "It's a kind of fish. But, hey, when that's what you've got." He shrugged. "I'd have eaten a, you know, dolphin, dolphin if I could have caught one. There were a couple of times I'd have eaten the *asshole* of a dolphin..."

"I'd have eaten the asshole of an asshole," Rusty said.

"You're like a string-bean pole," Stevens said. "How much did you lose?"

"Two hundred pounds," Rusty said. "I was kinda big when we got locked down."

"Oh," Stevens said, wincing. "In one of the cabins on the *Voyage*?"

"Yep," Rusty said. "One of the reasons I want to go do something is every time I walk in the damned cabin I'm afraid the door's going to close behind me and never open again."

"I thought I'd lost weight. I can't believe they cleared you for work."

"I just walked down here," Rusty said, shrugging. "The worst they can do is say no..."

"Stevens...?"

"You're still in very poor shape, Mister Bennett," the lady said. Like most he'd seen, she was pregnant.

"I really want to help out," Rusty said. "And I've got to get out of that fu... forking cabin, ma'am. I keep having nightmares that the door won't open."

"I took this job on the *Grace* because it's the biggest boat I could get on," the lady said, smiling. "Try having nightmares that you're back in a tropical storm in a life raft and you're suffering from morning sickness and starving."

"Yes, ma'am," Rusty said. "I'm good with my hands. But I'm not a mechanic or anything. I can shoot. I've been shooting my whole life. And I want to fight zombies, ma'am."

"You'd never make the medical requirements for clearance personnel," the lady said. "They carry tons of gear when they clear."

"I heard there's some thirteen-year-old girl that does it, ma'am," Rusty argued. "If she can..."

"Don't compare Shewolf to your normal thirteen-year-old girl," the woman said, laughing. "You haven't seen the video have you?"

"No, ma'am," Rusty said. "I haven't gotten out, much."

"If you go up to the lounge, you can probably find somebody who can show it to you," the lady said. "Shewolf *led* the boarding of the *Voyage*. She wasn't supposed to, but it happened. The *Dallas* had used a machine gun to clear some of the zombies but while she was going up more showed up. She went over the side, anyway. There was a Marine in a little bit better shape than you, not much but a little, who was supposed to go right after her and got bogged down climbing. One of the reasons they want people in the best possible shape for clearance. At that point, most of the copies . . . You know that song, 'I get knocked down, but I get up again . . . ?'"

. "Sort of?" Rusty said. "Kinda before my time."

"Go watch the video," the lady said, looking at her screen. "Since you know she made it, it's a hoot. But . . . I mean you can go try to track down Nurse Schoenfeld and get her to clear you. But I'd suggest something lighter. At least for now. And I'd guess you don't like enclosed spaces . . ."

"I don't mind if I know I can open the door, ma'am," Rusty said.

"Being on a small boat is physically wearing,"

the lady said, "but they need people for light clearance. Clearing life rafts and small craft. Not many people want to do it because you get beat up on those little boats. But..."

"Ma'am," Rusty said. "Being out in the air on a small boat... That'd be like heaven, ma'am."

"How strong of a stomach do you have?" the lady asked.

"I... pretty strong?" Rusty said.

"You're on the assignment board," the lady said, making a definitive tap on her keyboard. "Since you don't have a defined skill that anyone is looking for right now, you've got a week to find something. After that, you get put on boat cleaning or you can go into the hold with the lame and lazy. People who don't want to help out."

"Cleaning?" Rusty said.

"Cleaning up a boat after zombies have trashed it."

"I don't want to have to clean out a new boat," Sophia said, mulishly. "I've seen these boats. And I've cleaned them up. Rather get knocked around on a thirty-five."

Sophia "Seawolf" Smith was one of the founding members of the Wolf Squadron. As such, despite being fifteen, she was a shareholder and not a minor one, as well as being a member of the Captain's Board as skipper of the thirty-five-foot *Worthy Endeavor*. The boat had gotten beaten up by nearly six months at sea, not to mention the zombies that took it over, but it was still *her* boat.

"You won't," Fred said. "*You*, especially, won't."

Fred Burnell was the "Vessel Preparation and Assignments Officer" on the *Grace Tan*. The massive supply ship had an open center and rear deck. On it were, now, four "cabin cruiser" yachts on props in various stages of repair and refitting. Since all of them worked when they were brought alongside it was mostly a matter of cleaning them out.

"Things change," Burnell said. "We've got crews cleaning them up, now. But we're retiring the thirty-fives. They're just too small and don't have enough range."

"So, what am I looking at?" Sophia said.

"You don't remember me, do you?" Burnell said, smiling slightly.

"No," Sophia said, frowning. "Sorry. Should I?"

"No," Burnell said. "I guess seen one castaway, seen 'em all. The *Endeavor* plucked me off a life raft. So let's just say I owe you one even if you don't know it. There's a very nice 65' Hatteras Custom sitting out there. Not too beat up by zombies. The only ones on it were below, and we're changing out all the below materials. Good engines, low hours..."

"I appreciate it," Sophia said. "Sorry for snapping your head off."

"Not a problem," Burnell said. "Can't tell you

how happy I was when you blew that foghorn. Oh, you'll need two light clearance personnel and deck hands. Bigger boat."

"I guess I need to go do some scrounging," Sophia said. "What happens in the meantime?"

"Support for the clearance of the *Iwo Jima*," Burnell said. "I think you know how that works?"

"Hopefully better than the *Voyage*," Sophia said.

"Okay, okay, *seriously*?" Faith "Shewolf" Smith said. The thirteen-year-old had gotten her height from her father and it had kicked in young. Nearly six feet, slender and with some of the look of a female body-builder, her fine blonde hair was currently hanging limp and damp on her neck in the heat.

"You say that a lot," Sergeant Thomas Fontana replied.

The thirty-two-year-old black Special Forces sergeant had become fond of his . . . well he couldn't call her "protégé" since she'd taught *him* the ins and outs of close-quarters battle with infecteds. Partner was the right term but it was hard to apply to a thirteen-year-old girl, no matter how well she fought zombies.

"The middle of this ship is *missing*," Faith said, pointing pointedly. "There is a great big gaping hole in the *middle of this ship*. *Below* the waterline!"

The foursome were looking, in amazement in

Faith's case, at the USS *Iwo Jima*, an Amphibious Assault Carrier the size of a WWII "Fleet" carrier. The combination aircraft carrier, troop ship and floating dock, while not as big as the *Voyage Under Stars* was really, really big. Especially from the waterline looking into its cavernous well-deck.

"It's not missing," Fontana said. "It can't be missing if they never put anything there."

"That's the well-deck, Faith," her father said. Steven John Smith was six foot one, with sandy blond hair and a thin, wiry, frame. Although he was the putative commander of Wolf Squadron, so designated by the US Navy no less, he did clearance as well. They still had only four hard clearance personnel and he was good at it. Besides it burnished the reputation and this "squadron" was all about force of personality. "Obviously, it's where they pull landing craft in and out."

"That doesn't make it not nuts," Faith said. "I know nuts when I see nuts. Letting water into a ship? That's nuts."

"The good news is the well-deck *is* open," Smith said. "You don't have to climb a boarding ladder up to the flight deck."

"They dropped the stern gate when we abandoned ship, sir," Lance Corporal Joshua "Hooch" Hocieniec said.

Hocieniec completed the foursome that had only recently completed clearing the cruise liner *Voyage Under Stars*, listed as the world's second largest "super cruise liner." Larger than any passenger liner in history, it was best described as a floating Disneyland and just about as damned large. While the *Iwo* was big, as large as a WWII aircraft carrier and with much the same look, it wasn't the *Voyage*, thank God. The only larger ships on the ocean than the *Voyage* were supertankers, which had relatively small areas for zombies to inhabit and a supercarrier. God help them, the Hole was sort of hinting they'd like one of *those* cleared. Steve had flatly told them "Not until we've got *a lot* more Marines."

Hocieniec was the only survivor of the *Iwo* they'd picked up so far. There were sure to be more out there but all the life rafts from the amphibious assault ship found so far contained only the dead. And the few people picked up from the *Voyage* who might be potential reinforcements were still in too bad a condition to assist. With any luck there would be some Marines alive on the boat. They'd found that people were awfully inventive, given the slightest chance, at staying alive.

"And, look," Faith said, "a welcoming party."

Zombies, not so inventive. But very tenacious. It seemed like all zombies needed was fresh water. Which would seem in short supply at sea except their concept of "fresh" was about the same as a dog's. And if one died from the water quality, well, the survivors would just eat him or her.

Which was why there were at least thirty zombies waiting for them on the deck of a hover craft inside the ship. Which was more or less exactly where they were going to have to go. Fortunately, the stern gate was down and conditions were calm. Very calm.

The *Iwo Jima* had been, deliberately, "parked" in the Horse Latitudes zone of the Sargasso Sea. The Sargasso—the only sea not bounded by land—was surrounded by, but not affected by, the various currents of the North Atlantic. The Horse Latitudes were, in turn, a zone where there was always little to no wind and only very rare storms. They were the bane of early explorers of the Atlantic for the constant calm. They were called "the Horse Latitudes" because those were the latitudes where you had to eat the horses.

The combination, along with the somewhat entrapping sargassum weed that gave the region its name, meant that the assault ship was going to *stay* there. Except for the minor waves transmitted from distant storms, the area was pretty much flat calm, a nice change from the storm they'd left behind in Bermuda.

Since they'd gotten in contact with the Hole in Omaha, center for the Strategic Armaments Control, Wolf Squadron had found out that *most* Navy surface ships as well as many major commercial vessels had been similarly "parked" for the duration. The opinion of the "powers that be" prior to the Fall was that that way they'd be more or less impossible, or at least difficult, to find and they wouldn't be blown away by hurricanes or other storms. The commercial ships had apparently gone into the normally untraveled zone to avoid the Plague and have a place where they could maintain minimal power. As far as anyone knew, none of them had been uninfected.

On the horizon there was a supertanker full of Liberian crude. The normally empty zone was, relatively, chock with *big* ships full of H7D3 infected.

"You know," Faith said, musingly, "if we get this running we're going to have to rename it the *Galactica*, right?"

"Ouch," Fontana said. "Geek points galore."

"What?" Hooch said.

"Wait," Faith said. "Does that make the infected... wait for it... *Zylons*?"

"Ow!" Fontana said, snorting.

."With due respect, Staff Sergeant...," Hocieniec said. "What the *hell* are you talking about?"

"Shall I shoot the Zylons with my Barbie Gun?" Faith said, hefting a USCG M4.

Faith did not like the M4. Calling it a Barbie Gun was an indictment not a compliment. She also didn't like Barbie Dolls if for no other reason than her having a passing resemblance to the doll. Her main problem with the M4 came down to its round, the NATO 5.56mm.

It was hoary legend in the military that the 5.56 had been developed to wound the enemy so as to create a greater logistics burden on the enemy. The truth was that it was a light round with a high velocity, giving the M-16, the original of the M4, the ability to, ostensibly, fire accurately on fully automatic. The round also was light, permitting more of them to be carried by an infantry soldier as well as more moved logistically. And it, yes, did not "overkill" as had the previous .308 of the M14 much less the brute force .30-06 of World War II. It did *just enough* damage in the opinion of the technologist oriented defense department weenies and generals of the Vietnam era.

Faith's opinion could be summed up in one line, taken from a webcomic she'd enjoyed before the Plague: "There is no overkill. There is only 'Open fire' and 'Reloading.'" The first weapon she'd used for zombie clearance was a variant of the AK47 called a "Saiga" that fired 12-gauge shotgun shells. A zombie hit by a 12-gauge was not getting back up. When she ran out in a magazine and didn't have time to reload, she would switch to her H&K .45 USP. Zombies hit by .45 ACP also rarely stood back up. When they had run low on 12-gauge she had switched to her custom built AK firing the original 7.62X39 round, again a decent zombie killer.

When, desperate and with one of the largest cruise liners in the world still to clear, they had started using M4s and 5.56mm salvaged from a Coast Guard cutter, her normally sunny disposition had taken a downward turn. She disliked that she had to shoot zombies four or five times to get them to lie down and be good.

"Or we could use a, you know, machine gun," Fontana said.

"Ah," Faith said. "There's only like thirty of them. Back the *Toy* up to this tub and let's just shoot them off one by one."

"I thought you liked machine guns?" Fontana said.

"The whole belt fed is so last week," Faith said. "I still think it's a design flaw that you have to let up on the trigger."

"We're working on some you don't," Steve said.

"How?" Fontana said. "I mean, the only way to do that is coolant and . . ."

"Coolant," Steve said, nodding. "I've got the shop over on the *Grace* working on a water-cooled Browning."

"Doing the sleeve is going to be a bitch, sir," Hocieniec pointed out. "And that whole pump thing is . . ."

"Tech has changed remarkably since World War One, Hooch," Steve said, drily. "Think coiled copper tube and an electric pump. But that's for later. Shoot them off with aimed fire or break out the 240? As usual, I'm more worried about bouncers than anything. If we use the 240, even with these light rolls, we're going to have lots of bouncers."

"We could ask the *Dallas* to come up on it for us again," Faith said.

"That . . . Is not a bad idea," Steve said. The subs' hulls were made of thick, high-tensile steel, which was largely invulnerable to small arms fire.. "*Dallas*? You monitoring as usual?"

"*Wolf,* Dallas."

"Got a zombie entry problem again," Steve said. "You up for some kinetic clearance?"

"*We're out of seven six two, Wolf. Stand by...*"

"Standing by," Steve said.

"They floated theirs off for us," Fontana said. "Remember?"

"If it was during clearing the *Voyage*, the answer is 'It's all a blur,'" Steve said.

"*Wolf, bringing up the* Boise. *Be about twenty. You might want to clear your boats.*"

"Roger," Steve said. "Squadron Ops, you monitoring?"

"*Roger, Commodore. We'll send out the word.*"

"Get them well back and to the side," Steve said. "Five miles by preference. Stacey!"

"Moving!" Stacey Smith called. She put the *Tina's Toy* under full power and pulled away from the assault ship.

"Okay," Fontana said. "The *Dallas* has been in contact all along. Then the *Charlotte* tows the Coast Guard cutter down. Now it turns out the *Boise's* out there. How many fricking fast attacks are around us?"

"Your continued buildup of nuclear vessels in this region proves that you have access to vaccine!"

General Marshall Sergei Kazimov was the

acting commander of Russian Strategic Forces or, as he frequently referred to it, Soviet Strategic Forces. He had bluntly stated that he was Chairman of the Soviet Union. Also that if the "renegade Anglo-Sphere forces" did not immediately "vaccinate all his crews" he would "turn all of America's cities to ash."

Every time he used the term "nuclear vessels," Frank Galloway, National Constitutional Continuity Coordinator, tried not to break into a hysterical giggle. The general had no capacity at all to pronounce the "v."

"Mister Smith has stated, and our *very few* naval personnel who have gone through vaccination and quarantine have confirmed, that there are less than forty units of primer and booster in Smith's control," Galloway stated, again. It was always this way negotiating with the Russians. You just repeated the truth until they either gave in or the truth changed. "Our nuclear wes... vessels in the area are purely for what support they can provide to Wolf Squadron's clearance operations..."

"You lie!" Sergei shouted. "Wolf lies!"

"I wish he did," Galloway said, sighing. "I wish that he could immediately begin production of the vaccine. But until he has more clearance personnel and can clear a land base with the right facilities, that's impossible..."

"You will provide us with the vaccine or I will blow you to *hell!*"

"And we shall retaliate," Galloway said, trying not to sigh this time. "With what we have left. Which is, Sergei, far, *far* more than *you* have. You *will* be dead, I *might* be dead, there will be some radioactive wastelands that used to be infected-filled cities and what's the point? Oh, yes, there is the point that right now, Wolf is the only chance we have to get the world back in shape...!"

"Thanks, *Boise*," Steve commed.

"*You're welcome, Wolf Squadron,*" the *Boise's* commander replied. "*Please consider us for all your future kinetic clearance needs.*"

The team had rigged up while the *Boise* was potting zombies at long range with their MG240 and they now approached the wash deck of the assault carrier in a center-console inflatable.

Rigged up has a special meaning when zombie fighting. Troops in combat just thought they rigged up. Then there was "extreme hazard close-quarters biological clearance."

Each of the foursome were wearing multiple layers of clothes, including fire-fighting bunker gear, respirators, helmets and so many weapons and clearance tools it would have been ludicrous if they hadn't proven, at least once, that all of it was necessary. Not a single square inch of skin was uncovered or was in any way, shape or form "biteable." It was hot, it was heavy and it was cumbersome. It was especially hot in the Horse Latitudes, which were well inside the tropical zone.

It also meant that, as Faith and Hooch had proven, you could be absolutely dogpiled by zombies and still keep fighting. Faith, in particular, added a knife whenever she found a good one.

"Everyone remember where we parked," Faith said, stepping off the inflatable.

"Everyone remember to *drink*," Fontana said. "And how come you get to make the first landing, again?"

"I'm the cute one," Faith said. "You coming or not?"

"Faith, we've got to explain some language to you," Fontana said.

"Oops, live one," Faith said, as a zombie came loping down the catwalk above. She fired, missed and fired again. The second round hit but the zombie just stumbled then resumed running in their direction.

"Fucking *Barbie* gun . . . !"

—end excerpt—

from *To Sail a Darkling Sea*
available in hardcover,
February 2014, from Baen Books

1634: The Galileo Affair
by Eric Flint & Andrew Dennis
0-7434-9919-0 ✦ $7.99
New York Times bestseller!

1635: Cannon Law
by Eric Flint & Andrew Dennis
1-4165-5536-6 ✦ $7.99

1634: The Ram Rebellion
by Eric Flint with Virginia DeMarce
1-4165-7382-8 ✦ 7.99

1634: The Bavarian Crisis
by Eric Flint with Virginia DeMarce
978-1-4391-3276-0 ✦ $7.99

1635: The Dreeson Incident
by Eric Flint with Virginia DeMarce
1-4165-5589-7 ✦ $26.00

1635: The Tangled Web
by Virginia DeMarce
978-1-4391-3276-0 ✦ $7.99

Ring of Fire
edited by Eric Flint
1-4165-0908-9 ✦ $7.99
Top writers tell tales of Grantville, the town lost in time, including David Weber, Mercedes Lackey, Jane Lindskold, Eric Flint and more.

Ring of Fire II
edited by Eric Flint
HC ✦ 1-4165-7387-9 ✦ $25.00
PB ✦ 1-4165-9144-3 ✦ $7.99

Grantville Gazette
edited by Eric Flint
1-7434-8860-1 ✦ $6.99

Grantville Gazette II
edited by Eric Flint
1-4165-5510-2 ✦ $7.99

Grantville Gazette III
edited by Eric Flint
1-4165-5565-X ✦ $7.99
More stories by Eric Flint and others in this bestselling alternate history series.

Grantville Gazette IV
edited by Eric Flint
1-4165-5554-4 ✦ $25.00

Grantville Gazette V
edited by Eric Flint
978-1-4391-3279-1 ✦ $24.00